COLLISION!

At the upper edge of the viewport, Boba Fett saw one of the visible stars shimmer momentarily, vanish, and then reappear in the same location. Without conscious thought, but only pure reaction, his hand flew from the engine controls to the reverse thrusters. His palm hammered flat the thruster controls, giving them maximum power.

A split second later, *Slave I* hit the invisible object whose presence Fett had barely managed to detect.

The impact tore him from the pilot's chair, sending him tumbling across the curved bank of the cockpit controls. His spine struck the clear transparisteel of the viewport, a blow hard enough to send a shock of pain into the center of his skull, blinding him. . . .

Don't miss these other
exciting Star Wars® books:

X-WING
by Michael A. Stackpole
#1: ROGUE SQUADRON
#2: WEDGE'S GAMBLE
#3: THE KRYTOS TRAP
#4: THE BACTA WAR
#8: ISARD'S REVENGE
by Aaron Allston
#5: WRAITH SQUADRON
#6: IRON FIST
#7: SOLO COMMAND

THE BLACK FLEET CRISIS
by Michael P. Kube-McDowell
#1: BEFORE THE STORM
#2: SHIELD OF LIES
#3: TYRANT'S TEST

THE CRYSTAL STAR
by Vonda McIntyre

TALES FROM THE MOS EISLEY CANTINA
edited by Kevin J. Anderson

TALES FROM JABBA'S PALACE
edited by Kevin J. Anderson

TALES OF THE BOUNTY HUNTERS
edited by Kevin J. Anderson

THE BOUNTY HUNTER WARS
by K. W. Jeter
#1: THE MANDALORIAN ARMOR
#2: SLAVE SHIP
#3: HARD MERCHANDISE

CHILDREN OF THE JEDI
by Barbara Hambly

DARKSABER
by Kevin J. Anderson

THE ILLUSTRATED STAR WARS UNIVERSE
by Ralph McQuarrie
and Kevin J. Anderson

SHADOWS OF THE EMPIRE
by Steve Perry

THE NEW REBELLION
by Kristine Kathryn Rusch

I, JEDI
by Michael A. Stackpole

THE HAND OF THRAWN
by Timothy Zahn
SPECTER OF THE PAST
VISION OF THE FUTURE

THE BOUNTY HUNTER WARS
BOOK TWO
SLAVE SHIP

K. W. Jeter

SPECTRA™

BANTAM BOOKS
New York Toronto London Sydney Auckland

STAR WARS: SLAVE SHIP
A Bantam Spectra Book / October 1998

SPECTRA and the portrayal of a boxed "s" are trademarks of Bantam Books, a division of Random House, Inc.

ISBN 0-553-57888-X

Published simultaneously in the United States and Canada

Bantam Books are published by Bantam Books, a division of Random House, Inc. Its trademark, consisting of the words "Bantam Books" and the portrayal of a rooster, is Registered in U.S. Patent and Trademark Office and in other countries. Marca Registrada. Bantam Books, 1540 Broadway, New York , New York 10036.

PRINTED IN THE UNITED STATES OF AMERICA

OPM   20   19   18   17   16   15

To Andrew Slac, Mary Mayther Slac, and Gary Slac

Acknowledgments

The author would like to thank Sue Rostoni for gaffe-wrangling, Michael Stackpole for hardware expertise, and Geri Jeter, Graduate Gemologist (GIA), for gemstone reference.

1

Fear is a useful thing.

That was one of the best lessons that a bounty hunter could learn. And Bossk was learning it now.

Through the cockpit viewport of the *Hound's Tooth*, he saw the explosion that ripped the other ship, Boba Fett's *Slave I*, into flame and shards of blackened durasteel. A burst of wide-band comlink static, like an electromagnetic death cry, had simultaneously deafened Bossk. The searing, multi-octave noise had poured through the speakers in the *Hound's* cockpit for several minutes, until the last of the circuitry aboard Fett's ship had finally been consumed and silenced in the fiery apocalypse.

When he could finally hear himself think again, Bossk looked out at the empty space where *Slave I* had been. Now, against the cold backdrop of stars, a few scraps of heated metal slowly dwindled from white-hot to dull red as their molten heat ebbed away in vacuum. *He's dead,* thought Bossk with immense satisfaction. *At last.* Whatever atoms had constituted the late Boba Fett, they were also drifting disconnected and harmless in space. Before transferring back here to his own ship, Bossk had wired up enough thermal explosives in *Slave I* to reduce any living thing aboard it to mere ash and bad memories.

So if he still felt afraid, if his gut still knotted when Boba Fett's dark-visored image rose in his thoughts, Bossk knew that was an irrational response. *He's dead, he's gone . . .*

The silence of the *Hound*'s cockpit was broken by a barely audible pinging signal from the control panel. Bossk glanced down and saw that the *Hound*'s tele-sponder had picked up the presence of another ship in the immediate vicinity; according to the coordinates that appeared in the readout screen, it was almost on top of the *Hound's Tooth*.

And—it was the ship known as *Slave I*. The ID profile was an exact match.

That's impossible, thought Bossk, bewildered. His heart shuddered to a halt inside his chest, then staggered on. Before the explosion, he had picked up the same ID profile from the other side of his own ship; he had turned the *Hound's Tooth* around just in time to see the huge, churning ball of flame fill his viewscreen.

But, he realized now, he hadn't seen *Slave I* itself. Which meant . . .

Bossk heard another sound, even softer, coming from somewhere else in his own ship. There was someone else aboard it; his keen Trandoshan senses registered the molecules of another creature's spoor in the ship's recycled atmosphere. And Bossk knew who it was.

He's here. The cold blood in Bossk's veins chilled to ice. *Boba Fett . . .*

Somehow, Bossk knew, he had been tricked. The explosion hadn't consumed *Slave I* and its occupants at all. He didn't know how Boba Fett had managed it, but it had been done nevertheless. And the deafening electronic noise that had filled the cockpit had also been enough to cover Boba Fett's unauthorized entry of the *Hound's Tooth*; the shrieking din had gone on long enough for Fett to have penetrated an access hatch and resealed it behind himself.

A voice came from the cockpit's overhead speaker, a voice that was neither his own nor Boba Fett's.

"Twenty seconds to detonation." It was the calm, unexcited voice of an autonomic bomb. Only the most powerful ones contained warning circuits like that.

Fear thawed the ice in Bossk's veins. He jumped up from the pilot's chair and dived for the hatchway behind himself.

In the emergency equipment bay of the *Hound's Tooth*, his clawed hands tore through the contents of one of the storage lockers. The *Hound* wasn't going to be a ship much longer; in a few seconds—and counting down—it was going to be glowing bits of shrapnel and rubbish surrounded by a haze of rapidly dissipating atmospheric gases, just like whatever it had been that he had mistakenly identified, as Boba Fett's ship *Slave I*. That the *Hound* would no longer be capable of maintaining its life-support systems wasn't Bossk's main concern at this moment, as the reptilian Trandoshan hastily shoved a few more essential items through the self-sealing gasket of a battered, much-used pressure duffel. There wouldn't even *be* any life for the systems to support: a small portion of the debris floating in the cold vacuum would be blood and bone and scorched scraps of body tissue, the rapidly chilling remains of the ship's captain. *I'm outta here*, thought Bossk; he slung the duffel's strap across his broad shoulder and dived for the equipment bay's hatch.

"Fifteen seconds to detonation." A calm and

friendly voice spoke in the *Hound*'s central corridor as Bossk ran for the escape pod. He knew that Boba Fett had toggled the bomb's autonomic vocal circuits just to rattle him. "Fourteen . . ." There was nothing like a disembodied announcement of impending doom, to get a sentient creature motivated. "Thirteen; have you considered evacuation?"

"Shut up," growled Bossk. There was no point in talking to a pile of thermal explosives and flash circuits, but he couldn't stop himself. Under the death-fear that accelerated his pulse was sheer murderous rage and annoyance, the inevitable-seeming result of every encounter he'd ever had with Boba Fett. *That stinking, underhanded scum . . .*

The scraps and shards left by the other explosion clattered against the *Hound*'s shielded exterior like a swarm of tiny, molten-edged meteorites. If there was any justice in the universe, Boba Fett should have been dead by now. Not just dead; atomized. The fury and panic in Bossk's pounding heart shifted again to bewilderment as he ran with the pressure duffel jostling against his scale-covered spine. Why did Boba Fett keep coming back? Was there no way to kill him so that he would just *stay* dead?

"Twelve . . ."

It wasn't fair. He hadn't even had the chance to lean back in the pilot's chair and feel the warm glow spread through his body, the sweet tranquility that came with annihilating one's enemies. And Boba Fett had been his number-one antagonist; Bossk had lost track of the humiliations he had suffered at the other bounty hunter's hands. There had even been times when he had teamed up with Fett, and had still wound up the loser, gazing into the narrow visor of Fett's helmet and sensing a sneer of triumph on the face concealed by the Mandalorian armor. Granted, on one of those occasions when he'd gone in league with Boba Fett, Bossk's own secret agenda had been to kill him— but that he'd failed only went to show what a cruel, uncaring place the universe was. It was just as old Cradossk, his father, had instructed him in those long-ago days before being murdered by Bossk: *Nobody ever helps kill himself, even when he should . . .*

"Eleven," the bomb's voice said.

No time for self-pity. Bossk wiped all thoughts other than self-preservation from his mind. His pulse raced at the welcome sight of the escape-pod hatch directly in front of him. With one hand, Bossk pulled the pressure duffel higher up on his back as his other hand reached desperately for the entry controls at the side of the hatch, still a couple of meters away. There were no cross-passages in this section of the *Hound's Tooth*, no angle from which Boba Fett could leap out or take a blaster shot at him. He still had a chance to get away.

"Ten . . ."

The point of Bossk's claw hit the big red button for which he had been aiming. With a sharp hiss, the escape pod's hatch slid open, revealing the cramped, spherical space within; he'd have to be folded up, his knees in his face, the whole time he'd be in there. *Which beats dying*, Bossk quickly reminded himself. He threw the pressure duffel inside, then scrambled in after it.

"Ni—" The hatch zipping back into place cut off the bomb's relentlessly placid voice.

Bossk reached around the duffel and hit the pod's disengage and release buttons. His shoulders pressed hard against the curve of the hermetically sealed shell. The inadequate space was a humiliating reminder of another time when he had fled from Boba Fett in an emergency escape pod; the memory still rankled inside him.

Outside this pod, he could hear muffled clanking and creaking sounds, as the *Hound*'s machinery rotated the pod into eject position. "Come on . . ." Bossk's voice grated in his throat. The devices clicked through their programming with a sickening lack of haste. The noises changed to grinding and scraping, the pod shuddering as though it were about to come to a halt without even leaving the *Hound's Tooth* behind. He had never used this escape pod before, and had even considered yanking it out of the ship as useless deadweight; his basic Trandoshan nature had always made it an instinctual response, to stand and fight rather than turn and run. Factoring Boba Fett into the equation, though, yielded a different result.

This pod at least had a viewport. Through the tiny aperture, barely the size of his hand, Bossk suddenly saw an expanse of stars; the launchport on the exterior of the *Hound*'s hull must have finally irised open. His guess was confirmed when his spine was suddenly jammed back against the hatch behind him as an intense burst of thruster fire shot the pod out into space and away from the ship.

The stars shifted disorientingly in the viewport as the pod rolled to one side. Bossk wrapped his bare arms around the pressure duffel and ground his fangs together, fighting off the nausea evoked by the combination of random movements and the knot of fear at the base of his gut. Squeezing his eyes shut, he wondered what number the bomb's countdown had reached. Depending upon the amount and kind of explosives that Boba Fett had brought aboard the *Hound's Tooth*, and how fast this escape pod was hurtling through space, he still might not be in the clear; the bomb's explosion might wash over the pod like a planetary tidal wave, only of fire, not seawater. Bossk's claws curled into fists as he pictured himself being cooked inside the escape pod, like an unhatched egg being poached.

Wait a second. Another thought came to him. Boba Fett wasn't self-destructive; the other bounty hunter had undoubtedly gotten off the *Hound's Tooth* as soon as he had set the bomb ticking down to detonation. So his ship *Slave I*—the real *Slave I*, not the decoy that had given off the same ID profile—must still be in this immediate sector. *And* in range of an overlarge explosion. Bossk relaxed, letting his chest ease against the pressure duffel that he had wrapped himself around. That simple calculation dissipated some of the fear that had coiled around his spine. *He wouldn't set off something*, thought Bossk, *that would kill him as well.*

Another voice spoke aloud, in the confines of the escape pod. "Five . . ."

Bossk's eyes snapped open. His grip on the duffel tightened as his gaze darted from one side of the escape pod to the other.

"Four," said the calm, familiar voice of the bomb.

Terror made the voice inside Bossk's head nearly as expressionless. *It's in here.* Boba Fett had planted the bomb inside the escape pod.

"Three . . ."

A surge of adrenaline coursed through the Trandoshan's body. He shoved the pressure duffel away from himself, cramming it against the concave side of the sphere. His claws raked across the pod's interior, scrabbling to find the explosive device. Something smaller than his own fist would be enough to reduce him and the surrounding metal to dissociated atoms. *It's got to be here*, he thought furiously, *somewhere . . .*

Hot sparks stung his face as he yanked handfuls of circuitry loose from the escape pod's minimal control banks. An air hose, jerked free from one of its sockets, hissed and wavered in front of Bossk like an expiring snake. The stubby cylinders and curved module panels of the pod's auxiliary equipment battered against his forearms and chest as he swore and pulled at everything he could get his claws upon.

"Two . . ."

The unhurried voice came from a small blue cube that Bossk held between his hands. He knew that it was the bomb; it had been stuck to an atmosphere-scrubber grid with a spot of utility adhesive, not yet dry. Frantically, he looked about for some way to eject the box from the escape pod.

There wasn't any.

"One."

Inside the pod, the space was so tight that Bossk couldn't stretch his arms to full length. He shoved himself back against the ripped-apart junk, turned his face away—for all the good that would do—and thrust the bomb against the opposite side of the pod, near the tiny viewport.

Nothing happened.

He was still alive. Slowly, Bossk brought his gaze back around to the blue cube, held by his hands against the pod's curved wall. The device was silent, as though the last of its words had been drained from it. Clutching it in one hand, he drew it closer to himself and examined it.

One corner of the cube had popped open. Bossk cautiously inserted the point of one claw and pried it open.

Nothing inside—at least nothing that looked like an explosive charge. He peered into the empty space. The only contents were a miniaturized speaker and a few preprogrammed vocal circuits.

Bossk tossed the cube away from himself in disgust. It hadn't been a bomb at all. And he hadn't felt the impact of a bomb, in the distance outside the escape pod, so there probably hadn't been one placed aboard the *Hound's Tooth* either, of any size or destructive capability. If he hadn't given in to panic and hadn't abandoned the *Hound*— if he had stayed there and had gone toe-to-toe with Boba Fett, he might have settled his accounts with his enemy once and for all, and still have been in possession of his own ship. Now where was he? Bossk's elbows rubbed uncomfortably against the cramped confines of the escape pod, made even more so by the bits and pieces jumbled around him now. At least he hadn't damaged anything essential, as far as he could tell; there was still air to breathe, and the pod's navigational circuits appeared to be in operative condition. They had already locked on to Tatooine, the nearest habitable destination; the planet's familiar image now filled the viewport. It wouldn't be too long before the pod would descend through the atmosphere and land somewhere on the surface. *Probably,* brooded Bossk, *in some wasteland.* That was how his luck seemed to be going. Then again, there wasn't much besides wasteland on Tatooine, so the chances of anything else weren't good:

As he shifted position inside the pod, the contents of the pressure duffel poked him in the ribs. At least he had managed to get some things off the *Hound's Tooth*; valuable things. It was comforting to know that fear hadn't wiped out every other instinct inside his head. His natural Trandoshan greed had remained functioning. Whether he would be able to profit from what he'd salvaged—that remained to be seen.

He reached over and picked up the blue cube, the fake bomb that was mercifully silent now. Other emotions welled up inside Bossk as he gazed at the object resting in the palm of his clawed hand. A perpetual anger, which he always felt when he thought about

Boba Fett, was once again renewed in the dark reaches of his heart.

It had been one thing to scare Bossk off his own ship; that was a strategic gambit, worthy of the master that all the rest of the universe conceded Fett to be. But to stick this prankster module, this talking dud, inside the escape pod, just to rattle an opponent's head . . .

That was just plain sadistic.

Bossk crushed the empty blue cube into the center of his fist, then tossed it aside again. He wrapped his scaly arms around his legs and rested his chin against his knees. As the surface details of Tatooine grew larger in the viewport, Bossk's thought turned ever darker and more murderous.

Next time, he vowed. *And there will be one . . .*

On the great list of grievances that he kept next to his heart, every one with Boba Fett's name attached, another entry had been made.

2

"You let him get away."

Neelah turned from the viewport of *Slave I*'s cockpit. In the distance beyond, the escape pod with the bounty hunter Bossk aboard had been a point of light dwindling among the stars, then lost beyond the curve of the planet to which it was headed.

"You state the obvious," replied Boba Fett. His gloved hands moved across the controls in front of the pilot's chair.

"Yeah, well, I don't get it, either." That comment came from Dengar, standing in the cockpit's hatchway. His face was still shiny with sweat from his recent exertions. There had been a lot of stuff to move, and in a hurry, from this ship into the cargo module that had been launched from it. "That thug was trying to kill us."

"Not 'us,' " corrected Fett. "*Me*. In all likelihood, Bossk didn't even know you two were aboard."

That didn't make Neelah feel any better. Things had been happening fast—too fast, for her taste—even before Boba Fett's personal ship had lifted off from Tatooine's Dune Sea. *Slave I*'s swift, functional mass had come flaring down from the night sky like a magnified emblem of potentiated lethality, just in time to crush beneath its hot rocket nozzles one of the two men who had pinned her, Dengar, and Fett down with their blaster-rifle fire. Irritatingly, Boba Fett had kept his cool during all the shooting. *Easy for him,* Neelah grumped to herself. He was the one who had transmitted the signal to *Slave I,* up in orbit above their heads. So he had known it was coming. He just hadn't felt like letting his partners know.

If that's what we still are, thought Neelah. With her arms folded, she studied each of the two bounty hunters in turn. Dengar wasn't too hard to figure out; she could probably make a deal with him, and he'd stick to it. Especially if there was some chance of realizing a profit out of it. She even knew what he needed the money for; Dengar had told her about his bride-to-be, a woman named Manaroo, and his desire to make a big enough score to get out of the bounty hunter trade once and for all. *Smart man,* Neelah had decided. Or at least smart enough to realize that keeping company with someone like Boba Fett was a dangerous proposition. From what she had already picked up, Neelah knew that Fett's business associates tended to have lives as short as those of his enemies.

Whereas Fett might as well be immortal, for all that she could see. He had already survived falling down the gullet of the Sarlacc beast, at the gaping bottom of the Great Pit of Carkoon. The condition in which Neelah had found him, with his skin virtually dissolved from his flesh by the Sarlacc's gastric secretions, would have spelled out death for any other creature. It hadn't destroyed Boba Fett, though, but only seemed to have made him even tougher and more fearsome.

Just my luck. Neelah kept her own face expressionless as she watched Fett maneuvering the ship.

Her own fate had become bound up with one of the hardest creatures in the universe, the least likely to be swayed by threats or violence . . . or seduction. In some ways, she had been better off when she had still been in Jabba's palace, as one of the late Hutt's troupe of dancing girls. At least then she had known that her youth and beauty, and Jabba's taste for those enticing and precious qualities, would keep her alive. For a while, or until Jabba had grown either jaded with her dark-eyed looks or stimulated by the thought of tossing her to his pet rancor, the way he had done with that poor little Twi'lek Oola. She closed her eyes, barely able to suppress the shudder evoked by the memory of the girl's screams, the rancor's grunting snarl, and Jabba's slobbering delight at what had happened in the bone-littered pit in front of his throne. Whoever the ones that had finally bested Jabba the Hutt were—Dengar had told her names, Luke Skywalker and a Princess Leia Organa, that meant nothing to her—they had done a good job in ridding the universe of that massive, loathsome slug. Neelah supposed it would be asking a lot to have expected them or anyone else to have also restored her past to her, the darkly shadowed memories of who she had been and all that had happened to her before she had found herself in Jabba's palace.

It would be a lot to expect from Boba Fett as well. The bounty hunter trade was concerned with only one thing, delivering their precious bits of hard merchandise to the highest bidder. If that merchandise had thoughts and fears and hopes, or whether all that went to make up the merchandise's spirit had been scoured away by a deep-level memory wipe—that didn't matter. If Boba Fett was keeping her alive—he had in fact pulled Neelah out of their attackers' line of fire and aboard *Slave I* just seconds before it had taken off—then she had to assume it was being done on a bounty hunter's agenda, and not out of any concern for her welfare. *That's what I've got to figure out,* Neelah reminded herself. *What's in it for him.* Before anything else; more than her own survival depended upon the answer to that question. She knew that it was undoubtedly the key to unlocking all the other mysteries, all the way back to her own true name.

Another voice broke into her brooding thoughts.

"You still didn't tell us," said Dengar, "why you let that Bossk creature get away."

Boba Fett glanced over his shoulder at the bounty hunter standing in the cockpit's hatchway. "You know his name?"

"Of course." Dengar pointed to one of the data-screens beneath *Slave I*'s forward viewport. "I recognized the ID profile that came up when we were approaching his ship. Last I heard, the *Hound's Tooth* is still Bossk's ship."

"Correction," said Fett. "It *was* his ship."

"You're going to blow it up?" Dengar grimaced and slowly shook his head. "I don't know if that's such a good idea. I've had a few run-ins with Bossk before, and he can be a pretty ugly customer."

"That goes without saying." Neelah had stayed aboard *Slave I*, watching as Dengar had operated the transfer-port controls between the two ships. From the port's remote view-cam, she had caught a glimpse of Bossk as he had sprinted away from the apparition of his supposedly dead enemy, suddenly materialized aboard the *Hound*. She had even gotten a measure of grim amusement from witnessing the Trandoshan's panic. But she had also recognized his scaly, fang-mouthed image from her time at Jabba's palace. Bossk had been one of the many lowlifes and dealers in profitable violence that had drifted in and out of the late Hutt's employ. Every time Neelah had spotted him, a sick chill had set into her gut; the reptilian gaze that he directed toward her and the other dancing girls spoke silently of appetites that would leave welters of blood and splintered bones as signs of their fulfillment.

"I've had much more experience with Bossk than you have." Boba Fett's voice remained level and unperturbed. "He and I go back a long way. And believe me, I'm not concerned about any retribution at his hands."

"Fine for you," grumbled Dengar. "Maybe *you* can take care of him. I'm just worried about what happens when he comes after *me*. That guy isn't exactly known for being able to forgive and forget. He wakes up ready to bite other creatures' heads off."

"I can take care of him; I've done so in the past." A note of amusement sounded in Boba Fett's voice. "So as long as you stick with me—as long as we keep going with this partnership that we've agreed upon— then you don't really have anything to worry about at all, do you?"

The expression on Dengar's face indicated to Neelah that the end of the bounty hunter's worries was still far away.

She had to admit, though, that Boba Fett's claims seemed factual and not just boasting. He had been way ahead of Bossk, even as soon as they had all climbed aboard *Slave I* and sealed the entry hatch. "This ship is going to blow," Fett had announced. "Somebody's shoved a load of explosives aboard it."

"What?" Standing in the cargo hold, Dengar had gaped at the other bounty hunter. "How do you know that?"

Boba Fett had tapped the side of his helmet as he explained. "I've got an alarm relay, straight from the security systems I wired into the ship's perimeter web. Nobody gets in and out of *Slave I*, even when it's on autonomic standby, without my getting the details. The ship's computer has already done a spectrum read on the trade molecules in the air; there's some sloppy— but effective—high-thermal explosives somewhere around us, with a remote trigger charge attached."

It hadn't taken long to find the explosives: *Slave I*'s detector circuits had already done a preliminary search through the entire ship, narrowing the possible site of an unauthorized mass to somewhere behind the main holding cage. Boba Fett had quickly located the explosives, extracted them, and stuffed them aboard a cargo module. Neelah held a worklight up above her head, directing its beam into the space between the bulkhead's durasteel ribs, as Boba Fett and Dengar had unwedged the bulky object and dragged it out to the center of the compartment's floor.

Before jettisoning the module, Boba Fett had wired into its power circuits a small device that he had brought down from the cockpit area.

"What's that?" Neelah had pointed to the device.

"An ID overlay transmitter," Fett had replied as he'd closed the cargo module's hatch and stood up. "Programmed with *Slave I*'s identification codes. Strictly short range, and without the hard-encryption levels that would get it past a real ID inquiry. But it should be enough to fool—for just long enough—the uninvited guest who left this little package here."

The rest had been easy. Once the cargo module had shot out from *Slave I*, its navigation circuits had sent it homing toward the other ship lying in wait. Boba Fett had cut his own ship's thruster engines, holding back and keeping directly behind the cargo module, still traveling forward. The explosion, when Bossk had pushed the button, had given enough cover for Boba Fett to hit the thrusters with full power and come swooping up alongside the *Hound's Tooth*. He had been inside the other bounty hunter's ship, with his own surprises ready to go, before Bossk knew what was happening.

All of that fast strategizing had been easy enough for Neelah to follow. That was then, though; this was now. "I still don't understand," she said aloud, "why you didn't kill that Bossk or whatever his name is, instead of just throwing a scare into him like that."

"It's simple." Boba Fett didn't look over at her, but continued making adjustments to *Slave I*'s navigation coordinates. "Right now, the whole universe believes I'm dead. Or at least those parts of it that concern themselves with the fate of bounty hunters."

"That's true," said Dengar. "When I went into Mos Eisley, the story about you falling down the Sarlacc's throat was all over the spaceport."

"I anticipated that would be the case." Fett punched in a few more numbers. "Sometimes it can be a productive situation to be dead. Or at least to have creatures *think* you are."

"So you let Bossk get away? After he saw that you're still alive?" Neelah couldn't fathom what she was hearing. "Doesn't that defeat the whole purpose of this little charade? Once he makes his way into Mos Eisley, he'll blab the truth to everyone who'll listen to him."

"No, he won't." Boba Fett gave a single shake of his helmeted head. "You are not experienced with basic Trandoshan psychology. They are an egotistical species; the only creature worse in that regard is a Hutt. But then Hutts have more reason to be; they're considerably smarter than Trandoshans. Bossk is at least intelligent enough to realize that he benefits from a universe-wide belief in my death. With my absence from the scene, many will regard him as being the number-one bounty hunter still working the trade. Merchandise to be located and secured will come his way, and there are the benefits to the ego as well; those have always been a bigger motivation to him. If it's not credits in my pocket, I'm not interested in it."

Obviously, thought Neelah. She decided to keep her mouth shut, at least this time.

"For Bossk, it is a matter of pride," continued Fett. "He enjoys being fawned on and flattered; much of the animosity he bears me is due to his conviction that I somehow cheated him out of inheriting the leadership of the old Bounty Hunters Guild. That's a hard thing for him to forgive. He may hate my guts, but he's not going to relate any stories about my still being alive that make him look like a fool. When he gets to Mos Eisley, he's going to have a hard enough time telling the cantina habitués why he no longer has the *Hound's Tooth*; it's been his ship for a long time. He's not about to tell anyone that he got frightened out of it like a Biituian fen-hare."

"Okay . . ." Dengar nodded slowly as he mulled it over, leaning his shoulder against the side of the cockpit hatchway. "So you don't lose anything by letting Bossk go. But what do you *gain* out of it? That's worth having an enemy like that still aiming for you?"

"Simple—I gain an effective mouthpiece for the story of my death. There may be isolated sectors of the universe that haven't yet heard of that unfortunate event; some creatures may be very interested to find out about it. At the same time, some of the things in my immediate plans might inadvertently give rise to speculation that I *am* still alive. Better that we should have Bossk in a gossip den such as Mos Eisley, with every scoundrel on the inhabited worlds passing through and listening in as he does his best to convince everyone of just how dead I am."

Neelah was impressed, in spite of herself. *He thinks of everything,* she grudgingly admitted. It was no wonder that he had clawed his way to the top of the bounty hunter trade. The amount of bloodied corpses he had left behind himself must be equally impressive.

"You forgot about one thing." A smug expression showed on Dengar's face. "We're sitting, right now, aboard something that gives the whole game away. *Slave I* is known throughout the galaxy as being Boba Fett's ship; soon as other creatures spot it cruising into their systems, they're going to suspect—or they'll *know*—that you're alive. And up to your old trade again."

"I'm glad to see that I don't have a fool for a partner." Any trace of sarcasm was filtered out of Boba Fett's voice.

"So what are you going to do about it?" Neelah felt sure that the bounty hunter had already figured out the answer.

"That is a simple matter as well." Boba Fett raised one of his gloved hands from the cockpit controls and gestured at the bulkheads surrounding them. "Dengar is correct in his assessment that this ship reveals me to be still alive—but only if I'm actually in it. An abandoned *Slave I* reads out a considerably different message. If it's found drifting and empty, then most sentient creatures will make the logical assumption that I am in fact dead; the ship will confirm the stories they've already heard. For something as valuable to me as *Slave I*, the only way that it would fall from my grasp would be if I were no longer among the living. Or so most creatures will believe."

Neelah gave a nod; it made sense to her. "But you'll still need a ship," she pointed out. "You can hardly walk from here to where you'll want to go."

"How fortunate then that we have another ship available to us." With a simple gesture, Boba Fett indicated the cockpit's forward viewport. In the distance outside, framed by stars and the blackness of space, the *Hound's Tooth* floated. "Granted, it does not have the capabilities of this one—no ship does—but it'll suffice. Bossk was not such a failure at the bounty hunter trade that he didn't have the funds available to him to put together a decent enough system." Fett gave a slight shrug. "With a few minor modifications, it should serve our own purposes well enough. Once its ID profile is broken out and over-ridden, with a new ID programmed in, the ship won't even be recognizable as Bossk's—so no one will catch the discrepancy that the *Hound*'s original owner is somewhere back on Tatooine, while his ship is light-years away from there. That should provide us all the anonymity we require."

"I suppose that explains why you didn't just blow up Bossk's ship, with him still aboard." One thing still puzzled Neelah, in addition to all the other mysteries that still existed. "But why such a big need for secrecy?"

"Yeah," chimed in Dengar. "Your reputation is the biggest thing you've got going for you. There's a lot of creatures who'll just roll over and give up if they hear you're involved in something close to them. If you give all that up—if you give up your identity, your name—then you're starting from zero. Everything will have to be done the hard way, every time."

Boba Fett swiveled the pilot's chair around from the controls; his helmeted gaze, hidden behind the dark, narrow visor, took in each of them in turn. "You should consider yourselves unusually privileged," he said slowly, "that I've explained as much as I have already. I'm not in the habit of justifying my methods to anyone. But now I have a partner, so that requires a certain forbearance on my part. And as for you"—he pointed to Neelah, then nodded, as though in deep contemplation—"I have no objection to your listening in to what passes between Dengar and myself. But harbor no illusions: I saved you, and brought you along with us, for a reason."

Neelah glared back at him, feeling the anger inside her going up another notch. "Which is?"

"You'll find out soon enough. But for right now, you have value to me. Take comfort in that."

Sure, she thought to herself. *Right up until I don't have any value for you. Then what?*

That time might come at any moment. Neelah had already decided she would be ready for it, when it did arrive. Boba Fett might be the most dangerous bounty hunter in the galaxy—whether creatures believed he was dead or knew he was still alive—but if he thought she was just going to wait around for him to dispose of her in whatever way suited his plans . . .

Then he had made a fatal mistake. Neelah kept her face a mask as expressionless as the one into which she gazed. She didn't know how she was going to bring about that little surprise for Boba Feet, but the hidden workings of her brain were already in motion.

"And as for the need for secrecy . . ."

For a moment she thought he had somehow peered into her mind and read out some part of what he had found in there. Then Neelah realized that he was still answering the question that Dengar had raised.

"Some things are best accomplished in the dark."
Boba Fett's voice had gone low and brooding as he
turned back toward the cockpit's controls. In the forward viewport, the silent image of the *Hound's Tooth*
loomed closer. "There are many who wished me dead,
and who tried their best to bring that about."

That was true. The memory was still fresh in
Neelah's mind, of how the Dune Sea on Tatooine had
been pounded by the bombing raid, the fury of unknown forces—unknown to her—who sought to destroy Boba Fett, no matter what it took. Those forces
were still out there, somewhere amid the stars.

"Let's see how they like it . . ." Boba Fett's voice
was a dark whisper now. "When the dead return . . ."

3

The news had come a long way. From one side of the galaxy to the other; from the cold vacuum of space, just above one of the remotest backwater planets known to any sentient creature, to one of the Empire's brightest centers of power and wealth. And where power and wealth existed, there was also the irreducible, unavoidable elements of intrigue, conspiracy, and deceit.

"We live in a universe of lies," said Kuat of Kuat. One of his hands stroked the silken fur of the felinx cradled against his chest. The animal closed its eyes, content in its ignorance. Its master's words held no meaning for it. *Lucky thing,* thought Kuat. "We breathe in lies and exhale treachery, as though they were an essential part of the atmosphere."

"Sir?" Fenald, Kuat's head of security, stood next to him, close to the private reception area's great segmented viewscreens. From here, the construction docks and engineering facilities of Kuat Drive Yards could be seen, stretching out toward the range of stars spiraling in the limitless distance. Generations of the Kuat bloodline had first created, then transformed the corporation into the apotheosis of industrial production; at the fringes of Kuat Drive Yards, immense freighters disgorged the raw materials stripped from other star systems, all to be forged into the ships and weaponry of the Imperial Navy. Even as the multi-leveled disc of the corporation's physical plant slowly revolved on its axis, battle cruisers and destroyers bristled with yet-unfired armaments, the reinforced plates of the hulls welded onto the structural frames by articulated laser torches, the glare brighter than the depleted sun at the center of the former planet's orbit.

He was aware of the security head's puzzlement; the remark had come after a long brooding silence. All of Kuat Drive Yards' high-level employees, the innermost circle of trusted—and well-paid—associates, knew better than to interrupt these deep meditations. But sometimes, it helped to speak one's thoughts aloud. To a trusted listener; the head of security's instinctive loyalty was reinforced with a munificent salary. Nothing spoken would go beyond this sanctum's walls, carefully screened and swept as they were for hidden listening devices.

"What little genius that I have," Kuat of Kuat said at last, "is inherited from my father and from all my ancestors before him."

Fenald gave a slight smile; he had heard similar words before. "The Technician is too modest."

"Better that than too vainglorious." Overweening pride would, he knew, be the eventual downfall of his enemies. There had been a certain Falleen prince, with ambitions and ego nearly equal to that of Emperor Palpatine, whose fiery arc across the stars had ended in a fatal crash. "But as I was saying—there is more to that hereditary genius than the mere design and crafting of warships. If that were all I had to do," mused Kuat of Kuat, "then life would be an unending pleasure. But life for me, as it was for my progenitors, is not so simple."

"Sir?"

"Even under the old Republic, there had been political intrigues with which to contend." Kuat rubbed behind the felinx's pointed ears as he gazed out the curved bank of viewscreens. "And rival engineering firms that wished to supplant Kuat Drive Yards' position as the preeminent military contractor in the galaxy. It's always been that way." He nodded slowly. "But now, under the rule of Emperor Palpatine, the stakes involved in these intricate, unending games has reached a zenith of deadly seriousness. Our every move, on this board that spans the inhabited worlds, could have fatal consequences—not just for one man, but for even the mightiest corporations. I have little regard for my own fate, but the thought of the Emperor grasping all of Kuat Drive Yards in his fist, as has been done with so many other worlds and entities in the galaxy . . ." He fell silent for a moment as that thought evoked the renewal of a cold vow inside him.

That will never happen, swore Kuat of Kuat. "I would rather see Kuat Drive Yards, my heritage and the work of generations of Kuats before me, utterly destroyed and in ruins before letting it fall into the control of the Empire." He glanced over at his security head. "That's not an empty promise, either."

"As I am well aware, Technician." Fenald gave a single nod of acknowledgment. "I have personally supervised the necessary arrangements, to ensure another outcome. If that time should ever come, there will be no Kuat Drive Yards for the Emperor to take hold of."

There was a certain bleak comfort in Fenald's statement. *What can be built up,* thought Kuat, *can be leveled.* The same engineering and design skills that went into the construction of the Empire's warships had been turned to the means of annihilating the docks in which they were built. A vision came to Kuat of Kuat, not of the series-programmed, high-thermal explosions that would render all of Kuat Drive Yards into smoldering scrap, but the aftermath, when the twisted durasteel, the remnants of the cranes and immense grappling rigs, would be as cold as the stray atoms in the vacuum surrounding them. The KDY life-support systems, which kept the vacuum and the power-supply reactors' hard radiation at bay, would be shattered as well; no living creatures would be left among the rubble. The apocalypse would come upon them, the workers and servants of Kuat Drive Yards and their hereditary lord as well, in swift fury; they would all die at their stations, the lowliest machinist at a turret lathe's controls, Kuat himself reduced to an ashen corpse behind the torn-apart grid of the viewscreens that had looked out upon his domain. That would then be his monument, and the memorial to his ancestors, those who had also borne the title of Kuat of Kuat. Living observers on the nearest worlds would turn their gaze to the nighttime skies and see the shadow of the wreckage passing in front of the stars, writing a black glyph toward the horizon, an emblem of past glories that would need no translation to an alien tongue.

"I thank you for your faithful service," said Kuat of Kuat. "It means a great deal to me."

"If it eases the Technician's mind, then it's worth it." The Kuat Drive Yards security head stood with his hands clasped behind his back. The glow of true belief, as inherited as his superior's title, was evident in his eyes. "But the time of its use will never come; that is what I believe. Our enemies conspire in vain; Kuat Drive Yards will yet endure."

"Your confidence is also appreciated." Kuat wished he could be as sure. For there was more than just the

Emperor and his endless machinations to worry about. The Rebellion had complicated everything, as though the gameboard had been transformed from two dimensions to three. Kuat Drive Yards owed no allegiance to anything but itself, harbored no great ideals other than its own survival and independence, a state within whatever larger state prevailed beyond the corporation. If that other, encompassing state were the old Republic, the Empire that had overthrown it, or whatever vision of universal freedom that the Rebel Alliance wished to bring about—that meant nothing to Kuat of Kuat. Eventually, one side or the other would win out; if it was Emperor Palpatine, or Leia Organa and Luke Skywalker and the forces for which they had become both symbols and leaders, all that Kuat wished to make sure of was that Kuat Drive Yards was on a friendly—or at least neutral—basis with the victors. Whoever won, there would be a need afterward for cruisers and destroyers, and all the other fearsome equipage of interplanetary warfare.

"The Rebellion . . ." Kuat of Kuat mused aloud once more, voicing the deep currents of his thoughts. "Even if the Rebel Alliance is able to establish a new Republic—one with greater justice and harmony among the galaxy's sentient creatures than had prevailed before—certain aspects of human and nonhuman nature still would not change."

"Such is wisdom, Technician."

He and his head of security had discussed these things in the past. Mere greed and all the cascading layers of misunderstanding would be enough to dictate the presence of some kind of order-keeping force. And that meant armaments, and the ability to deliver their firepower across vast distances. The much-vaunted Death Star hadn't been a Kuat Drive Yards project—

Kuat of Kuat himself had forbade the organization even making a bid on any of its subsystems—but the reasoning behind it had been understandable.

"Not just wisdom," said Kuat. "But cunning." He repeated one of the lessons he had received from his own father, the Kuat of Kuat before him: *"Force and terror accomplish what reason and understanding cannot."*

The Kuat family had been in that business a long time, supplying the instruments of force and terror. His reluctance to get involved with any aspect of the Death Star's construction hadn't been based on a moral objection, but purely practical. Kuat Drive Yards' wealth and power came from building warships, and the Death Star, if it had succeeded in the Imperial admirals' purposes, would have wiped out much of the need for such expensive—and profitable—craft. A stupid creature fouls its own nest; only a suicidal one helps destroy it. With relief, and a measure of vindication, Kuat of Kuat had heard of the Death Star's own destruction at the Battle of Yavin. For the Empire to begin constructing an even bigger Death Star only meant that the admirals hadn't learned their lesson. *Speed* was not so important as *maneuverability*; the Death Star's hyperspace capabilities had not been enough to outweigh other elements of military force, such as *numerical superiority*. No Death Star could be made so powerful and impervious to attack as to outweigh the loss of those factors.

The security head displayed a thin, knowing smile. "Cunning prevails, Technician, where wisdom is powerless."

"Exactly so." That age-old principle was what kept him from placing the services of Kuat Drive Yards at the Rebel Alliance's disposal. True cunning required cold blood, beyond anything that ran in the veins of any of the galaxy's reptilian species. Kuat had seen ample evidence of that ruthlessness in the Emperor—but what of the Rebels? He had gone over the reports provided by Kuat Drive Yards' own intelligence teams, the compilations of details, facts, rumors, myths, anything that could be found out about the Alliance's leaders, particularly this Luke Skywalker that both the Emperor and his top lieutenant Lord Vader seemed so obsessed with. But Kuat had yet to be able to make a determination about their innermost nature. All that idealism dismayed him; it was precisely that which had brought down the old Republic and allowed Palpatine to come to power. And now, with this talk of Luke Skywalker being a Jedi Knight— what could be more foolish? Kuat's ancestors had seen all that bright parade of honor and dedication, of belief in things greater than that which could be grasped by mortal hands, gradually fade away while the Emperor's power had grown, an eclipse swallowing whole the suns it put into shadow. The mysterious Force that had shaped the Jedi beliefs did not seem able to prevail against those such as Vader, who could turn it to darker use, use that consumed one's spirit even while one's grasp upon the galaxy's fate tightened. *Better to trust in machines,* Kuat mused, *and in the powers that can be seen and felt and measured.* That simple cunning had ensured the survival of Kuat Drive Yards. So far . . .

"And yet," murmured Kuat of Kuat. "And yet, I would believe. If I could."

"Technician?"

He was aware of the other man peering at him, trying to decipher the meaning of the barely audible words. "Pay me no heed." The felinx shifted in the cradle of Kuat's arms, its lustrous green eyes shut, its wordless dreams of satiated appetite and endless warmth safe for the time being. That was all that mattered, to this small creature at least. *It's got things soft,* Kuat thought ruefully. If he had only his own desires, his own hopes and fears, to consider, then making the necessary decisions would be considerably easier. But with all of Kuat Drive Yards weighing upon his shoulders, with its fate weighing upon his shoulders, the lives of so many depending upon the moves he made in this game, the alliances he forged between himself and unproven allies, the annihilating hatred of enemies whose powers, revealed or in the shadows, spanned the galaxy . . .

The sleeping felinx stirred in Kuat's arms, as though sensing some wordless measure of his troubles. He stroked its head, soothing the creature back into the unworried sector of its slumbers. *I'll take care of you,* Kuat promised it. *One way or another. Win or lose.*

Beside him, Fenald turned away for a moment. The security head pressed his fingertips to his ear, listening intently to the buried whisper of his cochlear implant.

"The report has been decrypted and analyzed, Technician." Fenald dropped his hand from the side of his jaw. "Perimeter intelligence stations have confirmation from their sources, with a reliability factor in the high nineties percentile range."

"Very good." Kuat of Kuat had expected as much. He had issued continuing orders that he wasn't to be bothered with rumors and baseless speculation. At this point, only cold, hard facts—the accurate reporting of the moves made by the other players in the game—would help him formulate his own strategies and gambits. "And the details?"

"The ship known as *Slave I*, registered to the

bounty hunter Boba Fett, was found drifting in orbit above the planet Tatooine—"

"Found by whom?" That was the important part. Kuat was aware that there had recently been a large Imperial Fleet in orbit above the atmosphere of Tatooine; it had apparently been lying in wait for an expected rescue operation from the Rebel Alliance. The Imperial Fleet was no longer in the sector—if it had been, Kuat's own bombing raid on Tatooine's Dune Sea would have had to have been aborted. There was still a possibility, though, that the Imperial Navy might have left a few reconnaissance ships behind.

"*Slave I* was found by a routine security patrol of the Rebel Alliance." The Kuat Drive Yards security head's memory was enhanced by a loop-recall data-organizing module, controlled by the barely noticeable tensing of his facial muscles. "For some time now, the Empire has ceded control of that sector to the Alliance, inasmuch as it has little apparent strategic value. That may change, of course, when we deliver the new additions to the Imperial Fleet."

That was Kuat's own analysis of the situation. Tatooine was at the edge of the galaxy, far from the important and highly developed sectors that formed the core of the Empire. Palpatine could write off the entire zone and it would result in little real loss, either economically or militarily. At least in the short run—but leaving the sector in the hands of the Alliance would certainly give Palpatine's foes a development and staging area for the rest of their campaign against the Empire. Sooner or later, Imperial ships and troops would have to sweep through the sector and reestablish control; the Empire couldn't tolerate this festering—and rapidly expanding—wound in its side.

More than that, Kuat knew, would dictate the

eventual offensive, the deadly tools for which were even now being constructed in the Kuat Drive Yards docks. There was also the Emperor's own personality, if that term could be applied to something that had been so utterly consumed by unchecked egomania and the dark powers that he commanded. In some ways, it could be argued—and Kuat had certainly done so, in late-night conversations with his security head—that Emperor Palpatine, as such, had already ceased to exist. Kuat had heard the stories of Palpatine's dedication to what he termed the dark side of the Force; whether such a mysterious energy field, underlying the very fabric of the universe, actually existed or not was of no concern to an engineer and scientist such as himself. But to the self-schooled psychologist that Kuat was, and the political intriguer that he had been forced to become, it mattered a great deal. The Force might only exist in the minds of the Emperor and a few other die-hard believers in the old religion, such as Darth Vader; that made it real enough to demand Kuat's attention. He had had a few face-to-face encounters with the Emperor and the Dark Lord of the Sith, representing his inherited corporation in the business negotiations upon which Kuat Drive Yards depended. At the last such meeting, Kuat of Kuat had received the unsettling impression that the physical body of the Emperor, that hooded and wrinkled form, was no more than a shell, hollowed from the inside by the Force in which Palpatine had placed so much of his own psychic energy. The small eyes buried in their sockets of crepelike tissue had seemed to Kuat like holes poked through a mask worn by a no-longer human entity, something from which all life had been drained, leaving only ravenous hunger and the desire for control over those creatures that still breathed and moved of their own volition. Something still called itself Emperor Palpatine, and spoke with the same wily, mocking tongue—but the words were those of an entity not only dead but embodying Death itself, a Force that consumed the energies of Life as its food.

Kuat remembered something else from his last encounter with the Emperor: a deep sense of being offended, not so much as a living creature but as a businessman, the guiding intelligence of one of the galaxy's largest and most powerful corporations. *Where are the customers going to come from?* The problem with Palpatine's vision of the future, an Empire where his word and his will were the only ones that mattered, was that it was just not a commercially viable environment. What would be the point of Kuat Drive Yards, or any other of the galaxy's great manufacturing concerns, designing and creating products to be sold on one planet or a thousand, if there was no one on those worlds to buy them? More than anyone, Kuat of Kuat was aware of the destructive capability of the warships that his firm was constructing for the Imperial Navy. For the Emperor to succeed in his ambitions, his mania for universal control—and for him to turn back the threat of the Rebel Alliance—all that would mean the destruction of any number of inoffensive and otherwise prosperous worlds. *Potential clients,* mused Kuat—if not directly for his corporation's products, then for other companies with whom he had already done business. The Emperor had already shown his disregard for maintaining the galaxy's customer base, by sanctioning the late Governor Tarkin's destruction of the planet Alderaan with the massive firepower of the original Death Star. That had personally rankled Kuat; there had been an outstanding contract with the local government on Alderaan for a utility fleet of perimeter observation scouts and

orbital customs stations, all to be furnished at a considerable profit by Kuat Drive Yards. The units had
just been about ready to leave the KDY construction
docks and head off in a delivery flotilla to Alderaan
when the word of their destination being reduced to a
few charred ashes drifting in navigable space had
reached Kuat of Kuat. A near-total write-down for the
corporation, salvageable only in part by breaking up
the undelivered vessels and recycling some of their
components into the next order for Imperial battle
cruisers. For a while, he had considered presenting a
bill to Emperor Palpatine, for the losses sustained by
Kuat Drive Yards, but had at last decided not to push
the issue. *Better to leave the red ink on the books,*
Kuat had figured, *than make an enemy out of one's
biggest remaining customer.* Even with Prince Xizor
gone, things were still dangerous enough at Palpatine's court, with all the various levels of intrigue constantly going on, without handing another weapon to
the corporation's enemies.

"So the Rebel Alliance has Boba Fett's ship." Kuat
brought himself back to the situation at hand. The
deeper concerns over which he mulled would have to
wait a while longer for their final resolution. "And it
has been confirmed that this is in fact *Slave I*?"

It was a good question. Boba Fett's personal history was studded with occasions in which the bounty
hunter had passed off a ringer vehicle as his distinctive
ship. For someone whose skills consisted largely of
handing out other creatures' deaths, Fett had an unusual talent for faking his own demise. Or perhaps
that talent was to be expected—Kuat wasn't sure
which. Life and death were the same for a bounty
hunter; it was all merchandise, with different values
attached, depending upon the marketplace. Boba Fett
or any of his colleagues—they were all just as happy

to deliver a corpse as well as a living hostage, if the same payoff could be gotten for it. With that kind of attitude, it was no wonder that one's own death became just a matter of strategy and negotiation.

The head of security gave a single nod. "Our sources in the Alliance have concluded that there is no deception involved—as least as far as the identity of the intercepted ship is concerned. The subcode numbers on the engines' shield regulator devices have been read out—" He tapped the side of his head, where the cochlear implants were hidden. "Those were in the message that was received just now. I forwarded them to our records department; the numbers match up with the original construction manifest for *Slave I*."

"That settles the issue, then." Kuat of Kuat had personally supervised the design and assembly of Boba Fett's ship; there had been some custom features that still distinguished *Slave I* as a state-of-the-art job. An ID profile, the signal that was transmitted from one ship to another with the critical name and affiliation data, could be faked—not easily, but with enough determination and technical expertise, it could be done. Unbeknownst to the Empire or any other Kuat Drive Yards customer, every ship that left the construction docks had a trapdoor access routine hardwired into its onboard computers, for just that purpose. For Boba Fett to have overridden *Slave I*'s regulator subcodes, though, would have meant risking a catastrophic core meltdown; there wouldn't be a ship left floating around to be misidentified. *Ergo,* this ship was Fett's and no other. "Did our sources have any other information about the ship? The contents, perhaps?"

A shake of the head. "Other than it being unoccupied—nothing. The Rebel Alliance forces that found the ship are still examining it."

"They won't find anything," said Kuat of Kuat.

"What makes you so sure, Technician? Boba Fett was involved in a great many activities that depended upon maintaining secrecy." The security head clasped his hands behind the small of his back. "I would have thought it stood to reason that there might be some . . . *intriguing* traces of Fett's past aboard his ship."

"Oh, there very well might be." Kuat gave a shrug as he stroked the animal nestled in his arms. "And if you knew where to look, and if you had at least some idea of what you were looking for—*and* you were sufficiently motivated to begin with—you might be able to find them. But there's nobody associated with the Rebel Alliance who's capable of that kind of investigation. The Rebels are at a critical stage in their campaign against the Empire, and the crisis isn't likely to end anytime soon. They're not going to waste their precious time going over the ship of a dead bounty hunter—as they're likely to believe Boba Fett to be— with a fine-tooth comb. It'll be a moral issue with them." Kuat shook his head, pityingly. "As much disdain as the Imperial Navy has for bounty hunters and other semicriminal types, it's even worse with the Rebels. When you think you're finer and truer and more virtuous than your opponents, it's all too easy to fall into a blinding self-righteousness." That had never been a problem for Kuat himself; he was comfortable at any moral level, from the stars to the gutters, as long as it helped ensure the survival of Kuat Drive Yards. He could deal with anybody; doing business with Emperor Palpatine and his admirals proved as much. "The Rebel Alliance will give Fett's ship a cursory going-over," said Kuat, "and then they'll try to dispose of it as quickly as possible."

"Of course." The security head nodded slowly, digesting the other's superior wisdom. "I imagine they'll be able to get a pretty good price for *Slave I*. Considering what an expensive piece of goods it was to begin with—salvage value should be high. Any number of other bounty hunters would want it for their own personal vessel."

"Possibly," agreed Kuat. His head of security knew what he was talking about. When Boba Fett had ordered the construction and outfitting of the vessel, the bounty hunter had stipulated some expensive custom details. Kuat Drive Yards' accountants had demanded full payment up-front even before the ship's basic hull had been welded together. The design parameters that Fett had stipulated took the science—and the art—of small-craft development to a new level, one that Kuat himself had been only idly dreaming of, setting out a few concept sketches in his off-hours, before the actual job had manifested itself into reality. The advance payment had been for two reasons that had outweighed Kuat's innate desire to build such a ship: given the amount of time and resources that would be required to prototype, test, and finalize some of the unit's engine and maneuverability components, all the way from scratch to end product, and given the hazardous nature of the customer's line of work, said customer might well have been dead by the time *Slave I* had been ready to leave the docks. That would have been reason enough to demand the payment at the start of the process; the other reason lay in the nature of the ship itself, when it was completed. Anything that extreme in design was fully capable of killing the pilot on its first shakedown run, if the overpowered engines got away from him and tore apart the durasteel frame like a collection of wooden twigs. Better to collect the money well before the customer succeeded in annihilating himself.

That hadn't happened. The combination of Boba

Fett's pilot skills and Kuat of Kuat's design genius had resulted in *Slave I* being recognized—and feared—across the galaxy. A ship didn't have to be as big and overwhelming as an Imperial battle cruiser—or a Death Star—to have the necessary psychological effect.

Standing next to Kuat, the head of security raised an eyebrow. "I would have thought it a certainty," he said, "that the bidding for such a desirable item would be rather fierce."

"It would be—if the prospective purchasers thought there was nothing wrong with the ship." Kuat displayed a thin smile. "Of course, sentient creatures often get *interesting* ideas planted into their heads. Especially when someone such as Boba Fett is concerned—perhaps even more so now that he's thought of as the *late* Boba Fett. Bounty hunters and similar entities have their little superstitions, their fears and suspicions—not all of which are groundless, either. It's well known that Boba Fett had a considerable degree of security systems wired into *Slave I*; only a fool would assume that those had been deactivated by the original owner's demise. It's one thing to buy a used ship; it's another to buy a death trap."

"Ah." The security head nodded. "And if rumors, little hints about the unpleasant surprises that might be encountered by the new owner of *Slave I*, were to begin circulating in the appropriate territories . . ."

"Then the price might go down considerably." The felinx in Kuat's arms purred, as if it too were pleased by this notion. "And if the price goes down, so does the attention paid to the eventual sale—that's how psychology works for all sentient creatures. If they're no longer interested in a certain item, then they don't much care who is."

"Which would mean," said Fenald, "that when the Rebel Alliance finally puts *Slave I* up for sale, when they've finished their superficial examination of it, then the ship could not only be purchased for a bargain price, but also with a considerable amount of discretion."

"Exactly." Kuat of Kuat continued watching the launch preparations at the main construction dock. "Have one of our subsidiary corporations look into it—a components supplier, perhaps, but make sure that there isn't an obvious ownership trail back to Kuat Drive Yards. Transfer enough funds from one of my personal operating accounts, so that they'll be able to make the purchase when it happens. Instruct their chief negotiator to contact the Rebel Alliance as soon as possible, and see if they'll accept a preemptory bid; that way, the ship won't even come up on the open market and we won't have to deal with any other interested parties."

"And the rumor campaign? Concerning the dangers of purchasing Boba Fett's ship?"

"That should go into immediate high-speed propagation, to all points of the galaxy, radiating outward from Tatooine—that was where *Slave I* was last spotted. Make sure that the rumors penetrate all sectors controlled by the Rebel Alliance. The sooner they're convinced that *Slave I* is devalued merchandise, the more likely they'll be ready to listen to the preemptory purchase agreement. We've already got some listening-post agents planted in Mos Eisley, don't we?"

The security head gave a quick, affirming nod. "We just rotated a fresh crew into the spaceport."

"Fine," said Kuat. "They can start spreading the word. Have the covert operations department in our public relations wing come up with some negative-impact details about *Slave I*'s onboard security systems; perhaps some story about one of the Rebel Alliance investigating teams getting blown away as soon as they opened the main hatch. That way, when and if the Rebel Alliance indicates that the ship is going to be put up for sale, most sentient creatures' suspicions about it will be confirmed, whether they're true or not."

"By the time the rumor campaign is finished, Technician, the Alliance will be ready to *give* the ship to the first person that comes along."

"I'm not concerned about the nature of the bargain." Beyond the overarching curve of the segmented viewscreens, the last of the preparations for launching were nearly complete. Kuat could see the final checkout and clearance team departing from the battle cruiser, still shrouded beneath its net lines and pressurized construction canopies. "The only thing that's important in this regard is that we acquire *Slave I*— and its contents—as discreetly as possible. When our subsidiary corporation has gained title to the ship, it is to be brought here to Kuat Drive Yards in a shielded cargo transport, and no one outside of the KDY security operations is to know about it."

"That may be difficult to pull off, Technician." Fenald inhaled through clenched teeth. "The Imperial Navy has stepped up contraband-interception patrols in most of the navigable sectors between here and Tatooine. They've even been going over our regular supply shipments with a fine-tooth comb. Getting an entire transport past them, with its contents concealed, will take some doing."

The security head's statement didn't come as a surprise to Kuat of Kuat. He was already aware of slowdowns in the construction docks, due to the Imperial Navy's interference with the on-time delivery of necessary materials. Kuat Drive Yards had had to push back the delivery date on a number of the Empire's own orders. Since it was the fault of Palpatine's overzealous admirals, Kuat had been able to avoid any penalty rebates—for the time being, at least. But there had been no change in the ongoing situation, which indicated that the time-wasting searches must, at some level, have the Emperor's approval. Another psychological ploy: the Emperor was fully aware that Kuat Drive Yards wasn't doing any business with the Rebel Alliance, but ordering the searches to continue would indicate to Palpatine's underlings, and anyone outside the court on Coruscant, that the corporation was under suspicion.

Hard to tell what Emperor Palpatine was trying to achieve with a ploy like that, especially at a cost to himself of delaying these much-needed additions to his navy. With every time unit that passed, the Rebel Alliance was increasing in numbers and strength. Was tarnishing Kuat Drive Yards' reputation, and impugning its loyalty to the Empire, worth such a disadvantage? Kuat answered his own question: *It is, if Palpatine wishes to destroy—or take over—the corporation.* That was entirely consistent with the Emperor's lust for power and control. It wasn't enough to be a faithful ally to a madman like that; perhaps the time had finally arrived in the Emperor's carefully calculated plans, when he'd find it satisfying to consume those closest to him. The Emperor didn't want allies; he wanted slaves.

Perhaps I should go over to the Rebel Alliance. And take Kuat Drive Yards with him; the thought—and the temptation—had struck Kuat before. Was there any other option? Even if Kuat Drive Yards remained as the Empire's chief military contractor and was instrumental in achieving Palpatine's ambitions, what reward would there be for such service?

The same as there would very likely be for all of the Emperor's stormtroopers and admirals: annihilation, absorption, reduction into a will-less instrument of Palpatine's ego. Death, without the consolation of non-existence; life, where every atom of one's being was part of the prison into which the universe had been transformed.

Only one thing prevented Kuat of Kuat from following through on that notion, of taking Kuat Drive Yards over to the Empire's sworn enemies. What stopped him was the suspicion that that was exactly what Emperor Palpatine wanted him to do. All of the Emperor's actions regarding the corporation might be designed to push Kuat into the Rebel Alliance's arms. There were still forces in Palpatine's court that sought the destruction of Kuat Drive Yards as an independent entity. While Prince Xizor had been alive, he had whispered lies into the ear of the Emperor; perhaps Palpatine had finally been convinced by them. If Kuat made any move at all toward the Rebel Alliance, that could be justification enough for the Emperor to launch a full-scale assault against Kuat, placing the corporation's vast technical resources and construction docks under direct military control. There wouldn't be a Kuat Drive Yards after that; generations of engineering skill, the blood in Kuat's veins, would finally have come to an end, hissing into red steam under a stormtrooper's white-hot bolt of blaster fire.

"You might be correct about that . . ."

"Technician?"

"About bringing *Slave I* here to Kuat Drive Yards, once our subsidiary has acquired it from the Alliance." Kuat's deep musing about the dangers involved in his dealings with the Empire had connected with more immediate concerns. As delicate and ringed with hazard as the situation was, it might be a fatal mistake to be caught with such concrete evidence of being in touch with the Rebels; the enemies of Kuat Drive Yards would be sure to put the worst possible spin on it. "Perhaps it would be better if we secured some remote locale to which *Slave I* could be taken, and an inspection team could go there and examine the ship. We'd have to make sure, though, that they couldn't be identified as Kuat Drive Yards employees."

The security head nodded. "That could be arranged, Technician."

"See to it." Kuat stroked beneath the felinx's chin, perceiving in his fingertips the animal's contented murmur. "That will be all for now."

In the executive offices of Kuat Drive Yards, there was no need for the elaborate and obsequious rituals found at Palpatine's court. Fenald turned and strode away, bootsteps echoing on the matte-surfaced metal flooring.

Kuat remained gazing out the segmented viewscreens. Voicing his thoughts had helped sort them out, like examining a set of blueprints scrolling across a high-resolution CAD screen. Kuat Drive Yards' head of security was an unimaginative but thorough personality—Kuat had chosen and promoted him for precisely those reasons, plus an unflagging loyalty to the corporation that had nurtured him. There had been no need to remind Fenald of the importance of acquiring Boba Fett's ship—reacquiring it, actually, since the ship had been built here at KDY. Not because of any intrinsic value to the ship, but because of what it might still contain. It didn't matter whether Boba Fett was alive or not—and Kuat had the same gut feeling he'd experienced after the bombing raid on Tatooine's Dune Sea that Fett had eluded every force that would have brought about a lesser creature's destruction. Even if the unlikeliest event had occurred, and Boba Fett really was dead, there were very likely traces aboard *Slave I*, evidence of some of the deeper and more dangerous conspiracies with which the bounty hunter had become involved. Evidence that led back to Kuat Drive Yards; that was the real danger that had to be averted at all costs.

If Fett destroyed the cargo droid, brooded Kuat. *Or got rid of it somehow . . . then we might be safe.* For all his cunning, Boba Fett had almost certainly been aware of the value of the material that had fallen into his hands; he might have disposed of it before leaving *Slave I* in orbit above Tatooine. But if the big, awkward droid still existed, with its boxlike innards full of spy equipment and incriminating data waiting to be deciphered and analyzed—then a whole new level of trouble would begin for Kuat Drive Yards. All because of a holo-video of an Imperial stormtrooper raid on an isolated moisture farm on Tatooine, and the pheromone scent of the galaxy's most powerful criminal, the leader of the Black Sun organization . . .

Into Kuat's meditations came the image of Prince Xizor's face, with its violet eyes and cold, sneering smile. Even more than Emperor Palpatine, that had been the enemy all of Kuat Drive Yards had to fear. Xizor's death had not eliminated the dangers the corporation had to confront.

A signal flare, a quick streak of white light soaring up from the construction docks, cut short Kuat's musing.

He briefly took one hand away from the felinx and touched a miniaturized keypad on his opposite wrist. The circuitry controlling the viewscreens' time-aperture filtering went into activated status, synchronizing with the close-range signal from the micro-shutters implanted in his corneas. For a split second, the viewscreens flickered opaque, then became transparent again as the two optical systems locked in tight with each other.

No sound would travel through the vacuum between the docks and the arching viewscreens of Kuat's offices. But the glare of fiery light, if left unblocked, would be enough to startle the sleeping felinx awake. The creature was easily frightened; Kuat had no wish to have it clawing its panicky way out of his arms. There was still a white, threadlike scar under his own chin, from the last time that had happened.

The final signal flare, red this time, coursed across the field of stars above Kuat Drive Yards. That meant all KDY personnel had been cleared from the dock where the completed Imperial battle cruiser lay waiting, still shrouded in service lines and access canopies.

There was no need for a signal from him; everything happened automatically from this point. A simple imbedded fuse catalyzed the pyrogenic compounds interlaced in the shrouding material; the oxygen still captured inside the canopies' folds was sufficient for the christening of fire, the purging of everything that wasn't hardened durasteel.

In seconds, the battle cruiser had been wrapped in flames, churning in upon themselves, absent the rising convection effects that would have been caused by a surrounding atmosphere. The surrounding canopies had already blackened and been torn into great, ragged-edged sheets of ash, dissolving into nothingness as the last fiery glow dissipated. From the construction dock, the battle cruiser rose slightly, a perfect weapon, cleansed and tempered.

A few bits of ash, compelled outward by the force

of the vanished flame, drifted against the thick glass of
the segmented viewscreens. Kuat of Kuat stood with
the still-sleeping felinx cradled in his arms, the after-
image of fire shifting its spectrum behind the filters of
his eyes.

4

"You know how to pilot this thing?"

Boba Fett glanced over his shoulder at the other bounty hunter standing in the hatchway of the *Hound's Tooth*'s cockpit. "There are certain difficulties," he said evenly, with no apparent emotion. "But they can be overcome." He raised his own gloved hands from the control panel's distinctive forearm grooves. "Trandoshan operating interfaces are on the crude and awkward side, but the ship's configuration is otherwise standard. Anything of which those big claws are capable, I assure you is equally within my grasp."

I bet, thought Dengar. He leaned against the side of the hatchway, watching Boba Fett make some final navigation adjustments. He'd had his own encounters with Trandoshans, including the former owner of this ship, and they had all been unpleasant. Bossk had had a reputation for a hot temper even back in the days of the old Bounty Hunters Guild, when he'd had presumably less to gripe about. Cross him, and you were likely to get your head unscrewed from your shoulders like the lid of an emergency rations canister. That was what those claws were suitable for, not high-speed, pinpoint starhopping. Whereas someone like

Boba Fett could work over an enemy with equal finality *and* handle intimidatingly complex gear, from any kind of interplanetary vessel to that Mandalorian battle armor that Fett wore.

Dengar pointed to the cockpit's comm equipment. "What happens when somebody recognizes this ship, and they want to talk to Bossk? We might run into some old friend of his, somebody who can tell that this is the *Hound*."

"True," said Fett. He had turned his gaze back to the ship's controls. "But where we're going, we're not likely to encounter many acquaintances of Bossk's. He confined himself to a relatively restricted number of sectors, the worlds and systems where he was well known enough to command a certain measure of respect. That's what he liked. Bossk never showed much initiative about expanding his operations into new territories."

"If you say so." Dengar shrugged. "I guess that was his loss, huh?"

"Perhaps." Boba Fett punched another set of coordinates into the navicomputer. "Or it might be why he's still alive at all. Sometimes—for creatures like him—it's better to play it safe."

Yeah? And what about creatures like us? He found himself gazing at the back of Boba Fett's helmet, wondering what was going on inside it, what schemes and hidden agendas might be ticking away in the other bounty hunter's skull. It was no help to have seen Fett without the distinctive Mandalorian helmet—he supposed he was one of the few, along with the former dancing girl Neelah, who could make that claim. All that time down on Tatooine, when the two of them had been nursing Boba Fett back to health, keeping him from dying after he'd managed to explode his way out of the Sarlacc's gut—and Dengar was still no closer to figuring out the creature whose life he'd saved. And that was bad news, considering he was now supposedly partners with the deadliest and most feared bounty hunter in the galaxy; a partnership that Boba Fett had proposed and that Dengar had accepted, perhaps a little too quickly, now that he'd had a chance to think it over. *Why did I agree to that?* The ostensible reason was that the arrangement had seemed the quickest way to make a lot of money, pay off the huge debtload he'd been dragging around for years, and marry his beloved Manaroo—*if* she were still waiting for him, and *if* he returned to her as something other than a blaster-fried corpse.

Being out of touch with her was pure torment for Dengar; the depth of his love for Manaroo had not been completely apparent to him until just before he had left Tatooine in Boba Fett's *Slave I*. Dengar had contacted Manaroo and had instructed her to take his ship *The Punishing One* and go into hiding. She had done that job well; right now, he had no idea where in this galaxy Manaroo was, and no way of communicating with her. They had agreed together that as long as Dengar was partners with the notorious bounty hunter Boba Fett, it would be too dangerous for them to remain in contact with each other. There were too many creatures with well-nursed grievances against Boba Fett, or who would see some way of profiting by his death; if those creatures discovered that Fett's partner had committed his heart and spirit and fortunes to a female on her own, she would then be seen as the weak point in Fett's armor, the way of getting at him through his business associate. Manaroo would become the target of every low-life scum in the galaxy; she was smart and tough enough to evade and fight them off, but not forever—and Dengar wouldn't be there to protect her. That factor had tormented his mind and influenced his decision more than anything else.

But even that small measure of safety for his beloved had come with a price. Someday they would be together again—but only if they both survived, and if they found one another once more.

Those were big ifs, and getting increasingly bigger in Dengar's mind, the more time he spent hooked up with Boba Fett. Life as a bounty hunter had been hazardous enough, before now—which had been one of the main reasons he'd wanted to get out of this line of work. *And now,* he thought gloomily, *I've gone from the edges of all that danger right to the center.* If his luck—and his skills—had been nothing to boast of before, he had at least managed to keep himself alive. But there hadn't been mysterious, unidentified forces bringing a full-scale bombing raid down on his head, as had happened back on Tatooine. The raid obviously hadn't been meant to kill him; his death wouldn't even have been noticed by whoever was gunning for Boba Fett. That was the problem with hooking up with someone like that. Fett had whatever it took to survive under the most murderous conditions— even the Sarlacc hadn't been able to kill him. *Too bad,* thought Dengar, *for anybody else.* If you weren't at that level, you were dead meat.

And for what?

"So—" He tried again to get some useful information. "If we're not heading anywhere that Bossk used to hang out . . . where exactly *is* it we're going?"

Boba Fett didn't look around at him. "I prefer keeping that on a need-to-know basis. And right now, you don't need it."

A spark of resentment flared inside Dengar. "I thought we were supposed to be partners."

"So we are." Fett's gloved hands moved across the cockpit controls. "I consider myself bound by the agreement into which we both entered."

"Doesn't seem like much of a partnership, if you're making all the decisions." Dengar's voice tightened inside his throat. "I had the impression that somehow we were going to be on an equal footing. I guess I got that wrong, huh?"

This time, Boba Fett did swivel the pilot's chair around. The cold, blank gaze of his helmet's narrow visor fastened on Dengar. The rock that had formed in Dengar's throat now turned into a leaden weight, falling past his heart and into the pit of his stomach.

"You might have had some misapprehension along that line." The flatness of Boba Fett's words was scarier than any show of emotion would have been. "But if you continue to believe that we could somehow be equals, then I'm forced to disagree with my partner. There's no way that you and I could be thought of as equals. Not as far as being bounty hunters is concerned."

"Well . . ." The weight in his gut had gone cold, draining all the warmth from Dengar's blood. Boba Fett's hidden gaze seemed to press him downward, like a bug beneath the other's boot. "I didn't mean it exactly like that . . ."

"Good. I'd hate to think I had wrongly estimated my partner's value to me." Boba Fett's voice continued, as mild and threatening as before. "We do have some value to each other, Dengar. Even beyond your having saved my life, when you found me back there in the Dune Sea. But don't think that you're here, and my partner, simply because of gratitude. I assure you—I don't feel that kind of emotion."

Or any, thought Dengar. He could feel himself

sweating inside his own gear. Already, he had gone beyond wishing that he had ever broached this subject with the other bounty hunter.

"We can," said Boba Fett, "be very useful to each other. That's the only basis I know for a partnership. Of course, if you consider something else to be the case . . ."

Dengar stared back at the helmet's visor, as though hypnotized by the eyes concealed behind it. All words and thoughts had fled from his own skull.

"Then perhaps we should think about dissolving the partnership. Is that what you want?"

It took a while for Dengar to force a reply past his tongue. "No . . ." He shook his head. "That's not what I meant at all . . ."

"I'd advise you to think about what it is you want, then." Boba Fett leaned slightly forward in the pilot's chair, bringing the pressure of his visored gaze closer to Dengar. "Because if we're not going to be partners—our business relationship will be a lot different."

He's playing with me, thought Dengar. It didn't come as a relief to discover that Boba Fett was capable of emotion, or at least of cruelty. He raised his hands, palm outward, as if in surrender. "No," said Dengar hastily, "that's okay. I'm perfectly . . . satisfied with the way things are. You run the operations however you want, and that's fine by me."

Boba Fett was silent for a moment, then his helmet tilted in the barest nod of acknowledgment. "Very well," he said quietly. "There's no confusion now."

"Not in the slightest," agreed Dengar. He found he could breathe once more.

Boba Fett swiveled the pilot's chair back toward

the cockpit controls. "I'll make the decisions—and *you* carry them out."

The last remark puzzled Dengar. "Just what is it . . . you want me to do?"

"When the time comes, there'll be plenty. Don't worry about keeping up your end of the partnership. But in the meantime, why don't you just take it easy? Just relax."

Sure, thought Dengar to himself. *As if that's going to happen anytime soon.*

"Enjoy the peace and quiet," said Boba Fett as he continued his navigational adjustments, "while you can. It might be in short supply where we're heading."

"All right." Dengar stepped back from the cockpit's hatchway. "You're the boss."

"Close enough," said Boba Fett. "Go below and tell Neelah to strap herself in—you too, for that matter. We'll be making a jump into hyperspace in a few minutes."

He knew better than to ask the destination. Whatever coordinates Boba Fett had punched into the navicomputer, they didn't seem to be open for discussion. *That's a real partnership, all right*—Dengar turned away from the cockpit and grasped the ladder leading down to the minimal passenger space of the *Hound's Tooth*. It wouldn't be long before the ship would emerge into some sector of the galaxy, so uninviting that a Trandoshan such as Bossk had never frequented it. That made him feel about as comfortable as what being partners with Boba Fett had turned into.

He turned his head as he started down the metal treads of the ladder, looking back toward the cockpit. The other bounty hunter went about his self-appointed tasks, as though he'd already forgotten Dengar's presence.

Right, thought Dengar. If he'd had any doubts before about the exact nature of the partnership between himself and Boba Fett, they were cleared up now. *One way or another—*

His boot soles rang on the metal treads of the ladder all the way down.

She could barely believe what she had just heard. Overheard, actually—Neelah had tapped into the *Hound's Tooth*'s internal communications system through an access panel in the main personnel quarters aboard ship. The cramped space was furnished in Trandoshan taste, all dark tapestries over the bulkheads and a jumble of thinly padded sleeping pallets. The tapestries were fastened down at their corners, to keep them from drifting and tangling in case the ship's artificial gravity failed; they depicted various great moments in Trandoshan history and legend, all of them violent. Even while she had been fiddling with the comm equipment, with the specific intent of eavesdropping on Dengar and Boba Fett, she had been thanking fate that the *Hound's* original pilot wasn't still aboard.

Her gratitude faded a bit when she finally managed to listen in on the conversation up in the cockpit area. She was dismayed at the manner in which Boba Fett walked all over Dengar, for no more reason than a simple inquiry as to where they were all heading. *He's one,* Neelah thought disgustedly, *that's not going to be much use to me.* If things came down to a split between herself and Boba Fett—and she could already see how that was becoming increasingly likely—then having the other bounty hunter Dengar on her side wouldn't make much difference. Fett could eliminate them both, without any inconvenience at all.

If it hadn't been clear to her before, it was now obvious why Dengar wanted to get out of the bounty hunter trade so badly. *He just doesn't have the guts for it*, she thought with a rueful shake of her head. The kind of guts, and the conspicuous lack of nerves, that Boba Fett possessed. Better that Dengar should hang up his weapons and jettison his dwindling reserve of ambition, and settle down on some safe backwater world with his intended bride Manaroo, before he got himself killed or completely imploded from panic.

Neelah had her own conviction, reinforced now that she had listened in on Dengar and Boba Fett, about how matters would wind up going. *I'll have to do everything myself*. Wherever the *Hound's Tooth* was headed, and whatever was waiting for them there. She'd have to do it all, including saving her own and Dengar's lives—the cold lack of emotion in Boba Fett's voice assured her that he had no great regard for their survival. Dengar might have fallen for that partnership scam, but she hadn't. Neelah hadn't agreed to it, either; as far as she was concerned, she was an independent operator, with no one's skin but her own to watch out for.

The only problem with that was she still didn't know whose skin that really was. *I don't even know my real name*, mused Neelah bitterly. Her name, and everything that went with it: history, friends, enemies; who she might be able to ask for help, and receive; who would cut her throat at a moment's notice, if they knew she was alive and off the surface of the planet Tatooine. She had her suspicions, pieced together from logic rather than actual information. *Whoever dumped me off at Jabba's palace*—whoever it had been, that was the creature for whom she had to watch out. Or creatures in the plural; it might have been a whole conspiracy, any number of the galaxy's sinister forces leagued against her. They must have had their reasons for wiping her memory clean, all her past erased from inside her skull, disguising her as a simple dancing girl, and sticking her inside the fortressed headquarters of one of the most powerful criminal overlords to be found on any world. Perhaps Jabba the Hutt had known the whole story behind her being in his palace—but that didn't do her any good now. Jabba was dead, and all the secrets that the loathsome slug had kept to himself were gone as well.

Almost the only thing that remained from her past, a scrap of memory that had been left behind by the wipe process, was an image. No voice, no words, no other data, however fragmentary. Whoever had done it to her had been meticulously thorough. Perhaps it would have been better for her, though, if they had eradicated that last little bit as well. The image left in Neelah's obliterated memory was that of a face. Or rather a nonface; a mask. The image of Boba Fett's narrow-visored helmet, concealing the living face beneath its hard, inhuman gaze . . .

She had seen that masked face at Jabba's palace, and it had filled her with fear and anger then. Neelah had sensed that the bounty hunter hadn't been just guarding the Hutt as he'd been hired to do—Jabba had been one of the few creatures in the galaxy wealthy enough to have engaged Boba Fett's services like that—but she had also been sure that Fett had been following his own private agenda as well. He came and went from Jabba's court on mysterious errands, though he'd displayed a sure instinct for always being on hand in a moment of crisis, such as when Princess Leia Organa, disguised as an Ubese bounty hunter demanding the reward for a captured Wookiee, had brandished an activated thermal detonator right in front of Jabba. Boba Fett had snapped his blaster rifle up into firing position in less than a heart-beat, as most of Jabba's other guards had dived for cover.

Nobody had died that time, but it hadn't been for any lack of readiness on Boba Fett's part. Jabba had paid the bounty and the disguised princess had deactivated the explosive device—otherwise there wouldn't even have been ruins left of Jabba's palace. Neelah was sure, though, that Boba Fett would have survived somehow; he always did, no matter how many other creatures died around him.

And—strangely—she also knew that she would have still been alive, no matter what happened. *Let the fire fall,* thought Neelah; she would have emerged unscathed, carried to safety by . . . Boba Fett. Who else?

That was the meaning, she had little doubt, of the interest Fett had shown in her welfare, back at Jabba's palace. It hadn't taken her long to pick up on it, that every time the bounty hunter had returned from one of his mysterious errands, his helmeted gaze had turned in her direction, making certain that she was still there, alive and unharmed.

Which took some doing in a den of violence like Jabba's palace, where all the thugs and scoundrels took their cues from their master's own tastes in the suffering of other creatures. A Hutt like Jabba didn't count his wealth just in how many credits he kept heaped up in his treasure vaults, but also in how much pain and death he could inflict . . . and savor, like one of the squirming little delicacies that his tiny hands had stuffed into the lipless chasm of his mouth. A good number of Jabba's hirelings had worked for cheap—his favorite salary arrangement—with the understanding that they could indulge their cruel appetites as well.

Poor Oola had been one of the prettiest of the

palace's dancing girls, and thus reserved for Jabba's pleasure; that had been symbolized by the fine-linked chain he'd kept her on. *Not for me,* thought Neelah. She touched her face with one hand, her fingertips tracing the healed scar of the wound she'd received from the pikestaff of one of the Gamorrean palace guards when she'd made her own escape. Even before the honed metal had slashed across her jaw and cheek, she hadn't been of quite the same fragile loveliness as Oola had been. Given Jabba's sadistic tastes, the pleasure he had taken in seeing beauty viciously ripped to bleeding pieces, to be not quite so beautiful was a blessing; during her time in the palace, Neelah had seen prettier females than herself tossed to Jabba's pet rancor, and had heard their brief screams from the depths of the pit while Jabba's sniggering thugs had clustered around the edge, enjoying the sight nearly as much as their master had.

But there had been another reason for Neelah's longer life span within the thick stone walls of Jabba's palace. The first glimmerings of her suspicions had grown into absolute certainty. *It was him,* thought Neelah. *It was Boba Fett.* She glanced up again toward the cockpit area of the *Hound's Tooth.* An invisible connection stretched between herself and the helmeted bounty hunter piloting the ship. The same mysterious connection that had existed between them back in Jabba's palace. Without a word ever having passed between a mere dancing girl and the galaxy's most feared bounty hunter—at least, no word that her ravaged memory could recall—she had known even then that Boba Fett had been keeping watch on her. So that no harm would come to her—that is, none of a fatal kind. Life in the palace had had its numerous and imaginative unpleasantries, most of which had caused Neelah and the other dancing girls to wonder if a quick exit via the rancor pit wouldn't have been preferable. But Neelah had realized at some point that choice wasn't open to her. She'd had a guardian, of a sort; Boba Fett's careful and silent observation hadn't been trained just on his Huttese employer.

What would've happened, Neelah wondered idly, *if Jabba had gotten around to throwing me to the rancor?* A good question, even if it had been rendered moot by Jabba's death. The answer depended, she supposed, upon the exact nature of her importance to the bounty hunter. Was it great enough that Boba Fett would have interfered with Jabba's pleasures? Enough that, if the need had arisen, Fett would have swung his blaster rifle up and pointed it at Jabba's massive, jowly face, and the deep sepulchral voice from inside the helmet would have ordered the Hutt to let her go?

She wasn't sure, even now; Boba Fett played a complicated game, with the value of the pieces on the board shifting as rapidly as his stratagems. Whatever concern he'd shown for her welfare in Jabba's palace hadn't been based on any great love for her. Fett had already assured her—*and I believe it,* she thought grimly—that concern for other creatures' lives was a notion foreign to his mind. Even when he was ferrying a piece of hard merchandise, as hostages with prices on their heads were called in the bounty hunter trade, the only consideration that kept breath in their lungs was that live prey was usually worth more than dead ones to those who forked over the credits for their capture.

And what am I worth? That question still haunted her thoughts. *As any kind of merchandise.* Her worth, her value to Boba Fett; the reasons why he had been so intent upon her surviving her time in Jabba's palace—those were things that she still hadn't been able to figure out. If he had an interest in keeping her alive, then he undoubtedly had his reasons for it—and those reasons might not be any that were to her advantage.

There was one more question that was even more disturbing. *What happens,* wondered Neelah, *when those reasons come to an end?* When her life had no more value for Boba Fett, she could hardly expect a creature like him to keep her around out of mere sentiment. She had been no more than a dancing girl to Jabba; she was sure of that, having seen the slit pupils of the Hutt's eyes narrow upon sight of her, with the same malignant, destructive lusts that all things of beauty had evoked in his blubber-swaddled heart. Boba Fett wouldn't dispose of her just for the sake of whatever sick pleasure could be found in another creature's suffering, but for cold, hard credits. Neelah didn't find that to be any better arrangement. *I wind up dead,* she mused bitterly, *either way.*

Though there was another outcome possible. A long shot, but better than no chance at all. And much more to her liking. *Somebody winds up dead, all right.* She nodded slowly to herself. *But it won't be me . . .*

All she would have to do—if and when that final confrontation came—would be to take on the galaxy's number-one bounty hunter, a killing machine that other killers dreaded encountering. *Take him on,* thought Neelah, *and take him out.*

It wouldn't be easy.

But oddly, as slim as her chances might be—she found herself almost looking forward to that final encounter.

The course of Neelah's thoughts was interrupted by the clang of boot soles upon the treads of the ladder that stretched up from the cargo area to the cockpit of the appropriated *Hound's Tooth.* Neelah quickly started to close the access panel to the comm circuits, then relaxed when she saw that it was only Dengar climbing down the ladder.

"Nice job," said Neelah. She folded her arms across her chest and regarded him. "You pretty much let him wrap you up into a neat little package, didn't you?"

Dengar stepped off the bottom of the ladder. "What're you talking about?"

"Come on." She didn't care if Dengar knew that she had been listening in on the cockpit conversations. With her thumb, she pointed to the exposed wiring and the small listening device she had found in the ship's spare-parts locker and had spliced in. "I heard everything you said. And everything Boba Fett said back to you." Neelah slowly shook her head. "I can't say I was very impressed. At least, not with you."

With a sigh of pent-up breath, Dengar lowered himself onto a bare metal bench at the side of the cargo area. "He's a tough customer." The bounty hunter's shoulders slumped forward, in a full kinetic display of defeat. "That hunter might as well be made out of durasteel, from his skin into his heart. If he's got one."

"What were you expecting?"

Dengar shrugged. "Pretty much what I got from him."

"You idiot," said Neelah. "I mean, what were you trying to achieve? What were your plans when you started talking to Fett?"

" 'Plans'?" A blank look crossed Dengar's face. "Right now, I couldn't tell you."

"Great." Neelah's voice soured with disgust. "We're both possibly riding to our deaths—right at this moment—and the only ally I might have is completely brain-dead."

"Hey—" The bounty hunter straightened up from his slump. "That's not fair. You think it's so easy getting something out of Boba Fett, then *you* try it. I'll wait right here for you to come crawling back down that ladder."

"Take it easy. I'm sorry, okay?" As if her problems weren't bad enough, now she had to be concerned about this stressed-out creature's tender feelings. She'd just been reminding herself that Boba Fett didn't have any fragile sensibilities like that; why couldn't Dengar be the same? "Look," said Neelah, "you and I are going to have to stick together—"

"Why?" Dengar peered suspiciously at her. "What's in it for me? Hooking up with you, that is. I've already got a partnership going with Boba Fett. That's worth a lot more than being partner with someone like you."

"Really?" She couldn't keep an expression of wry amusement from showing on her face. "And that's why you were up there in the cockpit right now, talking things over with Fett—just like partners." Neelah gave another shake of her head. "I guess it just goes to show: there are partners, and then there are partners. And you're definitely one of the latter sort."

"Yeah? And what sort's that?"

"The disposable sort," said Neelah. "Just as disposable as I am, except I don't have any illusions about it." With one hand, she gestured at the various pieces of equipment festooning the bulkheads of the ship's cargo area. "See all this stuff? It used to belong to somebody else. That other bounty hunter—"

"Bossk. That's his name." Dengar nodded. "And you're right; this was his ship."

All of the equipment's controls and handles were sized for a creature with claws rather than humanoid digits; Neelah could have wrapped both her hands around some of the pieces that would probably have been swallowed up by a single one of Bossk's fists.

"And look what happened to him." Neelah indicated the cockpit above with a tilt of her head. "What Boba Fett did to him. It was easy, too; at least for Fett. And this Bossk, from all I've heard about him, was one tough customer as well." The Trandoshan bounty hunter had made a few appearances in Jabba the Hutt's palace during her stint as a dancing girl there, and she had listened in on some of the stories whispered about him. The tales might have indicated that Bossk was no genius, but his sheer viciousness and tenacity made up for any failings in the brain department. "And Fett still managed to turn him around and inside out, and send him on his way, minus this ship."

"That took some doing, all right." Dengar rested the palm of his hand against the cold durasteel of the bulkhead behind him. "The *Hound's Tooth* was Bossk's pride and joy. More than that: his weapons, his way of making a living. You couldn't have bought this ship from him, for any amount of money."

"Obviously, Boba Fett has another way of doing business." One corner of Neelah's mouth lifted in a humorless smile. "Too bad for the creature on the other end of the deal. And too bad for *you*."

"What do you mean by that?"

"Come on," said Neelah. "Don't be any more of a fool than you absolutely have to be. Isn't it plain to see? Your little conference just now in the cockpit should have made it clear to you just what your relationship is with Boba Fett. If you've fallen for that partners nonsense, you're even more of an idiot than you appear to be."

A scowl darkened Dengar's face. "That's hard talk, coming from somebody without a friend in the whole galaxy."

That remains to be seen, thought Neelah. For all she knew, with the ravaged state her memory was in, she might have friends—powerful ones, that would do anything for her—numbering in the legions. They could be looking for her right now. *If they think I'm still alive.* It all depended on just what circumstances had led to her being stuck in an out-of-the-way hole like the planet Tatooine.

It was a notion that continually resurfaced in her thoughts. But not one that she could spend any time dwelling on, right now. She had other, more pressing business to take care of.

"You're not an idiot; my apologies." Saying even that much grated against some deeply imbedded fiber in Neelah's character, a personality trait that had survived the memory wipe that had been performed on her. Other creatures were supposed to apologize to her, whether they were in the wrong or not; she felt certain that was the proper state of affairs. But for now, in this situation in which she'd found herself, she'd have to act otherwise. "But there's something you've got to understand." Neelah sat down next to Dengar on the narrow ledge of the cargo area's bench. There was barely room for the two of them on the shelflike space; her shoulder and thigh were pressed close to his, with an exchange of body warmth passing through their coarse, functional garb. "It's important," said Neelah as she brought her gaze down to meet his. "You and I—we *have* to stick together. If we're going to survive."

Dengar drew back, regarding her with suspicion. "I'll survive," he said after a moment's silence. "I can take care of myself—I have so far, at least."

"It's different now," said Neelah, her voice quiet and urgent. "Different from anything you've been involved with before."

"Maybe." The bounty hunter shrugged. "But if you've got doubts about what's going to happen to you—that's your problem. I've got enough of my own."

The urge to hit the thick-headed brute, to land her fist or some heavy piece of scrap metal against the side of his head, welled up in Neelah's breast. Muscles tensed, she fought the impulse back down.

"Look," she said. Leaning closer, she laid a hand on Dengar's knee. "It's not just your survival that's at stake. Right? If all you were concerned about was keeping your hide intact, you'd find a way to get yourself out of here, and as far away from Boba Fett—and me—as possible. That'd be the smart thing to do."

The suspicion in Dengar's gaze hadn't ebbed. But he hadn't pulled away from her touch, either; progress of some kind was being made. Or so Neelah hoped.

"Smart enough," conceded Dengar.

"But there's things you're trying to accomplish. All that you want to make possible for yourself and Manaroo." There had been time enough—back on Tatooine, while she and Dengar had been keeping their vigil over the unconscious Boba Fett, slowly healing from the near-fatal wounds he had received from the Sarlacc beast's gut—for Neelah to have heard all about Dengar's hopes and dreams for the future. A future that would include marriage to his beloved Manaroo, and the abandonment of this dangerous bounty hunter trade—but only if he could pull off the kind of financial score that would wipe out his debt burden and set him and Manaroo up in a new life. The only way to do that was to set himself right in the path of the greatest danger, to remain not only a bounty hunter but one allied with the most fearsome—and treacherous—bounty hunter in the galaxy. Neelah had seen at once the quandary in which Dengar was trapped: Boba Fett might indeed be his way out of the bounty hunter trade and into that bright, shining future that he wished to put together for himself and Manaroo. But Fett could also be the trap with no exit, a web of plotting and intrigue that could only be escaped through death. Dengar's death; he might not return to his beloved except as a corpse. "You can't trust Boba Fett," said Neelah, bringing her face even closer to Dengar's. "He's not concerned with yours and Manaroo's happiness."

"I don't expect him to be." Dengar spoke stiffly and guardedly. "He's a businessman."

"If that's all he were, we'd be safe. But he's a little bit more than that." Neelah tapped a forefinger against Dengar's knee. "With real businessmen, on any planet, partnerships are formed all the time; that's how business is done—"

"Oh?" Dengar seemed amused by her words. "You seem to know an awful lot about these things. For someone who has no memory other than that of being a dancing girl in Jabba the Hutt's palace."

"You don't need a memory," said Neelah, "to be able to figure out how things work." In Dengar's case, it seemed like an unimpaired memory was just so much excess baggage. "You just need to be smart enough to watch and listen. Come on, let's face it: if Boba Fett was interested in having a partner, he would have hooked himself up with some bounty hunter other than you."

"Such as?"

"Practically anybody." Neelah shrugged. "He could've made an offer to Bossk. They could've worked out their differences, if it meant good business for them. You've said yourself that's all Boba Fett is interested in. And Bossk is supposedly the toughest and hardest bounty hunter in the galaxy, after Boba Fett himself. Those two would have made an unstoppable partnership." Neelah's eyes narrowed to slits as she saw Dengar's reaction to her words. "What are you laughing about?"

"Sorry—" A derisive smile remained on Dengar's face. "But I find your ignorance amusing. You might not find your nonexistent memory a handicap, but others might. There are plenty of sentient creatures— especially in the bounty hunter trade—who are just a little more knowledgeable about Boba Fett's personal history than you seem to be."

An anger that had become all too familiar burst into flame around Neelah's heart. As smart as she might be—definitely smarter than this Dengar, possibly so in regard to Boba Fett—she still found herself at a disadvantage. *I have to figure out things that they already know.* It was a big galaxy surrounding them, in this little bubble of a stolen ship; Neelah had a lot of blanks to fill in before she would be on an equal footing with even the most ignorant back-worlder.

They didn't just steal my memory, Neelah mused bitterly. *They stole my ability—my chances—to survive.*

That was all the more reason for her to get Dengar on her side, at least for the time being. She could use him, both as an ally and as a source of information, until she had been able to find and fit enough missing pieces together, like assembling a primitive two-dimensional jigsaw puzzle inside her skull.

It would have been easier, she knew—something else you didn't need to be a genius to figure out—if Dengar hadn't already been involved with his intended bride Manaroo. That complicated things, especially any strategy Neelah might otherwise have had for getting him on her side. *Must be a real love match,* Neelah had decided; the more she had heard of Dengar's plans for his and Manaroo's future life together, when he had somehow found his way out of both debt and the bounty hunter trade, had convinced her of it. Dengar's obvious devotion to the woman—he had purposely sent her away, to keep her out of danger—aroused sparks of both envy and frustration inside Neelah.

But at Jabba's palace, she had found ways—she'd been forced to—of making life more endurable, ways that had depended upon her physical attributes. Not every male creature in that cesspit of depravity had responded to feminine beauty with the urge to destroy it in as bloody a manner as possible. Some of Jabba's underlings had been almost pathetic in their eagerness to be rewarded with a mere smile from her or any of the other dancing girls, evoked by the gift of some edible morsels filched from the palace's underground kitchens. An even better gift had been protection from the attentions of the more predatory sorts of scum that had found employment with the late Jabba. As much as Neelah had come to realize that she was under the watchful gaze of Boba Fett while she had been in the palace, she had still been grateful for any extra security that she and the other dancing girls had been able to wile out of the multispecies household staff.

None of that was possible now, when she needed it more than ever. That was the frustrating part. Neelah had already realized that there was no hope of her replacing the absent Manaroo in Dengar's affections. If anything, he was more in love with his betrothed now than when Boba Fett's *Slave I* ship had ascended from the surface of Tatooine's Dune Sea. And more dedicated to his mission of putting together a future life for the two of them, in some peaceful corner of the galaxy, far from the criminal dens and watering holes to which he'd previously been accustomed. Manaroo had already changed his life, one way or another; Neelah could see that. Without even being here aboard the *Hound's Tooth*, Manaroo was a critical element in all of Neelah's calculations. Worst of all, despite Dengar's vow to quit the bounty hunter trade, he still had just enough of a bounty hunter's mercenary toughness to complicate matters. *He'd get rid of me in a second,* thought Neelah, *if he figured that was best for him and Manaroo.*

The trick would be to convince Dengar that the road to that future life he envisioned with his bride was the one that led through Neelah's plans. She already had her notions of now to plant that idea in his head. The anger that had risen inside her, like a spark thrown on dry kindling, was carefully held in check for the time being.

"You've got me there," said Neelah, her voice carefully modulated. "Of course, there's things you know about that I don't. Even before—before they did this to me—" She laid her fingertips against the side of her head. "There were probably all sorts of things you knew about Boba Fett that I would never have heard of. That's the universe you've lived in. *His* universe."

"That's right." Dengar nodded in agreement. "It's his more than anyone else's. Boba Fett made it that way, bit by bit. If he'd wanted to—if it had suited his personal agenda—he could have taken over the entire bounty hunter trade instead of just the most profitable parts of it, the jobs that put the most credits in his pockets. There's still a remnant or two of the old Bounty Hunters Guild out there, but it's nothing compared to what it once was. Before he all but destroyed it, took it apart like a cheap astrogator device. Boba Fett could have set himself up at the top of the Guild, if he'd wanted to bother with it."

"You told me something before, about the Bounty Hunters Guild. Just a little while ago, right after Fett got rid of Bossk." Neelah searched her recent memory; it had been only a passing reference to the Guild, something hardly worth the effort to remember—at least, until now. "You said . . . something about Bossk. And the Guild. That the trouble between him and Fett went back a long way."

"Sure," said Dengar, leaning back against the bulkhead. He seemed amused by her efforts at assembling the past. "But it's no big secret. Everybody knows about it—or at least everybody who has any reason to be interested in the welfare of bounty hunters." Dengar's smile widened. "Not everybody is, you know. Bounty hunters aren't the most popular creatures in the galaxy. That's just another good reason for getting out of the business. Makes it hard to build up a lot of goodwill, when everybody else has this fervent wish that your whole category was lasered out of existence."

You don't have to tell me, thought Neelah. She had been hanging out with bounty hunters for only a little while now, and she already had serious grievances with them.

"So there is some kind of history—between Boba Fett and Bossk." Neelah intently regarded Dengar sitting next to her, as though she could read some additional clues from his face. "Something personal."

Dengar laughed. "You could say that. You could say a lot about the two of them, and it would all be true. At least, the more violent parts would be. Bossk has got a grudge against Boba Fett a parsec wide—and this latest embarrassment, getting booted out of his own ship, isn't going to make it any better. If Bossk hated Fett before, he's *really* going to be gunning for him now." Dengar shook his head. "Just goes to show what a tough hunter Boba Fett is. That's a dangerous game to play, letting an enemy as hard and determined as Bossk get away. You have to have some real confidence in your own abilities not to get a little nervous about a killer like that still floating around the galaxy, with your name at the top of his to-do list."

"Well, that's his problem, not ours." Neelah's brow furrowed as she tried to link up one tantalizing fragment of information with another. It was impossible; there were still too many pieces missing. Pieces that her own plans—and her life—might depend upon. "Look, you've got to tell me—"

One of Dengar's eyebrows raised as he looked back at her. "Tell you what?"

"Tell me *everything*." Neelah couldn't keep a pleading tone from her voice. "Everything that I don't know."

"That could take a while."

"All right; just about Bossk and Boba Fett, then." She was desperately clutching at anything, any key to the past. If her own life, all that had happened to her before Jabba's palace, was a mystery, she could at least dig out the true histories of those surrounding her. A key that would unlock all the dark secrets, or even a few, that Boba Fett kept behind the cold, hard gaze of his helmet—that could be worth a lot to her. *Maybe everything,* thought Neelah.

"Some of it you know already." Dengar made a one-handed gesture, vague enough to indicate a point in time rather than space. "Back when we were still on Tatooine."

That was true. There had been empty hours enough, while they had waited for Boba Fett's resurrection, for some of the blanks to have been filled in. Or at least those that pertained to the history of Boba Fett and the Bounty Hunters Guild. Boba Fett was still the same, as though he were some deathless, immutable construct, but the Guild had gone through changes. What existed now was only that which remained after the various interlocking conspiracies and schemes had finished with it. Conspiracies, all of which had had Boba Fett at their center. An entire war had broken out among the bounty hunters, and not all of them had survived. And if any could be said to have won that war, it would be Boba Fett himself.

Dengar had enjoyed telling those war stories; she had sensed the admiration in his voice. Admiration for Boba Fett, for the sheer ruthless efficiency of his plans and actions. An efficiency and a ruthlessness that Dengar certainly knew he could never achieve; he could only partake of it vicariously. *No wonder,* thought Neelah, *he fell for that partnership gambit.* Even close to death, lying half-digested by the Sarlacc on the barren rocks of Tatooine's Dune Sea, Boba Fett had been able to size up his target's basic psychology. Size it up, and then use it all to his own advantage.

That was a little tougher for her. At least, so far. But Neelah knew that whatever Dengar told her about Fett, about the past maneuvers in that war among and between the bounty hunters, the details would tell her as much about Dengar as anyone else. Which would suit her just fine. *That way,* she thought, *I'll find out about both of them.* Somewhere in there, she'd find something she could use . . .

"You're right," Neelah said aloud. "I know some of it. Thanks to you. Now how about the rest?"

Dengar regarded her in silence for a moment, then slowly nodded. "Okay." He leaned back against the bulkhead. "I guess we've got time. Though that all depends on where we're going, doesn't it?"

"Boba Fett didn't tell either one of us that." Neelah settled back, arms crossed over her breast. "So you might as well start, and we'll see how far we get."

A half smile formed on Dengar's face. "Maybe we'll just get to the good parts."

They're all good, thought Neelah. *As long as I get what I want.*

She listened as the figure beside her started talking . . .

5

"I've never been here before," said the emissary from the Bounty Hunters Guild. "Though, of course, it's been described to me many times."

"How flattering it is to me to be the auditory recipient of such notice." Kud'ar Mub'at folded another pair of his chitinous, spike-haired legs around himself. "To be spoken of in the corridors and nooks of the galaxy's intrigues and powers—such a pleasure! Always!"

The compound lenses of the arachnoid assembler's eyes watched in amusement as the Guild's emissary tried to keep from actually touching any of the web's fibrous—and living—structure. *Silly creature,* thought Kud'ar Mub'at; the amusement it felt was easily concealed behind its own narrow, triangular face. That was one of the advantages the assembler had over the members of nearly all the galaxy's sentient species: it could read them as easily as a primitive ink-and-paper datasheet, while its own emotions and calculations remained a masked enigma to them.

Kud'ar Mub'at supposed that was why he'd al-

ways enjoyed dealing with the bounty hunter Boba
Fett. With that visored mask on, the helmet of the
Mandalorian armor he bore, Fett was a constant challenge to decipher and manipulate. *A worthy opponent,*
mused the assembler. Even if he was already fated to
lose, enmeshed in a larger, invisible, and inescapable
web . . .

"You'll have to excuse me, if I seem a little . . . uncomfortable." The emissary's name was Gleed Otondon; his host couldn't tell from what miserably harsh
outlying world he had originated, but it was obviously
one that produced impressively bulky and well-
equipped residents at the top of its food chain—the
emissary was all leather-encased muscles with a horn-
spiked skull and proboscis atop. His clawed hands
twitched against his knees as he overwhelmed the
guest's chair near Kud'ar Mub'at's thronelike nest. He
glanced again at the densely intertwined fibers arching
over his head. "Are you sure this place is airtight?"

"My dear and most precious Gleed—allay your
fears." If outright laughter had been in the repertoire
of the assembler's emotional responses, Kud'ar Mub'at
might not have been able to restrain itself. "Reasonable as those apprehensions might be, I assure you
that they are most unnecessary." Perhaps even a little
insulting, though the assembler kept that reaction to
itself. It signaled to one of its corporeal-maintenance
subnodes, a miniature version of its own spidery
form. The wave of an upraised leg-tip was actually
unnecessary; the little node was tethered to the assembler's own central nervous system—as were all the
living bits and pieces of the web, the partially differen-
tiated inhabitants that Kud'ar Mub'at had spun from
his own inmost being. "But I'll check, just to be sure
for my most esteemed visitor."

Gleed Otondon shrank back, as though trying to

hide inside his own body armor, as the summoned node scuttled past his shoulders, trailing a whitely glistening filament of neural connector tissue behind itself. The node perched alertly on the angle of Kud'ar Mub'at's outstretched leg.

"Yes yes?" The node was all eagerness; it had been one of the assembler's favorite creations, though the bouncy mannerisms were starting to wear thin now. "What can I do do do for you you?" And the echoing whole-word stutter in its vocal circuits was *definitely* annoying. Kud'ar Mub'at made a personal mental note, in the unshared segment of its own cerebral cortex, to eliminate that flaw with the subnode's successor, after this one had been reingested. "Anything at all all?"

The curved walls of the web's central chamber seemed to move and shift, all of the gathered subnodes turning the varying levels of their communal consciousness toward the discussion taking place in their midst. A general alert had gone out over the web's neural fibers as to just how important these meetings were. Underneath a few dangling nodes, Gleed Otondon cringed at the sight of the bustling, enveloping activity.

"A status report, please." Kud'ar Mub'at made a show of giving orders to the subnode clinging to its extended leg. That was all for their visitor's benefit as well; there was no real need for courtesies being extended to things that were as much a part of the assembler as its own segmented abdomen and thorax. "Regarding our dear little home's atmospheric pressure—is all as it should be, pray tell?"

The subnode was silent for a few seconds as it shifted its minimal nervous system into communication with the rest of the web's bioengineering and homeostasis-maintenance nodes. Their wordless back-and-forth conference evoked a tingling sensation inside the tactile processors of Kud'ar Mub'at's central cortex. For a moment, it could feel the interlaced network of the web's outer sheath, as though its soft-abdomened body had expanded to the limits of its sensory perceptions.

Drifting amid the stars' cold points of light, the web's ropelike strands were studded with functioning scraps of various machines and spacecraft. Those bits and pieces were the only ones that the assembler hadn't spun itself but had incorporated into its extended being, usually as the final payments due from one extortionate scheme or another. The foreclosed-upon debtors were usually expelled through one of the web's annular exit ports, to deal with the vacuum as best they could. Kud'ar Mub'at's interest in them ceased at that point; the assembler thought it morbidly uncouth to collect scraps of corpses as trophies, the way those reptilian Trandoshans did.

"Normal pressure loss experienced—" At Kud'ar Mub'at's direction, one of the skittering voice-box subnodes took over from its exterior-maintenance web-cousin, still sitting on their parents' spider-jointed !eg. The stutterless voice box dangled within inches of Gleed Otondon's head; the emissary regarded it with evident dismay. "During reception of visitors and transfer from docking vessels, atmospheric generation stepped up two levels over subsequent time period, per standing orders for perimeter breach procedures." The voice-box node fell silent for a few seconds as it received more data from the exterior sensors. The voice-box nodes were little more than articulating mouths and imbedded vocal cords; they didn't possess enough separate memory to hold more than a few sentences at a time. "Internal web pressure currently at ninety-five percent of optimum volume; one hundred percent optimum within next hour."

"There. You see?" Kud'ar Mub'at gestured with its extended leg. The assembler spoke rapidly, to keep its visitor from thinking about and commenting upon the one word—"vessels," in the plural—that the voice-box node had let slip. *That's the problem,* thought Kud'ar Mub'at, *when you don't give your underlings enough brains to think with.* "Nothing at all to worry about."

"If you say so." The emissary from the Bounty Hunters Guild looked only slightly reassured.

The real worries, as always, belonged to Kud'ar Mub'at. *Life itself,* mused the assembler, *is a burden.* It was a constant temptation to design and create the web's subnodes with enough cortical matter to render them capable of independent thought and action; that would have taken a great deal of the load off the assembler's multiple shoulders. *It might also,* Kud'ar Mub'at reminded himself, *take my head off those shoulders.* The web had come to Kud'ar Mub'at as its inheritance, upon the death—murder, actually—of the arachnoid assembler that had spawned it. That might have been right and proper—Kud'ar Mub'at had never felt any guilt over the matter—but at the same time, it had no intention of making the same mistake itself, as its creator had.

"Ah, but I do say so." Kud'ar Mub'at enacted a semblance of a gracious humanoid bow, spreading wide two of its jointed legs and bending forward, eye-studded head lowered. The shifting of the assembler's weight momentarily lifted its pallid, wobbling abdomen from the living nest beneath; the concave subnode sighed and put its minimal intelligence to the task of reinflating its cushionlike bladder parts. "I make every effort for the comfort of my so highly esteemed guests. Such as yourself. Even if it did not facilitate the flowing conduct of business, I would still feel it incumbent upon me to do so, honored as I am by your presence."

"Don't bother." The emissary's unease shifted to annoyance. With a visible display of will, Gleed Otondon regained control of himself. "I've been informed about all your flattering language." His eyes narrowed into a focus of distrust. "It won't work on me."

Ah, thought Kud'ar Mub'at to himself, keeping his satisfaction hidden. *But it already has.* One way or another . . .

"I'm sure," soothed Kud'ar Mub'at, "that you don't mean that in a hostile way. But of course, if you wanted to, that would be fine with me as well. I try to be accommodating, as I hope you've seen." The assembler settled himself back down into the nest subnode's soft embrace. "May I prevail upon you for a very small, inconsequential kindness? If you'll excuse me for a moment, I must confer with a few of my tiny minions. Trifles, mere details; such an annoyance."

None of Kud'ar Mub'at's multiple eyes had lids, but a slight opacity filmed over their bright beadlike surfaces as the assembler relaxed their focus. It tucked its legs around itself as a further indication of having withdrawn its attention. One of its tiniest creations, an optical subnode barely bigger than a humanoid thumb, peered out from behind a tangle of the web's structural fibers. An unsheathed neural strand, white as spidersilk, conveyed a sharp image of the Guild emissary to the parent assembler's cortex. Gleed Otondon looked grumpy and uncomfortable, obviously irritated by even the slightest delay in taking care of business.

Let him stew awhile, decided Kud'ar Mub'at. The

assembler's full consciousness had already siphoned along the connecting neural fibers to another part of the web.

And to another visitor.

"You look different," said the Trandoshan bounty hunter. "From the last time I was here at the web."

"Ah, my dear and most esteemed Bossk." The web's owner and creator, the arachnoid assembler Kud'ar Mub'at, traced a gesture with one upraised leg, signifying a galaxy's worth of hard-won wisdom and regret. "You are still in the prime of a vigorous youthfulness. Is that not so? Whereas I myself . . ." The points of the tiny claws at the end of the leg tapped against a chitinous segment of exoskeletal carapace, just beneath the assembler's triangular face, and where a heart would have been if its anatomy were closer to humanoid or reptilian. "I grow old and tired. Just as your beloved father Cradossk did, may his memory be enshrined among the stars."

"Yeah, well, the old lizard isn't going to get any older now. That's for sure." A glow of satisfaction kindled in Bossk's own scale-covered breast. His father's bones, gnawed and picked clean, rested in Bossk's trophy chamber, where he could gloat and meditate over them, anytime he wished. *Served him right,* thought Bossk, grinding his fangs together as though retasting the memories of his predecessor. With Trandoshans, death was the penalty, not just for getting old and tired, but for getting in the way of the next generation—Bossk, specifically. If his father Cradossk hadn't tried to hold on so tightly to the leadership of the Bounty Hunters Guild, things might not have gone so gruesomely for him. Or perhaps they might have; recycling the protein and other constituents of one's elders was such a time-honored tradition among their species, it would have seemed a shame not to have carried it on, even if Cradossk had graciously surrendered the Guild's leadership to his heir Bossk. "He was a tough old lizard," mused Bossk aloud. His tongue traced the broken point of one of his own fangs. "In a *lot* of ways . . ."

"Deep is the measure of my own reminiscing," said the assembler, "when I recall your father Cradossk. Many were the dealings I had with him; much business did we do together. And most of it was highly and mutually profitable, I assure you."

"Believe me—I know all about that." Bossk folded his arms across his chest; his elbow nudged one of his holstered blaster pistols. "I was in on a lot of that business. The profitable stuff—*and* the unprofitable."

"Ah. What can I say?" Two of Kud'ar Mub'at's legs lifted in an approximation of a shrug. "It's a dangerous galaxy in which we live. Poor, struggling creatures that we are. Not everything works out as planned, does it?"

That's the truth, brooded Bossk. He had long harbored the notion—more than that, a cherished dream—that when he took over the Bounty Hunters Guild from his father's faltering claws, he would inherit a powerful and united organization, one that he would be able to rebuild into the dominant semilegal force among all the inhabited worlds. It could have been bigger than the great criminal syndicate Black Sun, inasmuch as the Guild had the ability to operate on both sides of the Empire's laws. Criminal overlords such as Jabba the Hutt hired bounty hunters, as did Emperor Palpatine, by way of his various underlings. In that sense, bounty hunters had always operated as sanctioned lawbreakers, to the degree that their clients either didn't care about or turned a blind eye to whatever methods were used to bring in the merchandise. *Just as long as the job gets done,* thought Bossk. It was a sweet arrangement . . . or had been.

The Trandoshan's musings turned bitter. *Real sweet* . . . Bossk nodded slowly. *Until Boba Fett screwed it up.* Not for himself—but for the Bounty Hunters Guild. And worst of all: for Bossk.

"You seem pensive," commented Kud'ar Mub'at, nesting across from where Bossk sat. "And so unfortunately melancholy. How that grieves me! Perhaps it would be better if we let the past be the past. And let go of those thorny memories that impinge upon the tender flesh of our bosoms."

"Easy for you to say," growled Bossk. As far as he could tell, nothing was poking at the assembler's globular abdomen hard enough to draw blood. Whereas he could just about taste his own, filling his mouth. It was in Kud'ar Mub'at's nature to have profited from the debacle that had befallen the Bounty Hunters Guild; Bossk wasn't exactly sure how the assembler might have gained from it, but he was sure that it had happened. No wonder the spidery creature could be so gracious; it was doing all right, as it always had. But for himself and the Guild . . .

Properly speaking, it wasn't even "the" Bounty Hunters Guild; not anymore, at least. That was more of Boba Fett's doing, the tragic result of having let him into the Guild in the first place—a perfect example of how senile old Cradossk had gotten, for him to have fallen for that gambit. Bossk had been suspicious of Boba Fett's intentions from the beginning. And his suspicions had turned out to be accurate: the outcome of Fett's joining the Bounty Hunters Guild had been to split the organization into two, neither one of them as powerful as the original, and both factions locked in combat with each other. One faction—the True Guild, as it called itself—was led by the elders that had been the original Guild's governing council behind Bossk's father Cradossk. The other faction was primarily made up of the younger Guild members, who had chafed for so long underneath the increasingly slow and inept leadership of the bold bounty hunters, and who had seized upon the internecine turmoil created by Boba Fett as their chance to break away and form a new organization.

Bossk had thrown his lot in with the latter group, the Guild Reform Committee. It was a committee in name only; group leadership had ceased upon the Trandoshan's assumption of its chairman position— now it was more of an efficient and brutal one-creature dictatorship, the exact image of what he had always intended the original Bounty Hunters Guild would become when his father Cradossk died. *And it will be,* Bossk had vowed. There was no room in the galaxy for two rival bounty hunter organizations; one of them would have to be exterminated. When that was taken care of—and Bossk had already set into motion his plans for accomplishing that particular task—then the Committee would resume the name of Bounty Hunters Guild. The one and only . . .

He had already removed a few personal obstacles to his control of the committee; if the bodies of some of the younger bounty hunters turned up in deliberately conspicuous places, it only served to illustrate the consequences of objecting to Bossk's one-creature, top-of-the-food-chain management style. And if some—quite a number, actually—of the Guild Reform Committee's rank-and-file decided that it was safer to go over to the old, stodgy True Guild, then Bossk considered it no great loss to his organization. Or to his plans. *Who needs them?* Bossk had long ago decided that it would be better to have fewer bounty hunters on his side, as long as they were also the tougher and more blood-thirsty and credits-hungry ones.

That had been the problem with the old Bounty Hunters Guild, one that he wasn't going to repeat when he had finished his campaign to take over and install himself as the head of what should have been his rightful inheritance all along. There had been just too many bounty hunters in the original Guild; sheer numbers had kept individual profits down, as well as making the whole organization slow and inefficient. It was small wonder that a private, non-Guild operator such as Boba Fett had been able to steal all their action. And even less of a wonder that when Fett had applied for membership in the Bounty Hunters Guild— and had been accepted by that fool Cradossk and his council of advisers—he had been able to split the organization into fragments in hardly any time at all. *Those other Guild members,* brooded Bossk, *they just weren't up to Boba Fett's speed.* They had fallen for Boba Fett's smooth line of talk—all that business about what the future was going to be like, and how they all had to work together—and they had suffered the consequences. The old Bounty Hunters Guild had been the only place where some—or even most—of those types had been able to survive . . . and without it, they were dead meat.

There weren't many, out of the number that had gone over to the True Guild faction, that Bossk wasn't going to let back into the reconstituted Bounty Hunters Guild. He had other plans for them, and their names on a list that he kept securely locked inside his head. Before it was all done, there would be quite a few corpses showing up in places where the right creatures would find out about them. Some might get dumped in the unlit doorway of the Mos Eisley cantina, back on that hole of a planet Tatooine. The silent bodies of onetime bounty hunters would serve as an effective message to all concerned: that Bossk was in business, and in charge of that business. All the galaxy's creatures—whether they were underlings of Emperor Palpatine or criminals in league with Black Sun, Huttese independent operators or members of the Rebel Alliance—if they wanted to do business with the Bounty Hunters Guild, they would have to deal with Bossk, and on his terms. And those terms would be rough for them—all of them—and sweet, and profitable, for Bossk. He had already decided that.

But right now, he had other business to take care of. With an internal push of will, Bossk ended his idle—but pleasant—imaginings. *Time enough later,* he thought, *for all that.* After his own plans and schemes had come to glorious fulfillment. There would be a lot of bones added to Bossk's memory chamber—including those of his archrival Boba Fett. That severed skull would be a particularly fine trophy, encased in its dark-visored helmet of a Mandalorian armor. But right now, if all those plans were to bear fruit, Bossk had to attend to his present business, no matter how unpleasant the surroundings. And repellent the creature to whom he had to speak.

Kud'ar Mub'at's high-pitched voice cut through the last fragments of the Trandoshan's reverie. "Please," spoke the assembler, "consider yourself under no unseemly obligation to hurry. At least, do not do so for my benefit. As your humble servant, I wait upon your convenience."

"Yeah, right." Bossk focused his slit-pupiled gaze on the arachnoid squatting across from him, its spidery legs tucked around the pale globe of its abdomen. He was already wondering if there was some way to include Kud'ar Mub'at in his plans, so that the assembler's hollowed-out exoskeleton wound up among his other trophies.

Kud'ar Mub'at watched . . . and approved.

The assembler's most trusted creation, the accountant subnode named Balancesheet, was doing a good job of handling the Trandoshan bounty hunter Bossk. Balancesheet took care of so many things now; the subnode's responsibilities had expanded far beyond those for which Kud'ar Mub'at had designed it. Simple number-crunching and tracking the ebb and flow of credits in the web's coffers—Kud'ar Mub'at should have known from the beginning, when he had just spun Balancesheet's essential brain matter from the assembler's own neurocortex, that the subnode would eventually turn out this way. *It's just like me,* thought Kud'ar Mub'at with an unavoidable trace of parental pride. *Cold and calculating, and so nicely devious.*

Deviousness was called for, when one had twice as many visitors to the web—and twice as much business to conduct—as a single entity could take care of. Even as versatile and multitasking a creature as the arachnoid assembler had its limits. Plus there were additional difficulties with this particular pair of visitors: much trouble would ensue if either one found out that Kud'ar Mub'at was engaged in talks with the other. Gleed Otondon was here representing the interests of the True Guild, the loyalist faction of the now-splintered Bounty Hunters Guild, and Bossk . . .

Bossk represents himself, thought Kud'ar Mub'at with an inward, appreciative smile. Any other claim was a useful fiction, both for the Trandoshan and any other creature doing business with him. The Guild Reform Committee's members might have been fooled, but Kud'ar Mub'at wasn't. Bossk was an ambitious and ruthless individual, much as his father Cradossk had been before advancing age had rendered the elder Trandoshan slow and gullible—and dead, at the claws of his own offspring.

Using the neural feed from the optical subnode perched in one of the web's smaller chambers, Kud'ar Mub'at viewed Bossk—and itself. The latter was also a useful fiction, though Bossk certainly wasn't aware of it. Some time ago, years or even decades of Standard Time Units, the assembler had shed its external carapace but hadn't discarded the hollow replica of itself. Kud'ar Mub'at had decided there might be other uses for the empty exoskeleton, and had even spun out from itself enough neurofiber and simple muscular tissue to turn its former shell into a controllable likeness of its own physical form. The masquerade was completed when the clever accountant subnode Balancesheet proved itself capable of crawling inside the shell, linking up to the neurofibers' synaptic receptor points, and performing a passable imitation of its creator, the original Kud'ar Mub'at. *Right down to my ornate language,* Kud'ar Mub'at had judged. *Such an apt pupil!* The assembler's own calculating nature was tinged for a moment with a warming emotional glow, a phenomenon otherwise unknown to him.

The simulated Kud'ar Mub'at, the carapace with the subnode Balancesheet inside, made its excuses to the grumbling Trandoshan. A moment later, the real Kud'ar Mub'at felt the tickle of the subnode's consciousness, like a tug on the neurofiber connecting them.

Well done. Kud'ar Mub'at directed its own thoughts toward the subnode. *You have this bounty hunter completely deceived.*

Balancesheet responded with appropriate and

becoming modesty. *Your praise is unearned. It was easy. He wishes to believe the things he hears. My speaking is but your words in another mouth.*

But nevertheless—performed with meritorious acuity. Kud'ar Mub'at had never lavished such words or thoughts on any of his other subnodes; that would have been like praising one of the compound eyes in the inverted triangle of its head or one of his multi-jointed legs, or any other mere part of itself. For that was all that the subnodes were, mere created extensions of the assembler's self. To make such statements about the little accountant subnode only indicated how different Balancesheet was from the others in the web, and how much Kud'ar Mub'at had come to depend upon it.

Another emotion, that of anticipated regret, welled up inside Kud'ar Mub'at's chitin-mantled breast. *I'll miss it when it's gone.* That thought was carefully kept from the subnode. Kud'ar Mub'at had no intention of letting Balancesheet discover the fate planned for it. The assembler had already decided that the accountant subnode's days were numbered, no matter how useful and important it had become. The mere fact that Balancesheet had evolved and taken on such importance, becoming Kud'ar Mub'at's most valuable creation, sealed its doom. Balancesheet already had developed more intelligence and independent volition than all of the web's other subnodes combined—that was why it could handle such a task as imitating Kud'ar Mub'at, from inside the otherwise empty carapace.

In the far reaches of Kud'ar Mub'at's memory, before it had become the galaxy's leading fixer, arranger, and go-between for the various worlds' criminal and semicriminal elements, it could remember having become just as valuable for the affairs of its predecessor, the arachnoid assembler that had spawned it as a mere subnode. That predecessor had wound up making the mistake that Kud'ar Mub'at had sworn not to repeat, that of letting one of its creations become too intelligent and independent. However valuable and convenient such a node's services might be, they weren't worth the price of eventual rebellion, mutiny, and murder. Patricide might be in the natural order of things for some species, an inevitable segment of the passage from one generation to the next—that was the way it was for Trandoshans like Bossk, from all reports. Whether it was the same for assemblers such as itself, Kud'ar Mub'at had no idea. The only other member of its species that Kud'ar Mub'at had known had been the one that had created it and that it had murdered and consumed in turn.

Those acts had seemed natural enough—or at least easy and satisfying—when Kud'ar Mub'at had done them. Sometimes though, in the web's dark and silent drifting between stars, in those brief intervals when there was no business to be conducted, the assembler allowed itself to wonder if it might be the exception, an aberration from the natural order. Perhaps its millennia-old predecessor had grown old and tired, and had created and groomed its chosen successor with an innate capacity to rebel, kill, consume, and usurp. Perhaps it hadn't been rebellion so much as fulfillment. The notion didn't bother Kud'ar Mub'at; in fact, it gave the assembler a little glimmer of hope, deep inside itself. Perhaps Kud'ar Mub'at *could* trust the little accountant subnode named Balancesheet, no matter how smart and independent it had evolved to be; perhaps Kud'ar Mub'at wouldn't have to destroy this most precious and worthy of all his creations, ingest its matter and spin out a new bookkeeping subnode, but one that could never replace dear little Balancesheet . . .

Kud'ar Mub'at pushed those thoughts away, as it had done so many times before. *I can't allow it.* Thoughts such as those were not the cold and precise calculations by which it had reached its present position of real if hidden power and influence. Kud'ar Mub'at knew that any emotions, even those directed toward its most faithful subnodes, constituted a trap. A trap with Kud'ar Mub'at's own death loaded into the catch of its spring.

Better it than me, Kud'ar Mub'at had already decided. Even though the assembler was connected by neural strands to all the web's subnodes, it didn't consider the whole lot of them to be identical with its own precious self. With the viewpoint from the dangling optical node, Kud'ar Mub'at regarded its own shed exoskeleton; the smaller form of Balancesheet, like a miniature version of its creator, was just barely visible, if one knew to look, behind the glossy transparency of the carapace's compound eyes. *How sad,* thought Kud'ar Mub'at. With intelligence came deceit. It was ever thus, Kud'ar Mub'at supposed, inside the web and throughout that larger galaxy beyond it.

Nevertheless, the resolve to eliminate the accountant subnode had to be delayed, at least for a little while. Necessarily so, and not out of mere weakening sentiment; at this stage in the complicated plans regarding Boba Fett and the remnants of the former Bounty Hunters Guild, the assistance of little Balancesheet was still required. Kud'ar Mub'at knew the dangers of the game it was playing. When the pawns on the gameboard were like the Trandoshan Bossk, the results of one's deceptive maneuvers being found out were inevitably fatal, and in the most unpleasant manner possible. Bossk didn't yet know—and Kud'ar Mub'at was determined that he never would—that

Boba Fett wasn't the only creature involved in the breakup of the old Bounty Hunters Guild. The scheme hadn't originated with Kud'ar Mub'at either, but had been brought to the assembler by that veritable eminence among plotters and double-dealers, Prince Xizor.

The Falleen noble was an altogether different type of creature from the so-easily hoodwinked Bossk. Both Falleens and Trandoshans were reptilian species, and equally cold-blooded. But a hot-tempered streak diluted the chill of Trandoshan blood; given the choice between successful scheming and disastrous violence, a creature such as Bossk would always go for the latter option. With Prince Xizor, as with all Falleens, nothing raised the temperature of his moods—the emotions that ran hot in other creatures, whether lust or other violence, were merely tools of Xizor's precise and merciless mind. That was what Kud'ar Mub'at appreciated the most about doing business with him. When Xizor had been here at the web, laying out the scheme against the Bounty Hunters Guild, Kud'ar Mub'at had perceived more than a mere business associate in the Falleen. Xizor at least was a worthy opponent on the other side of the gameboard.

This one, however—

Another thought leaked into Kud'ar Mub'at's central cortex. A moment passed before the assembler realized the thought wasn't its own.

This one, came Balancesheet's unspoken words, *is too easy.*

Another moment, as Kud'ar Mub'at recovered from its surprise. The accountant subnode's thoughts had broken into Kud'ar Mub'at's own, entirely unbidden. That had never happened before. And it had been in response to Kud'ar Mub'at's interior musing about the differences between Trandoshans and Falleens. Those thoughts, the contrast between Bossk and Prince Xizor, had not been directed out along the web's neural pathways, toward the subnode hidden inside Kud'ar Mub'at's discarded exoskeleton.

It was listening, thought Kud'ar Mub'at. *To me.* And then Kud'ar Mub'at was unable to keep from wondering if the subnode had heard that thought as well.

Kud'ar Mub'at stilled all its thoughts, creating a perfect silence inside itself. For a few moments, all it did was wait and watch, letting the image from the optical node fill the momentary vacuum of its consciousness.

What would you have me do now?

Balancesheet had spoken again, the words forming inside Kud'ar Mub'at's cortex, as real as the assembler's own thoughts. Across from the sheltering carapace, the bounty hunter Bossk sat in the web chamber, unaware of the silent conversation taking place.

Only a few seconds had passed since the accountant subnode, pretending to be Kud'ar Mub'at, had made its excuses to the bounty hunter Bossk. Given the impatient nature of all Trandoshans, it was probably not a good idea to make him wait much longer. Kud'ar Mub'at regained enough of his internal composure to address the waiting Balancesheet.

Proceed with the negotiations, spoke Kud'ar Mub'at along the neurofibers connecting him to the subnode. *The Trandoshan's confidence has obviously been gained, due to the excellence of your masquerade performance.* Kud'ar Mub'at kept the tone of its thoughts carefully unemotional and controlled, suppressing any sign of anxiety or suspicion on its part. *If that is easy for you, so much the better.*

The subnode's response held the same apparent lack of emotion. *As you wish,* thought Balancesheet, *and as you so wisely instructed me.*

For a few seconds longer, Kud'ar Mub'at watched via the optical node in the smaller chamber as the disguised Balancesheet resumed its cajoling flattery of the Trandoshan Bossk. The assembler kept its own thoughts hidden, disconnected from the strands that might have conveyed them to the accountant subnode or any other that Kud'ar Mub'at had created. Its resolve, that it had already made regarding the fate of Balancesheet, was even stronger now.

As soon as this business with the Bounty Hunters Guild is over, Kud'ar Mub'at assured itself. *Definitely.* The assembler allowed its consciousness to flow back from the extended neural fibers of its web and recondense in its own body. Kud'ar Mub'at was once again aware of the main web chamber surrounding itself, where it had left Gleed Otondon, the True Guild's emissary, waiting. *Better safe than sorry . . .*

"It's about time," Gleed Otondon grumbled as the assembler raised its head and blinked its multiple eyes. "I don't have endless Standard Time Units to waste on this matter."

"An infinity of apologies. My most profound regrets." Kud'ar Mub'at rearranged itself into the gently sighing, accommodating nest. The assembler performed another imitation of a humanoid bow, lowering the narrow triangle of its head before the visitor. "Farthest from my mind is any wish to seem other than entirely honored by your presence; believe me."

"Let's just try to wrap this up." The assembler's flowery language produced a sour expression on Otondon's sharply angled muzzle. "There's really only one basic issue that needs to be settled. And it's a simple one. Are you with us or not?"

"Pardon?" Kud'ar Mub'at spread wide two of its front legs. "What is the precise meaning of—'with'? I don't mean to imply that your words are not of pristine clarity, but—"

"Stow it.' Gleed Otondon's irritation was obvious. "You know what the score is. There are two factions that came out of the Bounty Hunters Guild, and there's only going to be one left, eventually. And the True Guild plans on making sure it's the one that survives."

"But of course," said Kud'ar Mub'at with a semblance of a smile on its triangular face. "Survival is such a lovely virtue. I've practiced it throughout the course of my existence."

"Then you'll want to go on practicing it, I bet." Gleed Otondon leaned forward, his hard glare reflected in the assembler's multiple eyes. "And the best way to do that is to make sure you're on our side. The True Guild isn't going to feel very friendly toward anyone who didn't help it put the Bounty Hunters Guild back together again. Those renegades in that so-called Guild Reform Committee—they're dead meat. And that's what will happen to anybody else who gets too cozy with them." Otondon turned his head to one side, peering more closely at the assembler across from him. "Just how cozy are you with Bossk and that bunch of his?"

"My dear Gleed." With its upraised forelegs, Kud'ar Mub'at made a fluttering gesture. "I understand the appropriate nature of your inquiry, but I *am* a trifle shocked by it, nevertheless. Suspicion is all very fine—in your trade, it's certainly a necessity—but I've never before been suspected of being an idiot. I *do* know how things work in this galaxy."

"I thought you might." Otondon's smile was made even uglier with its suggestion of brotherly conspiracy. "You really aren't an idiot, are you?"

But you might very well be. Kud'ar Mub'at kept his response unspoken. "I have not reached the advanced age and influential position that I possess by making poor choices as to friends and alliances." The assembler tapped the claws at the ends of his forelegs together. "So you and the others in the True Guild— and of course I regret not having the opportunity and the pleasure to address each and every one of them directly—may rest in the utmost assurance that I am, as you say, 'with' them in this regard. And while the bonds of friendship and the great admiration I have for such eminent and respected bounty hunters as the members of the True Guild would naturally dictate such a response on my part, I would like to ease and reassure your mind even further. It's good business as well, my dear Gleed." The assembler refolded its legs around its cushion-cradled abdomen. "Business that I wish to continue carrying out in the future, as mutually profitable as it has been in the past."

"I don't know about 'mutual,'" grumbled the True Guild's emissary. "It always seemed to put more credits in your coffers than ours."

"How grievously wounded I am to hear you say such a thing." Kud'ar Mub'at let himself sink down into the soft embrace of its nest, the better to indicate its mortification. "Perhaps, at that happy time to come, when the upstarts have been so righteously and inevitably vanquished and the original Bounty Hunters Guild has been restored in all its glory, then we can go over our account books together and come to a financial reconciliation." The assembler's voice became even more soothing. "If you yourself were to feel that you had suffered some *personal* hardship, you and I could talk about it . . . privately. Yes?"

Otondon scratched his elongated chin. "Are you talking bribery?"

"Oh! That's such a *crude* word, don't you think?" Kud'ar Mub'at shook its head. "I prefer to regard such practices as merely a matter of making our friendship—the one between just you and me—even more satisfying than it has been already. And of course, as a matter of friendship, if you were to return to the other members of the True Guild, whose interests you so ably represent, and you were to assure them of the avidity with which I wish to maintain business interests with them . . ."

"Yeah, yeah; I understand what you're getting at." Otondon gave a slow nod. "But I'm not going to do anything like that if it isn't true. The bit about you wanting to stay hooked up with the True Guild, and not having anything to do with Bossk and that Guild Reform Committee bunch."

"But, my dear Gleed, that *is* the truth." The assembler lifted one of its forelegs into the air with a dramatic flourish. "I swear it. Absolutely and unconditionally." Kud'ar Mub'at tucked the leg back with the others around itself. "That's not the sort of thing about which I'd even be *capable* of prevaricating."

"It'd better be true," said Otondon grimly. "Because it wouldn't be worth my life to tell the other True Guild members that you're with us, and then have them find out that you had handed us a line. Our kind of bounty hunters doesn't reward stupidity."

Too bad for you, thought Kud'ar Mub'at wryly. The assembler's visitor would have done well for himself, if that had been the case. "Rest assured, my most precious Gleed, that the relationship between myself and the True Guild—and the Bounty Hunters Guild, when it has once again come into existence—will be one of exclusivity and mutual profitability. You have my word on it."

"Good." Otondon gave a satisfied nod. "You

know . . . I kinda felt all along that we'd be able to do business together."

Fool. This was the easiest sort of negotiation: telling someone exactly what they wanted to hear. Part of Kud'ar Mub'at wished that they could all be this easy; and in fact, most of them were. It was only when the arachnoid assembler was matching wits with creatures such as Prince Xizor or Boba Fett that the game became both dangerous and interesting. That was what the other part of Kud'ar Mub'at appreciated, what made its own existence worthwhile. The assembler had lived for a long time in the drifting web that it had inherited from its murdered predecessor. Kud'ar Mub'at had been putting together complicated deals and intricate, self-serving schemes before any of the creatures it now encountered had been born. When that much time passes, the search for a worthy opponent becomes an obsession.

That was why it had been inevitable that Kud'ar Mub'at would have let itself become involved in the scheme to break up the Bounty Hunters Guild. Not so much for the profits that would accrue to the assembler's coffers—though the credits would in fact be substantial—but for the thrill of the game. *And* the quality of the opponents. Kud'ar Mub'at had been able to see past Prince Xizor, who had brought the scheme here to the web and laid it out before the assembler's multiple eyes, all the way to Emperor Palpatine, so far away on the planet Coruscant. Strings as delicate and intricately connected as any in the web were being pulled, and not all of them were in Xizor's hands. The Falleen noble enjoyed playing dangerous games as well—Xizor hadn't risen to the top of the galaxy-spanning crime syndicate Black Sun without having a taste for risk, and the skills to pull off those kinds of gambits. Kud'ar Mub'at was well aware of how deeply Lord Vader, the Emperor's black-robed fist, loathed and distrusted Xizor; the Falleen only had to make one wrong move, and every suspicion that Vader had planted in Palpatine's thoughts would be confirmed—fatally so, for Xizor. *When you play those kinds of games,* mused Kud'ar Mub'at, *for those kinds of stakes . . . you can't complain about what happens when you lose.*

In the minuscule heart inside its carapace, Kud'ar Mub'at felt sorry for the little accountant subnode Balancesheet. It had never played at that level, never developed those kinds of sharp, hard gaming skills. If Balancesheet had some notion of mutiny against its creator, as Kud'ar Mub'at had rebelled against its predecessor, it also had little idea of what it was risking. It might never know; the game, and its existence, would be over before it realized.

Such thoughts were pleasing, but there was business to be concluded. Kud'ar Mub'at turned its attention back to the True Guild emissary sitting before it.

"I'm sure your time is valuable, my dear Gleed." The assembler swept two of its legs out before itself. "Much more so than mine, which is only well spent when it is given to wait upon visitors such as yourself. With that in mind, are we at last in perfect agreement and harmony? The interests of you and the other True Guild members are identical to my own, as far as I'm concerned."

"They may not be identical," said Gleed Otondon, "but I guess they're close enough. For now."

"Ah. So wisely put. I trust you'll have no problem with going back to your fellow True Guild bounty hunters and assuring them that their friend and business associate Kud'ar Mub'at is indeed, as you say, 'with' them?"

"Maybe." Otondon shrugged. "There'd be even less problem if we settled that other business as well. You know, the bit about the bribe."

"That unpleasant word again." From deep inside the feathery mandibles of its exhalation apertures, Kud'ar Mub'at sighed. "But I do know what you're referring to. After all, I brought the matter up. A little more delicately, though."

Avarice showed in Gleed Otondon's smile. "If we could work it out right now, so that there were some *tangible* evidence along those lines . . . then I think we'd really be rolling. Got it?"

"Oh, yes. But of course." With one claw tip, Kud'ar Mub'at scratched the lowest point of its triangular face. The emissary's request for a transfer of credits, from the web's coffers into his pocket, actually raised some difficulties for the assembler. Its accountant subnode Balancesheet usually handled all those kinds of financial details—but right now, Balancesheet was busy impersonating Kud'ar Mub'at from inside the assembler's discarded exoskeleton. The Trandoshan bounty hunter Bossk was unaware that the actual Kud'ar Mub'at had been in simultaneous negotiations all along, with one of Bossk's enemies from the True Guild. And Kud'ar Mub'at had no intention of ending the masquerade; to do so would send both Bossk and Gleed Otondon into murderous rages, not directed at each other, but first at Kud'ar Mub'at. "Actually," said the assembler after a moment of silence, "I'm very embarrassed, inasmuch as I cannot presently fulfill your eminently reasonable request."

"What?" Gleed Otondon barked a harsh, skeptical laugh. "You gotta be joking. Everybody knows you're stuffed with credits out here. After all the business you've done, you must be sitting on piles of them."

"Sadly—that is not the case." Kud'ar Mub'at gave a slow shake of his head. Around him, the assembler's various subnodes gathered closer, like piteous orphans seeking shelter from cold stormwinds. Their various eyes turned toward Otondon's face. "Not all of my business ventures turn out so well, as do those where I have joined my feeble abilities with those of your profession. That is why I am so eager to renew the bonds of mutually profitable loyalty between myself and the true heirs of the Bounty Hunters Guild's mantle. There are so many untrustworthy and devious creatures in the galaxy, and I am but a humble go-between, a mere arranger of business between various parties . . . and I am so easily cheated out of what is rightfully due to me." The assembler dabbed at a few of its beadlike eyes with a claw tip, though moist displays of emotion were physiologically impossible for it. "And I have so many expenses." The tip of the claw pointed to the clustering subnodes. "Really . . . the upkeep on a place like this . . . it's practically more a medical than a business expense . . ."

"Spare me." The True Guild emissary gazed at the arachnoid creature with disgust. "You want to plead poverty, take up somebody else's time." Otondon began fastening the brass hooks of his outer cloak. "I don't want to hear it. But don't forget"—he stood up from where he had been sitting, then menacingly leaned over the assembler—"you owe me."

"A debt of honor," squeaked Kud'ar Mub'at, drawing back from Otondon's jabbing forefinger. "Every Standard Time Unit will begin with my recall of exactly this matter."

"Yeah, I bet." With his massive shoulders almost

scraping the chamber's curved, fibrous walls, Otondon looked around himself. "How do I get out of here? I've got to get back to the Guild. They'll be waiting for me."

Kud'ar Mub'at let one of the internal guidance subnodes scurry away and lead Otondon to the web's main docking area. There was another, smaller dock on the other side of the web; that was where the Trandoshan bounty hunter Bossk's ship *Hound's Tooth* was moored, safely out of Gleed Otondon's view. When Bossk had contacted Kud'ar Mub'at about coming out to the web, to have their business discussions together, the assembler had convinced him that there was a need for secrecy—powerful forces, hinted at but not named, were watching the web and keeping track of its visitors' comings and goings. That had been enough to convince Bossk to go along with the approach and docking arrangements that had kept him unaware of the True Guild's emissary entering the web at the same time. Gleed Otondon had been similarly hoodwinked, and just as easily.

Without leaving its nest in the web's main chamber, Kud'ar Mub'at reconnected with the neural input from the optical node he'd used just a little while before. The deeply suspicious face of the Trandoshan Bossk immediately came into view, just as clear as if the assembler had been in the other chamber with him, instead of the disguised accountant subnode Balancesheet.

"What's that?" Bossk turned his head, listening to some distant sound.

Over the elongated strand of silken neurofiber that connected them, Kud'ar Mub'at directed the optical node to refocus, so that the assembler's discarded exoskeleton could be seen as well.

"Pardon?" A voice identical to Kud'ar Mub'at's spoke from inside the carapace. The accountant subnode Balancesheet spread two of the exoskeleton's forelegs apart in a gesture of bafflement. "To what do you refer?"

"What I heard . . . just now." The nostrils on Bossk's scale-covered snout flared wider, as though he could breathe in some telltale molecules from the web's recycled atmosphere. "Sounded like a ship taking off."

In the vacuum of space outside the drifting web, the rush of the low-power docking engines from Gleed Otondon's ship would have been inaudible. But enough vibrations, from the disengagement of the docking subnodes, had traveled through the structural fibers of the web's exterior for Bossk's sensitive hearing to have picked up.

A smaller tremor, one of apprehension, moved inside Kud'ar Mub'at's chitinous body. If Balancesheet, inside the assembler's shed carapace, bobbled its response, then Bossk might very well leap to the conclusion—accurate enough—that the web had had another visitor while he had been here.

"Yes, it did sound like that, didn't it?"

All of Kud'ar Mub'at's spidery legs clenched around its nest, as it heard the distant subnode's words.

"But," continued Balancesheet's voice, "of course it wasn't. How could it be?"

In the view from the optical node, dangling from the ceiling of the smaller chamber, Bossk's slit-eyed glance turned toward the carapace with Balancesheet inside. "You tell me," said Bossk, "just why it wasn't a ship leaving here."

"It's simple enough," said Balancesheet mildly. "My dear Bossk, the only reason any sentient creature comes to my humble web is to conduct business with me. And very grateful I am for their visits. But you see me before you right now, don't you? And for all this time that we've been together, and that I have enjoyed to such a degree—is that not so? I couldn't very well have been discussing business affairs with any other creature, as you've had my undivided attention all the while." A set of the exoskeleton's shoulders lifted in a parody of a humanoid shrug. "So why would anyone else have been here? Really—I don't delude myself that my home has charm sufficient to attract guests for any other reason."

Bossk's eyes squinted even narrower, signaling deep distrust. The scales of his brow tightened as the brain behind them scrabbled at the problem. "So what was it, then?"

"Merely the waste disposal function here aboard my web." The Balancesheet-steered carapace slowly shook its head. "How embarrassing to talk of such things, rude plumbing and all! But I have the same housekeeping dilemmas as any other vessel that moves through such empty space as that surrounding us. Some certain waste products must be jettisoned, and for hygiene's sake, it's best to expel them with sufficient velocity to leave the navigational zone around oneself free of—shall we say?—*distasteful* impediments." The carapace's triangular face, a replica of Kud'ar Mub'at's own, displayed a slight smile. "Really, my dear Bossk, even the ships of Palpatine's Imperial Navy do very much the same thing."

"Oh. Yeah . . ." Bossk slowly nodded. "I guess you're right."

Not really, thought Kud'ar Mub'at to itself. Though the assembler admired the fabrication it had just heard the accountant subnode deliver, the truth was that the web completely recycled its constituent matter. Kud'ar Mub'at had an instinctive aversion to letting go of any particle, no matter how small or insignificant, that had ever entered the web's living construct. To do so would have been like losing a piece of the assembler's own body. *But,* it admitted, *as long as this Trandoshan is fooled, the truth hardly matters . . .*

When Bossk had finally departed the web, the *Hound's Tooth* released from the docking subnodes a safe interval of time after the other ship's disembarking, Kud'ar Mub'at complimented its creation on the quick and sure handling of the bounty hunter's suspicions.

"Well done," said Kud'ar Mub'at. Secure in the embrace of its pneumatic nest, the assembler let the accountant subnode perch on the claw tip of one raised foreleg. In the distant and smaller chamber, the shed exoskeleton was once again a hollow likeness of the assembler's physical form. "You handled the Trandoshan in a way to inspire pride amid the internal organs of your creator."

"Merely a matter of business." Balancesheet displayed no embarrassment at receiving such praise. "If I show a facility in that regard, it is because all interactions between sentient creatures can be reduced to a matter of credits, expenditures, and debits." One of the accountant subnode's limbs traced the outline of a zero in the air. "Sum and divide."

"And divide and conquer." Though, of course, "conquest" was rhetoric a little grander than absolutely necessary. Kud'ar Mub'at was perfectly satisfied with a higher than average rate of profit. "That's always the best advice."

Kud'ar Mub'at let the accountant subnode scuttle back into its usual resting place, deep in the internal corridors of the web. If the assembler wasn't careful, its rudimentary heart might soften once again toward the smaller replica of itself. Much had been accomplished with the subnode's assistance: the Trandoshan bounty hunter Bossk had gone away, convinced of the same thing that his opponent Gleed Otondon was, that Kud'ar Mub'at and all its devious scheming was allied to the interests of his fragment of the old Bounty Hunters Guild. *Let them go on believing that,* thought Kud'ar Mub'at. When they found out otherwise, it would be too late for them to do anything about it. Whether the True Guild or the Guild Reform Committee won their battle with each other, that mattered little. As long as Kud'ar Mub'at won . . .

The assembler folded its legs around itself, and meditated over what the next steps in its scheming should be.

6

"Here is the report, Your Excellency."

Slouched in the form-chair in his private quarters, Prince Xizor extended his hand and took the single sheet of flimsiplast that the bowing lackey offered to him. The lackey tucked the silver tray under his arm and withdrew, still bowing. The creature's existence was already banished from the Falleen prince's mind, even before the tall, ornately worked doors closed once more.

Xizor preferred solitude in moments such as this. Not so much to maintain secrecy—the throne room was surrounded by minions who were, out of fear or loyalty, as dedicated to the Black Sun organization as he was—but to have the course of his thoughts undisturbed by the clatter of other creatures' words. Those from different planets and genetics—they were for amusement or profit. Xizor had had ample reason to congratulate himself in the past, for having found ways of combining those goals. Falleen pheromones had a powerful effect on the female members of most of the galaxy's sentient species—and enough of those were sufficiently satisfying to Xizor's tastes that he could pleasure himself with these easy conquests. If at the same time, he could advance his own and Black

Sun's agenda by overpowering a high-ranking female diplomat or envoy, either from the old Republic or this new upstart Rebel Alliance, then so much the better. But when everything he wished had been accomplished, the same cold smile would cross the sharp-edged angles of his face, the deep violet of his reptilian eyes vanishing behind mocking slits, as with a simple gesture of farewell he would make it clear that the female's desperate obsessions were no longer any concern of his. For a Falleen, sexual conquest was best savored in memory, like a trophy installed in the labyrinthian corridors fortressed inside his green-hued skull.

As cold-blooded as the reptilian Falleen physiology was, there actually was a hot-blooded element to their psyche. In this, the species was similar to the Trandoshans, however grossly ugly those creatures' scaly and large-fanged appearance. By contrast to a Trandoshan, a Falleen such as Xizor exhibited a haughty, fine-boned elegance that was as much a factor in their legendary sexual prowess as the powerful pheromones exuded from their silk-grained skin. What the two species shared, though, was the speed with which their satiated appetites returned, as hungry as ever. For Trandoshans, hunger was centered in their gut; their brains, what there were of them, were servants to a basically primitive carnivore nature. To best an enemy was to eat him. *We Falleens,* thought Xizor, *are a little more subtle than that . . .*

The anticipation of his next pleasures would have to wait, there was more immediate business at hand. Words were already forming on the surface of the flimsiplast, darkening into legibility.

While a species characteristic, the exuded pheromones differed enough from one individual Falleen to the next that they could function as a coded trigger for security devices. The chemical reaction taking place in the fibers of the flimsi could only have been initiated by physical contact with Prince Xizor's fingertips. He raised the sheet in his hand, holding it at a comfortable distance from his gaze.

It was a report from one of his chief lieutenants in the Black Sun organization, the Kian'thar named Kreet'ah. *Vigo* Kreet'ah, to use the title of honor he had earned through his faithful service; always loyal, occasionally cunning, and often violent. Kreet'ah had some excellent sources of information planted throughout the galaxy; Kian'tharan family and liege relationships were so intricate—their reproductive processes required fertilized ova to be handed down through three generations of nonconsanguine affiliate clans before birth—that outsiders had little chance of sorting through all the levels of cousin and sibling status on the Kian'tharan home planet. At the same time, the entire species had deceptively honest faces, which made it easy for them to work their way into other sentient creatures' trust. As had more than one of Kreet'ah's sub-α kin, inside the various widespread financial institutions that serviced the galaxy's less-than-savory business enterprises. Those businesses included the arachnoid assembler Kud'ar Mub'at's activities as a go-between for bounty hunters and their clients. Kreet'ah's agents reported to him on a regular basis, about every significant piece of information that came past their multilensed eyes.

This particular datum was one for which Prince Xizor had been waiting. He had specifically ordered the information to be determined by Kreet'ah's sources. It pleased him to know what other sentient creatures were up to, especially when the data was stolen right from beneath their noses, if they had them.

BOTH REMAINING FACTIONS OF BOUNTY HUNTERS

GUILD IN COMMUNICATION WITH KUD'AR MUB'AT—
Xizor appreciated brevity and conciseness in such reports. OTONDON OF TRUE GUILD AND BOSSK OF GUILD
REFORM COMMITTEE SIGHTED ABOARD WEB.

How intriguing, thought Prince Xizor. Not that
the news surprised him. More than anything, it confirmed both the excellence of his own plans and his
ability to predict just what the other players in this
game would do. All that was left was for him to decide
his own next move.

Only a few seconds had passed from Xizor's examination of Vigo Kreet'ah's report to his complete
understanding of all that it meant. The subtle pheromones exuded by his body had another effect on the
keyed chemicals imbedded in the flimsiplast. All the
words were suddenly hidden by a burst of flame, as
the flimsi's fibers self-ignited. In a moment, the report
was a rose flower of black ash, curling in Xizor's
palm. The momentary heat was a trifle, barely a test of
his rigorously maintained self-control; his martial
training had inured him to pain much greater than
this. Even before the flames had died, he crushed the
remnants of the burning flimsi into a smear of dust inside his fist. The message it had contained was now
safely extinguished from the universe.

Or almost gone. The words still resided in Prince
Xizor's memory—and that of his trusted lieutenant,
Vigo Kreet'ah. There was power in knowledge, especially the knowledge of secret things. Other creatures'
secrets; and when the information was something that
was of interest and importance to Emperor Palpatine,
then the secret was very powerful indeed. *A shame,*
mused Xizor, *that it should be diminished by anyone
else being a party to it.* Secrets had finite energy; each
sentient creature added to the knowledge diluted that
strength. Even a Black Sun Vigo such as Kreet'ah, who

supposedly had the organization's interests at heart just as much as his overlord did—Xizor would have to make a strategic decision about that. A personnel decision; granted, Kreet'ah's loyalty was proverbial inside the Black Sun ranks . . . but there were younger, up-and-coming foot soldiers who would welcome the chance at a promotion. *If* a vacancy at the top should some day appear . . .

Xizor brushed the vanished report's ashes from his hand; the black flakes drifted, almost weightless, against the folds of his cape. For another few seconds, he weighed Vigo Kreet'ah's existence in the delicately balanced scales of his thoughts—and made his decision. Kreet'ah would live, at least for a while longer. An underling's unswerving loyalty deserved some consideration, after all—at least enough to purchase someone like Kreet'ah a little more life and breathing space.

Besides, there were other matters to think about, even just in connection with what Kreet'ah's report had told him. The lids of Xizor's violet eyes drew down to mere slits as he turned the datum over in his mind, as though he were examining every facet of a rare but toxic gem. In his own private vaults, separate from Black Sun's treasure-laden coffers, were inert-metal cylinders that safely held inside the rarest of green diamonds. There were other gemstones in the galaxy that were even rarer, more valuable, and more beautiful—a diamond, after all, was nothing more than carbon. But to hold one of these on the palm of one's hand for even thirty seconds was to receive a lethal dose of radioactive emissions. That was what made them so precious in Xizor's estimation.

On a few occasions, he had bestowed one as a gift upon one of his mistresses, when the affair had been over in his mind but not in hers. At a safe distance, of course—the tiny box would be sent by an expendable messenger, who would also perform the service of hanging the gem on its platinite chain around the female's elegantly formed neck. And then, at the appropriate time, a more valuable Black Sun member, a stealth-burglar with expertise in hazardous materials, would fetch the green diamond back, when it had done its task of creating such a beautiful corpse.

It had occurred to Prince Xizor that some types of valuable knowledge were exactly like those toxic gems in his collection. Much to be desired, and with their undeniable uses—but sometimes deadly to those who held them. A truism throughout the galaxy: corpses were the best sharers of secrets.

Xizor nodded slowly to himself, his hands nervelessly still upon the arms of the form-chair. There was a risk to himself that came with such valuable knowledge. Emperor Palpatine still seemed to be unaware that one of his own most trusted lieutenants was also overlord of the galaxy's supreme criminal organization—even though Lord Vader had voiced his own suspicions in that regard to the Emperor, and more than once. *But Palpatine must know,* brooded Xizor. It was impossible to believe that the Emperor, with his near omniscience about everything that happened in the galaxy, would *not* know something like that. *So,* thought Xizor, *he must have his own reasons for wanting it to appear otherwise.* Emperor Palpatine was a master of subtle strategy; perhaps it suited his purposes to allow Black Sun a free hand for the time being. If Palpatine were to make a move against the criminal organization at a time like this, he would find himself in that worst of all possible military and political situations, a two-front war; even the Empire, with all its resources, could find itself grievously stretched by combating the Rebel Alliance and Black

Sun simultaneously. And Palpatine could not eliminate Prince Xizor from his court and at least the appearance of his confidences without triggering hostilities with Black Sun.

Obviously, for Emperor Palpatine it would be better to leave Xizor untouched—for now. But Xizor was not such a fool as to think himself thereby immune from all danger. Any indiscretions on his part—if the galaxy at large were to learn of his being the head of Black Sun—and the Emperor's hand would be forced, no matter what the cost. Palpatine's control over his dominions was not yet so strong that he could risk the Empire appearing to have traitors at its very heart.

He knows, thought Xizor, *but others don't.* That was the important thing. It was not for the sake of deceiving Palpatine, but for maintaining the galaxy's ignorance, that it was crucial no connection could be made between Vigo Kreet'ah's network of spies and the ultimate recipient of their information, Prince Xizor himself.

If the trail of data could be determined, from Kreet'ah's sources, then to the Black Sun organization—then it would be very difficult to avoid having the connection made, even without any hard evidence, between Black Sun and Xizor himself. The Emperor might ignore it, as he had ignored other evidence before. But others—such as the Rebel Alliance—might not. And that might be the point when Emperor Palpatine would finally act, with swift and fatal results.

There were more difficulties involved in keeping these matters secret, Xizor knew, than just keeping his own silence. A link in the chain leading to him had to be destroyed, vaporized as if struck with a blaster bolt. He had already decided that Kreet'ah was still worth more to him alive than dead. So some other link would have to be eliminated. Kreet'ah himself could take care of that; a Black Sun Vigo could easily arrange for the sudden disappearance of a few of his own information sources. Then it would just be a matter of Kreet'ah rebuilding his network of spies inside the Rebel Alliance, with a few more barriers between them and Black Sun—troublesome, but not impossible.

Xizor had already made a mental note as to what instructions he would give to Kreet'ah. He expected no objection from the Kian'tharan; it was more a matter of standard operating procedure than anything else. Standard . . . and familiar. A smile played at the corner of his mouth. *Even*, thought Xizor to himself, *somewhat enjoyable*.

That was his one regret about sparing Kreet'ah's life. Now he wouldn't have the pleasure of taking it.

7

A moment comes, when a target is sighted and locked upon, and all one has to do is press the trigger stud underneath one's thumb. Boba Fett had had many such moments in his career, enough so that there was no longer any physiological response, no speeding of the pulse, no tightening of the breath beneath his dark-visored helmet, no trickle of adrenaline into the veins of the body that bore the Mandalorian battle armor . . .

But there was still a deep sense of satisfaction, an almost spiritual glow at the core of his being. It was what he lived for, even more than the credits that all his hard work brought in.

In the cockpit of *Slave I*, Boba Fett's gloved hands moved swiftly across the navigation controls. The ship's velocity was already max'ed out, the thrust from the custom-designed—and expensive—Mandal Motors engines ramped to overload. A shimmering vibration traveled through *Slave I*'s structural frame, blurring the gauges and readouts beneath Boba Fett's fingers. In the cockpit's viewport, against a backdrop of unwavering stars, could be seen the trailing jets of the ship that Fett pursued. *He's good*, Boba Fett thought grudgingly. *But not good enough*.

The other ship, an Incom Corporation Z-95 Headhunter, was perfectly suited for just such high-speed chase and evasion maneuvers. This particular one had been modified with an additional passenger area, reaching from an expanded cockpit and along the main fuselage. The ungainly structural addition would create a negative aerodynamic drag inside a planet's atmosphere, but in the vacuum of space there was little effect on the craft's speed. Boba Fett knew who the pilot was, a free-lance hunt saboteur named N'dru Suhlak; a kid who had washed out of the Rebel Alliance's Tierfon Fighter Base not for lack of flying skills, but an excess of insubordination. The expertise and training that Suhlak had picked up while he was hanging out with ace pilots like Jek Porkins and Wes Janson, plus his own natural abilities—there were just some things in this galaxy that you had to be born with—had quickly gotten him to the top of his chosen speciality. It was one for which he commanded top credits: a hunt saboteur's trade was essentially the secure transport and delivery of hard merchandise, one creature at a time. Suhlak made the claim that he could get any sentient creature with a bounty posted on its head—that was what "hard merchandise" meant, in bounty hunter jargon—from Point A to Point B without getting intercepted, no matter who was gunning for the cargo.

Big talk, thought Boba Fett as he punched in another course micro-correction to stay on the Z-95's tail. But the kid had proved he had the pilot chops, getting past even the few other bounty hunters for which Fett had any respect at all. IG-88, the droid bounty hunter, had been blitzed so fast that the optical processors inside its durasteel head hadn't even spotted Suhlak getting past its interceptor stakeout point. Most of the other bounty hunters, even before the

Bounty Hunters Guild had split up into its two main factions, had made it a general rule not to pursue Suhlak's ship, the pursuit being a waste of time and fuel—and one's life. Not all of Suhlak's escape maneuvers were based on speed alone.

Boba Fett punched in an override command, diverting *Slave I*'s excess atmospheric-maintenance functions to the cooling system for the main thrust engine. If there had been anyone in the holding cages below the cockpit area, they would have been asphyxiated in a few Standard Time Units. But *Slave I* wasn't carrying any passengers, willing or unwilling, right now. Fett's ship had been lurking in the debris shadow cast by a ring of wrecked and stripped star freighters above the toxic atmosphere of the planet Uhltenden; he had been waiting, with all propulsion systems in abeyance-trigger mode, for Suhlak's Z-95 to show up. When it had, the chase was on.

N'dru Suhlak had been either lucky or smart so far not to have crossed Boba Fett's path. The merchandise that Suhlak had ferried had all been below Fett's threshold of interest. Letting the kid get away with it, for as long as there was no impact on Fett's business interests, had been a good way of letting Suhlak grow overconfident. Any misestimation of one's skills—or one's luck—was a fatal error when Boba Fett was involved. *You've made your mistake now,* Fett silently told the ship speeding through the vacuum ahead.

He kept one gloved hand hovering close to *Slave I*'s hyperdrive controls. No astrogation coordinates had been read out of the navicomputer and locked in yet, but the tracking devices and targeting computer were ready to go. If Suhlak had made one more mistake, that of taking the little Z-95 into hyperspace, he would have found *Slave I* right on top of him when he emerged back into realspace. Nobody escaped from Boba Fett that easily. *He must know it's me,* thought Fett, *right behind him.* The helmet of the Mandalorian armor nodded slowly as its bearer gazed out the cockpit viewport. His nod indicated both satisfaction and anticipation; the pursuit and the inevitable capture would be all the better now.

The Z-95 suddenly disappeared from sight.

Fett's hand darted closer to the hyperdrive controls, stopping a fraction of a centimeter before hitting them. The tracker lock-on signals hadn't flared red yet. *He's still here.* Boba Fett leaned forward in the pilot's chair, bringing his visored sight closer to the cockpit's forward viewport. His appreciation for Suhlak's skills had gone up a notch. It'd been a smooth maneuver, and one that Fett hadn't encountered before. If he'd been fooled into jumping into hyperspace, even for a moment, by the time he'd gotten *Slave I* back out to this navigational sector, Suhlak could easily have gotten an insurmountable lead. Or if not insurmountable—Fett didn't admit that possibility; it hadn't happened yet—then one that would have taken a lot more work and time to overcome. That cut into his profits, a notion that was the only one that could evoke his anger.

He quickly scanned the bank of tracking indicators, while pushing forward the linear aperture control from near vicinity to far. The thermal and radiation trackers showed no sudden bump in the emission profile of Suhlak's Z-95; if he had taken some sharp vector away from his previous course, those trackers would have picked up the additional thrust necessary, even if Suhlak had been able to conceal the visual flare from his ship's engines.

The puzzle of N'dru Suhlak's sudden disappearance, along with the hard merchandise he was carrying aboard his ship, intrigued Boba Fett on a coldly rational basis. He wasn't concerned—yet—whether he'd figure out the answer in time to catch the fleeing hunt saboteur. *If he's here*—and Suhlak had to be— *then I'll find him . . .*

It wouldn't do to overshoot whatever hiding place the Z-95 had found. Boba Fett reached over and damped the main thrust engine. The slight vibration in *Slave I*'s frame ceased as the ship immediately lost speed.

That was what saved him.

At the upper edge of the viewport, Boba Fett saw one of the visible stars shimmer momentarily, vanish, and then reappear in the same location. Without conscious thought, but only pure reaction, his hand flew from the engine controls to the reverse thrusters. His palm hammered flat the thruster controls, giving them maximum power.

A split second later, *Slave I* hit the invisible object whose presence Fett had barely managed to detect.

The impact tore him from the pilot's chair, sending him tumbling across the curved bank of the cockpit controls. His spine struck the clear transparisteel of the viewport, a blow hard enough to send a shock of pain into the center of his skull, blinding him. If he had still been carrying the back-mounted weapons he wore when outside the ship, their sharper edges would have crushed his cervical vertebrae and left him paralyzed, helpless against whatever happened next.

The pain ebbed a fraction, enough for Boba Fett's blood-reddened vision to clear. At the limits of his consciousness, he could hear *Slave I*'s perimeter-breach alarms sounding with high-pitched, ululating cries. The vertical, tail-downward flight position of his ship—the engines' thrust-ports were all mounted on the hull side opposite the rounded curve of the cockpit—had resulted in the main viewport being the part to take the brunt of the collision with the unseen obstacle. Or seen too late to prevent a crash; the memory of the brief glimpse Boba Fett had caught, the telltale shimmer and reappearance of a star at the edge of the viewport, was still vivid.

At least, he had been able to slam on the reverse thrusters in time. There was an inherent limit to transparisteel's toughness; there had to be, for it to have enough of a glasslike refractive index to be used in viewports. If *Slave I* had been traveling any faster, the rounded exterior shape of the cockpit would have shattered like a crystal egg. Boba Fett would have found himself breathing vacuum, surrounded by glittering shards.

The ship's artificial gravity was still working; he managed to scramble back down to the pilot's chair from which he had been thrown. The alarm signals were still shrill and loud in his ears. That meant *Slave I* was still losing internal atmospheric pressure. Boba Fett made a quick visual scan of the viewport arching before the control panels. There was no crack in the transparisteel, but the crash had been hard enough to loosen a section of interstitial bond between the clear material and the surrounding durasteel of the hull.

"Activate emergency weld sequence." The procedure was one of the few keyed to a voice command for the onboard computer. Fett had anticipated that if it had ever become necessary, he might not have been able to reach the cockpit controls at a time when speed was of the essence. He quickly gave the structural coordinates for the leaking section of the viewport bond; every millimeter of *Slave I* was precisely charted in Boba Fett's memory, as clear as if he had been looking at the original blueprints and design parameters. "Initiate thermal ramp—*now*."

He could feel the glow of heat through the dark,

T-shaped visor of his helmet as the circuits laid in the cockpit's surrounding bulkhead powered up. A moment later the durasteel next to the viewport leak turned red, then white-hot; the crystalline structure of the metal turned ductile, just enough for the seal to reform around the transparisteel. The perimeter alarms fell silent as the loss of atmosphere tapered down to just a few molecules hissing out into space, then none at all.

The whole emergency repair process had taken only a few seconds. *Slave I* was like a living organism, designed in its essence to heal itself. Boba Fett could feel in his own nerve endings when that happened, just as any wound to the ship's fabric was sensed as a wound to himself. The only things closer to him, even more of a perceived extension to his spirit, were the weapons he carried. Those were as much a part of him as his own hands, instruments of his will.

Losing even a few seconds in the pursuit of N'dru Suhlak and his cargo was irksome. And to have it caused by a trap like this one turned Boba Fett's durasteel-like resolve even harder and colder.

The mechanics of the trap were close enough now for him to easily discern. Floating in space just in front of *Slave I* was a sheet of mass-altered, optic-filterable transparisteel, its jagged edges reaching out wider than the ship's hull. Suhlak must have gotten it from the ring of transport wreckage in orbit around Uhl-tenden; Boba Fett recalled that some of the wrecked freighters had been hijacked supply ships bound for the construction docks of Kuat Drive Yards. Chances were good that they might have been carrying advanced armaments-technology supplies—and that Suhlak had put them to use for his own escape route scheme.

Optic-filterable transparisteel hadn't been developed for observation purposes, but for armor plating of heavy destroyers and cruisers in the Imperial Navy, as well as tactical camouflage. The light transmitted through it could actually be routed, through interior "bucket-brigade" datalinks, from one side of a ship to another, effectively passing on the visual perceptions to an outside observer. A crude form of simulated invisibility, but with one important strategic advantage. The nano-tech datalinks could also be programmed to *filter out* any specific visual data, such as the presence of other navy ships . . . or the trail of a speeding Z-95 Headhunter. The optical image sent through the filterable transparisteel would show the distant stars on the other side of the barrier, and nothing else. Boba Fett realized that had been how N'dru Suhlak had managed to disappear from view, while the thermal and radioactive profiles from his small ship had continued to register on *Slave I*'s tracking systems. A perfect trap . . . or almost. The only thing that had saved Boba Fett from a fatal crash into the floating barrier had been his lightning-fast reactions and the quick response of *Slave I*'s reverse thrusters.

That still left the small matter of catching Suhlak's Z-95, which had an even bigger lead now than it had before.

Or did it? Boba Fett's preeminence in the bounty hunter trade was based on more than mere weaponry skills. Psychology played a significant part as well. Without ever having met him face-to-face, he had a good notion of how Suhlak's brain worked. *Cocky,* thought Fett as he reached out toward the cockpit's control panel. *And not quite smart enough to play it safe, and just run when he's got the chance.*

With a few quick adjustments, Boba Fett extended *Slave I*'s docking claw; the sharpened points of the pincerlike extension dug hold of the huge piece of optic-filterable transparisteel. Fett slammed the joystick control hard to one side, simultaneously releasing the claw's grip. Through the forward viewport, he saw the distant stars shimmer and then become clear and focused once more, as the jagged-edged sheet of armor-thick, glass-clear material tumbled to one side of the ship.

There he is. Straight ahead through the cockpit's forward viewport, Boba Fett saw Suhlak's Z-95. Closer than it had been when he had been chasing the smaller craft, and with its powerful thruster engines damped down to standby level. Suhlak had turned his ship around, angling it back toward the vector it had previously traveled, so that he could get a clear view of *Slave I* crashing into the barrier trap he had set in place. And a perfect shot of Boba Fett dying in that crash. *Only,* thought Fett, *it didn't work out quite like that.*

And now there was no place for Suhlak to run. This close, he would never be able to maneuver his ship around, rev up its thruster engines, and hit top velocity before *Slave I* would be able to catch up with him.

Boba Fett slammed his palm down upon the thruster controls of his own ship. In its viewport, the Z-95 loomed closer and larger, like a bull's-eye target under high magnification.

The first crash had been satisfying enough to watch. N'dru Suhlak had smiled to himself, imagining the famous bounty hunter tumbling head over heels inside the cockpit of his ship, caught by an invisible trap.

The second crash was glorious.

"You see?" Suhlak turned away from the Headhunter's viewport and displayed his self-satisfied smile to his only passenger. "So much for your unstoppable, implacable pursuer, the great Boba Fett."

Beside him, the Twi'lek Ob Fortuna, former major-domo at the headquarters of the Bounty Hunters Guild, leaned closer toward the transparent curve of the viewport. The Twi'lek's eyes, like those of all the males of his species, were usually half-concealed behind their lids, perfectly suiting his darting, sneaking gaze. But now those eyes were opened wide in amazement. "I . . . I never would have thought such a thing possible." One of Ob Fortuna's pale, long-fingered hands reached out, coming within a fraction of an inch of touching the viewport's concave surface. "He's gone. Absolutely . . ."

Suhlak's smile split open, emitting a harsh laugh. "You can say that again."

He turned his own gaze back toward the viewport. The churning light from the explosion was just beginning to fade, but it was still bright enough to have tripped the protective glare shields lining the curving transparisteel. Without those shields, both he and his fare-paying cargo would have been blinded. *It would have been worth it,* thought Suhlak. *Almost.* The glare from what had been Boba Fett's ship *Slave I,* now being consumed by the unleashed fusion of its impact-shattered engines, was almost tangible, a warm thermal glow across the intervening vacuum and onto Suhlak's smiling face.

"How did you do it?" Wonderment had filtered into Ob Fortuna's voice as well. "It's impossible . . ."

"Nothing's impossible," said N'dru Suhlak. He let his smile curdle into a sneer. "Unless you start believing your own mythology. Then everything starts to get a little difficult—least if I'm around." He nodded toward the viewport. "I had this Boba Fett character figured out from the beginning. Somebody like that always figures he's the only one with brains. Real brains, that is. So if he falls into a trap and gets out of it, he figures that's the only trick you had up your sleeve."

"But . . ." Ob Fortuna's brow creased as he labored to comprehend. The heavy, fleshy masses of a male Twi'lek's double head-tails rolled across his shoulder as he tilted his head. "He hit that optic-filterable transparisteel you set up. And he managed to hit his reverse thrusters in time, so his ship wasn't damaged . . ."

"Exactly." Suhlak shook his own head in disgust. These Twi'leks had a knack for simpleminded skulduggery and flattering more powerful sentient creatures, but anything else was a stretch for them. "You just don't get it, do you? That wasn't the only piece of armor-grade transparisteel I set out there for him to run into. Look, Boba Fett's dead now, but that doesn't mean I underestimated him. I knew he had the kind of smarts and reflexes that would keep him from a fatal crash—the first time, that is. So I put out a *second* piece of transparisteel, only I didn't set up any optical filtering on it; that way, Fett would see us just sitting here, waiting for him to come and get us. He wouldn't be able to resist gunning his engines and coming right for us—and he didn't. At that kind of speed, the mass of the second piece of transparisteel was more than enough to crumple that ship of his into scrap metal and blow his thruster cores into fusion overload. There probably aren't two atoms of the great Boba Fett left connected to each other by now."

"That's . . . that's very clever." Ob Fortuna gazed wide-eyed at him. "I would never have come up with something so . . . final."

"Yeah, right." The last thing Suhlak wanted was to hear any oily Twi'lek flattery turned his way. "You just keep remembering that. Then you won't mind paying me."

"Ah, but it's a pleasure to do so. Even if all I bargained for was to just get past Boba Fett. Not have him eliminated totally."

"Whatever works." Suhlak shrugged. "Sometimes speed does the job . . . and sometimes you gotta do a little extra. Besides . . . knocking off somebody like Boba Fett is good advertising for a person in my trade. It never hurts for creatures to know that you're the best." In the viewport, the fiery, roiling glow from the crash was almost gone. Nothing was visible of the wreckage of the late Boba Fett's ship; the explosion had vaporized every fragment. "Enough of this," said Suhlak, reaching for the Z-95's controls. "Let's get out of here. I've got other business to take care of."

Times like this, he wished his craft were as big as Boba Fett's ship had been, something with enough space aboard that he could have stowed his fare-paying merchandise somewhere else. Most bounty hunters had cages in the cargo areas of their ships, where they kept their hard merchandise safely out of the way until delivery. To outrun a bounty hunter ship, though, required something much lighter and faster. The old Z-95s weren't so tightly designed as the T-65 X-wing starfighters that had replaced them, and thus had more modification possibilities. For his hunt sabotage purposes, he had stripped out all the heavy armament and weapons systems, and had bubbled out the passenger space—not all hard merchandise was as compact as humanoid life-forms.

Even with the extra space gained from those modifications, the net result was that passengers—or merchandise; Suhlak was beginning to use the same language as bounty hunters—still wound up right in the already cramped cockpit area of the Z-95. *And this Twi'lek,* thought Suhlak, *is really getting on my nerves.* All those oily, unctuous mannerisms, plus Ob Fortuna's ratlike smile and weaseling words, were right in his face. Suhlak felt the impulse to take the Twi'lek's floppy head-tails and pressure-tape them to the far bulkhead, just to keep from seeing them all the time he was trying to navigate. *Well, he won't be on my hands much longer . . .*

Suhlak readied the Z-95's main thruster engine, then reached for the vector-align controls. Once the headhunter was safely away from this sector, with all its drifting transport debris, he'd be able to make a clean jump into hyperspace.

His hand froze above the controls as he looked up to the viewport. Inside Suhlak's throat, his breath was stilled as well.

"What's that?" From behind him, Ob Fortuna's voice was a terrified squeak. The Twi'lek's pale hand reached past the side of Suhlak's face, pointing to what was now revealed, floating in space before the Z-95.

"It's . . . Boba Fett's ship." Suhlak spoke the words, a simple statement of fact. But one that sent his heart plummeting down toward his boot soles, at the same time his spine contracted in apprehension. "He's not dead."

There was more proof of that as the image of *Slave I*, the ship that was as much the emblem of Boba Fett as the dark-visored Mandalorian helmet he wore, turned slightly in the viewport. It seemed to loom upright in the vacuum, the large curve of its cockpit centered in the elongated oval of its hull. And between its two main laser cannons—their dark, menacing apertures swung directly toward the Z-95, and locked on to their target.

Two bolts of coruscating energy struck the Headhunter. The viewport filled with the white glare of their impact; their force sent the smaller craft tumbling. Blinded, N'dru Suhlak felt himself tumbling backward, out of the pilot's chair and landing heavily against the insufficient cushioning of his passenger.

"Don't do anything stupid." Another voice spoke, from the comm unit mounted on the cockpit's control panel. Boba Fett's voice, unmistakably so, even on a tight-beam relay from his ship. "You've got something I want. I'm coming over to get it." The voice's lack of perceptible emotion made it all the more intimidating. "Right now."

Dazed, but with his vision slowly coming back, Suhlak placed a hand against Ob Fortuna's muscleless chest and pushed himself upright. He grabbed hold of the back of the pilot's chair and dragged himself toward the Z-95's controls.

"What . . . what are you going to do?" The Twi'lek sounded close to panic.

"Like the man said." Suhlak damped the main thruster engine. And prepared for a visitor. "Nothing stupid."

The hunt saboteur looked just as Boba Fett had expected. On the dark and lean side, wearing Tierfon Fighter Base fatigues with all identifying insignia stripped off. Suhlak's sharp-angled face was both avaricious and—at the moment—sullen.

"I make it a rule," said Boba Fett, "not to interfere with other creatures' business. Except"—he stood in the opening of the transfer hatchway extending from his own *Slave I*, not wanting to step into the already crowded quarters of Suhlak's Z-95—"when they interfere with mine."

"Really." N'dru Suhlak gave an ostentatiously weary sigh. "I don't need a lecture on operating practices from you."

"You don't need me to kill you, either. But I'd be happy to do it." Boba Fett had donned his usual arsenal before crossing over from his ship. He didn't bother drawing his blaster or reaching over his shoulder for any of the higher-powered weapons; their mere presence, silent and intimidating, was enough. "And believe me—it would be just business. Nothing personal."

The kid didn't make a reply. A weapons belt, with a standard-issue Imperial Navy blaster pistol in its holster, was slung from a protruding angle of the Z-95's structural frame. It was within easy reach of Suhlak, but he continued to stand with his arms folded across his chest, chin lowered, and eyes glaring.

Good, thought Boba Fett. *That shows he's not completely stupid.*

"And as long as we are talking business . . ." The bounty hunter turned toward the other sentient creature in the Z-95's cockpit. The Twi'lek Ob Fortuna cowered back against the bulkhead, his hands raised toward his face in cringing supplication. "You and I have some unfinished matters to take care of."

"I . . . I don't know what you mean." Ob Fortuna's hands crawled over each other like blind, hairless animals. "I am but dirt beneath your boot soles, Boba Fett. Nothing but a poor—and currently unemployed—servant to those with real power. Ever since the esteemed Cradossk died—"

"Correction. Cradossk didn't *die*; his son Bossk killed him. And then he took care of the remains the way Trandoshans do those things."

A visible shudder ran through the Twi'lek. Even the scowling Suhlak appeared a little sick at the mention of Trandoshan dynastic practices. By now, the late Cradossk's bones, complete with gnawed tooth marks, were treasured items in Bossk's personal trophy chamber.

"Well, then . . ." What was meant to be an ingratiating smile appeared on Ob Fortuna's face. He lifted his empty hands, palms upward; his shrug raised the pendulous weights of his head-tails. "You can hardly blame me for wanting to seek other employment. I had been Cradossk's major domo for a long time; it would have been too traumatic for me to have undertaken those same services for his son Bossk."

"Seems reasonable to me." N'dru Suhlak's shrug wasn't as encumbered. "Give the guy a break, why don't you?"

The gaze from the helmet's T-shaped visor was as cold and hard as the half-forgotten legends described the Mandalorian warriors, long vanquished by the Jedi Knights, as being. Boba Fett was well aware of the effect that dark gaze had on other creatures; it was as much a weapon as any other slung behind his back. "I've already given you a break," he said quietly to the hunt saboteur. "You're not dead. Yet."

Suhlak leaned back against the pilot's chair. He glanced over at Ob Fortuna, then slowly shook his head. "That was my best shot."

"But . . ." Panic obliterated every other emotion in the Twi'lek's eyes as he looked back toward Boba Fett. "You have to understand . . ."

"I understand a great deal," said Boba Fett. "That's not the problem. And neither is your not wanting to work for Bossk. I don't even care to work with a creature like that. The problem is who else you were working for when you were in Cradossk's employ."

The skin of Ob Fortuna's head-tails took on a

sweating translucency, as any remaining color drained from his face. "But that . . . that's insane. It's a lie!" His desperate gaze swept in the hunt saboteur, as though an ally could be found there. "I was completely loyal to Cradossk! I swear it!"

"Loyal in your way. As loyal as any Twi'lek is." Boba Fett didn't need to step forward from the transfer hatchway to keep Ob Fortuna pushed against the Z-95's bulkhead. "And that's just about as much loyalty as credits can buy. Anybody's credits." He turned his visored gaze toward Suhlak. "How much were you getting paid for safe delivery of this merchandise?" He used the bounty hunter terminology, even though it was technically incorrect in this case; no bounty had been posted for Ob Fortuna.

Suhlak looked back coolly at him. "Enough."

This time, Boba Fett did step forward. He dug into a small, belt-mounted pouch and extracted a few credits, then slapped them into Suhlak's palm. "There," he said. "Consider it delivered."

The hunt saboteur inspected the credits. "Looks a little short." He glanced up. "Know what I mean?"

A few seconds passed before Boba Fett answered. "You've got an excess of nerve," he said slowly. "That's not a bad thing, given how you're trying to make a living. I can even admire that. But let me give you some advice." Fett had returned to the transfer hatchway that led back to the waiting *Slave I*. "Don't try it on me—"

"No!" A shrill cry cut across Boba Fett's words. The few scraps of control remaining to Ob Fortuna had suddenly evaporated; his face distorted and mottled by fear, he flung himself across the cramped space of the Z-95's cockpit area. The weight of the Twi'lek's head-tails lifted clear of his robed shoulders. His clawing hands reached out, not for Boba Fett's throat, but for the holstered blaster hanging near the pilot's chair. Ob Fortuna's rushing flight propelled him into Suhlak's chest, sending them both sprawling across the cockpit's metal-grated floor. The bounty hunter kicked himself free of Ob Fortuna, then scrambled as far away as possible, shielding his face with an up-raised arm.

Ob Fortuna got to his knees, fumbling with the un-familiar blaster. Both his long-fingered hands wrapped around its grip; the barrel wavered, pointing wildly in all directions. Before he could find the weapon's trig-ger stud, a sharp hissing sound hit against the bulk-heads, followed by the Twi'lek's gasp of pain as the blaster was torn from his grasp.

The blaster was snared in the thin line of mono-linked filament running from the wrist of Boba Fett's battle armor to the small, nonexplosive projectile he had fired. He drew back his outstretched arm, at the same time retracting the line to its source reel; the blas-ter flew as rapidly as Ob Fortuna's panicked rush. Boba Fett deftly grabbed hold of the weapon.

"Not a smart move," said Fett. Though from the way the Twi'lek had been sweating and twitching, it was exactly what he had expected. He pulled the blaster free of the line's tangle, then slung it toward Suhlak. The hunt saboteur had uncoiled himself into a sitting position, and now caught the blaster with both hands. "Hold on to that," instructed Boba Fett. He knew that Suhlak was at least smart enough to sit tight and not provoke any further demonstration of his skills.

Crouched into a whimpering ball, Ob Fortuna cowered back against the cockpit's farthest bulkhead. His pallid face was luminous with sweat, the head-tails drawing damp, sluglike trails across the front of his robe. He shrieked and tried futilely to compress himself into an even smaller mass as Boba Fett stepped forward and reached down. Grabbing hold of the robe's collar, he pulled the unresisting Twi'lek upright.

"Let's go," said Boba Fett. He stepped back toward the transfer hatchway, dragging Ob Fortuna along with him.

"Where . . ." Ob Fortuna's hands clung to his captor's forearm. "Where are we going . . ."

"That's not really your concern anymore." He turned and shoved the Twi'lek into the hatchway, toward the other ship waiting at the other end of the connecting passage. Ob Fortuna stumbled and landed on his hands and knees.

"Hold it."

Boba Fett heard the simple command from behind him. He brought his dark-visored gaze around, looking back over his shoulder. He saw N'dru Suhlak standing in the middle of the Z-95's cockpit area, the blaster held unwavering toward the transfer hatchway. The weapon was aimed directly at Fett.

"Now what?" Boba Fett held himself motionless.

"Isn't it obvious?" Suhlak's lopsided smile appeared. "You screwed up. Now you're going to do what *I* say."

"Oh? Why should I?"

"Because—" The smile showed how much pleasure Suhlak took in the explanation. "If you don't, I'm going to drill a smoke-lined hole right through your gut."

Boba Fett shook his head. "You're not doing it with that piece." He held up one gloved hand, displaying the power cell he had deftly palmed from the blaster, before he had tossed it away. "If I'm not a fool the first time, I'm not likely to be the next time, either."

"Guess not." Suhlak glanced at the useless weapon in his hand, then lowered it. He looked back up at the bounty hunter. "So answer me something."

"Make it short. I've already wasted too much time here."

"How'd you do it?" Suhlak appeared genuinely puzzled. "I mean—how come you're not dead?"

"Simple," said Fett. "I knew there'd be another piece of armor-grade transparisteel floating out there. The best traps—the kind a clever barve like you would lay—always have two sets of teeth in them. So just before I hit the transparisteel, I took my ship in a hard one-eighty degree roll, so my main thruster engines were pointed straight at it. Put the engines at maximum, dropped a high-thermal explosive charge, and jumped to hyperspace before it went off." Boba Fett's emotionless voice made it sound easy. "While you were still looking at what was left, my ship was jumping back into realspace, just on the other side of you. Then all I had to do was wait."

"Huh." In the cockpit area of his own ship, Suhlak nodded in admiration. "That must be why you're letting me go, then. So I can tell everybody I run into about what a tough customer you are."

"Tell them whatever you want. I don't need the advertising. I'm letting you go on your way for one reason only."

"What's that?"

Boba Fett tossed the blaster's power cell into the Z-95's cockpit; the small object clattered across its flooring. "You're the best hunt saboteur I've come across, at least recently. And if you're the best there is right now . . . then I don't have to worry about you interfering with my business."

"Maybe," Suhlak said quitely, "I'll be even better next time."

"I'll worry about it then."

With one finger, Boba Fett punched the control pad mounted on the sleeve of his battle armor. The transfer hatchway rised shut, sealing itself from the Z-95. He turned as the hatchway disengaged and began retracting the short distance back into the hull of *Slave I*.

The Twi'lek Ob Fortuna had saved him some trouble. Boba Fett found him with a length of thin cable, part of the line that had snared away the blaster, wrapped around his throat and pulled tight with his own hands. The look of fear frozen in the dead creature's eyes was mute testimony that self-asphyxiation was preferable to whatever fate he'd imagined would be delivered by his captor.

It didn't matter to Boba Fett. This was one of the few times when something he had hunted down was worth more dead than alive. *He knew too much,* thought Fett. Specifically, about what had gone on behind the scenes with the break up of the old Bounty Hunters Guild. And, just like a Twi'lek, he'd always talked too much. *Now he won't.*

There was one task left to take care of, as far as the late Ob Fortuna was concerned. Other sentient creatures, much more important and powerful than a sniveling, opportunistic Twi'lek majordomo could ever have been, were interested in silence being maintained about certain matters. They would want proof of that silence. Boba Fett extracted a few sharp-edged tools from one of his uniform's pouches, then knelt down beside the still-warm corpse.

He left Ob Fortuna's stiffening body in the transfer hatchway. Once back inside *Slave I*, he slung the sealed bag he carried into a storage locker, then mounted the ladder to the ship's cockpit. Seated in the pilot's chair, Boba Fett hit the hatchway's atmospheric purge button; the quick blast of air pressure was enough to expel the corpse out into the vacuum, drifting close enough to Suhlak's ship that the hunt saboteur would be able to have a last good look at it.

Fett hit the main thruster engines control, heading out of the sector while simultaneously punching in the coordinates for his next jump. There was plenty more business to take care of, before he was done.

There was *always* more business.

8

Someday, thought Prince Xizor. *Someday he and I will meet face-to-face.* Either here on Coruscant, in the Imperial throne room itself, or in some bleak, remote corner of the galaxy—that moment would surely come. *For the last time.* And then the little war, deadly and personal, between himself and Darth Vader, the Dark Lord of the Sith, would be at an end.

One way or another.

He strode through the vaulted corridors of the palace, the reddening twilight of Coruscant's sun casting angles of blood-colored light across the richly inlaid floor ahead of him. A single unbraided rope of Xizor's night-black hair, drawn back from his bare skull like a glistening viper, swung across the flaring shoulders of his robe with each stride.

Xizor focused his thoughts as he came closer to the great doors of Emperor Palpatine's throne room. The concerns of dominion—both Palpatine's Empire and Xizor's own Black Sun criminal organization—were manifold and urgent, made even more so by the rise of the impudent Rebel Alliance. And now, he was summoned for this audience with the galaxy's ruling power, a power in the shape of a wizened old man.

If it weren't for the eyes set in that gaunt, wrinkled face—eyes that were as cold and commanding as Xizor's own violet-colored ones—he would never have thought the Emperor to be more than a cloaked beggar, if he had come across him in some dark passageway of the Empire's capital on Coruscant. But once having looked into that gaze, so bereft of any of the tender emotions that sentient creatures were prey to, Xizor could understand how the former Senator Palpatine had climbed astride an Empire built out of the old Republic's ruins. If there had been any last barriers to Xizor's own ruthless ambitions—any weakness or sentiment within himself—he had been inspired by the Emperor's example to root it out. Whether the mystical, universe-spanning Force of which Palpatine and Lord Vader talked was real, Xizor had no idea—or at least not enough to believe in it over his own strengths and cunning. But the dark side of that Force was something he could attest to. He had seen it beneath the hood of the Emperor's cloak, like twin gravitational wells that could absorb and crush a weaker creature's spirit.

The high, intricately patterned door swung open before Xizor. Once more, he found himself in the presence of that dark strength.

"Xizor . . ." The Emperor's simple throne turned, bringing his hooded gaze and his thin, humorless smile toward the center of the cold, empty space. The ancient-appearing figure sat deep in the throne, as though the weight of his thoughts and schemes were crushing him toward the planet's core. "As much pleasure as there can be found in one's scurrying underlings, I find in you."

The throne room was both empty and occupied by another. Without turning his head, but with just a glance from the corner of his eye, Xizor saw a dark apparition. The holo image of Lord Vader, insubstantial yet oppressive, stood at one side of the throne room.

He brought his gaze back to the Emperor. "You honor me with your praise, my lord."

One corner of Palpatine's bloodless lips twisted in a sneer. "I do not praise you, Xizor. As with all my servants, you neither surprise nor disappoint me. I expect foolishness and incompetence, and I find I am richly rewarded in those things."

The Emperor's tongue-lashing was in his usual manner. Xizor had grown used to it, though the words still rankled his proud spirit. *Someday, old man.* His thoughts were a silent and carefully guarded promise inside the chambers of his bare skull. *Your precious Force and all your servants won't be able to save you.*

In the meantime, though, the show of servility had to be maintained.

"If I fail you, my lord—" Xizor bowed his head. "Then the regret truly is mine."

The holo image of Lord Vader spoke up. "Do not be deceived by this one." Bands of visual static flickered through the black figure, as one holographically reproduced arm rose, its hand pointing toward Prince Xizor. "His speech is elegant, my lord—as always— but it is as hollow as his unfulfilled promises."

"Bold words, Lord Vader." Xizor allowed himself a flash of anger. "Especially from one who has assured our Emperor that the Rebel Alliance would be crushed long ago. The Rebels seem to have made a mockery of the assurances you made to your master."

If Darth Vader had been physically present in the throne room, those words might have been worth Xizor's life. He knew how dangerous a game he was playing; he could see the visible reaction in Vader's image, the black robes swelling like the sun-obscuring clouds of an advancing stormfront, the gaze from the dark lenses beneath the helmet flashing as sharp as lightning bolts.

"I would caution the prince—" Thunder, ominous and deep, sounded in Vader's speech. The harsh rasping of his breath was just as audible, transmitted from the bridge of the *Executor*. He had only recently taken possession of this new flagship, which had replaced the previous *Devastator*. If anything, the threat of his powers seemed enhanced by the greater arsenal surrounding him. "His ill-advised rashness might be excusable in one as young and inexperienced as himself. But my patience with him grows thin."

Xizor sensed a pressure at his throat, like an invisible hand tightening against his windpipe, cutting off the flow of blood and air to his brain. He didn't know if he was imagining it, if some weakness not yet rooted out from the core of his being had allowed a trace of unreasoning, wordless fear into his thoughts, or whether Vader's powers could reach this far. He had had previous encounters with the dark lord's undeniable strength, the ability to reach out and crush the life from those creatures Vader considered lesser to himself. To annoy him, to fail to carry out instructions or thwart his plans in any way, was to court an unpleasant death by asphyxiation.

Black spots, the first signals of anoxia, were already beginning to form and coalesce in Xizor's vision. The invisible grip seemed undeniably real now, like a fist beneath his throat, shoving his head back, lifting him onto the balls of his feet. The passage of time, measured by Xizor's own pulse, slowed to a crawl and then stopped.

The Emperor had always intervened before this

point, as though he were commanding a guard beast to heel. Perhaps this time, he would let the process reach its fatal conclusion.

A single thought emerged through the darkness welling inside Xizor's skull. *I wasn't summoned here for an audience with the Emperor . . . but an execution. My own . . .*

The darkness was torn open by a red surge of anger, from deep within Xizor. Anger, and the hunger to survive.

"Patience . . ." Prince Xizor barely managed to squeeze the word past the encircling constriction at his throat. The effort dizzied him; the surrounding throne room dissolved out of focus. "Patience is a virtue . . . the rewards of which . . ." He was close to blacking out, losing consciousness entirely. But he knew his doing so would be followed by his death. "Are for the Empire . . ."

"Well spoken, Xizor." A trace of amusement sounded in Emperor Palpatine's voice, barely audible at some place in the black-tinged haze. "Rest assured that I find others in my service even more burdensome than yourself. Your little amusements weary me, Vader; release him."

As though the knot of a primitive gallows rope had snapped, the pressure on Xizor's throat—imagined or real—was suddenly released. He barely managed to keep himself from falling to his knees, the invisible fist suspending his weight now gone. With an effort of sheer will, Prince Xizor held himself upright, drawing in a breath that filled his lungs and threw his shoulders back.

He kept his face a mask as well, to conceal the furious hatred he felt for both Vader and the Emperor. To be toyed with, whether with mind games or this mystical Force of which they professed mastery, was infuriating enough. But to be humiliated by Vader, the instigator of the biological weapons experiment that had killed so many hundreds of thousands of Falleens back on their homeworld—a slaughter that had included Xizor's own family, his parents and uncles and beloved siblings—that made the filtered air of the Imperial throne room burn like acid with each inhalation.

"As you wish, my lord." Vader spoke again, his holo image standing with arms folded across its chest. "Though I would be doing the Empire a service if I were to permanently remove Prince Xizor from its court."

"That may be so, Vader." The Emperor made a dismissive gesture with one languid hand. "But I will be the one to determine that. And I will decide when it happens. Until then, I desire that there be a cessation of this squabbling among my servants. You quarrel with each other while the Rebellion festers and grows." The expression on the wrinkled face darkened. "Must I take care of all these matters myself?"

"Only if you forbid me to fight on your behalf, my lord." Xizor spread his hands wide, palms upward. "Every atom of my being is at your command."

"How pleasant it would be, Xizor, to believe that. But I am not such a fool." The Emperor made a quick gesture, cutting off the holo image of Darth Vader before it could voice its approval. "For one of your devious nature—and high ambitions—to be totally loyal would be a miracle beyond the scope of the Force itself. Even without the Force, I would be able to see well enough into your heart. You are not so devoid of self-interest, Xizor, as you would have me believe. If you wish to see the Empire achieve its fated glory, for its dominion across the galaxy to be total, then such a desire is due to your own lust for glory and power. You tie your ambitions to the Empire, because you know that is the best way to achieve them."

Xizor looked straight back into the Emperor's eyes. "I will not deny it, my lord. But should not a faithful servant be rewarded for all that he does on his master's behalf?"

The Emperor had turned in his throne while Xizor had spoken. For a moment longer, Palpatine gazed out the high arched viewscreens that looked out past the Imperial city and beyond to the star-filled skies. Then he turned back toward Xizor and the holo image of Vader. "Oh, you'll be rewarded well enough; have no fear of that." His hands lay like dead things on the arms of the throne. "When the Rebellion is crushed and all that resist my will are annihilated, those who have served me will have the greatest reward of all: the opportunity to continue serving me and the Empire. Until you are broken by age and the rigors of that service, and I will have no further use for you. Such is the nature of my loyalty, to those who have earned it."

Once again, Xizor bowed his head. "I desire nothing more than that, my lord."

"Whether you do or not, it matters little. Nothing matters, but *my* will."

From the corner of his eye, with his head still bowed, Xizor looked over at the holo image of Darth Vader. Even at this remove, with his enemy not even physically present in the throne room, he could still sense the dark lord's disdain and suspicion. *He knows,* thought Xizor, *but he cannot prove it. Yet.* And it might not matter, even if Vader could prove it. All of Vader's accusations of treachery counted for nothing against the Emperor's own convuluted strategies, that gave the seeming appearance of trust in the Falleen prince. The actual words *Black Sun* had been spoken by Vader on other occasions—Xizor's spies at the court had informed him so—and the Emperor had dismissed them with a wave of his bony hand, as though the words were no more than scraps of rumors and lies.

But does Palpatine know, wondered Xizor, *that I know?* If the Emperor thought that Xizor was taken in by this charade, then the Emperor was the greater fool. It was just a matter of who got caught out first. The Black Sun criminal organization, controlled by Prince Xizor, had its own agenda, its own plans for expansion and dominance throughout the galaxy, as though it were an enveloping shadow of the Empire; where Palpatine's reach extended, so would Black Sun's. And the Emperor was old, visibly so; this vaunted Force, whatever its nature, could not keep him alive forever. Even before then, Black Sun might emerge from the darkness, a power in its own right, and claim the larger empire for its own, a treasure plucked from Palpatine's withered hand.

If there's one thing I've learned from the old man, thought Prince Xizor, *it's that ambition is as infinite as the universe itself.*

That was a lesson much to Xizor's own liking. He could endure a good deal of petty humiliations, at Palpatine's and Vader's hands, in order to see the day when he would put that education to use.

Patience, the control of one's anger and thirst for vengeance, was one of the greatest of all martial skills. And the most difficult to master: he had but to glance at the holo image of Lord Vader standing in the Emperor's throne room, for his own hands to clench into tight-knuckled fists.

Someday, Xizor told himself again. *Until then—watch and wait.*

"As you wish, my lord." Xizor brought his gaze up to meet that of the Emperor.

"Perhaps," spoke the holo image of Darth Vader, "the Emperor would care to determine the quality of Prince Xizor's service. It was not so very long ago that Xizor told us of his great plans to destroy the Bounty Hunters Guild, and all the benefits that would thus flow to the Empire." Vader's image looked contemptuously toward the Falleen prince. "Surely by now, those plans would have shown some results. Or were they as insubstantial as the prince's loyalty?"

"Excellent, Vader." The Emperor nodded in approval. "You anticipate my desires; such is the true sign of a valued servant." Palpatine's gaze sharpened as he peered at Xizor. "So? Your speech then, Xizor, was most . . . entertaining. By virtue of its grand conceits, I granted you my permission to carry out your scheme. I would be disappointed to hear that there has been no progress in this matter of disrupting the bounty hunters' organization. And yet . . ." The Emperor's eyes narrowed to slits, like small knife wounds in the wrinkled flesh. "I have already received contradictory reports, concerning what has come from all your plans." He turned toward the other figure in the throne room. "Is that not so, Lord Vader?"

"That is exactly the case, my lord." A note of triumph sounded in Vader's rasping voice. "I previously advised against investing any of your time and energy in these vain, pointless pursuits. The Rebellion must be our first priority; it grows in strength while Prince Xizor squanders our resources on a quest that, even if it were successful, would give us nothing."

"Control your anger, Vader. You come perilously close to questioning my wisdom when you continue to attack the merits of Xizor's scheme. I saw it as sufficiently intriguing, when he first presented it to us, that I found your protests to be founded more in spite and jealousy than in true strategic analysis."

Vader made no reply, but Xizor could detect in the holo image a stiffening of the spine inside the black robes, an indicator of the Emperor's words having struck their mark.

"Perhaps," Xizor said mildly, "the difference between Lord Vader and myself is that I have no doubt of the Empire's imminent victory over the Rebel Alliance. That is why I find it worthwhile to turn our attention to the governing of the Empire after its dominion has been established as an irrefutable fact."

He could tell that his words pleased the Emperor; a thin smile lifted one corner of Palpatine's mouth.

"You see, Vader?" The Emperor gestured with one hand toward Prince Xizor. "That is why my mastery of the Force is greater than your own. There can be no true power without certainty. It is not enough to *try* to suppress the Rebellion, we must *do* so."

Vader's holo image stood unflinching against the Emperor's tongue-lashing. "You speak of the difference, my lord, between Prince Xizor and myself. Yet there is another difference that must be considered. And that is the difference between a childish faith and wise preparation. Even the admirals of the Imperial Navy, with their trust in mere technological contrivances such as the Death Star, still know they must fight and destroy the Rebels before the Empire's victory is accomplished."

That, thought Xizor with a mixture of both disbelief and satisfaction, *was not a good move.* It had always been clear to him that Darth Vader considered himself as being above the niceties of diplomatic speech. For all his loyalty to the Emperor, he was still capable of angering his master. And Vader had surely done so now: the Emperor's face darkened with fury.

"Even a child," said Palpatine in a low, ominous voice, "should know how foolish it is to contradict one such as myself. You consider yourself wiser than that, Vader, do you not? Yet you persist in bestowing your unwanted advice upon me, even after I have warned you of the consequences."

"I do so, my lord, not to contradict, but to—"

"Silence!" The single word of command snapped through the throne room's air like a whiplash's cutting tip. "I know better than you do yourself just what your intentions are." The Emperor's hands tightened upon the arms of his throne. "Your thoughts are an open book to me, with the words written large enough for an idiot to perceive. You have let your hatred of Prince Xizor lead you into a dangerous territory, one where the life of an unruly servant such as yourself is mine to crush within my fist." The Emperor raised one hand, its clawlike fingers compressed into a rigid, white-knuckled ball. "Your usefulness to me, Vader, is not such that I can tolerate your insubordination."

As Xizor watched, his own heart filled with the gloating pleasure that accompanies an enemy's humiliation. Darth Vader's holo image stood like a black rock at the edge of a storm-lashed sea, enduring silently the waves dashing against it. But when the Emperor's wrathful words ceased, Vader's image lowered itself onto one knee, its black-helmeted head bent in submission.

"As you wish, my lord." All emotion was drained from the image's relayed voice. "Do with your servant as you will."

"All in good time." Palpatine's voice actually sounded sullen, as though he were barely satisfied with Vader's acquiescence. "Until then, you still have some measure of worth for me."

I've won, thought Xizor. *This round, at least.* He hadn't even had to do much for it to happen this way, merely let the arrogant Lord Vader dig his own grave. The Dark Lord of the Sith was so used to other sentient creatures, all of whom he considered inferior to himself, giving way before his undoubted powers that the least resistance threw him off balance. That was what had led to his saying such rash and ill-advised things to the Emperor. *His only mode is to attack,* Xizor had judged correctly. For a combatant to have no capacity for strategic retreat, to bide his time and wait, was a liability rather than a strength. As long as Emperor Palpatine was so much stronger than he was, Vader could be easily maneuvered into incurring that scathing wrath. *Which deflects it from me,* thought Xizor with pleasure. A fall from grace, however temporary it might be for Vader, was a comparable elevation for his opponents.

The only thing that Xizor had to remember, that he could never allow himself to forget, was that such a momentary advantage came at a considerable price. Whatever enmity Darth Vader had borne him before was now magnified many times over. For Xizor to have witnessed Vader's humiliation, that proud spirit crushed beneath the Emperor's boot sole, was to have had his own death warrant sealed—if Vader could bring that about. And Xizor knew now, even more than before, Vader would turn as much of his powers as possible to that task. The only thing that could divert Vader from his commitment to Xizor's destruction was the growing threat of the Rebel Alliance to the Empire. If the Rebellion should be crushed—and Xizor felt the chances were good that it would be—then in whatever aftermath followed, Xizor would have a formidable enemy indeed, facing him.

The prospect didn't alarm him.

I'll be ready, thought Xizor, glancing over at the

half-kneeling image of Vader. The thought of that final encounter—so long delayed, so long anticipated—made the blood pulse in his veins.

Emperor Palpatine's voice broke into Xizor's thoughts.

"Enough of this bickering." The Emperor pointed a bony finger at Xizor. "Do not delude yourself that your thoughts are hidden to me. You flatter yourself if you believe that I am taken in by all your maneuvering, Xizor—or if you believe that I find no merit at all in Lord Vader's criticisms of your schemes and actions. You promised much from your plan to break up the old Bounty Hunters Guild: a seemingly endless supply of the type of servants that the Empire requires, sharp and agile mercenaries, to take the place of the dull inefficiencies with which I am afflicted." Palpatine leaned forward in his throne, fixing his cold, incisive gaze on the figure standing before him. "I have had various reports come to me of the progress of your scheme against the Guild. But the outcome of that scheme appears rather . . . clouded. What say you, Prince Xizor?"

A bow of his head, then he looked back into those dead-seeming eyes. "The explanation is simple enough, my lord." Xizor spread his hands apart. "The campaign against the Bounty Hunters Guild is not yet complete. There still remains much to be done—"

"As there always will be," spoke Vader's holo image. "These plans are doomed to ignominious failure."

The Emperor shot Vader a stern warning glance, then looked back toward Xizor. "I do not recall," said Palpatine, "anything you said about the scheme proceeding in stages. When you proposed it to me, you made it sound as if it were a relatively simple matter. Merely insert the well-known bounty hunter Boba

Fett into the Guild, and it would then dissolve of its own accord."

"Your memory is accurate, my lord." Xizor made a nod of acknowledgment. "And I confess my error now: I did not anticipate the current state of affairs with the Bounty Hunters Guild."

"Which is?"

You know already, old man. Xizor was sure of it, and that the Emperor amused himself at his expense. "The Bounty Hunters Guild has not yet completely disappeared. It has broken into two rival factions, the True Guild and the Guild Reform Committee. The latter is effectively under the control of the bounty hunter Bossk, the son of the original Guild's leader Cradossk."

"I see." The Emperor's hands lay unmoving upon the throne's arms. "Reports have come to me that the elder Cradossk was in fact killed by this Bossk."

"That is indeed the case, my lord."

The Emperor displayed an unpleasant smile. "It sounds as if the bounty hunter Bossk is exactly the sort of creature you thought would be of greatest service to the Empire. Ruthless and ambitious, is he not?"

"Those are hereditary traits, my lord." The flaring shoulders of Xizor's robes lifted in a shrug. "But it requires cunning as well to be a perfect instrument of your will."

"Cunning such as yours, I suppose."

Xizor returned the smile. "I cannot deny such an evident truth."

"Just as," said the Emperor, "you cannot deny that the old Bounty Hunters Guild has not dissolved into a myriad of independent agents, from which we could pick and choose as served our purposes best.

You show yourself capable of admitting your errors; why not confess as well that your scheme has been a failure? I see no great advantage in there being two guilds where there was only one before. If anything, it merely compounds our difficulties in dealing with these creatures."

"There is no failure, my lord." Xizor allowed his reply to become heated. "Unforeseen difficulties arise; they are to be dealt with." He came close to saying that the Emperor himself had not anticipated the Rebellion, but checked himself in time. Why risk angering someone who possessed the power of life and death? "As I intend to deal with these."

"So we are to hear yet another grand scheme." The holo image of Darth Vader spoke with contempt. "Schemes on top of excuses, covering failures. There's no end to such things with you."

"Measure your own failures, Lord Vader." There was nothing to lose in firing a retort back at the dark lord. It was impossible for Vader's malice to become any greater. "I at least have the means for changing a temporary failure to lasting victory. Do you?"

Vader's holo image stood with its arms folded across its chest. Mindful of the short leash—even shorter now—that the Emperor kept him on, Vader made no reply to the taunt.

"And just what are those means, Xizor?"

He looked back toward the Emperor. "They are simple enough, my lord. The Bounty Hunters Guild is not what it was; with one blow, we have cleaved it into two opposed segments, factions filled with murderous hatred for each other. Whatever pretense to brotherhood the bounty hunters may have once maintained, that sham at least has been ripped away. Now we must complete the process of fragmentation. Each individual bounty hunter must be turned against all others, in whichever faction they currently reside. They must have no interests in common, but only enmity for each other."

"That may be the goal," said the Emperor, "but it is not the method. You have not answered my question, and I grow impatient. Tell me now just how you propose to shatter these two factions into their constituent atoms."

Unflinching, Xizor returned the Emperor's hard, cold gaze. "By the very element that motivates these creatures, that made them decide to become bounty hunters in the first place. A powerful, galaxy-spanning force in its own right." Xizor hesitated a moment, in an intentional dramatic effect. "Greed," he said. "That will do it."

The Emperor's smile grew even less pleasant than before. "There is a wisdom—even a certain justice—in turning a creature's own nature against itself. Much of my own rule depends upon exactly that tactic." Palpatine nodded slowly. "Let me hear the precise details you have envisioned, Xizor."

That was when he knew he had won another round in this game. Even before Xizor had finished relating the plan to the Emperor, he was sure that it would be approved. He would be empowered to carry out the next step in his plans.

And as long as the Emperor thought that those plans were entirely to his benefit, and to the benefit of the Empire . . . so much the better. *Soon enough,* thought Xizor, *he'll find out the truth.* But by then, it would be too late.

"And what say you, Lord Vader?" The Emperor turned his gaze toward the holo image at the other side of the throne room. "I expect that your silence does not indicate a wild enthusiasm for Prince Xizor's suggested plan."

"You know my thoughts, my lord." Vader's image stood stiff and inflexible. "I see no point in repeating my words. But if you wish to hear them, so be it. This scheme of Prince Xizor's, just like his previous failure, is a waste of time and energy. Your attention would be better placed elsewhere, on the true concerns of the Empire."

"Just as I expected," said Palpatine wearily. "You confirm my estimate of the jealousy you bear toward any other servant of mine." The Emperor raised his hand, in a gesture directed toward Xizor. "Proceed with your plans against the remnants of the Bounty Hunters Guild. But bear in mind, Xizor: failure is no longer an option for you. There is only success—or death."

Xizor bowed his head. "That is as I prefer it, my lord."

The hem of his heavy robes swirled against his boots as he turned from the gaunt, ancient figure on the throne. He strode toward the high doors that led out of the room in which the galaxy's ruler sat.

All the way, and even to the vaulted corridors beyond, he was aware of Vader's gaze at his back, like the sharp point of a vibroblade, waiting for the chance of a fatal thrust.

9

"You make it sound as if you had been there." In the narrow space aboard the *Hound's Tooth,* Neelah folded her arms across her breast. She gazed skeptically at the other figure with her. "How would you know so much about what went on in Emperor Palpatine's throne room?"

"There's ways," said Dengar. He sat on the floor's metal grate, his back against the bulkhead. "How do you know I *wasn't* there with the Emperor, and Darth Vader and Prince Xizor?"

"They wouldn't have let you in." Neelah leaned against the structural beam behind her. "I know that much, at least." There had been plenty of other things she hadn't known, which Dengar had had to explain to her; the story he had been relating to her, about all the bad blood in the past between the Trandoshan bounty hunter Bossk and Boba Fett, wouldn't have made sense otherwise. Who Emperor Palpatine was, and even Darth Vader, the entity known as the Dark Lord of the Sith—those things she'd had a rough idea of before Dengar had started with the story. Neelah had kept her ears open while she had been one of the dancing girls in Jabba the Hutt's palace; in a place like that, with its unrelenting atmosphere of ennui and malice, gossip about the galaxy's politics and dominant personalities had been just as endless. Most of the sentient creatures in the palace, from the lowliest scullery hands to the top-level mercenaries, had been constantly on the lookout for some way to scrabble up the chains of credits and power that seemed to link the stars together like an invisible web. Loyalty to any one employer was strictly a mercantile commodity, to be bought and sold like all the other temporary services.

So Topic A of conversation, in all the barracks and corridors and slop pits, had always been about who was up and who was down, who had managed to wangle a way closer to the center of the Imperial court, who had gone over to the Rebel Alliance, who was for sale to the highest bidder—and who was dead, all the scheming and maneuvering having reached an end with a blaster bolt to the head. Disloyalty might be more profitable in this universe, but it also had its price.

"All right," said Dengar. "I wasn't there. But other creatures were; the Imperial court is full of eavesdroppers and snoops. Just like Jabba's palace." Neelah had told him about how much she had learned in that viewless fortress back on Tatooine. "If you're not listening, you're not surviving—that's how those places are set up. It's not a matter of spies, so much— though there are always plenty of those, some of 'em talking to the Rebels, some reporting to Black Sun— as it is just sentient creature nature. And I know how to keep my ear to the ground as well, you know." Dengar pointed with his thumb toward the ship's cockpit deck above them. "I may not be quite the bounty hunter that Boba Fett is, but I got at least a few of the necessary skills. You can't get anywhere in this business without being able to work your info sources. I got some lines into the Imperial court *and* Black Sun—some of them official, the stuff they *want* you to know, and some of them out the back door."

Neelah raised an eyebrow. "And you trust them?"

"No more than I have to." Dengar gave a shrug. "Some information I paid for—hey, it's a business expense—and that's usually got at least a little reliability factor to it. If you get killed because you trusted something they told you, you're not going to be coming back to buy any more from them. And some things you can get confirmed from more than one source—even when it's something to do with somebody dead, like Prince Xizor. The problem with running a criminal organization is that you've always got a lot of less-than-honorable creatures working for you, and knowing all about your business dealings. So when you're gone, they'll always talk for a credit or two." A half smile showed on Dengar's face. "Why do you think creatures like me spend so much time in dumps like that cantina back in Mos Eisley? It ain't the food, and it *sure* isn't the gnardly music they got going there. No, what creatures go to a place like that to hear is information, pure and simple. Keep your ears open and you can find out all sorts of things."

"If you say so." Neelah was less than impressed. As far as she could tell, Dengar was entirely too trusting. *Probably just as well,* she thought, *that he's getting out of the business.* Still, she had the odd conviction that the story—or at least as much of it as he'd told her so far—was true. A sudden, disturbing notion came to her: *Maybe I already knew some of these things.* From before, from that life that had been stolen from her, that had been hers before her memory had been wiped clean and she had been enslaved in Jabba the Hutt's palace. If that was true, it meant that she had been something quite different from a simple dancing girl and potential rancor-fodder.

But I knew that, too—deep inside her spirit, in some place where an unquenchable spark of fire had remained glowing in the surrounding darkness, she had been absolutely sure that her true identity was something higher and greater than the lies in which she had been trapped. Even before she had discerned that Boba Fett had been watching out for her in the palace, making sure that nothing too horrible—or at least fatal—happened to her. Some strange twisting fate had brought her to that place, and some other destiny lay beyond it—if she could find it and hold it tight to herself. Everything that had been taken from her, the very self that had been erased, like a name written on a scrap of flimsiplast and set on fire, reduced to crumbling ash; she would either find it or die in the attempt. In some ways, it didn't matter which; that was what left her unafraid of the helmeted figure up in the *Hound's Tooth*'s cockpit. The worst Boba Fett could do was kill her; the other death, in which her identity had been destroyed, had already happened to her, long ago.

"You can believe it or not," said Dengar. "Doesn't matter to me. But you could get the same story from plenty of other creatures in this galaxy; now that all that stuff is over, the whole war among the bounty hunters, most of it's not exactly a secret." With an upward tilt of his head, Dengar again indicated the cockpit above them. "Boba Fett made sure of that."

"He helped spread these stories—is that what you mean? Why would he do that?"

"Anything that adds to his reputation, he figures is a good idea. He won big out of that whole bounty hunters war, and against some pretty fierce opponents. Hey"—Dengar laid a hand on his own chest— "*I'm* pretty impressed. It's the kind of thing that when a lot of other creatures, bounty hunters or not, meet up with Boba Fett, they just roll over and play dead from the start. No sense in actually winding up dead. So it saves him a lot of time and effort, being preceded by that kind of well-known history."

Neelah supposed that made sense. Though it raised some other questions as well. If Boba Fett saw some advantage to grooming his reputation, using the myths and legends about him as a weapon against other creatures, then where did the process stop? A convenient lie or exaggeration would serve his purposes just as well as the truth. And once that possibility was admitted, then nothing about him could be trusted. Nothing that he couldn't back up with his own actions. *There's the problem,* admitted Neelah. *You guess wrong, and it would cost you your life.*

"So then what happened?" Neelah sat back down at the base of the ship's structural beam, across the small space from Dengar. "Come on—the story doesn't end there." All the while that the *Hound's Tooth* had been traveling through space, toward its unrevealed destination, she had been listening to him. She had lost track of time, of how many Standard hours had gone by. "What went on next with Boba Fett and all the other bounty hunters?"

"I don't know if I should bother telling you." Dengar had rooted around in the *Hound*'s storage area and had found an empty cargo duffel. He wadded it up into a makeshift pillow. "Not if you're going to be so skeptical about everything. What's the point?"

Spare me, thought Neelah. She rolled her eyes upward in exasperation. Someday, if he lived that long, this supposedly sentient creature would be on the hands of some other female, his bride-to-be Manaroo. Neelah didn't envy her.

"All right." She barely managed to control her anger. "You have my apologies." Neelah would have liked to have given him more than that, and hard enough to hurt. "I don't doubt a single thing you tell me." *For the time being,* she promised herself. But before the *Hound's Tooth* reached wherever Boba Fett was taking them, she needed to have more hard information. She wasn't sure she'd find out what she needed from this complicated history of the war among the bounty hunters, but right now it was her only lead. "So why don't you go ahead and tell me the rest of what happened?"

"Maybe later." Dengar stretched out on the floor, tucking the wadded-up duffel behind his head. "I'm exhausted." His eyes closed. "Besides—I don't feel like wearing my throat out, telling old stories to unappreciative brats. Especially sarcastic ones."

The urge to violence nearly overwhelmed her. Her eyes narrowed as she gazed at Dengar, either already asleep or pretending to be. A swift kick to the head would either wake him up or put him out for good. *It's tempting,* thought Neelah.

With the last vestige of self-control, she decided on another course of action. With a final withering glance at the recumbent figure of Dengar, Neelah turned and started up the ladder to the ship's cockpit.

He heard someone coming up, from the ship's main hold below. There was no need for Boba Fett to turn away from the navigation controls of the *Hound's Tooth*; the mere sound of the steps upon the ladder's treads, lighter than they would have been for the other bounty hunter Dengar, indicated which of the ship's passengers it was.

"So where are we?" Just as he had figured: the female Neelah's voice spoke from behind him. "Still out in the middle of nowhere? Or are we getting close to this mysterious destination we're supposed to be heading toward?"

There was an obvious level of irritation in her voice. Boba Fett turned his visored gaze away from the cockpit's viewport and glanced over his shoulder at her. "It's a good thing," he said with deliberate mildness, "that you're not planning on going into the bounty hunter trade anytime soon. For us, patience isn't just a virtue—it's a necessity. If you rush your shot, you can wind up in a galaxy of trouble."

"I'll try to remember that." Neelah stood in the cockpit's hatchway; a simmering anger, barely controlled, showed in her dark eyes. "I'll tuck it away with all the other free advice everyone's been giving me. Since that seems to be *all* that I get around here." Her expression darkened. "Or anywhere else, for that matter."

The female's bad mood reminded Boba Fett that there were definite advantages to transporting hard merchandise, the kind of sentient creatures that bounties had been posted on. *Those,* thought Fett, *you can always throw into a holding cage.* There was never any question of who was in charge, not just in the big things but right down to the smallest details. The situation was a little more confused with Neelah; at some point, he was likely to need her cooperation. Even when she had been a dancing girl in Jabba the Hutt's palace, she had still retained some of the haughty personality traits that had been part of her former highborn social position. Those ran so deep that not even the most thorough memory wipe could root them out. So now, if she were to develop a grudge against him, getting her back on his side might take some considerable doing. *Rules out the cage,* decided Fett.

There were other considerations as well that he had to take into account. Neelah was already starting to piece together the tantalizing, infuriating fragments of memory that had been left to her. Dengar had told him all that she had talked about, back in the cavern hiding place on Tatooine; things that Dengar himself did not know the significance of—but Fett did.

Nil Posondum, thought Boba Fett. She had remembered that name. Fett wasn't surprised. That former accountant, who had then become hard merchandise in *Slave I*'s holding cage, was the key to all that had happened to Neelah. If she were to connect that memory fragment with the enigmatic message that Posondum had scratched into the metal floor of the holding cage, a great many mysteries would be resolved for her.

Boba Fett wasn't ready for that to happen; not yet, at least. The scratched message no longer existed, except as an image that had been inside *Slave I*'s onboard databanks, that had now been transferred here on the *Hound's Tooth.* The image, and the information in the scratched message, was still safely locked up. And that was how it was going to remain.

In the meantime, though, he had one seriously annoyed female standing in front of him.

"It's too bad," said Boba Fett, "that you've had

your fill of good advice. Because I was just about to give you some more."

"Yeah?" Leaning against the side of the hatchway, Neelah raised a skeptical eyebrow. "What is it?"

"Simple. Take it easy. We've got a long way to go yet, and there's a lot that can happen at the other end. So you should relax while you can."

"Oh." Neelah gave a slow nod, as though thinking it over. "Really? That's what you do? 'Relax'?" The next sound she made was a short, scornful laugh. "The only time I ever saw you relax was when you were unconscious, right after you got vomited up by that Sarlacc beast. If that's what you mean by relaxing, it doesn't seem like such a good idea."

If he had been capable of amusement, the female's comment might have done the job. "That wasn't relaxing," said Boba Fett. "That was dying." And it would have ended with his death, lying there half-digested on the hot sands of Tatooine's Dune Sea, if it hadn't been for both her and Dengar. Owing anything, let alone one's life, to another creature was a new experience for him. How to pay off debts such as those was a problem he was still thinking about. Without that consideration, he would undoubtedly have been harsher toward the other passengers aboard the *Hound's Tooth*.

"Maybe," mused Neelah, "I just don't know what a creature like you considers 'relaxing.' I guess killing other creatures is something that suits you."

"Not as much as getting paid for it."

Neelah fell silent for a few moments. Turning away from her and back toward the cockpit's control panel, Boba Fett made a few more navigational calculations. As he had anticipated, Bossk's former ship was neither as technologically advanced nor as well maintained as his own ship *Slave I*. That sloppiness had taken him a while to get used to, and it still irritated him. He found it little wonder that Bossk had never been able to reach the top of the bounty hunter trade; the Trandoshan had tried to substitute sheer ruthlessness and violence for careful planning and investment in equipment. *That never works,* Boba Fett told himself. Ruthlessness and violence were necessary, all right; they just weren't enough.

The female's voice broke into his thoughts. "Maybe I'd be able to relax, if I could break open your head."

Boba Fett didn't look around at her. "What's that supposed to mean?"

"You heard me. I wish I could crack that helmet of yours as though it were an egg." Neelah's words turned vehement. "I'm sorry I didn't take my chance when you were lying there on your deathbed. Then I could have cracked open your skull as well, and I could've found out what I need to know. About myself."

"That may not be what you want at all. Especially when you do find out." Fett lifted his shoulders in a minimal shrug. "It might not be to your liking."

"Those chances," said Neelah, "I'd rather take. Instead of not finding out."

"Don't worry about it. You'll find out soon enough."

Neelah's voice turned ominously quiet. "I'd rather not wait."

She managed to take him by surprise. Boba Fett had reached out across the controls, to access the navicomputer display positioned awkwardly high on the cockpit panel. He felt a slight, almost imperceptible tug at the equipment belt of his Mandalorian battle armor. That alone was enough of a signal to trigger his turning sharply about in the pilot's chair to face Neelah.

But the female had already darted back to the cockpit's hatchway. Neelah raised the blaster pistol that she had managed to lift from its holster at Boba Fett's waist. Holding the weapon in both hands, she aimed it directly at the center of Fett's dark-visored helmet.

"I wasn't joking," said Neelah. The thin smile at the corner of her mouth was a grim indicator of her intent. "When I said I'd like to crack your head open. I wonder . . . just how many bolts from this thing do you think it'll take?"

Boba Fett leaned back in the pilot's chair. "Congratulations," he said. He had stowed most of his weaponry for safekeeping, to avoid the various pieces of his portable arsenal from interfering with his activities in the cockpit. The small blaster pistol had been the only weapon he had kept with him. He gestured toward it, as it stayed unwavering in Neelah's grasp. "Not many creatures have pulled off a trick like that. Getting the drop on me is a pretty rare occurrence."

A sneer twisted the corner of Neelah's mouth. "It was easy."

He had to admit that she had gotten the weapon away from him with a surprising show of deftness. Or perhaps not so surprising; with what he knew of her background, her identity before she had wound up as a memory-wiped dancing girl in Jabba the Hutt's palace, skills like this were more common than not. She was far more than a mere child of aristocracy; if he failed to remember that, it was at his own peril.

"Perhaps so," said Boba Fett. "That doesn't mean it was a good idea. You may have some pretty fast moves, but trust me—they're nothing compared to mine. Before you could press the firing stud on that piece, I'd be out of this chair, and my forearm would be against your throat. And after that, things would get even more unpleasant for you."

"I'm willing to risk it." Neelah shrugged. "What have I got to lose? You're not telling me what I want to know. What I *need* to know. At least this way, if I get off one good shot, I'll have the satisfaction of getting a good reason for you clamming up on me. Think of it this way: being dead is the perfect excuse."

Boba Fett had already calculated the precise distance between himself and the female, the exact angle, speed, and direction of the moves necessary to get the weapon away from her. He could do it without even getting winged by the one blaster bolt she would be able to fire in that microsecond interval. *Better,* he told himself, *if I don't have to do that.* For one simple reason: a wild shot inside the confines of the ship's cockpit could have some serious consequences. Even now, the *Hound's Tooth* wasn't in the operational shape he would have preferred; its previous owner's sloppiness had seen to that. He would be able to repair any structural damage the bolt would cause—the weapon didn't have enough power to pierce the hull—but if it took out any of the control panel, tracing and patching the unfamiliar circuits would take time. And time was a commodity that was in short supply at the moment. There was business to take care of, a long way from here.

"I've been close enough to dead," said Boba Fett, "that I'm not eager to repeat the experience."

Neelah raised the blaster a little higher, sighting

over its barrel at her target. "Then you better start talking."

"No—" Boba Fett gave a single shake of his head. "I don't think so."

"What?" The female's brow creased. "What do you mean?"

"It's simple." Boba Fett gestured toward her. "You've got as much to lose as I have. Kill me, and you'll never find out what you want to know."

Tilting her head to one side, she peered closer at him. "Maybe with you out of the way, I'll be able to find out the truth from someone else."

"Maybe." Boba Fett gave another shrug. "But if you guess wrong about that—if I'm the only one that knows the score about who you really are—then you'll have knocked off the only person with the answers. Sure that's a risk you want to take?"

For a few seconds more, Neelah seemed to be considering her options. Then she lowered the blaster. "I suppose not." Her angry expression hadn't faded. "Looks like you talked your way out of this one."

"You'll thank me for it later." He held out his hand. "I'll take the piece back, if you don't mind."

Neelah shook her head. "I've still got a use for it."

He watched her as she turned in the hatchway. With the weapon at her side, she started back down the ladder to the ship's main hold.

At least, thought Fett, *she knows what she wants.* Getting it was the only problem.

He swung the pilot's chair back toward the controls. He had his own concerns to take care of.

A boot in his ribs woke Dengar up. He blinked, then came swiftly to full, startled consciousness as he

166 / STAR WARS

found himself looking into the business end of a
blaster pistol.

"Time to start talking," said Neelah. She had the
weapon aimed straight at his forehead. "I want to
hear the rest of the story."

10

"You gotta admit," said Bossk, "it's a nice place for a meeting."

He enjoyed his own grim humor. Keeping the claws of one hand resting on the grip of his holstered blaster, Bossk watched as Boba Fett looked around the moldering crevices and dry cliff faces of the ancient sea trench. The oceans of Gholondreine-β had been sucked down to the last molecule of saline liquid, then transported by a fleet of massive Imperial freighters to an orbital catalysis plant near Coruscant. Economy hadn't been the motivating factor—it was more expensive to ship that amount of water than to synthesize it—but punishment had been. The coastal and inland democracies on the planet's land masses had been irritatingly slow, in the eyes of Emperor Palpatine, to divest themselves of the last vestiges of allegiance to the old Republic. Now, beneath the flat glare of cloud-purged skies, dust wound through the cracked and empty streets of the deserted cities. Neighboring worlds in this sector had received a valuable object lesson in how to respond to the Emperor's commands.

The shell of some long-dead marine animal

crunched beneath Boba Fett's boot sole. His ship, *Slave I*, stood several meters away, the rounded dome of its cockpit transparisteel glinting in the angle of light that managed to penetrate the sea trench. The cleft in the planet's desiccated surface was deep enough that in less than a Standard Time Unit, it would be cast into near-total darkness. That was all right with Bossk; the business that he had to transact with his rival Boba Fett wouldn't take long.

"It's all right." Boba Fett had completed his visual survey of the site, in tandem with the various data readouts on one forearm of his Mandalorian battle armor. The indicator lights had gradually shifted from red to yellow, then finally to green as *Slave I*'s multi-sensor threat-alert systems had finished scanning the area for hidden traps and ambush devices. Bossk had left his own ship in a lowered standby condition at the other end of the trench, so its onboard weaponry wouldn't trigger the other bounty hunter's suspicions. "Though it's not quite as private as you might think," said Fett. One gloved hand pointed toward the surrounding cliffs, their crumbling faces towering above the humanoid figures below. "I'm picking up signs of quite a few organic life-forms up there."

Bossk emitted a short, harsh laugh. "I don't think we have to worry about them." He slung his blaster rifle from behind his back; bracing the weapon against his hip, he fired a maximum-power bolt into the cliff directly above where he and Boba Fett stood. The bolt shattered the dry stone, sending a rain of powdery white dust and shards down to the trench floor. "Check it out," said Bossk. Using the toe of his own boot, he poked through the rubble. A hissing noise came from the needle-fanged mouth of a centipedelike creature, writhing and uncoiling to nearly a meter in length; its yellow eyes blazed with a ferocious malice as it whipped itself around Bossk's ankle. Before it could sink the points of its fangs into his shin, he had clubbed it off himself with the butt of the blaster rifle. Another blow snapped the creature in two; the separate halves spattered a greenish-black ichor across the trench floor as they spun about in knotting contortions. "Pleasant little things, huh? They're not even good to eat. Taste like recycled flange oil."

No reply came from Boba Fett. He had turned the gaze of his dark-visored helmet up toward the cliff face. What had been still and seemingly lifeless before now shimmered in the sunlight's flat glare with intertwining motion, like maggots in rotting flesh. The bolt from the blaster rifle had roused nests full of the many-legged creatures, exuding from holes chewed into the soft, crumbling stone. The sonic impact had been enough to startle the creatures on the other side of the trench as well; for a moment, the walls on either side of Bossk and Boba Fett crawled with coiling insectoid forms and hungry yellow eyes.

"Standard operating procedure for the Empire." Boba Fett displayed no signs of unease as the small shadows of the creatures wavered in the glare reflected from his helmet's visor. "Especially when the Emperor's in his punitive mode. These things aren't native to this planet; they're a laboratory hybrid from an Ithorian root-source, genetically enhanced for a zero-moisture environment."

The dead creature had left a black smear on Bossk's boot. He bent down and wiped it off with his thumb-claw. "The Empire seeded them here?" He straightened, looking up at the churning stone above him. "What good are they?"

"They're not any 'good' at all," said Boba Fett. "They exude bio-toxins with a molecular breakdown rate that can be measured in centuries. The levels eventually get high enough to kill them off as well. But by then the entire surface crust of this planet will be riddled with their poison-filled bore holes. There're some refugee colonies of Gholondreine-β natives on the surrounding system worlds, but they won't be coming back to their homeworld for a long time. Palpatine's seen to that."

Bossk felt slightly ill; he figured it was from the effects of having taken an exploratory bite of one of the centipede creatures. *That'll teach me,* he thought glumly. The thought of anyone deliberately concocting an unpalatable life-form irritated him; in Trandoshan philosophy, eating other creatures, including one's own species, was the whole point of existence, at least one worth living. Cold vindictiveness, such as the kind in which the Emperor indulged himself, didn't sit well with Bossk, either. Even reptiles had more of a capacity for hot-blooded, noble, and annihilating anger.

"You still want to talk business?" Boba Fett sounded amused by Bossk's apparent nausea. "You look like you're about ready to lose your lunch."

"Don't worry about me," snarled Bossk. "I sent for you to come here for a reason. We got a chance to make some major credits. Big-time stuff."

He hadn't seen Boba Fett in the flesh since they had both been back at the old Bounty Hunters Guild headquarters. The Guild had just started its process of falling apart, right after Bossk had killed his own father, Cradossk. He had been too busy since then, keeping his own faction of younger bounty hunters, the Guild Reform Committee, from splintering any further, to have paid much attention to Boba Fett's comings and goings. Even so, his suspicions had been aroused when Fett had vanished from the old Guild's headquarters, just as if he had finished the job he had been sent there to do. Bossk had heard a lot of rumors since then. The whispered accounts had it that Boba Fett had actually been responsible—intentionally so—for breaking up the Bounty Hunters Guild. Bossk couldn't quite figure out why Boba Fett would have wanted to do that. *But if he had,* Bossk decided, *then he did me a favor.* His father, Cradossk, would still be alive and running the show otherwise, and he'd still be waiting for his chance.

"What 'we' are you talking about?" Boba Fett folded his arms across his chest. "I've already worked with you once. That's more than I'm in the habit of doing."

Boba Fett's lone-wolf reputation was well deserved; it was the main reason that Bossk had been so amazed and distrustful when Fett had shown up at the Bounty Hunters Guild headquarters and had applied for admission to the organization. But Boba Fett had gone in with Bossk and a couple of the other Guild members—Zuckuss and the droid IG-88—on a team operation. Fett had even brought in one more creature on the operation, the walking animate laser cannon called D'harhan. That had been some genuinely hard merchandise, out on the Shell Hutt world of Circumtore; most of the team had been lucky to get out alive.

As it was, for D'harhan it had been the end of the line. Which proved that teaming up with Boba Fett was not necessarily a good idea; Bossk had vowed to himself to never even consider it again. There were some situations that Boba Fett was willing to walk into, only because that barve was confident that he'd walk back out of them eventually. And if that meant the death of an associate from long ago, like D'harhan, then for Boba Fett that was a price he was more than willing to pay.

Time—and greed—had eroded Bossk's resolution, though. *Just too many credits to pass up,* he'd told himself. He'd learned his lesson about going in with Boba Fett on an operation like this: *Watch your back.* That would be easier, Bossk had figured, with just the two of them, instead of a whole team.

"Come on," said Bossk. "Why don't we try to talk on a friendly basis?" The scaly muzzles of Trandoshan faces weren't designed for any kind of smiles, let alone ingratiating ones. In expressing positive emotions, Bossk was as handicapped as if he'd been wearing Boba Fett's dark-visored helmet. "Things worked out pretty well the last time."

"You didn't think so then." Fett's voice was flat and emotionless. "The way you carried on during that whole Circumtore job, I would have thought you had the last of any team operations."

"I changed my mind." Trying to talk another creature into something was way out of Bossk's line; he preferred threats and/or violence. But the chances of either one of those working with Boba Fett were well below zero. "Besides—some jobs are just too big for one bounty hunter."

"Speak for yourself."

He had a good idea that Boba Fett knew what he was referring to. The word about this particular piece of hard merchandise had gone through the bounty hunter grapevine at close to hyperspace velocities.

"All right," said Bossk. He decided to drop any pretense of friendliness. That approach was obviously not working. *Should've known,* he thought grimly. *This guy has always been durasteel-plated.* "Let's just approach it as a business deal. I got a good idea that you and me can pull this one off—*if* we work it together. Or we can go solo, and both wind up dead."

"As I said before—" Boba Fett didn't even bother giving a shrug. "Speak for yourself."

Bossk could feel his own eyes narrowing into slits as his spine tensed with anger. The impulse to launch himself at the other bounty hunter, with his clawed hands going for Boba Fett's throat, was almost overwhelming. The only thing that stopped him was the certainty that while he was still in the air between them, he would already have a hole burnt by Fett's blaster rifle through his chest and out his back. He'd land at Fett's boots as a corpse.

"That does it." *Why did I even bother?* thought Bossk. This whole meeting was a waste of time. Boba Fett followed no creature's rules but his own. "You go your way and I'll go mine. We'll see who gets killed first."

He turned on his heel and started back toward the waiting *Hound's Tooth.* Shadow had started to fill the dry marine trench, as Gholondreine-β's pallid sun shifted from its overhead zenith. On the trench's darkened wall, the yellow eyes of the centipedelike creatures glinted from their bore holes.

"Wait a minute." Boba Fett's voice called after him.

Bossk glanced over his shoulder, glaring at the other bounty hunter. "What?"

"I didn't say I wouldn't go in with you on this one." The razor-edged shade cut diagonally across Boba Fett. He stood unmoving among the dead and hollowed-out shells of the vanished ocean's inhabitants. "I was just giving you the facts about the arrangement."

A cold wind had started to roll down the length of the trench, cutting through the scales of Bossk's flesh and into the bones beneath.

The other bounty hunter's words evoked a slow

nod from Bossk. "We better settle the rest of it, then."
He nodded toward the *Hound's Tooth*. "Might as
well talk about it aboard my ship."

Boba Fett shook his head. "That's not a good
idea."

"What's the matter?" The refusal of his invitation
offended Bossk. "I'm not trying to set a trap for you. I
just want to talk business."

"Oh, I trust you all right." Boba Fett had already
started walking back toward his own ship. "Just not
enough. Besides"—he stopped and turned the visored
gaze of his helmet over his shoulder—"I've got something to show you. That you'll find interesting."

Whatever, thought Bossk. He followed after Boba
Fett. Dealing with him was a continual, unneeded
education in hostility.

The interior of *Slave I* was exactly as Bossk remembered it from the team operation on Circumtore.
He glanced around the bulkheads and holding cages
with visceral distaste; Boba Fett kept his ship in a state
of maintenance that Bossk personally found offensive.
It was like paying a visit to the surgical ward of an Imperial Navy medical crew, with every surface stripped
to bare metal and sterilized. As far as Bossk was concerned, a bounty hunter's ship should be an extension
of his personality, with every aspect of his spirit having seeped into the structure, right down to the engine
ports and the cockpit controls. He was proud that
walking around inside the *Hound's Tooth* was like
walking inside the bone limits of his own skull.

Then again, thought Bossk with a sneer, *maybe
this* is *Boba Fett's personality.* All business—credits
and merchandise—and no passion, no actual enjoy-
ment of the violence and terror that came with the
bounty hunter trade. *What a waste . . .*

"Have a seat." Boba Fett pointed to a bench near one of the holding cages. He sat down on one at the opposite side of the space. "So you want to go after this renegade stormtrooper. Right?"

At least with an all-business type like Boba Fett, there was no wasting time. "That's right," said Bossk. "It's the job of a lifetime."

That was an understatement. When the bounty had been posted, in an official wide-band relay from the Emperor's palace on Coruscant, the amount of credits offered had been thought to be some kind of transmission error, too many zeroes added on to whatever the real sum was. Bossk remembered thinking, *I could buy a small, unindustrialized planet for that many credits—if the Empire was putting any up for sale.* Both of the factions from the old Bounty Hunters Guild, the Reform Committee and those senile creatures that called themselves the True Guild, had contacted the Emperor's communications center and had asked for a clarification as to the actual amount of the bounty being offered.

And they had been told that there had been no transmission error. The amount given in the original message was for real.

The effect on bounty hunters throughout the galaxy, in every seedy spaceport dive and in the headquarters of the two Guild factions, had been electrifying. Greed worked miracles when it came to getting sentient creatures' attention. For Bossk, it had been like laying his bared claws straight upon an unshielded power generator, one big enough to drive an Imperial battleship through hyperspace; every scale on his body had seemed charged.

This would settle everything—that was the dominant thought that had sprung up inside Bossk's head.

To capture the renegade Imperial stormtrooper for which Emperor Palpatine had posted such a colossal bounty would determine once and for all, in Bossk's eyes and those of every other sentient creature in the galaxy, just who was the number-one bounty hunter. The Emperor wasn't putting up that kind of credits because it was going to be an easy job. This particular stormtrooper wasn't one of the trigger-happy rank-and-file, good for little more than simple terrorism and carrying out the orders of his commanders. Trhin Voss'on't *was* one of the commanders, right at the top level of the Imperial stormtrooper hierarchy, a strike-force leader in one of the elite Strategic Insertion battalions—or he had been right up until he had dumped the personnel of an Imperial Star Destroyer at blaster point, commandeering the vessel with a hand-picked skeleton crew of accomplices.

Initial speculation about what the motives of Voss'on't might have been centered around the possibility of his having defected to the Rebel Alliance, taking the Destroyer and its complement of weapons, code databases, and crypto-secured Imperial technology as an addition to the Alliance's growing arsenal. That theory had been largely abandoned when the destroyer had turned up drifting in an uninhabited navigational sector between star systems, with the corpses of Voss'on't's accomplices aboard. They had been efficiently executed in standard Imperial stormtrooper disciplinary fashion, a single laser hole at the back of each one's skull. The Destroyer had been stripped of whatever pieces were most easily and profitably salvaged; thruster engine parts with the appropriate molecular-level code numbers started turning up almost immediately in various black-market salvage operations, having filtered through an untraceable chain of scavengers and intersystem scrap dealers. Whatever credits had been paid out had enabled Voss'on't to pull off a complete disappearing act.

"What *I* think"—Bossk leaned forward from where he sat in *Slave I*'s main hold—"is that this Voss'on't had been planning this move for a long time. And then when he had everything lined up just right, he jumped on it."

"That's obvious," replied Boba Fett. "Nobody gets away with an entire Imperial Destroyer without making preparations."

"You gotta wonder, though, about why he did it." Bossk scratched his muzzle with one of his claws. "Whatever credits he made from scrapping the ship, he's probably had to pour right into making his escape. There's a lotta bribes to be paid out, and a lot of creatures you gotta arrange to get killed, before you can just vanish like that. And Voss'on't had to get rid of the Destroyer at a rate of ten decicredits to the credit, actual value—it's not like he's making a profit on the whole deal and setting himself up in style for the rest of his life."

Boba Fett gave a dismissive shrug. "What does it matter why he did it? Maybe he got tired of being under Palpatine's thumb. A lot of other creatures in this galaxy feel the same way. There wouldn't be a Rebellion going on, otherwise. The only thing that matters is that he did it—and that the Emperor will pay to get him back."

"Yeah, but you gotta get inside this trooper's head if you're going to have any chance of tracking him down." Bossk put the full force of his intellectual powers on the problem. He could feel his scale-covered brow corrugating with the effort. "I mean, his motive has got to be an important factor."

"For you, maybe." Fett remained unimpressed. "But not for me. The only thing that's important with hard merchandise is the price that's paid. Everything else, all the other factors—those always remain the same. The whole point is to track the merchandise down, then turn it over and collect the bounty. You start worrying about what the merchandise is thinking, then you're just handicapping yourself." The dark gaze of the other bounty hunter, the helmet visor that was such an unmistakable part of the Mandalorian armor, fell unwavering on Bossk. "That's why you're at a certain level in the bounty hunter trade . . . and I'm at a different level."

Given Bossk's hair-trigger temper, it seemed odd even to him that Boba Fett's slighting remark didn't evoke an angry reaction. *Maybe,* he mused, *I can learn something from this hunter.* Maybe Fett was right; maybe he did think too much. All that ratiocination got in the way of being an effective hunter. *That's my problem,* thought Bossk. *I'm too much of an intellectual.*

"So—do we have a deal going?" Bossk leaned back against the bulkhead behind the seat. "You wouldn't be talking to me, otherwise. Right?" He felt proud of himself for having figured out that much. "You and me, we're forming a team, a partnership, to go after this renegade stormtrooper. What's his name . . . Trhin Voss'on't. That's the deal?" Bossk looked hopefully toward the other bounty hunter.

Boba Fett gave a single nod. "Strictly a onetime operation. Don't anticipate anything permanent. I've had enough of hooking up with other creatures. That's why it didn't break my heart when the old Bounty Hunters Guild fell apart."

That was another whole issue; Bossk figured it would only blow the working relationship if he brought it up now. Besides—even if Boba Fett had deliberately set out to break up the Guild, did it matter what his reasons might have been? No more than what Voss'on't's reasons for bailing out of the Imperial stormtroopers were. *I've already learned something,* thought Bossk. This minimalist attitude he'd picked up from Boba Fett simplified things enormously, cutting them down to the essentials like a vibroblade through unprotected flesh.

"Wait a minute." A suspicion had formed inside Bossk's brain. "You don't like going in with other bounty hunters—you just said so." He peered closer at Boba Fett. "So why team up with me now? Are you that afraid of this Voss'on't barve?"

"Not at all," said Boba Fett. "Fear is an emotion that I have a certain appreciation of; I can see it in other creatures. And it's a useful thing to use against them; it muddies their reasoning processes, so they fall prey to panic and random, chaotic behavior patterns. Then you can drive them before you like herd beasts." Fett's voice had lowered in tone, as though he were reading off the tomb inscriptions of his prey. He nodded slowly, then resumed speaking. "But other than that, I have no *personal* awareness of such a thing; it does not exist inside me."

"You didn't answer the question." Bossk wasn't going to let himself be diverted by some elaborate speech. "Why are you agreeing to team up with me?"

"The answer is simple." Fett pointed a single gloved finger toward him. "You're useful to me right now. This job is at a whole new level; nothing like it has ever come up before. This is hard merchandise that can do much more than just run and hide; it can protect itself. Voss'on't has all the military skills that come with his having been a member of a Strategic Insertion team. He's got the resources—the training, the experience, the weapons—to put up a good fight. He's not some scared little bookkeeper cowering in a hole on some backwater world."

"So you *need* me." Bossk marveled at the concept— and that the notorious Boba Fett, the most feared bounty hunter in the galaxy, would admit such a thing. "Huh."

"I didn't say that; I said you're *useful* to me." Boba Fett drew his hand back, then folded his arms across the chest of his battle armor. "I could bring in this Voss'on't by myself; that's not a problem. I might even enjoy it; I don't often get such a challenge presented to me. But it would be easier with a partner. A matter of strategy: wherever Voss'on't is hiding out, he's going to be expecting bounty hunters to be coming after him. He's undoubtedly aware of the price that Palpatine has set on his head. And he'll be expecting that the bounty hunters will form partnerships and teams for this operation." Boba Fett's voice turned quiet again. "He'll be expecting that from all the bounty hunters—except one. And that's me."

"So you figure this is the only way to take Voss'on't by surprise?"

"No—" Boba Fett shook his head. "There would be other ways. But none that will get him to lower his guard in the same way. He's got to be made to think that he's the one that is running the game, that he's calling the shots. That's his weak point: he's used to being in command. And authority in the Imperial stormtroopers is both an absolute and an addictive matter; the other stormtroopers that Voss'on't gave orders to were expected to give their lives, if necessary. That kind of loyalty from underlings has a corrosive effect on a sentient creature's thinking. It makes him believe—deep down—that the whole universe is his to command. When wise creatures say that absolute power corrupts, they mean more than just a moral issue. It interferes with your intelligence as well."

"Hold on." Bossk frowned, trying to incorporate the other's words into the workings inside his own skull. "I thought you said you didn't believe in trying to figure out what went on in the heads of the merchandise you went after."

"I don't," replied Boba Fett. "This isn't psychology; this is just hunting. That's all. I don't care *why* the merchandise does what it does; I just take note of its behavior, how it reacts and moves. I've spent a lot more time at the Imperial court, and at places like Jabba the Hutt's palace, than you have; my skills are appreciated and paid for there." The voice coming from the helmeted figure held a dark, ominous certainty in its tone. "I've seen the same thing in the admirals of the Imperial Navy, and in Jabba the Hutt and Emperor Palpatine. What starts out as a tool, a weapon in their hands, winds up as a cancer in their minds. And then . . ." Fett slowly nodded. "Then it takes them over. And they become easy prey."

Bossk drew back on the bench, keeping a wary eye on the other bounty hunter. Fear might have been an unknown emotion to Boba Fett, but his words had managed to evoke a disturbing unease inside Bossk.

"Maybe you're right," said Bossk. "But I don't think anybody's going to be knocking over Emperor Palpatine anytime soon."

"Is that so?" Boba Fett's voice had returned to its normal inexpressive tone. "It's not something I'd make any wagers about, one way or another. The Rebel Alliance has too many hopeless optimists in it to be much of a threat to Palpatine."

"Anyway—maybe that's why Voss'on't went renegade. So the same thing wouldn't happen to him."

"If that's the case," said Boba Fett, "then he's smarter—and more dangerous—than I've given him credit for."

"So what's your plan?" All that weird talk had made Bossk nervous; for a moment it had felt as if the bare durasteel bulkheads of Boba Fett's *Slave I* had been closing in on him. "I mean, other than forming a team when he's not expecting you to do that."

"Simple—as all the best plans are. We *don't* form a team."

"I don't get it." Now Bossk was genuinely confused. "What've we been talking about, then?"

"What we're talking about," said Boba Fett, "is what we want Voss'on't to think we're doing. Oh, we'll form a team, all right—we're going in together on this job, all right—but the first thing we'll have you do is betray me. When we make contact with Voss'on't, when we find out just where he's hiding, then you'll stab me in the back."

"You're joking." Bossk peered intently at the other bounty hunter. "Aren't you?"

"I don't mean literally stab me in the back. I mean you'll communicate with Voss'on't on the sly. And you'll offer to go over to his side, to work for him. It's an old trick among criminal types: the best way to get past your target's defenses is to make him think you're betraying someone else."

Bossk shook his head. "I can see some problems with this scheme right from the start." He had expected better; was this the limit of Fett's strategic thinking? "First, how am I going to convince him that I'd even *want* to work on his side? The last bunch that went along with him all wound up dead. Unless I'm feeling suicidal, I'd have to be an idiot to go in with somebody with a track record like that."

"I'm not saying that you'll tell Voss'on't that you *trust* him. Of course you don't trust him; why should you?" Boba Fett's voice remained level and patient—to the degree that was possible. "He'll know that you'll be watching your back the whole time you're dealing with him. Just as he'll know that you should be able to take care of yourself; you're an experienced bounty hunter and you've been in dangerous situations before. Whereas the crew that helped Voss'on't steal the Imperial destroyer obviously did trust him; that's why he was able to get the drop on them, and they paid the price with their lives. So you and Voss'on't will know where you stand with each other; you'll be able to make deals like actual business creatures."

"Then that's the other problem," said Bossk. "I can see what he'd want from me—mainly, that I'd set you up somehow so you wind up dead and he doesn't wind up as hard merchandise in one of your holding cages." Bossk pointed with his thumb-claw toward the metal-barred structures on the other side of the hold. "Voss'on't doesn't want to wind up on his way back to the Emperor. But what's in it for me? What does Voss'on't have that makes it worthwhile for me to deal with him? Like you said, he's probably already spent most of the credits he got from the scavenger operations that he pieced out the Destroyer to."

"Voss'on't has got plenty left to deal with. Maybe not credits on hand, but in his own kind of merchandise. Do you really think that Emperor Palpatine wants him back—and has posted that kind of bounty for him—just out of wounded pride, or something like that? The Emperor doesn't have that kind of emotional involvement in his stormtroopers; they're just tools for him, and if one goes bad, it's no big deal. There's plenty more to fill in the gaps in their ranks. If

Palpatine wants Voss'on't caught and brought back to Coruscant so badly, there's a good reason for it. Voss'on't stole more than an Imperial Star Destroyer. He stole the code databases for all of the Imperial stormtroopers' Strategic Insertion teams; that's what the Emperor wants to get back into his possession."

"Codes?" Bossk gazed back at Boba Fett in disbelief—and disappointment. "That's the big deal? What's so important about operational codes? That's the sort of thing that can be changed almost instantaneously if they fall into the other side's hands. Security breaches happen all the time in the Empire." Bossk shook his head. "For that level of code, all the Empire has to do is send out a cancel-and-nullify signal to its military units, then send out a secured-and-encrypted relay with the replacement codes. It may be a complicated procedure, but it's cheaper than the bounty Palpatine has set up for Voss'on't's return."

"That's the procedure, all right." Boba Fett leaned forward slightly. "For all of the Empire's military units—*except* the Strategic Insertion teams. Those units, like the one Voss'on't was part of, are not in constant communication with the Empire's communications centers. The Strategic Insertion teams are in deep cover; that's what they were designed for. When they're on a mission, especially in some remote sector of the galaxy, they can go for a long time without being in touch with any part of the chain of command above them. They're virtually independent operatives; that's why they're so few of them in the Empire. So they can't receive a cancel-and-nullify signal from their superiors, at least not in time to do any good. They have to stay with the original codes that they were sent out with—and those were the ones that Trhin Voss'on't took with him. And *that's* what the

Empire needs to get back, enough for Palpatine to have set up that kind of bounty."

"I got it now." The situation had started to become clearer for Bossk. "Scrapping the destroyer was just to get the credits that Voss'on't needed to go into hiding; the real credits are in the code databases."

"Exactly," said Boba Fett. "Voss'on't will try to cash in on those codes. He can either sell them back to the Empire, or he can see if the Rebel Alliance will pay him what he wants for them. He's under some pretty severe time pressure; the longer he goes without making a deal for the code databases, the less valuable they are. As the different Strategic Insertion teams finish their operations and return to their originating bases, then they can be fitted out with new operational codes. But in the meantime, Voss'on't has got some pretty valuable merchandise in his possession. If he can avoid getting picked off, and he can make the deal he's shooting for, he'll be set. With those kinds of credits, he can buy a lot of protection. But he still has to make the deal. He has to survive long enough to do that."

Bossk nodded, a little more excitedly. "And that's where we come in."

"Exactly. I'm his main concern. I'm the only bounty hunter that Voss'on't is really worried about—"

"Wait a minute," protested Bossk indignantly. "What about me?"

"Come on. Let's face reality." Boba Fett held up a gloved hand, as though trying to placate his partner. "I've got the reputation, and I've got the skills to back it up. You don't."

Sullenly, Bossk grumbled a few Trandoshan words under his breath.

"You've got enough of a reputation," continued

Fett, "that it's just about plausible that I'd be willing to team up with you. We'll be able to convince Voss'on't about that. And once we've got him believing the setup, then we're on our way. If you're supposedly teamed up with me, then you're in the position to double-cross me. All these Imperial military types have a low opinion of bounty hunters; Voss'on't will fall for this story in a fraction of a Standard Time Part. For a cut of his eventual profits from selling the code databases, you can make sure that I won't be able to interfere with his plans. Or at least that's what you'll tell him. And that's what he'll believe."

Nodding slowly and thoughtfully, Bossk mulled over the details of the plan. "How am I going to convince him that I can do that? That I can stop you from catching him?"

"That's the simplest part of all." Boba Fett spread his gloved hands apart. "You'll kill me."

"What?" Bossk stared at the bounty hunter sitting across from him. "Is that some kind of a joke?"

"I don't tell jokes," said Boba Fett, "even when I'm not working. That's the plan. You're going to take care of Trhin Voss'on't's number-one problem for him. You're going to eliminate me—or at least that's what he's going to believe. And that's when he'll relax; that's when his guard will go down. And then he's vulnerable. He'll be an easy pick-off, then."

Bossk drew back from the helmeted figure, as though in an instinctive reaction to have wandered too close to a gaping precipice. His spine pressed against the cold durasteel of the bulkhead behind him, as deep and ominous suspicions formed inside his mind. *What does he know?* The brain inside the Mandalorian armor's helmet, and all of its cunning, intricate workings, was as hidden from him as though it had been concealed on the other side of this barren planet. Yet at the same time, he could feel Boba Fett's gaze penetrating him, inspecting each of his secrets, one by one.

With a force of will, he shook off the feeling. *You're being paranoid,* Bossk told himself. There's no way that Boba Fett would have been able to determine what Bossk's own agenda was. *He's an ordinary, mortal creature like yourself.* Like turning the key in a hidden lock, Bossk reached down into the core of his being and let his innate Trandoshan anger emerge. His father, Cradossk, if he were still alive, would have been embarrassed to see his own spawn being intimidated by any other living thing, including the notorious Boba Fett. The slitted pupils of Bossk's eyes narrowed even farther as the hormones of his anger seeped through his veins, tightening the heavy muscles they surrounded. It didn't matter, decided Bossk, whether Boba Fett knew anything about his real plans, about his intentions after the matter of pulling in Trhin Voss'on't was taken care of. When that time came, he would have a few surprises for Boba Fett. The other bounty hunter might think he was smart, but this time, Bossk was sure that he had finally gotten ahead of him.

"So how do we start?" The surge of anger brought along an equal amount of impatience. Bossk was tired of talk; he wanted action. "How are we going to prove all this stuff to Voss'on't?"

"First," said Boba Fett, "we'll need some concrete proof that you're willing to kill your partners. Some kind of proof that Voss'on't will regard as impressive. You'll never be able to get into his confidences unless we have that."

Why anybody would doubt the murderousness of a Trandoshan was beyond Bossk. His species had conclusively demonstrated its violent tendencies all through the galaxy. *And proud of it,* he thought. Who wouldn't be?

"What did you have in mind? Unless"—one corner of Bossk's fang-lined mouth lifted in an ugly version of a smile—"you were planning on having me kill you right now." He nodded, as though pleased with the idea. "That would probably work."

"I told you—I don't joke around." A laserlike glare seemed to emerge from behind the helmet's dark visor. "I'd appreciate it if you took this seriously as well."

"Okay, okay; sorry." Bossk held out both his palms, as though fending off a blow. "So what are we going to do?"

"We need proof—real hard proof—that you're serious about betraying your partners. So we need one more partner, just for the purpose of giving us that proof."

"Another partner?" Bossk scowled. "I don't feel like cutting in anyone else on this deal."

"We won't be cutting anyone else in. That's already been taken care of." Boba Fett rose from the bench on which he'd been sitting. "Come over here. I told you outside that I had something to show you. Something that you'd find interesting."

Bossk followed the other bounty hunter over to the storage lockers at the hold's other side. He watched silently as Boba Fett punched a key sequence into the pad beside one of the square locker doors. A red light flashed and the drawer slid open.

"Take a look at this." Boba Fett grasped the edge of a cloth sheet covering some large, uneven object. "This is all the proof you'll need." He pulled the cloth aside, revealing what was underneath.

"What the—" Startled, Bossk gaped at the figure

lying face upward in the drawer. "Zuckuss!" The insect-like face, with its immense goggling eyes and inter-twined breathing tubes, was as familiar to him as his own. Bossk looked over at Boba Fett. "What happened to him?"

The sound of Zuckuss's name being spoken aloud hadn't caused the figure in the drawer to stir. The round, glassy eyes continued to stare upward at the hold's metal ceiling.

"Simple," said Fett. "It's all part of the plan. We needed a dead bounty hunter, someone that you can tell Trhin Voss'on't was part of our team. So I provided one."

The unemotional coldness of Boba Fett's explanation amazed Bossk. *It really is all business with this barve,* he thought. *No wonder he's on top of the bounty hunter trade.* "He's dead?" Bossk pointed to the unmoving figure. "Really dead?"

"See for yourself."

Bossk leaned down closer to the unmoving object in the drawer. He didn't feel sorry for Zuckuss—pity was another emotion foreign to Trandoshans—but at the same time, there was an odd trace of regret in seeing him like this. There was no sense of friendship or other tender feelings wasted among bounty hunters, but Zuckuss had been part of the team on the Circumtore job. Things had gone badly enough then that Bossk had felt like killing Zuckuss . . . but he hadn't. And to realize that Boba Fett had done so, as a matter of cold and hyperrational business practice, part of his scheme for bringing in this renegade stormtrooper—that didn't sit right with Bossk. To kill in anger was one thing, even a fine and noble thing. But Boba Fett's way of doing it without emotion struck him as essentially . . . evil. *That's it,* realized Bossk. He had rarely, if ever, meditated so deeply on a moral issue. *That's it, exactly.* And now here he was, teaming up with Boba Fett. The implications of that were something he didn't want to think about, now or ever.

Automatically, to keep his thoughts safely submerged, Bossk went about verifying Zuckuss's death. Checking the body's neck, where the most visible blood vessels were located, he found no pulse; at the filtered openings of the breathing apparatus, where the exterior tubes looped toward the chest, no signs of respiration were detectable. The latter convinced Bossk more than anything else; one of the more irritating things about Zuckuss, when he'd been alive, had been the slight, constant noise that went with his inhaling and exhaling. *Won't have to hear that anymore,* thought Bossk.

"He's dead, all right." Bossk straightened up from his examination of the corpse. "If what you wanted is evidence to show Voss'on't that bounty hunters are getting killed, then you sure got it." The only problem was that the cover story that went with the corpse had it that Bossk himself had killed Zuckuss. He preferred taking the credit only for his own violence. That raised another question in his mind. "How am I supposed to have killed him? He looks in pretty good shape. I mean . . . considering everything. Usually if one of us Trandoshans knocks somebody off, they really show it."

"Tell Voss'on't you suffocated him." Boba Fett pointed down to the corpse's face. "With those exterior breathing tubes, it's a relatively easy thing to do."

Bossk glanced over at Boba Fett. *That must be,* thought Bossk, *how he did it.* Just like that; cold and effective. "And why did I do it? What's the line going to be on that?"

"Just as you said before—you didn't feel like splitting up the credits with any more partners than necessary. I've already started the story in circulation about Zuckuss teaming up with you and me; it's probably already reaching Voss'on't's ears by now. So when we track him down, and you talk to him, you can feed him the rest of the line."

"Which is?"

"That you don't feel like splitting the credits with me, either." Boba Fett punched the bulkhead-mounted control pad again, and the drawer slid back, taking Zuckuss's lifeless body with it. "And that you've figured out that you'll do better financially if you sell me out to Voss'on't rather than sticking with me as a partner. After all"—Fett turned back toward Bossk—"I'm not as famous for being trustworthy as I am for other things. Am I?"

It took Bossk a while to figure out whether or not Boba Fett was breaking his ban on joking around while doing business. If it was a joke, it made him as uneasy as seeing Zuckuss laid out dead. *I'm in deep here,* thought Bossk as he gazed into the dark visor of Boba Fett's helmet. He was beginning to wonder exactly how deep.

"No," said Bossk slowly. "I guess you're not . . ."

"Then it's settled." Boba Fett punched a control sequence into the pad on the forearm sleeve of his Mandalorian battle armor. On the other side of the ship's hold, the hatchway irised open. "We're partners." Outside, night had filled the dry marine trench of what had once been Gholondreine-β's planet-girdling ocean. "And we have a plan. Don't we?"

"Right." Bossk's nod was just as slow. "We sure do . . ."

All the way back to his own ship, the *Hound's*

Tooth, waiting at the other end of the trench, he could feel the yellow eyes of the centipedelike creatures in their bore holes, carved into the cliffs towering in darkness above him. Bossk knew it was only his imagination if he thought he could hear them laughing at him.

11

This is easy, thought Bossk. Almost too easy . . .

As if such a thing were possible. The Trandoshan bounty hunter felt a surge of gloating pleasure, welling up from the depths of his gut, as he sat at the rickety table, his claws wrapped around a chipped stoneware mug. Whatever gratification he felt hadn't come from the mug's contents, a sour inebriant that had briefly numbed the tongue behind his fangs when he had sipped it. This watering hole's drinks were both strong *and* disgusting.

"We could take him now," growled Bossk under his breath. "Why don't we just go ahead and *do* it?"

He was alone at the table. The voice that answered his question sounded from deep inside his ear. Trandoshans, as a species, lacked external pinnae such as most humanoids had; beyond the small aperture of his ear canal, a cochlear micro-implant device had been precisely inserted with the point of a surgical needle. That piece of equipment had been just one of the preparations for this job.

"Not as simple as that," said Boba Fett's voice, both near—right inside Bossk's head—and distant. The other bounty hunter was currently located somewhere far from this ratty watering hole; Fett might still be aboard *Slave I*, out past this backwater world's atmosphere, for all Bossk knew. "Do you really think our target doesn't have some kind of defenses in place? He's not a complete fool, you know."

A snarl of glowering impatience settled on Bossk's face. He resisted the urge to scratch with his heavy claws at the implanted device itching inside his head, like some kind of burrowing parasite above the hinge of his jaw. He didn't want to do anything that might give him away, even though this dump was so poorly lit as to seem like some underground cavern. The slit pupils of Bossk's eyes were dilated as wide as possible, and there were still shadowy figures, hunched over their drinks at other wobbly tables, whose features his normally sharp eyesight couldn't make out at all.

Trhin Voss'on't, though, he'd been able to spot right off, as soon as he'd descended the worn stone steps into the watering hole. The renegade Imperial stormtrooper—ex-stormtrooper, Bossk reminded himself—was right where Boba Fett's information sources had said he'd be. Bossk had to admit that when it came to tracking down hard merchandise anywhere in the galaxy, Fett had a network of contacts second to none. It was no wonder that Boba Fett had always been able to get a jump on any of the members of the old Bounty Hunters Guild, for scooping up a prize bit of merchandise and delivering it before most of the others in the business had any idea of what was going on. And when Fett had put the word out to his virtual eyes and ears, stationed on every inhabited planet, that he was looking for this former stormtrooper, it hadn't been very many Standard Time Parts before the necessary info had come back to him.

"What's our target doing?"

"Drinking," growled Bossk. "What else is there

to do in a dive like this?" He was able to keep his muttered responses down low enough that the miniaturized throat mike could pick them up, yet not be overheard by any of the other patrons of the establishment. And Trandoshan faces were not so expressive that anyone glancing his way, in these shadows, would be able to detect the speech motions of his scaly muzzle. He would have preferred the auditory cover of a jizz-wailer band like Figrin D'an and the Modal Nodes, back at the Mos Eisley spaceport on Tatooine—that combo created such a racket, you could blow somebody away in one of the cantina booths with hardly anyone noticing. This world's hangouts were entirely too quiet for Bossk's tastes.

"I'd be drinking, too," said Bossk, "if I could stomach their well hooch."

A burst of solar flare static rasped inside Bossk's head, like a swarm of Nimgorrhean saber wasps, and loud enough that he couldn't stop himself from pressing the butt of his palm against his ear opening. That didn't do any good; Bossk winced and ground his fangs together until the noise from the implanted device faded away. It proved at least that Boba Fett and his *Slave I* ship were off-planet. This unattractive and remote world—Bossk had already forgotten its name—had an unstable sun, with emission bands wide enough to play havoc with all sorts of comm systems, even the expensive narrow-beam equipment that Boba Fett could afford to use. The two of them would have a hard time coordinating this operation if another flare broke the link between them at some crucial point.

". . . stay low." Boba Fett's unnaturally calm voice faded back in. "Try not to draw any attention to yourself."

"I'm already doing that," snarled Bossk. Those

were the same instructions that Boba Fett had given him when he'd told him of this new plan, before he'd stuffed himself into a one-way, single-passenger drop ship and had piloted away from Fett's *Slave I*. The drop ship was now out in the wastelands beyond the encircling slag heaps of what had once been an Imperial mining-and-refinery colony; the fact that the mines had been abandoned as worthless didn't surprise Bossk. As he had made his way on foot, past enormous, scavenger-ready drill units, gross tonnage excavators, up-ended conveyor lines, and surrounding slag heaps, then into the midst of the shabby plastoid buildings that had become by default the planet's only inhabited zone, it had struck him that even the dirt and rocks here were of an inferior quality. "So when are we going to make our move?"

"Soon enough," replied Fett. "There's still a few things that have to be checked out." The voice of the distant bounty hunter spoke with infuriating patience and logic. "We can't allow ourselves any mistakes. We're only going to get one shot at this guy. If we spook him and he dives into whatever escape route he's got lined up—and he's sure to have one—we won't be able to track him down again. We'll have lost him."

That possibility made Bossk's blood run even colder than its normal homeostatic temperature level. He had everything riding on this job, on bringing in Trhin Voss'on't and delivering the renegade stormtrooper to Emperor Palpatine. Whatever would happen to Voss'on't at that point, it was no concern of Bossk's; he imagined it wouldn't be pretty. The Emperor wasn't known for looking kindly upon mere failure among his ranks; actual treachery was sure to merit treatment way beyond harshness. A shudder moved across the scales of Bossk's shoulders and spine. As ruthless, and inured to ruthlessness, as all Trandoshans were, he had nevertheless made a personal vow—long ago, at the beginning of his career as a bounty hunter—*never* to cross the Emperor. *That way,* Bossk reminded himself, *lies a serious amount of grief.* Let those high-minded Rebels take the beating that was so surely coming to them.

And let me, thought Bossk, *collect the bounty for this piece of hard merchandise.* All his plans, for freezing out the True Guild faction and re-forming the old Bounty Hunters Guild, with himself at its head, depended upon raking in that mountain of credits that Palpatine had put up for Trhin Voss'on't's hide—and the return of the codes that Voss'on't had absconded with. From long experience, and from looking inside his own reptilian heart, Bossk knew how bounty hunters' minds worked. That amount of credits could buy a lot of loyalty. There was no point in being a bounty hunter unless your nobler instincts were up for sale to the highest bidder.

Though, of course, there were high bidders . . . and then even higher bidders. Bossk took another sip of the acrid fluid in the mug before him, not even tasting the stuff as he mulled over his weighty concerns. *Depends on just how many credits you have.* He nodded slowly to himself. *You can never have too many.* Even with the enormous bounty on Trhin Voss'on't's head, there was no denying that a half share of those credits wasn't the same as getting all of it. From the beginning of this job, it had struck him as a shame that Boba Fett—who didn't have anywhere close to the need for the credits that Bossk did—was going to get such a hefty slice of the bounty. *A real shame,* thought Bossk. Especially considering that he was down here doing all the work and taking all the risks, within spitting distance of a dangerous ex-stormtrooper, while Boba Fett wasn't even on the planet's surface, but out beyond its atmosphere somewhere.

The contents of the mug had ignited a wet, smoldering fire in his gut; he ignored it. He had a lot to think about.

Bossk let those interwoven thoughts stew at the back of his mind, while he kept a surreptitious eye on Trhin Voss'on't. Whatever else could be said about Boba Fett, the man was right about one thing: the renegade stormtrooper must have some kind of defenses in place. It would be suicidal otherwise for Voss'on't to be sitting out here in the open like this. Bossk imagined he could feel the sloping, crudely plastered walls and the low, smoke-darkened ceiling of the watering hole pressing in on him, as though they were the disguised machinery of some Trandoshan-sized trap.

The close confines of the place and its stale, sweat-smelling air didn't seem to bother Voss'on't. With his elbows planted on the small table at which he sat, the ex-stormtrooper nursed along a mug filled with the same near-lethal concoction that Bossk had tasted. Boba Fett's intelligence reports had described Voss'on't as spending the bulk of his time here. From what Bossk could tell, it didn't seem to be for the purpose of getting drunk. Voss'on't carefully paced his intake so that the drink had no apparent impact on him; either that, or he'd had his liver biochemically enhanced to neutralize the intoxicants in the thick, heavy liquid. His sharply angled face, as hard and expressionless as the masklike full helmet he'd worn when he'd been in the Emperor's service, contained eyes narrowed into a permanent squint, surrounded by skin wrinkled and creased as old, flayed leather. White scars showed through the graying buzz-cut that clung to Voss'on't's skull; some of them undoubtedly dated all the way back to his basic training days.

Becoming an Imperial stormtrooper was no easy process; few had a chance of enduring the violent hammering-in of the military skills that went with the deathly white armor. Those who didn't make it all the way to the end, whose bodies or minds broke under their drill sergeants' sadistic regimens, washed out of the program as corpses. An unquestioning loyalty and obedience to superior officers went with the training; any resistance to commands, however destructive or fatal they might be, was rooted out like diseased nerve tissue.

For someone like Voss'on't, who had gone through all that and had then served with distinction in one of the stormtroopers' elite units, to have kept hidden deep inside himself a vestige of another nature, one that could even contemplate treason—that spoke of a dark core that was harder and more determined than all the ranks of the other stormtroopers combined. Voss'on't might have been waiting for years, not divulging his plans to anyone around him, as he watched for the perfect opportunity. And then when it had come at last, he had swung into action without hesitation or remorse, applying all his hard-won stormtrooper skills to the task. And if others had to die in the process, for him to make his escape with the codes that would buy his safety, he wouldn't be likely to even give a second thought about it.

Not bad. Bossk gave a tiny nod of appreciation as he contemplated the narrow-eyed figure sitting at the distant table in the watering hole's gloom. Trhin Voss'on't was exactly the sort of tough, murderous scum that he could admire. If circumstances had been different, he could have imagined teaming up with the ex-stormtrooper rather than with Boba Fett. Voss'on't would have made a worthwhile addition to the ranks of the Bounty Hunters Guild, once Bossk had succeeded in putting the organization back together again. He supposed it was just one of the ironies of life in this galaxy that the price of re-forming the Guild was going to be paid out of Voss'on't's hide. Once Emperor Palpatine got through with him, after the renegade had been captured and cashed in, there wouldn't be enough left to even make a decent trophy out of him—by all reports, the Emperor wasn't given to the same sentiments about keepsakes as Trandoshans were.

Boba Fett had broken the comm connection; the cochlear implant in the side of Bossk's head had gone silent. The other bounty hunter, wherever he was at the moment, was presumably busy, setting up the rest of the plans for snaring Voss'on't. *He'd better be,* thought Bossk grumpily. There wasn't so much traffic in and out of this dump that Bossk's presence here wouldn't be eventually noticed and commented upon. Trhin Voss'on't had given him a suspicious glance when he had come into the gloomy confines of the watering hole, then had looked away, as though satisfied that the newcomer presented no threat to him. Voss'on't might change his mind about that assessment if Bossk hung around much longer, without some other creature joining up with him. The only credible reason for hanging out in a place like this was for the purposes of conducting business, usually far enough on the shady side of the law that any illumination at all would be unwelcome. There wasn't a species in the galaxy so depraved or devolved as to come here for the atmosphere or the quality of the drinks. Bossk was beginning to regret having drank as little of the foul-tasting fluid as he had.

He also figured that it would be a dead giveaway

if he spent too much time keeping watch on Trhin Voss'on't. Creatures in a place like this demanded some measure of privacy, even when they were sitting at a table right out in the open. Minding anyone's business other than your own was a sure route to a blaster bolt through one's gut. And somebody on the run from Emperor Palpatine would likely be even jumpier about being snooped around.

Voss'on't wasn't even facing in Bossk's direction, but the preternatural awareness he was likely to possess would be the equivalent of having eyes in the back of his head. There were plenty of species in the galaxy like that, with a 360-degree field of view around themselves—but it took a deep level of suspicion for a humanoid to achieve the same effect.

Holding the stone mug in both his clawed hands, Bossk shifted his gaze over to the other patrons of the watering hole. Most of them seemed to be personnel left over from the planet's brief period as an Imperial mining colony. *Stupid barves,* thought Bossk dismissively. They had gotten what they deserved, for being either stupid or unlucky enough to have been conscripted for a tour of duty like this. When the colony's mines had been abandoned as unprofitable, they had been left behind like so much discarded machinery, not worth the cost of freighting to any other location. Now they sat hunched over their brain-numbing potions, slowly trickling out the last of their wages for a few moments of thought-dead oblivion. Even if any of them could afford to get off-planet, there was no place for them to go, no world with a need for their marginal skills. Most of the former miners had let themselves be surgically altered, just for the privilege of rooting beneath the planet's rocky crust for whatever the Empire had once deemed valuable. Their skulls were thickened with massive layers of hormonally induced bone growth, as a form of subdermal safety helmet suitable for mining work, extending nearly to the width of their shoulders; their faces were masked with intricate folds of spongy air-filtration ciliae, dangling like pink and white moss over their throats—that was the Imperial bio-modification clinics' idea of protection against silicosis and other lung-fouling diseases. Even their hands had been altered, the fingers replaced with curved sections of durasteel, that meshed with another to form sharp, scooplike appendages, the better for scrabbling in the rocks and loose gravel of the quarry tailings. But not much good for any other use; the former miners had to clumsily grasp the stone mugs in front of them between the edges of their surgically transformed hands, in order to lift the drinks to their hidden mouths. With their labor-hunched spines and dull, sodden eyes, they looked like some enlarged subspecies of Venedlian sandmole, with just enough brains buried in the recesses of their gargantuan crania to be aware of their own degradation. Even as he gazed at the poor creatures, Bossk dismissed them as being of no more importance than the daubs of faded decorative paint on the watering hole's walls. The Empire left victims wherever its reach extended; these were just more of them.

"You looking for someone?"

A harsh, flat voice broke into Bossk's thoughts. He turned and looked up. And found himself gazing straight into the face of Trhin Voss'on't.

The former Imperial stormtrooper stood at the edge of the table bearing Bossk's drink. Voss'on't placed both his hands against the table's surface and brought his face down close to the Trandoshan's. Bossk could see even more clearly the old scars that straggled through the close-cropped hair on Voss'on't's skull.

"Did you hear me, pal? I asked you a question."

Bossk's initial impulse was to drop one of his own hands down to the side of his belt, pull out his blaster pistol, and bring its cold muzzle up against the bridge of the ex-stormtrooper's nose. He was stopped from doing so by the sure feeling that it would be a bad idea. Either he wouldn't move fast enough, and he would find himself looking into the business end of Voss'on't's weapon, or he would have to blow away a valuable piece of living merchandise. Either way, his profits or his ability to go on breathing, he would lose out.

"Why do you care?" Bossk kept any sign of his thoughts or emotions out of his voice. The ex-stormtrooper had caught him off-guard—Voss'on't had moved so stealthily and quietly that Bossk didn't have any warning of his approach. "You mind your business, and I'll take care of my own."

Voss'on't leaned in closer to the Trandoshan. "My business," he said softly, "is remaining alive. I don't like anyone interfering with it."

"What makes you think—"

"Shut up." Voss'on't's expression had started out as one of simmering anger, and that hadn't changed. "Keep your hands flat on the table, where I can see them. I get nervous when creatures have both their hands and their weapons where I can't keep an eye on what's going on." The cold eyes narrowed their gaze. "Believe me—you don't want me getting nervous."

Bossk unfolded his claws from around the stone mug and flattened them against the table. "There. Satisfied?"

"Not very. I still want to know what you're doing here." The next words came out as a snarl. "Bounty hunter."

Great, thought Bossk disgustedly. *He must've spotted me as soon as I walked into this place.* The whole time that Bossk had been sitting and nursing along the revolting drink he'd been served, believing he was pulling off his end of the operation, nobody had been fooled at all. Or at least the target of the job hadn't been.

"That's a new one," said Bossk with as much mildness as he could summon up. "I've been accused of being a lot of different things, on a lot of different worlds, but that's the first time anybody's called me one of those." One corner of his scaly muzzle lifted in an approximation of a smile. "Sure you're not just looking for a fight?"

"I don't fight; I'm a very peaceable kind of person." Voss'on't either didn't bother to smile or was incapable of it. "I just kill people. Especially creatures who mess around with me."

"Good thing I'm not in that category." Where was Boba Fett? Bossk felt the scales across his shoulders tightening with irritation. The whole operation was blowing up in Bossk's face—perhaps literally, if Trhin Voss'on't reached for his own blaster pistol—and the other bounty hunter was nowhere to be found. *He's off-planet somewhere,* seethed Bossk, *and I'm about to be killed by the hard merchandise we came here to collect.*

"You can be in the category of dead, if I don't like your answers." Voss'on't turned his scarred head to one side, peering closer to Bossk. "Now, some creatures might think I've done some stupid things. And I could even agree with them; getting on the wrong side of Emperor Palpatine isn't a recipe for longevity."

Bossk nodded. "That's more problems than I've got."

"I'm the only problem you've got right now. And that's enough. Because one stupid thing I *didn't* do is get myself into a situation where I knew there'd be a bounty placed on my head, without compiling a little personal database of just who was most likely to show up looking for me."

"Ah. I see." The thoughts inside Bossk's head raced at an even faster clip. Now would have been a real good time for Boba Fett to have turned up. "I suppose . . . that would be the smart thing to do."

"That's right . . . *Bossk*." The ex-stormtrooper practically spat out the name. Keeping his gaze on the Trandoshan, he reached behind himself, grabbed the chair from an empty table, and pulled it around; he sat down, leaning over the back of the chair. "How's things with the Bounty Hunters Guild these days?"

Bossk managed a shrug. "Could be better."

"That's your name, right?"

There was no point in lying. "You got it."

"Your old man used to run the Bounty Hunters Guild." A sneer crept into Trhin Voss'on't's words. "Guess you're not quite up to that, huh?"

Bossk's cold reptilian blood went up a couple of degrees. "Look—" He was close to not caring about the consequences of reaching for his blaster. "Let's just leave Guild politics out of the conversation, okay? That doesn't have anything to do with you."

"It might," said Voss'on't with a trace of amusement. "Especially if it gave somebody like you the desire to score a huge bounty. A bounty like the one Palpatine's got riding on me. You could do a lot with that kind of credits, couldn't you?"

"What if I could?" Bossk eyed the man with deepening suspicion. "Anybody could. That's probably why the Emperor is willing to spend the credits. You know? To motivate creatures, to get them to do what he wants—that's what credits are for."

"Huh. Believe me, pal—the Emperor has other ways of 'motivating' creatures. I know; I've been motivated plenty of times in the service of the Empire. And those ways aren't all as pleasant as credits in your pocket."

Bossk shrugged. "Those other ways don't work on bounty hunters. Credits are the only thing that motivates us."

"Good for you." Voss'on't gave a slow nod. "I forgot; you're all rough and tough, fearless types."

"Fearless enough."

"Let me tell you something else. All the credits in the galaxy won't do you any good, if you're not alive to spend them." Voss'on't's gaze narrowed even farther. "And I can arrange that. I've already done it for a couple of others in your line of work, who showed up out here on my doorstep."

"So I've heard." The reports, from Bossk's subordinates in the Guild Reform Committee, had come to him while he and Boba Fett had still been tracking down Voss'on't's hiding place. At least half a dozen other bounty hunters, all of whom had gotten a jump on making a try to capture Trhin Voss'on't, had gotten this far, to this backwater world and this crummy dive—and no farther. Bossk supposed the bodies had been hauled out and dumped in one of the abandoned quarries at the edge of the slowly disintegrating colony structures. There had never been any concern in Bossk's mind that any of the other bounty hunters might actually collect the bounty posted for Voss'on't. None of them had ever had a chance.

"Then you're a slow learner," said Voss'on't. "You should've paid attention to what happened to those other bounty hunters. Right now, you don't even know what you've walked into. I had a lot of credits to spend, when I got done selling off what I stole—and there wasn't anybody I had to split those credits up with, either."

"No—" Bossk slowly shook his head. "Not by the time you got done with them."

"You would've done the same, if you were in my situation."

"True." Bossk shrugged. Getting rid of one's partners was all in the course of ordinary business, if you could get away with it. "Who wouldn't?"

"Nobody with any sense," said Voss'on't grimly. "And I had sense enough to spend the credits making sure that some top-level bounty hunter such as yourself wouldn't be hauling me back to Coruscant and the Emperor's palace anytime soon."

That remark puzzled Bossk. *If he spent the credits on some kind of defenses*—it was the same question that had puzzled Bossk before—*then where are they?* Either they were well hidden, or Voss'on't had gotten cheated on them.

He was willing to bet that it wasn't the latter. Those other bounty hunters, the ones that had already come this way, wouldn't have gotten killed so readily if Voss'on't's defenses were illusory.

Besides . . . it was always wiser to assume that when somebody boasted of their ways of arranging your death, they weren't lying. Especially when it came from a former Imperial stormtrooper.

Bossk cut short his mulling over of the situation. "Now what happens?"

"It's been nice talking to you." Voss'on't spoke with a distinct lack of emotion. "Just like I enjoyed talking to those other bounty hunters that came around here. Your type of scum is close enough to that of my former associates—the kind of work we do—that we had something to talk about. For a while, at least. It made for a little change of pace for me." He tilted his head in the direction of the hunchbacked, molelike miners at the watering hole's far tables, with their shovel hands folded around their drinks. "I'm afraid these dirt-grubbers here aren't very stimulating conversationalists. So believe me—it's not without some real regret on my part that I'm going to have to kill you. Just to be on the safe side, you know."

"Yeah, right." Bossk felt seriously annoyed. He knew that things were going to get ugly, real quick—and Boba Fett still hadn't deigned to show up on the scene. *Some partnership,* groused Bossk to himself. For all he knew, Fett had succumbed to an attack of nerves—it had never happened before, as far as Bossk knew, but it wasn't impossible—and had decided not to tangle with the ex-stormtrooper at all. Fett's ship *Slave I,* with Fett in the cockpit, might be already hitting hyperspace, heading for remoter and safer planetfalls—and leaving Bossk sitting here, holding the bag. *Typical,* thought Bossk. *Can't depend on anybody—unless they're dead.* When he got the Bounty Hunters Guild up and running again, with himself at the top of it, he was going to make sure that he got the respect he had deserved for so long, and had never yet gotten. In the meantime, he was going to have to blow away a prime piece of hard merchandise—the biggest bounty ever posted, as far as Bossk could recall—just to keep from getting killed himself. And even that would take some doing. *Unless . . .*

An idea had struck him. "Before you do that," said Bossk, "could you tell me something? Did you spend all the credits?"

"What's it matter to you?"

"Well, the truth is that you've got me wrong." Bossk tapped his chest with a single claw. "Sure, I know who you are and what kind of price has been put on your head. Everybody in the galaxy probably knows that by now. But I didn't come here to try and haul you in. Do I look like a complete idiot?"

Voss'on't peered suspiciously at him. "Keep talking."

"Come on—" Bossk spread both his clawed hands apart. "Let's face it. The bounty hunter trade isn't what it used to be. At least, not since the old Guild broke up. So creatures have got to find new ways of making a living. You're not the only scum who wants to survive. And I'm not such a fool that I'm likely to think I've got a chance of bringing in a former stormtrooper—especially one who's gotten himself set up the way you have." Using words like this was a new thing for Bossk; the process made him feel a little dizzy. Always before, he had solved problems and gotten out of sticky situations in the standard Trandoshan manner: enough violence to leave *somebody* dead on the floor. He had lied before—as recently as when he had talked Boba Fett into going in as partners with him on this job—but never at a moment's notice like this. Even though it had been part of the plan from the beginning, he still hadn't prepared himself for it. Bossk plugged ahead, regardless; he had no option otherwise. "So . . . I figured, why not cut myself in on a good thing, just from a different angle?" The sheer recklessness of his words was having more of an intoxicating effect than the nauseating fluid in the stone mug could ever have had on him. "There's more than one way to make some credits in this galaxy." He put his hands back down on the table and leaned closer to Voss'on't. "Let's face it—there's going to be a lot of bounty hunters coming after you. The kind of price you've got on your head—it's guaranteed. And all it's going to take is for one of them to get lucky, and then you're not an ex-stormtrooper any-more. You'll be hard merchandise, on its way back to the Emperor."

"They'd have to get *very* lucky for that to happen."

"It's a strange universe we live in," said Bossk. "All kinds of things can happen. Who would've thought that the Rebel Alliance would have had any chance of taking out the Death Star? But one lucky shot, and that thing was so much molten scrap."

Bossk could see that his words were having an effect on Voss'on't. That last argument had been particularly well aimed; a military mind like Voss'on't's would naturally have had a lot of faith in the invincibility of a pile of weaponry like the Death Star battle station.

"So you need a little more," continued Bossk, "than what you've already got set up. If you're going to stay alive and healthy, and out of the Emperor's hands. That's what I figure, at least." Once he had gotten started at this business of lying off the top of his head, it had turned out surprisingly easy. The words were coming faster and easier. "You need all the help you can get—and that you can pay for." Bossk leaned back in his chair. "That's where I come in."

"You?" Voss'on't gave a derisive snort. "What can you do for me?"

"I can tell you just how any of those bounty hunters out there are going to make their moves—*before* they happen. I didn't spend all that time in the old Bounty Hunters Guild without learning all the tricks of the trade. And I know all those hunters; I know how their minds work." Bossk started to warm to the subject. "You see, they all have their individual styles, their ways of working. Now, somebody like IG-88—that one's a droid—he's got sort of a cold, logical, *precise* way of setting out his strategies for hunting down merchandise. Whereas the ones who take after my kind of tactics, they're a little more *instinctive*. You know? They kind of sniff out their prey. Whatever works, that's all. If one kind of bounty hunter can't catch you, then another kind will. Unless . . ." Bossk nodded slowly, with his own personal version of a wise smile. "Unless you know what to anticipate from them."

"Ah. I see." Voss'on't looked at him with distaste. "And that's what you're planning on selling to me, I take it. Your expertise on bounty hunters."

"You got it." Actually, now that Bossk had had a few more seconds to mull over what he had just said, it didn't seem like such a bad idea. *Maybe,* he thought, *I should look into this.* There were a few sentient creatures out in the galaxy who specialized in getting merchandise past whatever bounty hunters were looking for it, but that was basically a matter of running and dodging, making a delivery from one point to another. To actually go into business, though, as a sort of counter-bounty hunter, matching one's capacity for violence and intrigue *against* bounty hunters—that held a certain appeal for Bossk. For one thing, it struck him, there would undoubtedly be enough bloodshed to suit his tastes; bounty hunters weren't known for taking kindly to any other creature impinging on their operations. Plus the credits that could be made—that had a definite attraction for him. "That's what I can deliver, all right." Bossk let his smile widen across his muzzle. "For a price."

"A good price, I suppose."

Bossk shrugged. "I'm worth it."

"I bet you are," said Voss'on't. "But you're a business creature, right? You know how things are when it comes down to business. Everything's negotiable."

"Well . . . to a point."

"Because," continued the former stormtrooper, "I have my own notions about what you're worth."

That didn't sound good to Bossk. "Like what?"

"Like this." Voss'on't reached inside his jacket and pulled out a blaster pistol. In one quick, fluid motion, he had it pointed directly at Bossk's forehead. "I think we have a deal."

All thought ceased, and Bossk went into pure reaction mode. With his hands flattened against the top of the table, and a blaster aimed at his skull, his options were limited.

But not totally—he threw his weight back in the chair, toppling it and himself with it. At the same time, Bossk thrust his legs straight, his clawed feet coming up hard against the table's underside. The table flew up, striking Voss'on't's weapon arm and throwing off his aim. As Bossk's spine struck the watering hole's littered floor, a sizzling bolt lanced through the empty air above him and struck the ceiling. Ashes and dust fell on Bossk as he quickly rolled onto his hands and feet, and dove toward the tables crowding the far side of the space.

That's what I get for being smart—Bossk's thinking processes rose in tandem with his self-disgust. *Next time*— Chairs flew clattering as his momentum knocked the watering hole's contents in all directions. *Next time, I'll just reach over and pull somebody's head off.*

Another bolt from Voss'on't's blaster pistol seared an inch above Bossk's scales. He rolled onto his shoulder, unholstering his own weapon and firing even before he had a chance to aim. The bottles of off-planet liquors, arranged in rows behind the watering hole's bar, shattered into wet splinters as the humanoid barkeeper dropped to the floor. Most of the other patrons, the molelike former employees of the mining colony, had already scattered out of the way of the blaster fire, covering their heads with their shovel hands and hurriedly lumbering with an awkward, hunchbacked gait toward the worn steps leading up to the surface level, or crouching down behind over-turned tables.

"Move over—" Bossk elbowed aside one of the miners. From across the chaotic, vacated space of the watering hole, Voss'on't's next shot hit the vertical tabletop shielding the pair of kneeling figures. "Don't worry—he's not trying to get you." Bossk leaned around the edge of the table and laid down a quick barrage from his blaster, aimed well enough this time to force Voss'on't toward the arched opening of the watering hole's rear exit. Between his fire and the ex-stormtrooper's, most of the establishment's chairs and other contents had been reduced to singed and smok-ing rubble.

"Bounty hunter!" Voss'on't, hidden in the shad-ows at the edge of the watering hole, called out. "If you think this is how you're going to get out of here alive, you're mistaken."

My mistake, thought Bossk bitterly, *was coming here at all.* Especially by himself—why he had ever agreed to Boba Fett's notion of splitting up was now beyond him. If they had double-teamed Voss'on't, as the original plan had been, they might have had a chance of taking him. Zuckuss's death now seemed needless; that should have aroused his suspicions right there. The only point to the present arrangement that he could see—and it was a realization not without irony—was that if Fett had been trying to eliminate him, so there would be a clear shot at taking Voss'on't solo and not having to split the bounty, that much at least had been accomplished.

"Tell you what, Voss'on't—" Bossk pressed his

spine against the shield of the overturned table, one shoulder jammed against the silent form of the miner next to him. His shouted words bounced off the watering hole's ceiling. "We could both walk out of here alive if that's the way you want it. That'd be an easy deal to make." Bossk kept the barrel of his blaster pistol pointed upward, the weapon's warmed metal almost touching the side of his head. "But if I'm not leaving in one piece, then neither are you."

"Big talk, bounty hunter." The voice from the hidden Voss'on't drifted back, mockingly. "It's easy to see that you never served in the Imperial forces. Bragging without being able to back it up is grounds for disciplinary action. You don't even know what you're facing, pal."

"As far as I can see," Bossk called back, "you've got a blaster and I've got a blaster. And there's one of you and one of me here." He turned past the edge of the table and left off a bolt in the direction of the other's voice, then quickly scrambled back before Voss'on't could return fire. "Considering how the Imperial stormtroopers usually make up in numbers what they lack in marksmanship—I'd say I've got the advantage."

A quick pair of bolts charred the rim of the table above Bossk's head, sending hot splinters across his shoulders. "You're forgetting something, bounty hunter." The same sneering tinge as before sounded in Voss'on't's words. "I may not have spent all the credits, but I spent enough of them. Enough to make sure there's plenty of surprises in store for someone like you."

"Yeah?" Bossk glanced at the weapon in his upraised hand, to be sure of its charge level. The indicator gauge showed that it held more than enough to disintegrate the entire structure of the watering hole, shot by shot, if necessary. "Like what?"

"Like this."

Those words confused Bossk for a moment. They seemed to be from Trhin Voss'on't's mouth, but much closer, as if the ex-stormtrooper had managed to sneak up right next to him. He turned away from the edge of the table and toward the unemployed colonial miner. His glance was just in time to see one of the huge shovellike hands come swinging down toward his skull.

Bossk's blaster went spinning across the floor of the watering hole as his shoulder knocked the table upside-down. Stunned nearly unconscious, Bossk barely felt his arms flop loosely across the wreckage of the shattered chairs, their sharp-ended pieces caught underneath his spine. His vision was just clear enough, even though tinged with swirling red at its limits, to see both Trhin Voss'on't and the anonymous miner looming over him.

"You see?" Voss'on't smiled down cruelly at him. One hand held a blaster pointed down at Bossk. With the other hand, the ex-stormtrooper reached over and lifted a miniaturized comm device that dangled on a cord beneath the wrinkled, fungoid breathing filter that masked the miner's face. The eyes obscured by the heavy goggles, two round lenses beneath the heavy brow ridge of the helmetlike skull, gazed dully ahead as Voss'on't triggered a matching device in his own free hand. "I spent the credits where they would do the most good." This time, Voss'on't's voice was picked up by a throat microphone, almost identical to the one Bossk had on, which then sounded from the tiny speaker of the device tethered to the hulking miner. "There isn't a single creature in this colony that isn't on my payroll. They're *all* looking out for me. I like it that way." He switched off the throat mike, and his voice came unamplified from his own mouth once again. "They're smart enough to work for me, but not to operate any kind of sophisticated communications gear, so I had to rig up a system that I could do a live transmit of my own voice; that way I could give them their orders personally. Plus it's great for little jokes like this one."

Upper-level stormtroopers had a reputation for gratuitous sadism; Bossk could see why now. He raised himself onto his elbows and gazed up sullenly at Voss'on't. "So what are you going to do with me?"

"Same thing I did with the others that came around here." Voss'on't let the blaster dangle loosely in his hand. "And that I'll do with all the others that think they're going to get rich from my hide." He motioned with the blaster to the miner standing across from him. "Stand this fool up."

The two big shovellike hands slipped under Bossk's arms and brought him unsteadily to his feet; the effects of the earlier head blow hadn't completely faded away. Bossk managed to remain standing as the miner let go of him and stepped back a pace.

Now Bossk found himself looking directly into the muzzle of Voss'on't's upraised blaster.

"All right, bounty hunter." Voss'on't's ugly smile showed behind the weapon's barrel sight. "Don't think I didn't give your little business proposition some serious thought. I did—but I'd already heard it from the last two bounty hunters that came through here." His thumb settled on the weapon's trigger stud. "And I'd already decided that I didn't need their services, either."

"Wait a minute—" With his vision still blurred, Bossk spread his hands apart. "We could still work something out—"

"*We* could," said Voss'on't. "But since you're leaving us right now—for good—who exactly am I supposed to be dealing with?" His hand tightened on the blaster's grip, thumb beginning its pressure on the trigger.

"How about dealing with me?"

Bossk figured that the blow from the miner must have knocked something loose inside his head. Those last words hadn't come from either himself or from Voss'on't.

And he recognized the voice that had spoken them. It was Boba Fett.

Squinting, Bossk managed to bring his sight into focus, well enough to see Trhin Voss'on't holding up his throat mike unit and looking at its tiny speaker in puzzlement. Fett's voice had come from there. "But that can't be," murmured Voss'on't. "That would mean—"

"Exactly." One word, cold and emotionless—but not from Voss'on't's throat mike unit. Boba Fett's voice, unamplified and real, came from behind Bossk. He saw Voss'on't look past him in surprise, just as one of the miner's broad shovel hands pushed him aside. Stumbling, almost falling to the watering hole's floor, Bossk saw the miner's other hand separate into its tapering durasteel fingers, like a bouquet of ancient military sabers. The fingers, each of them nearly a half meter in length, seized upon Voss'on't's hand and forearm. A single bolt, from the blaster trapped inside the miner's massive fist, lit up the open seams of the metal. Then Voss'on't's scarred face distorted with pain and rage, as the miner's hand turned, twisting and nearly pulling Voss'on't's arm from its socket. Voss'on't crumpled on top of the broken chair debris that lay scattered across the floor.

"Here." Fett's voice spoke again as the miner's

durasteel hand opened flat and held out the ex-stormtrooper's captured blaster. "Don't let him move."

Bossk grabbed the blaster and kept it aimed at Voss'on't, sprawled out before him. From the corner of his slit-pupiled eye, he watched as the miner disguise was shed in pieces, revealing Boba Fett beneath it. The first to go were the shovellike hand attachments; they fell to the floor with a doubled clang. Boba Fett's own hands, in the gloves of his distinctive Mandalorian battle armor, next unfastened and discarded the large, hunchbacked mass that had covered his shoulders; that allowed him to stand up straight, with his usual traveling arsenal visible at his back. His helmet, with its T-shaped visor mask, became visible as Fett peeled off the wrinkled, mossy breathing filters and oversized protective goggles that had concealed his identity. The bony mass of the miner's overdeveloped cranial shell followed the rest of the disguise, the hollowed-out bits and pieces strewn across each other as the side-mounted antenna on Boba Fett's helmet swiveled back into its usual position.

"So what was all that about?" Bossk's normal Trandoshan disposition had reasserted itself; he felt more irritated than relieved as he looked at his partner in this operation. "I thought you were still up above somewhere, out beyond the atmosphere, in *Slave I*."

"That's what I wanted our merchandise here to believe," said Boba Fett. "I knew he'd be monitoring our communications. With the equipment he was able to outfit himself with, there would have been no chance of masking or encrypting our relay. So I recorded and synthesized a few audio signals, static and the like, to patch in with my communications to you; that way, Voss'on't believed the same thing you did, that I was safely out of the area. But in fact, I was here the whole time, disguised as one of the former colonial miners that he had put on his payroll."

"I get you." Bossk nodded in appreciation of the strategy. "We needed to have him drop his defenses—and nothing does that like believing you've just bested one of your enemies." He knew the feeling, the glow that came with one of these victories over another sentient creature. The only thing better was the actual moment of a foe's death, when his carcass became a source for another grisly trophy in one's memory chamber. "And you already paid off the other miners?"

"Of course. I don't like bystanders interfering with my plans." Boba Fett's shoulders lifted in a slight shrug. "And loyalty that's been purchased once is always the cheapest to buy again."

"Nice plan." A surge of resentment suddenly mounted inside Bossk. "Except for one little thing—*partner*. You just about got me killed."

"Every plan has its risks." No apology was apparent in Boba Fett's voice. "You knew that from the beginning."

"Sure—but how come I'm the one that winds up taking them all?"

"You have nothing to complain about," said Fett. He had unholstered his own blaster pistol and now used it to point down toward the former Imperial stormtrooper. "We've got what we came here for."

"Think so?"

Another voice had spoken.

Bossk glanced quickly down at Voss'on't. The ex-stormtrooper's face was streaked with blood, his brow slashed open by the shovellike hand that had knocked him sprawling. Through the trailing red web, his gaze was both furious and somehow triumphant. Before the Trandoshan or Boba Fett could stop him, Voss'on't had torn aside the sleeve of his jacket, revealing a small control pad strapped by two bands to his forearm. There was only a single button on the pad, which Voss'on't jabbed his index finger down upon.

The watering hole—bar, what was left of the tables and chairs, the walls and ceilings—came apart like so much cheap plastoid. Bossk found himself tumbling backward in air, clawed hands scrabbling to catch hold of anything in this suddenly erupting world. The planet's sulphurous daylight poured through the crumbling pieces of the structure whose close spaces had been encircled around him only a fraction of a second ago.

His spine slammed hard into a sheet of durasteel. The vibrations of immense heavy machinery were as tangible as a seismic catastrophe, rumbling through his flesh and setting his bones jangling against each other. Before Bossk could tell where he was, what machinery he had landed upon, the durasteel tilted out from under him. He barely managed to catch hold of a row of bolt heads, his claws digging into a seam in the metal. More debris from what was left of the bar rained across his shoulders as he held on. A glimpse toward the revealed horizon showed more and more of the terrain at the foot of the craggy mountains, and Bossk realized that the machinery to which he clung was surging upward.

A voice sounded inside his head, from the cochlear implant. "Don't try to jump," came Boba Fett's voice. "These things will crush you like an insect."

Bossk pulled himself higher on the sloping metal flank, managing to get a better view of the grinding treads beneath him and the whirring cone at the machine's prow, studded with durasteel teeth. Each metal triangle was twice his own height, the total moving with a force capable of grinding his own ship *Hound's Tooth* to ragged shrapnel.

"What's going on?" Against the machinery's howling noise, Bossk shouted into his throat mike. "What is this thing?"

"Autonomic crust-piercer." Fett's voice snapped back the answer. "For deep-core mining operations—"

A shudder ran through the metal that Bossk's torso was pressed against. He clung with even more determination to the bolt heads and seam, aware that if he were to be shaken loose, he would slide straight into the massive, gear-driven treads only a few meters below him.

"Voss'on't must have wired it up," continued Boba Fett's voice, "for one more defense system. With a doomsday button, in case anybody did manage to get the drop on him."

"Where are you?" Bossk scanned across the land scape far below; the buildings of the abandoned Imperial mining colony looked like mere rounded bumps set into the barren, rocky ground. He could see a few figures of miners running on foot, trying to get out from beneath the shadow of the uprearing machine.

"Don't worry about me—"

"I'm not—" If Boba Fett's voice hadn't been implanted right inside his head, Bossk wouldn't have been able to hear him past the roar and howl of the crust-piercer.

"I managed to hit the ground," came Fett's voice. "Voss'on't has to be around here somewhere."

Bossk lifted his head from the durasteel and strained to look past the treads clanking beneath him. A churning cloud of dust obscured the ground below. Boba Fett was still hidden from view, but he caught a glimpse of another figure, one that he could recognize even at this elevated distance.

"Voss'on't!" Bossk shouted again into the mike at his throat. "I see him!" The crust-piercer's shadow gave a rough indicator of direction. "He's to the north! North of me—" Bossk had no idea of where Boba Fett might be in the dust cloud mounting below. "Toward the foothills and the colony gate!" For a moment, he lost sight of the tiny figure below, then spotted him again. "Now he's moving west—"

There was something else that Bossk could see, a glint of dark metal in Trhin Voss'on't's hand. At some point in the chaos that had followed the mining equipment bursting up from beneath the watering-hole, the ex-stormtrooper had managed to scoop up a blaster pistol.

"He's armed—"

The need for informing his partner of that fact was eliminated as Bossk saw Voss'on't crouch down, weapon arm raised, and fire a quick barrage of blaster bolts into the dust cloud before him.

"Fett?" Bossk called into his throat mike. "You still there?"

Nothing but silence came from the cochlear implant inside Bossk's head.

Well, thought Bossk, *guess I won't be splitting any bounties with him—*

The mining equipment to which Bossk clung, the enormous, clattering, and howling bulk of the crust-piercer, had reared up far enough from the planet's surface that it had become hard to see exactly what was going on down below him. Voss'on't had gone from being a doll-like figure to an insect. Bossk could just discern the ex-stormtrooper's movements as he stepped forward, blaster still poised and ready, to investigate his kill.

Two things happened then—

Voss'on't's tiny figure was suddenly knocked off

its feet as a propelled dart with line attached zipped out of the dust cloud. The line wrapped itself around Voss'on't in a microsecond, pinning his arms to his sides; sprawled on his back, the ex-stormtrooper kicked furiously, trying to stand up again. Boba Fett emerged from the dust cloud at the crust-piercer's base, lowering the dart weapon from its braced position against his shoulder. As Bossk watched from on high, his partner pulled the line tight with one gloved hand, jerking the furious Voss'on't over onto his face and away from the blaster pistol on the ground.

The second thing was that the crust-piercer finally emerged all the way from the planet's surface. Enough momentum had been built up in the machine's enormous mass, from the speed of the treads grinding up through the rocky substrata, that for a moment it separated from its shadow spilling across the ruins of the abandoned mining colony. The crust-piercer hung suspended a dozen meters or more above the ground, its gouging prow and propulsive gears spinning free of contact with any substance other than the air itself.

On the ground, Boba Fett turned his visored gaze away from his captive and up toward the durasteel construct, looming as big as a flying mountain range above him.

This is not good, Bossk told himself as he clung to the machinery's bolt-studded flank. *This is going to hurt—*

He felt himself going from a near-vertical position to lying prone, pinned by gravity, on the metal surface against his chest, as the crust-piercer lost the force of its momentum and tilted forward in the air. The machine's metal-toothed, conical snout was now parallel to the ground, with the treads directly beneath its mass, equivalent to that of a small Imperial fighting ship, but without the means to keep itself aloft.

Chewed-apart boulders, the last of the subsurface that the crust-piercer had ripped up and carried with itself, now tumbled away from its gears and shielding panels, spinning and raining across the shadowed area below.

That shadow suddenly loomed closer, as the crust-piercer began its fall, like a metallic stratosphere breaking apart and rushing toward the planet's core. Atop the machine, as though he were an ant stranded aboard a child's toy, Bossk braced for the impact.

He felt it, through every fiber and cell of his body. The grip of Bossk's claws was torn away from the bolt heads and the seam in the metal flank; a jutting projection of an auxiliary engine-exhaust pipe above kept him from flying completely off the immense machine. His outstretched forearms and torso struck flat against the metal, the blow knocking the wind from his lungs, dizzying and anaesthetizing him from the roar and fury of the crust-piercer's destruction of itself and whatever lay beneath it.

Bossk came to a second later, and wiped blood from his muzzle. Black smoke billowed upward into the sky, pouring from the crumpled and ripped-apart flanks of the crust-piercer. He ducked instinctively as muffled explosions sounded from deep within the machine, its shattered power sources igniting into flames and arcing, meteorlike sparks, dragging white trails behind them.

It's gonna blow, Bossk told himself. *Get going—*

Pushing himself up on his bruised hands, Bossk managed to scramble to the edge of the panel beneath him. The metal was slick with lubricating oil, bubbling and hissing with the heat from the explosions farther inside the machinery. He let himself fall, not caring what the distance to the ground was.

That turned out to be only a couple of meters;

flopped on his back, Bossk saw that the gears and treads of the crust-piercer's propulsive devices were buried three-quarters of their height into the ground. Loose dirt and gravel sifted toward him as the crust-piercer's mass lay at the bottom of the wide funnel-shaped depression into which the abandoned mining colony had been transformed. A few of the ruined buildings perched teetering on the rim of the bowl. *Hollow,* realized Bossk. *That's it.* The terrain beneath the mining colony had been tunneled out, as layer after layer of ore had been extracted and the shafts and underground quarries had been left empty. He would otherwise have been killed by the impact of the crust-piercer's landing, if it had struck solid ground, with no way of dissipating even part of the crushing force.

Bossk got to his feet and staggered toward the front of the machine, away from the fires and continuing small explosions in the power units toward its tail section. The weight of those had set the crust-piercer at a tilt, its conical prow, stilled now, rearing up and pointing toward the sky.

He stood still, his breath and pulse gradually slowing as he brushed away the bits of rock that had imbedded themselves in his scales. The acrid odors of flame and burning oil stung his flared nostrils. He was alone in what was left of the mining colony; whatever inhabitants had been left were probably still fleeing through the surrounding hills. And nothing could have survived being buried under that many tons of durasteel falling out of the skies . . .

Something moved underneath the prow of the crust-piercer, halfway between the rectangular plates of its treads. Rocks and dust shifted, sliding into a dark space below.

As Bossk watched, a gloved hand emerged, clawing its grip into the dirt. Then a forearm swathed in rags of battle gear, dragging the attached shoulder out into the light. A familiar helmet, even more dented and scraped than it had been before, showed its cracked T-shaped visor.

Bit by bit, as though rising from the grave, Boba Fett crawled out from beneath the smoldering wreckage.

When Fett was halfway out, Bossk recovered from his astonishment, enough to reach down and grab the other bounty hunter by the wrists, tugging him the rest of the way free and getting him to his feet.

"You okay?" Bossk peered into Boba Fett's dark visor.

Boba Fett didn't answer the question. "Come on." He pointed back to the scraped-out hole from which he had just emerged, with the bulk of the crust-piercer towering above it. "Voss'on't . . . he's right there. We have to get him out."

The job was made easier by the ex-stormtrooper being both motionless and still bound by the cord that Boba Fett's dart weapon had looped around him. Bossk backed up from the hole beneath the machinery, dragging Voss'on't with him. He stretched him out on the ground, a few meters away from the crust-piercer.

Fett knelt down and did a quick check of vital signs, then stood back up. "He's still alive." Fett glanced over at Bossk. "We've got our merchandise."

Exhausted, Bossk squatted onto his haunches. Beside him, Boba Fett managed to activate his comlink and signal his ship *Slave I* to descend and pick them up.

"I don't know . . ." Bossk slowly shook his head. Every breath hurt, and he was sure there were at least a few bones broken inside him. "I don't think I want to work with you anymore . . ."

12

When news comes from far away, it sometimes accumulates power on its journey. Like a tidal wave on the surface of an aquatic planet, that rolls uninterrupted and gathers greater and greater force in doing so, until it can wrench that world off its spinning axis—or sweep up on its curving face and then crush any leviathan creature smaller than itself.

Such dark, brooding meditations came easily to those of the Falleen species. Prince Xizor stood at the small viewport, gazing out at the stars and the emptiness in which they were held; the thumb and forefinger of one hand stroked the sharp angles of his chin as his thoughts progressed through their courses. He had already heard the news, the fulfillment of the next step in his intricately woven plans, before he had made the return journey to this place. Indeed, he had been expecting the news at any moment, as he had waited in the private quarters of his ship *Virago. Some things,* he mused, *are as certain as the galaxy's own slow rotation.* Many of his own actions and schemes were based upon a cold assessment of calculated risks; the most dangerous of those added a blood-stirring excitement to his life. To stake all upon the turn of a card, to use the most ancient gambler's metaphor—

everything, including the very life he savored at such moments—was the ultimate sport. But that was not the kind of lower-keyed satisfaction he derived from betting on a sure thing. And in this universe, as had been demonstrated over and over again, nothing seemed as certain as one Boba Fett, bounty hunter.

A sound of scrabbling claws and a slight motion caught the corner of Xizor's eye. He turned and saw one of Kud'ar Mub'at's subnodes, a little crablike thing tethered by a whitely glowing neurofilament to the web's communication fibers. "Yes?" Xizor raised an eyebrow as he regarded the semi-independent creature clinging to the wall in front of him. "What is it?"

The subnode's mouth, nearly humanoid in size, opened and emitted words. "Your presence is desired, my lord." Its voice was a squeaky approximation of its own master's. "In the main throne room and conference area."

"Very well." He gave a single nod of acknowledgment. "Tell Kud'ar Mub'at that I will be with him shortly."

Xizor let the subnode lead the way, through the cramped angles and turns of the web's internal corridors. The rough-textured walls, with their structural fibers of varying thicknesses compressed to a solid mass, were faintly illuminated by the phosphorescence of other subnodes dangling at intervals above, idiot creations of their assembler parent. They had no more intelligence than was sufficient to monitor the slow catalysis and decay of the light-producing compounds in the globular bodies, each barely larger than the span of Xizor's palm. When their glow had dwindled sufficiently, the instincts with which they had been designed and extruded would send them creeping back to Kud'ar Mub'at to be reingested by their creator. Xizor felt no pity for them; he shared the attitude that lesser creatures were for the service of their masters.

He ducked his head to make his way through one of the lower-ceilinged areas in the web. His broad, heavily muscled shoulders scraped against the matted walls on either side. Aboard the *Virago*, even the narrowest passageways were wider than he could have reached with his hands fully outstretched; his own personal quarters on the ship were as luxuriously appointed as the reception hall of many a planet-bound ruler's palace. It was a test of his will to voluntarily return to Kud'ar Mub'at's space-drifting web and enter its dank, claustrophobic spaces; only the prospect of successfully concluding some long-standing business schemes was enough to entice him anywhere near the arachnoid assembler and its scuttling, scurrying brood of subnodes.

"Ah, my most precious Xizor! Sunlight of my drab existence!" Kud'ar Mub'at perched on the pneumatic cushion of the subnode that served as its throne. The assembler's spike-haired forelimbs lifted and waved in a grotesque parody of a welcoming gesture. "How deeply embarrassed am I, to have kept one of your exquisite eminence waiting! Please accept my most humbly prostrated apologies—"

"No need for that." Xizor could already feel his own patience draining away inside himself. The assembler's flowery language always irritated him, suspecting as he did that every word that came from Kud'ar Mub'at's mouth was tinged with venomous sarcasm. He stood before the assembler, arms folded across his chest. "I was told upon my arrival here at your web that important news had just been received, and that was the reason for delaying our meeting." His vibroblade-sharp gaze took in Kud'ar Mub'at and the various subnodes clustered around it or perching on various limbs. "If the news had that kind of urgency for you . . . then I wonder if it could possibly have some bearing on *our* mutual interests."

All of the multiple eyes that studded Kud'ar Mub'at's face shifted uneasily for a moment, as if revealing the agile contortions of the mind that lay behind them. Then the assembler creaked out an unpleasantly high-pitched laugh. "Why is it, my so esteemed Prince Xizor, that you already know all about this news that I've just heard? Granted, your native intelligence is of a nature many awesome degrees above my own. But still . . . for you to acquire such information before me . . ." Kud'ar Mub'at shook one of the tiny subnodes from its forelimb, then used the exposed claw-point to scratch the tip of its chin. "How it *grieves* me to harbor suspicions against one so uniquely dear to me as yourself! The pain! Nevertheless—" Kud'ar Mub'at's two main eyes peered closer at its visitor. "I would hate to believe that your information-gathering sources, the great and efficient network of your Black Sun organization, had been monitoring developments in this little matter independently from my own favorite and trusted spies. That would tend to indicate—oh! The horror!—that you, dear prince Xizor, did not trust *me*."

"I trust you, all right." One corner of Xizor's mouth lifted in a grim smile. "There are some things that I can absolutely depend on to happen when I'm dealing with you. Given any opportunity, you will lie, cheat, embezzle, and in other ways seek to gain an advantage over a business partner. Withholding or changing a few important details about some matter in which we both have an interest—that would be one of the lesser offenses you would commit."

"Hm." The assembler appeared nettled; it turned its narrow face away from Xizor and spent some time fussing with its nestlike throne, poking and prodding it with its lower sets of limbs. The pneumatic subnode bore the assault with dull patience. "Very well; be that as it may." Kud'ar Mub'at finally settled its globular abdomen back into the nest beneath it. "If I'm to be criticized for being a business creature, and taking care of business the way I should—no more, no less— then I shall just have to accept that as my lot in this universe."

"Spare me," said Xizor. He didn't know which was worse, Kud'ar Mub'at's unctuous flattery or its occasional spasms of self-pity. "You've done all right by yourself." Xizor gestured with an upraised hand, indicating the matted fibers of this tight space and all the smaller ones beyond. "Consider the treasures you've accumulated."

"True . . ." Kud'ar Mub'at's beadlike eyes glittered as their gaze darted around the area. Here, just as throughout the web, the structure's fibers were intertwined with various bits and pieces of machinery and high-level comm gear, all of it filched and salvaged from various spacecraft that had been unfortunate enough to have fallen into the assembler's control—usually to pay off the owner's debts, the invariable cost of doing business with such a clever and avaricious creature. "I have so many *pretty* things . . . pretty and rare, and expensive as well . . ."

Idiot. Xizor didn't bother to conceal the sneer that showed on his face. Some of the scavenged gear in Kud'ar Mub'at's web worked—that was how the assembler managed to keep track of his many far-flung schemes on different worlds—but the rest were inert and useless. Useless, except to one of its solitary species; the assembler seemed to value the process of acquisition as much as the results. Constantly absorbing things, both dead and alive, into its network of self-generated neural fibers, making them as much a part of itself as the subnodes that it designed and extruded for its service—that was the sum of Kud'ar Mub'at's existence. Its complex schemes were woven for the same reason as the physical web that it squatted in, drifting past the stars and their circling worlds: because it had no other way of existing separate from the strands of that web and those schemes. It exuded both, the way other creatures breathed. Xizor glanced at the thickly matted strands near his shoulders; it struck him again that he was standing, almost literally, inside another creature's head, its thoughts having taken on an animated, tangible form. That realization filled him, as it always had before, with a subtle nausea.

"But," said Xizor aloud, "there are so many more things you'd like to have. And *that* is why we're in business together."

"Exactly so, my dear Xizor." Kud'ar Mub'at's face split into a jagged grin. "Forgive me for ever having doubted your so deeply held distrust and low opinion of me. Be assured: it's mutual."

"Then let's get down to it. Now that you've heard what I already know. There's hard merchandise on its way here. Boba Fett has captured Trhin Voss'on't."

"Did we anticipate anything else?" Kud'ar Mub'at imitated a humanoid shrug with the rising of a pair of forelimbs. "Boba Fett never fails. That was why we made him an integral part of our plans. If Fett goes out after a bounty, he always collects. And a bounty such as the one that the Emperor offered for Voss'on't . . . well . . ." Another shrug, slightly less exaggerated. "It was a certainty that he would go after it."

"As would every other bounty hunter in the galaxy," Xizor pointed out. "That was the other part—the other *predictable* part—of the scheme. Even as we speak, the other bounty hunters—the few that are left of them—are still at each other's throats, back-stabbing and conspiring against one another. The news has not reached them yet that the inspiration for all their unbridled greed is already in the hands of Boba Fett. By the time the other bounty hunters learn that Trhin Voss'on't has been captured, it will be too late for them to escape the consequences of their actions. There are no longer two factions of bounty hunters—the True Guild and the Guild Reform Committee are finished. Avarice has the power to accomplish such things, to turn one creature against another, who a moment before had been calling themselves family." The savoring of that accomplished fact was like a rich, intoxicating liquor on Xizor's tongue. He had always despised the tendency of lesser creatures to form themselves into would-be protective groups, whether it was the old, vanished Bounty Hunters Guild or this new Rebel Alliance that was enjoying its brief moment in the sun. "There was a time," continued Xizor, "when these bounty hunters had considered themselves bound by their so-called 'Hunters' Creed,' as if that little pact would have been enough to keep their enmity for each other in check. Well, that precious fiction is gone at last—and good riddance. There may be a few left who give it lip service, but the rest have discovered the truth about themselves and each other."

"Indeed they have." Kud'ar Mub'at nodded his triangular head in agreement. "So excellent and foresighted was your scheme, my dear Xizor! I congratulate you on its success—not that it was ever in doubt, of course. Between you and Boba Fett, how could it have turned out otherwise?"

Xizor ignored the assembler's flattery. It was superfluous, at any rate; he had set out to destroy the old

Bounty Hunters Guild, and had done so. Boba Fett had been no more than the tool in his hand, as sharply efficient as a sculptor's honed chisel. The first blow had been enough to divide the Guild into two rival factions; this final one had smashed those into their constituent atoms. There wouldn't be very many of those left alive, by the time the process had reached its end; bounty hunting was a ruthlessly competitive trade, one in which the best way to assure one's survival was to eliminate as many of the others in it before they had a chance to eliminate you. However stodgy and inefficient the old Guild had been, it had at least managed to hold down the level of mayhem among the individual bounty hunters. Now, without even the two remnant splinter organizations around, it was open season in the trade. The corpses were already starting to pile up. Of course, that was also to Prince Xizor's liking: only the toughest and most capable bounty hunters would survive such a winnowing-out of their numbers, and the skills of those would be even sharper and more enhanced by it. Perhaps there would never be another bounty hunter the equal of Boba Fett; so be it. But now there would be others, harder and more murderous in their quick, bright, lethal grace. They would be perfect, not just for the uses of Palpatine's Empire, but also for that of the darker empire that lay in its shadows, which was so fittingly known as the Black Sun.

"Yes," said Xizor, nodding slowly. "It could have been no other way. Even if we had not made sure of the outcome ourselves."

The assembler emitted a harsh, cackling laugh that was taken up and echoed by the piping voices of the subnodes clustered around it. "Poor Boba Fett!" Overcome by its hideous glee, Kud'ar Mub'at waved its forelimbs. "Think of how much trouble he might have saved for himself, if he had known that Trhin Voss'on't, the supposedly renegade stormtrooper, was acting on Palpatine's direct orders the whole time!"

As much as he admired Boba Fett, Xizor couldn't help feeling a certain pleasure at having hoodwinked the famous bounty hunter. And it had been accomplished just as Kud'ar Mub'at had said.

The whole thing had been a setup, and *all* the bounty hunters had fallen for it. Xizor knew that that had been a major part of the attraction for Emperor Palpatine—and why he had agreed to the subterfuge, as long as Xizor had put up the bounty stake from his own personal fortune. Far from being a renegade and a traitor, Trhin Voss'on't was actually one of the Emperor's most loyal soldiers; loyal enough—and obedient enough—that he had been willing to follow orders that resulted at least temporarily in the blackening of his reputation among the ranks of his fellow Imperial stormtroopers. And more than that: to fully establish his cover story of being a renegade, ruthlessly following his own personal agenda, the others involved in the hijacking of the Imperial ship had to be killed, and by Voss'on't's own hand. Those orders he had carried out with no hesitation as well. The stolen codes had been a minor issue compared to that; before the plan had even gotten under way, measures to eliminate the damage caused by the sale of the obsolete data had already been in place. Just as Xizor had anticipated, the final result of his preparations was a perfect enticement to the greed of the individual bounty hunters, and more than enough to dissolve the two remaining factions into which the old Guild had splintered.

That final collapse into every-creature-for-itself anarchy, the remnants of the old Bounty Hunters Guild disintegrating into nothing but memories, had been a result that Emperor Palpatine had been glad to hear of. Before coming here to Kud'ar Mub'at's drifting web, Xizor had had another meeting with the Emperor in his throne room on the planet Coruscant, and had received the Emperor's congratulations on a job well done. All the while, the holographic image of Lord Darth Vader had fumed in silence, unable to make any protest without risking either the Emperor's mockery or his wrath—or both. Xizor had savored the moment of triumph, even while aware that whatever enmity Vader had previously borne him, it was now multiplied many times over. The only thing worse than failing in a contest of wills between oneself and the Dark Lord of the Sith was to win out over him. Vader did not take the humiliation of defeat lightly.

There will be consequences, Xizor assured himself. The day of reckoning between himself and Vader had only been postponed. When it came, only one of them would be alive afterward.

He would be prepared for that confrontation. Xizor knew that he was in an even stronger position than he had been before.

Now, Xizor mused, *Palpatine thinks he's gotten what he wanted.* A tougher, harder breed of mercenary bounty hunters, all of them ready to do the Empire's dirty work, for a price. And without the old Guild keeping them noncompetitive, and fat and lazy. *That's good for the Empire,* Xizor nodded slowly to himself. *It's even better for Black Sun.*

"You've done well for yourself, my dear Xizor." Nestled before him, Kud'ar Mub'at had discerned the course of Xizor's silent thoughts. "You've more than proved your value to Palpatine. That will stand you in good stead in the future, with all the rest of your plans and schemes. The Emperor's favor will shine down upon you like the warming sunlight of a tropical world. He's known for rewarding cleverness . . . and loyalty."

"Not as much as you might think," replied Xizor. "I have no illusions in that regard. The Emperor will keep me at his right hand as long as he considers me to be a valuable instrument of his will. If anything should happen to dispel that sense of value, then I will be just that much closer to him, so that he—or Darth Vader—can crush the breath from my throat."

"Needless worries; needless, I say." Kud'ar Mub'at bestowed its jagged smile on the web's guest. "Whatever obstacles are arrayed before you, in your traversal of the maze that is Emperor Palpatine's court, I'm sure you'll negotiate them with your usual and commendable alacrity."

Xizor returned the smile. "I'm sure I will, as well." He tilted his head in a mocking half bow toward the assembler. "How can I fail to, with an accomplice such as yourself on my side?"

"Ah! How sweet of you to say so! Then may I take it that all issues of distrust between ourselves are dispelled?"

"Of course not, you idiot." Xizor shook his head in disgust. "The day I trust a creature such as yourself will be the day I sign my own death warrant. But enough of that—let's get down to business."

"Whatever," sulked Kud'ar Mub'at. "As you wish." It gestured with the tip of one forelimb. "Please proceed."

"It's one thing to congratulate ourselves on having achieved the objective of our plans, the total disintegration of the Bounty Hunters Guild. If you wish to bask in the warm glow that comes with such an accomplishment, then do it when you're by yourself, Kud'ar Mub'at." Voice turning harder, Xizor leaned toward the assembler. "But right now, there's plenty of work left to be done, if we're to enjoy the results of our schemes. One doesn't put plans such as these into motion, without creating certain—shall we say?— *messes* that need to be cleaned up."

"Indeed." Kud'ar Mub'at nodded judiciously. "It is exactly as you say, my dear Xizor. We have brought some participants into these intrigues, who might not be exactly pleased to find out the role they've been un- wittingly forced to play."

That much was true; Xizor had already admitted as much to himself. "The stormtrooper is not much of a problem," said Xizor. "The fact that Trhin Voss'on't carried out the orders that he was given, and played his part in this little masquerade, indicates a certain naiveté on his part. That's often the case with these military types; they're trained to trust their superiors. The Impe- rial stormtroopers could not survive if they allowed any doubt within their ranks. And in Voss'on't's case, he was promised a great deal in addition, if he played his role well."

"Really?" The assembler tilted its head to one side. "What exactly did Emperor Palpatine promise Voss'on't?"

"Retirement." Prince Xizor shrugged. "A mod- est pension, based upon his years of service in the stormtroopers. You have to remember, very few of their number live long enough to enjoy those things. Given what they have to go through, and what they have to do along the way, a little peace and quiet is all they want for their last days."

"How touching. And what will Trhin Voss'on't receive instead?"

"Leave that to me," said Xizor coldly. He bore the stormtrooper no ill will; whatever happened to Voss'on't now was a matter of simple necessity. Voss'on't had become a loose end, something that had to be cleaned up and disposed of—before he could create any embarrassment for those who had devised the scheme in which he had played so vital a part. Old soldiers tended to talk about their adventures. A few indiscreet details leaking out, concerning how other stormtroopers had been duped and killed, would have serious impact on the morale of those still serving in the Emperor's forces. The Rebel Alliance could use that kind of information as a way of encouraging mass defections, merely by offering any survival-minded stormtroopers a safe haven out of the reach of their commanding officers and their murderous Emperor. For that reason alone, Trhin Voss'on't was not going to receive the peaceful retirement that had been promised to him; he knew too much. Xizor had already assured the Emperor that Voss'on't would be taken care of—permanently.

"And what about Boba Fett?" A note of amusement sounded in Kud'ar Mub'at's voice. "Wrapping up that particular loose end might be just a little more difficult. He is, after all, not quite the same sort of trusting individual as Trhin Voss'on't."

"That's my problem. And I'll take care of it." Xizor had already given the matter its due consideration. Unfortunately, for both himself and Boba Fett, the only possible solution was the same one that would be applied in the stormtrooper Voss'on't's case. Xizor made it a general rule of business never to create a situation where someone else had an advantage over him. *Only a fool,* he had long ago decided, *hands a weapon over to a potential enemy.* It was just as foolish to leave a weapon lying where an enemy might find it and pick it up. And in the universe he lived and operated in, everybody was an enemy, sooner or later—it was just safer to make that assumption from the beginning.

Boba Fett had one of the most carefully groomed networks of information sources in the galaxy; that was a big part of his success as a bounty hunter. It was only reasonable to expect that some of those sources might be located in the ranks of Black Sun itself. Fett might not know it now, but the truth might be discovered at any moment: that it had been Prince Xizor who had instigated the Bounty Hunters Guild's destruction. To allow even the possibility of Boba Fett, with his devious mind and appetite for gain, acquiring such a damaging piece of information to hold over him—that would be madness. Even if he then eliminated Boba Fett, the problem remained of all the others who might have learned the truth from him. Too many creatures would bear Xizor a grudge then; even if he managed to evade every bounty hunter who had some remaining vestige of loyalty to the old organization, to do so would endlessly complicate his existence. And it would only take one of them, with a stroke of luck, and all his plans for Black Sun would expire along with his own life.

No, thought Xizor. The decision had already been made. Fett's silence and the bounty hunter's death were one and the same thing. And too valuable not to bring about.

"I'm entirely confident," purred Kud'ar Mub'at, "that it will be taken care of, and in your usual efficacious manner. Of that I have no doubt, my dear Xizor. The only question is when. I prefer to sleep soundly here in my humble web, safe among my treasures, my dreams undisturbed by the awareness of bounty hunters with a grievance against me. My only wish is to coexist with my fellow creatures of the galaxy in as harmonious a manner as possible. The thought of Boba Fett, still on the loose somewhere, and bearing uncharitable thoughts toward me—that would impinge itself most ungraciously upon my slumbers."

"Don't worry," said Xizor grimly. He had already made his decision about that part of the matter as well. When there were messes to be cleaned up, they had to be taken care of, right down to the tiniest detail—or the potentially most valuable. The bounty hunter Boba Fett would undoubtedly have had his uses in the future, for both the Empire and for Black Sun; in some ways, Fett was one of the most irreplaceable creatures in the galaxy, with a necessary function to serve, as long as one had the means to pay for it.

Plus, Xizor had to admit to himself, he felt a certain admiration for the hunter. Boba Fett's efficiency and ruthlessness were truly inspirational qualities, which Xizor had pointed out to his underlings in Black Sun on many occasions as models worthy of their emulation. The galaxy would be a kinder, gentler place with Boba Fett removed from it—the notion filled Prince Xizor with disgust.

How paradoxical, he mused, *that ruthlessness requires that the most ruthless be exterminated.* Still, if it came down to a choice between his own survival and that of Boba Fett, then the bounty hunter was already history.

"I am," sighed Kud'ar Mub'at, "a creature given to worry. It's my nature." The assembler gestured with his forelimbs toward the subnodes clustered around it. "I have so many responsibilities. That's why I'm forced to admit that I have grave concerns about your plans for 'taking care' of Boba Fett. Others have tried to 'take care' of him in the past, and things did not turn out well for those improvident creatures."

"That's the difference between them and me.

When I take care of something, it remains that way. Don't forget: I have the resources of not only the Empire, but Black Sun behind me as well. Boba Fett has never come up against a combination such as that. To prevail against a lot of slobbering Hutts and similar creatures, with their shabby, insignificant networks and spheres of influence, is one thing, to survive against the forces I command is quite another."

"Your confidence, my dear Xizor, is so powerful as to evoke awe in one such as myself."

"It should be." The Falleen prince reached over to the edge of his cape and drew it across his chest. He was ready to leave the web now, to make sure of his other preparations. "Your only true concern, Kud'ar Mub'at, is playing out your own role in this last stage of our plans."

The assembler drew back on its pneumatic nest. "My thespic skills are so dreadfully limited . . ."

"You've done all right so far," said Xizor. "It was your expert lying that got Boba Fett involved in the scheme against the Bounty Hunters Guild in the first place. He fell for it then, as he had no reason to disbelieve you. Similarly, he has no reason for distrust now. Fett has in his possession certain hard merchandise, as he and the other bounty hunters like to refer to their captives; namely, one Trhin Voss'on't, assumed to be a renegade Imperial stormtrooper. You, the assembler Kud'ar Mub'at, are holding in escrow the bounty payment for the delivery of that merchandise." Xizor glanced up toward one of the larger subnodes that held on to the fibrous wall near Kud'ar Mub'at. "Is that not so?"

"That is a true and verified statement," replied the subnode called Balancesheet, "regarding certain credit funds now on deposit in this web. The entire amount of the bounty for the Imperial stormtrooper Voss'on't is at this moment in our possession. Just as you say, Prince Xizor."

"And *that* is precisely something I'm nervous about." The subnode's creator fidgeted in its nest. "That is a considerable amount of credits for me to be sitting on; perhaps the largest amount that's ever been here at one time in my web. I've always considered it to be a prudent policy to shift my financial assets into reputable planetary banking establishments, within the controlled boundaries of the Empire. Otherwise I'm just too much of a target, out here alone in empty space."

"Nobody would ever rob you, Kud'ar Mub'at; your go-between and escrow services are too valuable for too many creatures. Besides, I've stationed my own *Virago* close at hand, along with several other craft from Black Sun's operational fleet. Their firepower should be more than enough protection for you, until the bounty is safely out of your hands."

"That may be . . ." Kud'ar Mub'at didn't appear entirely satisfied with the answer. "But is it enough to protect me from Boba Fett?"

"Leave the bounty hunter to me," said Xizor. "All you have to do is play your part. For someone to whom lying comes so easily, it should not be a task to strain your capabilities."

He turned away, having had more than his fill of the assembler's protests. As he headed down the shoulder-cramping space of the web's central corridor, Xizor could hear the assembler sputtering and fussing behind him.

A short time later, another voice spoke to Xizor as he waited in the web's docking area for the small shuttle vessel that would return him to the *Virago*.

"Excuse me—" The small voice spoke from close by Xizor's head. "I wonder if I might have a word with you. Just by ourselves . . ."

Xizor glanced beside himself and spotted the accountant subnode Balancesheet, dangling upside down from the matted ceiling of the area. "What do you want?"

"As I said." The subnode's voice was a carefully modulated whisper. "A word with you. On subjects that would be of mutual—and profitable—interest to us."

"Profitable to your master Kud'ar Mub'at as well." Xizor shook his head. "I'm familiar enough with how the assembler's web is constructed. Everything here is spun directly from Kud'ar Mub'at's own neural tissue." Looking into Balancesheet's bright beadlike eyes, Xizor knew that he might as well be looking straight into the assembler's sharp, avid gaze. Why Kud'ar Mub'at was going through this pretense, sending one of his semi-independent nodes after him like this, was beyond comprehension. *Does he think I'm so easily fooled?* "I've already said to him all that I care to for the moment."

"I think you have misapprehended the situation," said Balancesheet evenly. "As well as exactly whom you're talking to." Upside down, the subnode crept a little closer to Xizor. One of its tiny claws held up a glistening white strand of neurofiber. The strand was broken, connected only to Balancesheet but not to the structure of the web. "You see? I'm an independent agent now. When you talk to me, Kud'ar Mub'at knows nothing of it. Unless I want Kud'ar Mub'at to know."

Xizor regarded the subnode with suspicion. "You've managed to unplug yourself from the web? That's very ingenious of you—but how is it that

Kud'ar Mub'at is not aware of one of his valuable subnodes having separated itself from the larger organism?"

"Simple." Balancesheet reached over and picked up another, larger strand of fiber that led directly into the intricately knotted structure surrounding them. At this fiber's tip was another subnode, smaller and with claws almost too delicate to be seen. "Kud'ar Mub'at is not the only one here who can create subnodes; I have mastered the art as well. This is one of mine." Balancesheet held the tiny, tethered organism out for Xizor's inspection. "Its only function is to masquerade as me, to send neuro-signals into the web that falsely indicate that I'm still attached and subservient to Kud'ar Mub'at. Trust me; the old assembler has not the slightest clue as to any of this."

"Indeed." Xizor was impressed, both with the subnode's ingenuity—and the possibilities it presented. Kud'ar Mub'at had been getting on his nerves for a long time now. Perhaps the assembler's usefulness was already coming to an end. "You're right about one thing . . . ."

"And what is that?" Balancesheet's bright, round eyes peered into Xizor's gaze.

"We do have a lot to talk about."

13

He couldn't stop thinking about the bounty hunter.

Kuat of Kuat knew that he was wasting time; the past was the past, and couldn't be altered. *There are messes that must be cleaned up,* he told himself as he gazed out at the Kuat Drive Yards construction docks. That cleaning-up process had to happen now, in real time; the longer it was delayed, the more grievous the consequences would be. Everything that he had worked to achieve, that the Kuat bloodline had built this corporation into, might yet be wiped away by the forces that conspired against him.

He knew all these things, they weighed upon his spirit with the grinding mass of planets, yet he still found his thought returning, as though pulled by some even greater gravitational force, to the bounty hunter Boba Fett, and all that had happened in the past.

Fett was the key to it all. The key to what had happened then, and what must happen now if Kuat Drive Yards was to be saved.

There were things that all the galaxy knew about that past, the story that had grown to almost legendary proportions, about the breakup of the old Bounty Hunters Guild and the things that had come about after that. The capture of the renegade Imperial stormtrooper Trhin Voss'on't, and what had happened when Boba Fett had gone to collect the bounty for him . . .

Those matters were public knowledge. Or at least some of them were.

And other ones were secrets, locked inside the skull of Kuat of Kuat. He had to make sure they remained secret.

If doing so demanded the death of other creatures—specifically, Boba Fett—then that was a regrettable necessity. Business was business.

He would agree with me about that, thought Kuat as his gaze lifted to the cold stars above the docks. Boba Fett would hardly be able to blame him for taking care of business in as efficient—and deadly—a manner as was needed.

Kuat turned away from the high, segmented viewscreens. It irked him that there was so much that had to be dealt with, as soon as possible, and yet he still had to bother with distractions such as a summons to a convocation of the planet Kuat's ruling households. With a burden-laden sigh, he lifted the heavy robes from the carved stand upon which they hung between such events.

So simple a matter, and he was transformed.

All it took was for Kuat of Kuat to don the formal robes, the garb that signified his position at the head of the noble families of this world. He so rarely left the headquarters of the Kuat Drive Yards and his austere suite of offices looking out over the construction docks that his simple coveralls had become his unconscious preference. The same as that which the corporation's engineering and security staff wore, with no signs of rank attached to them; if those beneath him obeyed his orders, it was because they knew he had earned authority through more than just genetic inheritance.

Even the felinx, the silky-haired creature that he cradled in his arms, had trouble recognizing him in the robes, with their sweep of intricate, golden-threaded embroidery falling from his shoulders. Kuat of Kuat, the master of one of the most powerful corporations in the galaxy, had had to kneel beside his lab bench and coax the animal out with soothing, enticing words. *Poor thing,* thought Kuat as he stroked the special place behind its ears; a purr of induced bliss sounded from deep in its throat. As with all the members of its decorative, pampered species, the felinx believed itself to be the master of this domain; it took interruptions to its expected schedule with an ill grace.

As do I. Kuat of Kuat had carried the animal to the office suite's arching, segmented viewscreens; he gazed out at the ships being built or readied for launch, massive commissions for the Imperial Navy of Palpatine. Enough weaponry studded the hulls to intimidate all but the most foolhardy of foes; the laser cannons being mounted into the open skeletal frames required bracing and recoil-dissipation casings that would have withstood explosions measured in the giga-tonnage range. Anything less, and a single shot fired in battle would rip a destroyer or battle cruiser in two, a victim of its own lethal strength. The contemplation of such an event brought a wry grimace of self-recognition to Kuat's face.

"We must always be careful," he whispered into the felinx's feathery ear, "not to blow ourselves up with our own weapons."

The felinx stirred drowsily in Kuat's arms. As far as it was concerned, all of its plans had succeeded admirably; it was fed, warm, and content. Kuat wished that he could feel the same about all his schemes and machinations. Even now, forces that he had set into motion were circling about him and the Kuat Drive Yards, like the iron teeth of some invisible trap, greater than the worlds and corporations it seized upon.

He heard the tall doors of the office suite open; without disturbing the felinx, Kuat glanced over his shoulder. "Yes?"

The head of security for Kuat Drive Yards stood in the angle of light from the corridor outside. "Your personal transport is ready." As with all of the corporation's staff, Fenald spoke without elaborate formalities. "To take you to the gathering of families."

"I don't need to be reminded," said Kuat, "about where I'm going." The assembly of the planet Kuat's ruling households was the reason for his having donned the formal robes. And for his bad temper. "I'm sorry—" The security head was one of his most valued staff, and had done nothing to merit sharp language. "But this is all coming at a very inconvenient time."

That was an understatement. Even if all Kuat of Kuat had to worry about was the stepped-up pace of construction at Kuat Drive Yards, the constant pressure from Emperor Palpatine to supply the Imperial Navy with the ships needed to crush the burgeoning Rebellion, he would have had more than enough on his mind. But with those other concerns, some of which were secrets that he alone bore the weight of on his shoulders . . . it was a crushing burden.

Or to be more exact, it would have been a crushing burden for almost any other sentient creature. Kuat of Kuat closed his eyes, his fingertips automatically

stroking the felinx's fur. If he was not as other creatures were, it was because he had been born this way,
the hereditary chief executive of Kuat Drive Yards; the
blood flowed in his veins of the other engineers and
leaders who had preceded him. All that he had done,
the schemes that he had devised, had been for the sake
of the corporation. There were so many in this galaxy
who sought the destruction of Kuat Drive Yards, who
wished to disassemble it into bits or swallow it whole.
The corporation's own best customer, Emperor Palpatine himself—and Palpatine's chief henchman, Lord
Vader—were among that number. Kuat Drive Yards
had had at least a few friends among the leaders of the
old Republic; those had been swept away in the
course of Palpatine's rise to absolute power. Now
everything, the very survival of the corporation, depended upon the wits and courage of those who shep-
herded it.

And now, with all that going on, to have the ruling
households getting on his case . . .

"No apology necessary." The security head
showed a wry smile. "When, if ever, would there have
been a convenient time to deal with them?"

"You're got a point there," admitted Kuat. The
felinx protested as he peeled it away from his chest
and deposited it in a fleece-lined basket near the work-
bench. With its tail huffily erect, the animal jumped
from its bed and went stalking for its food dish. Kuat
brushed away the silken hairs it had left on the front
of his robes. "All right," he said wearily. "Let's get
this over with."

Fenald closed the office suite's door behind them,
then followed Kuat toward the docking area. "I've
gotten as much advance information on the meeting
as I could." Among his other duties, Fenald was in

charge of surveillance—or in blunter terms, spying—upon the planet's ruling households. "From all indications, it appears that the Knylenn Elder will be there. In person."

"That old fool?" Kuat shook his head as he walked. The Elder had always been his chief opponent in the households' deliberative council. Of all the families, the Knylenns had fought hardest—and over centuries and generations—against the Inheritance Exemption by which the Kuat line maintained its hold over Kuat Drive Yards. "I'm surprised they managed to pry him out of his life-support systems."

"The younger members of the family are using the Elder as a front. So they had a new portable life-support system designed and built, just so the Elder could come to an emergency meeting like this." The security head raised an eyebrow. "A *very* expensive system, too; it apparently has several redundant layers of first-degree droid intelligence built in, with constant real-time monitoring of all bodily functions. And get this: it even has cryo-storage of all-important organs, with total immune-reaction suppression at the cellular level, ready to go at any sign of cardiopulmonary or renal-hepatitic failure. The Elder could be getting a heart transplant as you were talking to him, and you wouldn't even know it except for the little blinking lights on the front of the unit."

"Charming," said Kuat. "Of course, that presupposes that he started out with one inside him." He could see the docking area attendants up ahead, standing by the open hatchway of his personal transport. "Who else is going to be there?"

"The usual cabal—all of the Knylenns, their *tel-buns* and their affiliates; the Kuhlvult clan and their morganic allegiances; probably a good deal of the Kadnessi."

Kuat stopped in the middle of the corridor and looked at his security head. "That's more than the usual."

The security head nodded in agreement. "This is the big one, Technician. The Knylenns have been trying to overturn the Inheritance Exemption since before your grandfather ran this corporation. They've called in all the favors that any of the other ruling households might owe them—because they think they can do it now."

"Maybe they can." Kuat paused beside the transport's hatchway as the attendants drew back. "Maybe I should let them. Then dealing with the Empire and all the rest would be someone else's problem." He pulled the formal robes tighter around himself to facilitate getting into the tight passenger space of the transport. He looked over at Fenald. "What do you think?"

"That would be your decision to make." Standing with hands clasped behind his back, the other man gave a single nod. "But it would be the end of Kuat Drive Yards as an independent corporation. No one else in the ruling families has the ability—or the courage—to stand up to Palpatine."

"I sometimes think," said Kuat, "that courage is simply another name for foolhardiness." Gathering up the broad and inconvenient hem of the robes, he stepped into the transport. "I'm old and tired—or at least that's the way I feel, so it might as well be true." He had to duck his head down to look back at the figure standing outside the hatchway. "Perhaps instead of going and dealing with these tiresome creatures, I should pilot this ship straight to Coruscant. I could make a deal with Palpatine: if I give in now and just let him take over Kuat Drive Yards, I'd save him a lot of trouble. Perhaps in gratitude, he'd pension me off with enough credits to eke out a comfortable existence on some obscure planet."

"It's more likely, Technician, that once Emperor Palpatine has what he wants from you, that he would simply have you eliminated."

Kuat managed a grim half-smile. "I believe you're right." He settled into the transport's two-person passenger area. "So I don't have any choice then, do I, about going and dealing with the Knylenns and all the rest of the ruling households?"

"No," replied Fenald. "You don't."

"Then," said Kuat, "my duties and my actions are one and the same." He turned toward the transport again.

Fenald laid a restraining hand on Kuat's forearm. "However, Technician, you are not obliged to face this particular duty by yourself."

Kuat looked back at his head of security. "What do you mean?"

"It's madness for you to go there alone. The Knylenns and the others are obviously planning some unpleasant surprise for you. You'll need all the help you can get."

"Perhaps so. But that doesn't mean I can have it."

"I hope you'll forgive any rashness on my part, Technician. But I took the initiative of contacting the Master of Etiquette for the ruling households." Fenald gave a slight nod as he withdrew his hand from the sleeve of Kuat's formal robes. "And he gave a different ruling on that point of protocol. Since the Knylenns are bringing their *telbuns* to this gathering, the normal restrictions do not apply. Under the ancestral household code, the *telbuns* are technically outsiders; not quite true family members. So to maintain strict reciprocity, the household of Kuat is thereby permitted to bring in an outsider as well."

"I see." Kuat mulled over the information. "And your suggestion is that you should accompany me."

"More than a suggestion. It is, Technician, my most urgent advice."

Kuat peered closer at the security head. "Why are you so concerned about coming to this gathering? The ruling households of Kuat are hardly an entertaining crowd."

"As I said before—they're up to something."

"And what is your evidence—your hard evidence—for that suspicion?"

Fenald was silent for a moment before answering. "No evidence," he said quietly, "other than what I feel in my gut."

The security head's reply disturbed Kuat. Fenald had never before been one to act upon anything except facts as cold and hard as the durasteel employed in the Kuat Drive Yards construction docks. But still . . .

"All right," said Kuat. He pointed toward the hatchway of the personal transport. "We'd better be on our way. They'll be waiting for us."

A few Standard Time Parts later, the pilot of the personal transport was skimming the craft over the densely forested land masses of the planet Kuat. For Kuat of Kuat, looking out at the green organic material was less pleasing than contemplating the hard, cold shapes of laser-welded durasteel in the Kuat Drive Yards construction docks.

One of the junior members of the Kuhlvult clan, barely having achieved adult status, had come out to meet Kuat's personal transport. "There are those among us," said Kodir of Kuhlvult, "who will be glad to see you." Her movements in the formal robes, as she led the way to the ruling households' gathering hall, were more graceful than Kuat's could ever have been. "Not everyone is happy with the Knylenns' agenda for this meeting."

"Really?" As he walked beside her, Kuat searched the young woman's face for some clue as to her intent. "And why would that be?"

Kodir's smile was more sly than friendly. "We know how the Kuat household runs Kuat Drive Yards; your family has kept this world one of the richest in the galaxy for generations. It did so under the old Republic, and it continues to do so under Emperor Palpatine. Such skill deserves its own reward; that was why the Inheritance Exemption was passed by the other households so long ago." She tilted her head, eyes lowered in respect. "And that is why some of us would wish to keep it that way."

In silence, Kuat walked on beside the young woman; his head of security trailed a few steps behind. *The Exemption,* mused Kuat. *That's what it all comes down to.* It had, for a long time.

The wise among the ruling households, as Kodir of Kuhlvult had indicated, wished to keep the Inheritance Exemption. The ambitious, such as the Knylenns, wished to eliminate it; the Exemption was what kept them from achieving supremacy among all the ruling households, and from taking control of Kuat Drive Yards, this world's preeminent source of wealth.

Alone among the planet Kuat's ruling households, the lineage of the Kuat family was the only one that was passed down from parent to child by direct genetic inheritance; that was the sole intent and effect of the Exemption. For all the other households, a strict disruption in the genetic chain prevailed: the heirs of the ruling households were not the children of the current adult members, but rather of the *telbuns* that were chosen to perpetuate the line. Unfortunately, such an arrangement had begun to show its faults when *telbuns,* chosen more for their physical beauty rather than the high intelligence and other favorable genetic factors that would produce the engineering and corporate leadership skills needed to run Kuat Drive Yards, had threatened to take the corporation into bankruptcy through their incompetence. Thus the Inheritance Exemption that effectively kept the Kuat bloodline, with its innate tendencies necessary for the success of the business, in charge. The Inheritance Exemption, as Kuat of Kuat well knew, had the additional benefit of checking the viciously squabbling ambitions of the ruling households, and keeping any of the world's nobles from conspiring and murdering to place an actual son or daughter at the head of Kuat Drive Yards.

If only, thought Kuat of Kuat, *that was the end of the matter. And the end of ambition and conspiracy.* It hadn't been; the Knylenns had long chafed under the limit that had been placed on their household's ability to rise to the absolute top of their world's power structure. The Knylenns had been the most aggressive about circumventing the restrictions, by choosing their *telbuns* from a limited pool of candidates. Rumors abounded in the other households that some of the Knylenn *telbuns* were in fact the children of the already existing Knylenn adults, born in secret offworld locations and smuggled back to the planet Kuat, infant princes in disguise. Certainly, over the last few generations, the physical resemblance between the Knylenns and their appointed heirs had grown suspiciously close.

Whereas this heir to the Kuhlvult clan, walking next to Kuat of Kuat, had obviously been chosen for her beauty and her lean-muscled, athletic grace—he had to exert himself to keep up with the long strides that billowed her formal robes out behind her. She had obviously come into her inheritance only recently; Kuat remembered having heard, most likely in a report from his security head, that one of the Kuhlvult Elders had recently died and his heir had assumed that preeminent rank in the household. Kuat was grateful that whatever the reason had been for her parent's initial selection as a *telbun*—the Kuhlvults had long been notorious for its weakness for attractive faces—the result had been the elevation of someone with enough intelligence to see through the Knylenns' schemes.

Whether that would be enough—and whether there was a sufficient number like this Kodir of Kuhlvult in the other households—remained to be seen. Kuat strode on toward the meeting place, concealing his own grim apprehensions about what was to come.

Fortunately, none of the Knylenns or their associates made any objection to Kuat of Kuat's security head attending the gathering of the ruling households. It would have been a bad move strategically, to have started off the gathering with an officious reference to the tradition-bound codes that governed the families' interactions. *Better,* thought Kuat, *to at least pretend that we're all friends—for the moment.* And let the Knylenns suffer the consequences of the first hostile move.

"Kuat, your presence is appreciated."

The voice was familiar to him, from the last time he had left the productive sanctuary of Kuat Drive Yards in order to return to the homeworld. He turned and gave a nod of recognition. "I understand," said Kuat, "that we have much to talk about."

"True." The hatchet-sharp face of Khoss of

Knylenn showed a thin-lipped, humorless smile. The formal robes hung easily on his frame; they were obviously his preferred garb. "I hope you . . . *enjoy* hearing the words of your equals." He gestured toward the head of security standing just behind Kuat. "I know how tedious it can be, surrounded only by underlings and their too-often flattering but misleading voices."

A roseate, shadowless glow suffused over the robed figures—more than two score of them, the largest number of ruling household members that Kuat had ever seen gathered together—as the perfect opalescent dome diffused the sunlight outside. In that gentle illumination, even the most withered and cronelike Elders, of either sex, appeared as benign, attractive creatures. The younger ones and the appointed *telbuns* seemed to be almost godlike in their preening splendor. It had been inevitable that such lying arts, enhancement to the point of deception, would have evolved to such a degree on the planet of Kuat. The revenues from the ship-building industry of Kuat Drive Yards, preeminent supplier of military vessels to the Empire, enabled the ruling households to concentrate on all that they considered most important: the gloss of surfaces, the mechanics of deceit. Kuat of Kuat wondered why any of them would consider overturning the financial arrangements of such a system merely to fuel the Knylenns' ambitions.

"I don't," said Kuat, "surround myself with flatterers. When it comes to engineering, it's better to hear the truth, no matter how unpleasant. If a ship being built has a stress fault that will cause it to implode at full thruster force, I would rather know before a client such as Emperor Palpatine has a chance to find out."

"Ah." Khoss nodded in feigned appreciation. "Very wise. As you value the truth, then I'm sure

you'll find our meeting today to be *very* rewarding."
He turned away, his formal robes swirling at the heels
of his boots. A phalanx of younger Knylenns and their
telbuns turned their smug gazes upon Kuat before following after their kinsman.

"You realize, of course, that he hates your guts."
Kodir of Kuhlvult leaned her head close to Kuat's
while keeping an eye on the Knylenns striding away. "I
don't think I'm surprising you with that information."

"He's always hated every Kuat family member."
Kuat shrugged. "That's his own legacy from his predecessors. And it's why I'm pretty sure that the Knylenns
have been circumventing the inheritance restrictions.
You can't learn that kind of hatred; you have to be
born with it, right in your genetic material."

Before Kodir could reply, Kuat's security head
gave him a discreet nudge. "Here comes the Knylenn
Elder. The party's about to start."

The light filtering into the pearllike dome shifted
in color. A flock of wind-orchids, the rootless semi-
vegetative denizens of Kuat's deepest forests, had
drifted across the convex exterior of the dome; their
rich hues of violet and azure fell across the forms of
the ruling household members like a soft optic rain.
The air currents outside lifted the wind-orchids and
sent them slowly tumbling away; the warmth of the
blurred sunlight reentered the dome.

Kuat of Kuat saw a flurry of activity at the other
side of the gently illuminated space. The crowd parted
way before something larger than a mere human
figure.

"That's the life-support system I was telling you
about," said Kuat's security head. "It wasn't just the
functional parts that made it expensive; they had to
decorate it."

A vertically oriented cylinder was surmounted with the grey-bearded visage of the Knylenn Elder; his snow-white hair, braided into two thick ropes, looped over the shoulders of the segmented metal encasing his arms. A trembling palsy shook the vein-gnarled hands left bare, restrained by flexible straps from tripping any of the controls and gauges studding the exterior of the system's casing. Bright red arterial blood percolated through a network of tubes and oxygenating devices; above the tank treads that moved the portable system forward, patches of condensed moisture indicated the cryo-storage bins, with their valuable soft-tissue contents inside.

The Elder's age-yellowed gaze scanned the gathering's faces, the eye muscles twitching in their wrinkled sockets. At last, the Elder fastened upon Kuat of Kuat, standing several meters distant.

"Are you . . . surprised, Kuat?" The voice emerged from the amplified speaker at the front of the portable life-support system, a few gasping syllables at a time. "That I've . . . lived so . . . long?"

Kuat walked forward and stood before the Knylenn Elder, gazing up at the face elevated by the machinery that had consumed the aged body. "Nothing you do surprises me." He could hear the gurgle and hiss of the life-support system's various components, the fluids moving constantly between sterilized metal and flesh arrested in its slow decay. "When I was but a child, and you already in the prime of your manhood, you swore before our biological mothers that you would outlive me." He smiled politely up at the Elder. "You might make it yet."

The laugh that grated from the speaker sounded like sheets of corrugated durasteel grinding against each other. "With your . . . help, Kuat. As you . . . shall see . . ."

Spittle had flecked the side of the Knylenn Elder's face, and shone damply in the tangles of the beard draped across the metal collar encasing the wattles of his throat. The younger Khoss of Knylenn mounted a built-in step at the side of the life-support system and reached up with a silken cloth, dabbing away the wetness as tenderly as if the old kinsman were made of crumpled paper. From his perch on the gurgling machinery, Khoss looked down at Kuat of Kuat. A spark of simmering contempt showed in Khoss's eyes.

Kuat turned away from the Knylenns. A single nod was all the communication that he needed to exchange with Fenald.

"Nobles of this world! My fellow kinsmen!" Khoss had not dismounted from the side of the Knylenn Elder's life-support system, but instead had climbed onto the flat area just behind the upright cylinder. The slight effort had brought an excited flush to his face; he steadied himself by reaching down and placing both his hands upon the metal-sheathed shoulders of the Elder he stood behind. The Elder's white braids were draped at the level of Khoss's knees. "I beg your indulgence—but urgent matters have brought us together at this time!" His voice rang against the glowing limits of the dome. "The very future of the world that we share among us; that future lies in jeopardy!"

The overt theatricality in display offended Kuat of Kuat. He shook his head in distaste, a gesture that was noticed by Kodir standing next to him.

"You're right," she said. "They've all rehearsed their parts. Just look at them."

In the gathering place's opalescent light, the Knylenns and their affiliates had taken up positions on either side of the Knylenn Elder. With their *telbuns*, they constituted an obvious majority of those present, the weight of the ruling households' authority manifested by the confident, even smug expressions on their faces. They stood, male and female alike, with their arms folded across the embroidered fronts of their formal robes, their booted feet spread apart as though they had been transformed into warriors.

"That's handy," Kuat of Kuat remarked dryly to his head of security. "Now at least we know exactly what we're up against."

Kodir of Kuhlvult laid a hand on his shoulder and spoke close to his ear, turning her own back on the massed figures. "The Knylenns have been sending out their emissaries and negotiating teams to the other households for a while now. In fact, ever since Emperor Palpatine dismantled the old Republic. That was when Khoss of Knylenn decided the galaxy's politics had changed enough for him to make his move."

"I see." Her words didn't surprise Kuat; he'd already had his own Kuat Drive Yards intelligence teams report the Knylenns' maneuverings to him. The shift in the power structure among the inhabited worlds, the rise of the Empire and Palpatine's concentration of authority in his own hands, had had inevitable consequences in every council hall and parliament scattered among the stars. At the last gathering of the planet Kuat's ruling households, Khoss of Knylenn had tried to whip up a rebellion against the Kuat bloodline and their administration of the Kuat Drive Yards business. The accusation had been that Kuat of Kuat had shown a disastrous favoritism toward the Rebel Alliance by keeping Kuat Drive Yards out of any involvement with the construction of the Empire's new Death Star weapon.

There had been other military contracting firms, on other worlds, that had reaped both the Emperor's favor and the huge profits that had come with building the Death Star; Kuat of Kuat had been aware that Palpatine himself had commented—with malign suspicion—about the reasons for Kuat Drive Yards not even bidding on the smallest part of the project. Palpatine's misgivings had been soothed away by the simple expedient of Kuat Drive Yards absorbing an unplanned cost overrun, by Kuat of Kuat's personal orders, on the design change orders for an operational wing of a half-dozen new Imperial battle cruisers. That had cut deeply into the corporation's profits for the fiscal quarter, but it had also maintained Kuat Drive Yards' inside relationship with the Empire.

Only later, when the Death Star had turned out to be something less than invulnerable—after the Battle of Yavin, the Imperial admirals' ultimate weapon had been little more than smoldering scraps floating in the vacuum of space—had Kuat's enemies among the ruling households been forced to acknowledge his wisdom. Kuat Drive Yards' preeminent position among the Empire's military contractors was even more secure now, with Emperor Palpatine placing greater trust in Kuat of Kuat's engineering expertise. Whatever plans the Knylenns might have had for taking over the administration of Kuat Drive Yards were put on hold—until now.

Which raised a single question in Kuat of Kuat's mind. *Why now?* he wondered as he looked at Khoss of Knylenn, perched on top of the Knylenn Elder's portable life-support system. What had changed? Some element in the delicate balancing act of power and ambition, either here or somewhere offworld, must have altered slightly, enough for Khoss and the rest of the Knylenn household to believe that they had another chance for realizing their goals. But nothing

that had come to Kuat of Kuat through his own intelligence sources had alerted him to any new development. Either the long years of frustrated waiting had
driven Khoss of Knylenn insane, or the usurpers and
their affiliates had developed contacts and espionage
networks that exceeded Kuat's own. The latter possibility bordered on paranoia, but inevitably so for
someone in a position such as that held by Kuat,
where sheer information dictated one's survival. *What
do they know?* His gaze narrowed as he watched
Khoss and the rest of the Knylenns. *Or worse—what
do they know that I don't?*

Those questions were soon to be answered. Khoss
of Knylenn gestured with an outflung arm, silencing
the murmuring hubbub from the crowd assembled
around him. His hand lowered again toward the
shoulder of the ancient, withered figure embraced by
the life-support system's machinery. "Let the Elder
speak!" Khoss's shout rang against the glowing limits
of the gathering space. "Listen to what *he* has to say!"

On either side of the life-support system's segmented treads, the Knylenns and their affiliates turned
their respectful faces up toward the Elder.

"This ought to be good," muttered Kodir of Kuhlvult, standing next to Kuat. The sour expression on
her face made her distaste for the proceedings evident.

The eyes in the age-wrinkled face reminded Kuat
of Emperor Palpatine's cold scrutiny. But the Emperor's eyes were at least animated by the deep, con-
suming appetite that existed behind them, the hunger
for power over all the universe's sentient beings. By
contrast, the Knylenn Elder's gaze was dulled beneath
the accumulated layers of time, as though any remaining spark were clouded by dust and cobwebs.

"Would that I were at rest . . ." The rheumatic
voice crackled from the amplified speaker at the front

of the cylinder. One corner of the Knylenn Elder's mouth pulled downward with each spoken syllable, the palsy showing a few yellowed teeth. "Would that I were at rest *forever* . . . in the tomb of those who preceded me, for these many years . . . than that I should live to see such treachery . . ."

"Hear him!" Khoss raised both hands from the Knylenn Elder's shoulders and held them wide above his own head. "*This* is why we are gathered at this place!"

"Treachery . . ." The Elder's voice continued, each word like gravel scraped across metal. "When treason is committed . . . by those to whom much power has been given . . . in whom much trust has been placed . . . is greater treachery possible?"

Another murmur sounded from the Knylenns and their affiliates, rising into quick, angry shouts.

The last of Kuat's patience had been exhausted. Before either the Knylenn Elder or Khoss standing behind him could speak again, he strode forward. "Don't waste my time with your cheap theatrics." Kuat of Kuat stood in front of the life-support system's massive durasteel prow, looking up at the faces of both the Knylenn Elder and Khoss of Knylenn. "If you're referring to me, then say so. And if you have charges to make, then state them. Or am I expected to defend myself against nothing more than the hatred you've always shown toward my bloodline?"

"Very well—" Khoss of Knylenn glared down at him. "No one here is surprised that you merit accusation; yourself, least of all. The head of the Kuat household should know better than anyone else just what iniquities he is capable of."

"Iniquities such as fomenting distrust and rebellion toward one who has done no more than serve and enrich this world's heirs?" Kuat of Kuat shook his head in disgust. "Whatever evils I know of are the ones I've observed in you." He gazed round at the Knylenns and their affiliates, ranked on either side of the hissing machinery. "They're easy to see when they're reflected in so many other black hearts. Envy is a mirror that reveals its bearer's face more than anything else."

The Knylenns' murmurs and shouts had been stilled for a moment as Kuat's words had stung home. But now they broke once again into uproar, with threats and imprecations directed at the target who stood before them, unflinching.

"You speak bravely—" Khoss's impassioned voice rose above the others. "For one whose deeds have put him in opposition to all the rest of this world's ruling households."

"Speak for yourself." Kodir of Kuhlvult stepped up beside Kuat. "And speak for those you've fooled and cajoled onto your side." One of her hands gestured toward the sagging scowl of the Knylenn Elder. "And for those too senile to realize the folly of the words you've placed in their mouths. But you don't speak for me, or for any of the Kuhlvult household, when you attack one whose bloodline has brought nothing but wealth and honor to the planet of Kuat."

Kuat looked over at the young female. "This may not be your best move," he said quietly. "They've got the numbers."

"So?" Kodir gave a shrug with her reply. "What does that matter, if they're wrong?"

Atop the portable life-support system, Khoss of Knylenn ordered his followers to silence. "You wished for an accusation?" He directed a sneering smile at Kuat. "Your own knowledge of your deeds is not enough? That is as we expected. It's not likely—or even possible—that one so mired in treachery would voluntarily confess and repent. But that is not necessary for us to have sufficient and convincing evidence of the crimes committed by the bloodline of Kuat, the dagger thrust into the hearts of all the ruling households." Khoss turned where he stood and gestured toward the back of the gathering place. "Bring it forth."

That accusations would be made, Kuat of Kuat had fully expected. But the exact nature of whatever supporting evidence might have been fabricated—that was something of which he could still be surprised. He watched as a three-dimensional holoprojector was wheeled by a pair of Knylenn affiliates into the middle of the domed area.

"What's this?" Kuat pointed to the device. "Do you seek to enlighten or entertain us?"

"I'm sure you'll find it . . . amusing." Khoss reached down and was handed a remote-control keypad by one of the affiliates. "It may not show you at your best, but it captures your likeness well enough."

With a single press of the controls, the holoprojector was activated. In the cleared space before the machinery of the life-support system, light shimmered and coalesced into perceptible forms. A segment of the past came into view, as though summoned from a realm of ghostlike spirits. But the past shown was one that Kuat of Kuat recognized.

He found himself standing less than a meter away from a reproduced hologram of himself. The image wasn't dressed in the formal robes that he himself wore now, but in the simple coveralls of all those who labored for Kuat Drive Yards. Enough details of the space surrounding the hologram were visible that Kuat could see it had been recorded in his private working area. The hologram image was bent over some object on the lab bench, intently prying it open with delicate tools.

Even before the object yielded to the holographic Kuat's probe, the real Kuat could see what it was as he stood in the gathering place of the ruling households and watched his image from the past. The gleaming metal object on the lab bench was a hyperspace messenger unit, which contained in turn another miniaturized holoprojector. The real Kuat watched his past image activate the projector, and another re-created scene appeared, held inside the larger one.

That scene, which the image of Kuat intently regarded, was from inside the palace of the late Jabba the Hutt. With a twist of the probe in the hyperspace messenger unit's controls, the Kuat image froze the holo scene. The real Kuat continued to watch as his past image responded to the events in the re-creation of Jabba's throne room.

You're dead, aren't you? The holographic image of Kuat spoke to the frozen hologram-within-hologram image of Jabba the Hutt. *That's such a shame. I hate to lose a good customer.*

The real Kuat remembered saying those words. Just as he remembered everything else he had done back then, when the hyperspace messenger unit had arrived from the distant planet of Tatooine and he had opened it up to hear the secrets it had brought to him. The holographic re-creation of the scene in front of him, of himself in the past watching another hologram, was like walking around inside his own head, in that space where his memories were kept.

The rest of the scene played out, showing the image of Kuat carefully inspecting the other figures besides Jabba the Hutt that could be seen in the hologram-within-a-hologram. The scene that had been recorded in Jabba's palace ended with Princess Leia Organa, disguised as an Ubese bounty hunter, facing down the Hutt with an activated thermal detonator. That had been amusing to witness. Before that, though, there had been less pleasant things to watch, such as the grisly death of one of the Hutt's dancing girls, by being dropped into the rancor pit before the throne. To re-create Jabba the Hutt's court was to summon from the past a particularly nasty piece of the galaxy.

In the hologram that had contained the other one, the image of Kuat of Kuat extracted the probe tool from the hyperspace messenger unit on the lab bench, and the silvery ovoid self-destructed, its casing and innards melting down into smoldering scrap.

"You're right," said the real Kuat, the one who now stood in the gathering place of the ruling households. "That is interesting."

Not for what the holographic playback had shown him; his memory was clear enough about having opened up the messenger and watching what it had to show him. But for what was implied by the mere existence of the hologram, and it being in the hands of the Knylenns. The hologram had been recorded surreptitiously, in Kuat's most private and guarded sanctuary. Recorded by some hidden device, without his knowledge, and then transmitted to Khoss of Knylenn and the other conspirators against the bloodline of Kuat. That meant a major breach of security, within the actual organization of Kuat Drive Yards. A breach that only one individual would be capable of creating.

Kuat of Kuat turned and looked over his shoulder at Fenald. His gaze was met with one that looked straight back into his eyes, without making any effort at aversion.

Then the head of security for Kuat Drive Yards gave a single nod. That was all that was necessary, even before he spoke. "Now you know," he said.

"Yes—" For a second longer, Kuat regarded the man he had trusted more than any other sentient creature in the galaxy. "I suppose I do." Many things were clear now, including why Fenald had been so insistent upon accompanying him to the gathering of Kuat's ruling households. *He wanted to be here,* Kuat thought bitterly, *to make sure he got paid.* However much the Knylenns and the others had offered for this treachery . . .

He turned back toward the others assembled in the gathering place. Kodir of Kuhlvult gently touched Kuat's arm. "You don't look too good," she said.

For a moment Kuat wondered if she was speaking about herself. During the holographic playback, he had heard a sudden gasp behind himself; he had glanced over his shoulder and had seen Kodir turn pale, eyes widened with surprise, as she had watched those re-created events from the past. He didn't know what had struck her so forcefully, and right now there wasn't time to find out.

"Don't worry about me." Kuat of Kuat slowly nodded. "I've got a lot of thinking to do."

Kodir peered closely into his face. "Are you sure? Maybe we can get this meeting postponed; there might be enough members of the other households who aren't completely tied in with the Knylenns who'd let you off for reasons of health. You really do look like you've just had a heart attack."

"No—" Kuat brushed her hand away from the sleeve of his robe. "It's better if I get it over with now. Besides . . ." He managed to smile at her. "I've got a few surprises of my own that Khoss and his bunch know nothing about."

Kuat lifted his gaze toward the leader of the Knylenns, perched aboard the portable life-support system. He had to assume the worst about what the Knylenns were aware of, regarding his own schemes and actions. Whatever they had bribed his head of security with—*former* security head, Kuat reminded himself—it had obviously been enough to give them effective access to everything that had gone on inside the headquarters of Kuat Drive Yards. *If* they had known what to look for . . .

There was only one way to find out.

"You must be joking," said Kuat. "Is it treachery for me to keep an eye on one of Kuat Drive Yards' customers? We sell our wares to any creature who has the credits for them—as long as we can do so without incurring the wrath of the Empire. Some of our customers need a good deal of watching; I would have been a fool to have blindly trusted someone like Jabba the Hutt. You should be grateful to me for taking such precautions."

"Precautions, are they?" Khoss of Knylenn's voice took on a sarcastic edge. "And what cautious nature of yours led to the saturation bombing of a sector of the planet Tatooine's surface known as the Dune Sea? Don't try to deny that it happened. We know all about it, and that the bombing raid was personally directed by you, from aboard your Kuat Drive Yards flagship."

So they possessed that knowledge as well; Kuat's security head had done a thorough job of selling him out. "That's none of your concern," said Kuat stiffly. "Some things are necessary, the reasons for which cannot be revealed publicly. As long as Kuat Drive Yards is a profitable concern—and you reap your share of those profits—then all prying into these matters does nothing except hinder my running the corporation."

"Ah!" Khoss leaned forward, above the grizzled head of the Knylenn Elder. "You wish to keep secrets from those closest to you, those with the greatest right to know." A sweeping gesture of his arm took in the gathering place and those it held. "The representatives of this world's ruling households are like children to you, incapable of understanding all your great schemes and maneuvers. Tell me, Kuat of Kuat—" Khoss spoke with icy scorn. "Are we supposed to be *flattered* by such an attitude on your part?"

This time, Kodir of Kuhlvult spoke up. "You can be as flattered or as offended as you choose," she said. "But the truth is as Kuat tells it. The ruling households long ago chose to put their trust in his bloodline. We created the Inheritance Exemption specifically so that the Kuat family, from one generation to the next, could continue to manage the corporation from which our wealth comes. Are we now to revoke that trust, for no better reason than that Kuat of Kuat runs it as he sees fit?"

"Our little Kuhlvult cousin has made it clear just whose side she has taken." Khoss directed his withering sneer at her, then spread his hands to the crowd around the base of the life-support system. "She was given the chance to join with the rest of the ruling households, those who desire justice and are not swayed by facile arguments about endangering the sources of our wealth. Perhaps she has her reasons for making such a choice. Why should treachery be limited to those of the Kuat bloodline? With the power that he commands, Kuat of Kuat has his ways of tempting the greedy and foolish into being his allies."

The speech from Khoss of Knylenn was met with angry shouts from his assembled supporters. But another voice managed to rise above them.

"Nothing tempts me but the desire to make you

eat your own words." Kodir of Kuhlvult looked as if she were ready to climb up onto the life-support system and achieve her wish by force. "If there were any substance to them, it would make quite a mouthful for you, I'm sure. But they're nothing but air. Nothing but lies and little hints and rumors, none of which add up to anything real."

"My dear cousin," said Khoss with feigned politeness, "it takes wisdom to measure the weight of things as subtle as Kuat's treachery. He's too smart to pursue his twisted ambitions openly, where anyone might see them."

"So you bribe your way into my private quarters." Kuat gestured toward his former head of security. "And you set spies onto those who have done you no harm."

"I do what is necessary," replied Khoss. "If it were what is required to uproot the evil that has taken root among us, I would embrace the darkest energies that could be found in this universe. But you've already beaten me to that, haven't you?"

"You talk nonsense."

"Do I?" The brows rose high above Khoss's eyes. "Is it nonsense to wonder about the meaning of not only Kuat's own espionage, but also an unexplained bombing raid upon the surface of another planet? A planet which rumors have already been swirling about, throughout the galaxy? You might not be aware of the nature of those rumors and tales, but it seems clear enough that this certain planet known as Tatooine had already taken on a great importance in the eyes of both Emperor Palpatine and the most feared instrument of his will, Lord Darth Vader himself. And it is no great feat of espionage to have learned that the Rebel Alliance has gained a new and valuable leader in the form of one Luke Skywalker, whose home planet is this same Tatooine. Are we to believe it a mere coincidence that of all the inhabited worlds in the galaxy, the schemes of Kuat of Kuat should also revolve around Tatooine? Or is it not a greater likelihood that those schemes, regarding which Kuat asks us to trust him, have through his rashness and folly gotten our own world and our inheritance fatally enmeshed with the struggle between the Empire and the Rebellion?" As if on cue, the mutterings and shouts from the Knylenns and their affiliates rose to a higher pitch. "We don't even know what purpose is served by all of Kuat's scheming—he doesn't consider us fit to be trusted with these vital secrets; only *he* should know these things. That is why Kuat has also concealed from us that he has received other messages from Tatooine, concerning the welfare of a certain notorious bounty hunter named Boba Fett. This bounty hunter may have also been a customer of Kuat Drive Yards at one time, but he's rather more than that now." Khoss jabbed a finger toward his adversary standing before the portable life-support system. "Is that not true, Kuat?"

The breach in security was more extensive than Kuat had originally feared. *They've gone off-planet,* Kuat realized. The Knylenn household had obviously been in touch with intelligence sources elsewhere in the galaxy, and had paid for what they wanted to know; that meant there was a good chance they had traced out a few more connections that Kuat would have preferred to keep hidden.

But what exactly had the Knylenns found out? That remained to be seen.

"Since you seem to know so much—" Kuat's hand swept a gesture toward Khoss. "Why don't you tell us what is true? Or what you *think* is true."

"It's not a matter of thinking, Kuat; it's a matter of knowing. Or knowing *enough*; enough to be concerned about where your schemes have led us to."

"And where is that?" Kuat kept his tone mild and even somewhat amused.

"You have kept much hidden—you show an undeniable talent, Kuat, for secrecy. But secrets can also be found out; truth has a way of revealing itself." Khoss straightened himself behind the encased torso and scowling head of the Knylenn Elder, and folded his arms across his chest. "For is it not also true that these schemes also entangled you—and by extension, Kuat Drive Yards—with the criminal organization known as Black Sun? You've said that you value the Empire as a customer, and yet you also had secret dealings with the very creatures who continually circumvented Emperor Palpatine's authority in the galaxy. I would call that a risky game, one that tried to play both sides against each other. That's not good business, Kuat; that's madness."

So they don't know everything, decided Kuat. Whatever intelligence sources the Knylenns had used, whatever information they had paid for, it hadn't been enough to reveal all of his schemes and maneuvers. If Khoss of Knylenn had known exactly what had gone on with the Empire and Black Sun—and even the Rebel Alliance—he would have already used that knowledge against Kuat. Some of those schemes, such as Kuat's attempt to link Prince Xizor, the leader of Black Sun, with the Imperial stormtrooper raid that had killed Luke Skywalker's aunt and uncle, had gone beyond all reasonable concepts of risk—yet they had been necessary as well as part of Kuat's calculated campaign to eliminate the threat that Xizor represented to Kuat Drive Yards. The scheme had failed—

Kuat had already admitted that to himself. All his efforts now, including the bombing raid on Tatooine's Dune Sea, were concentrated on eliminating the evidence of that scheme before the truth of it leaked out to Emperor Palpatine. *Maybe I'm too late*—if the Knylenns had gotten wind of even these few scraps of information, there was no telling what Palpatine, with his vastly superior intelligence organization, might already be aware of.

"Very well." He had heard enough from Khoss of Knylenn. The state of the Knylenns' perception of his secrets was clear. "I don't care to tell you more than you already know. If you believe these matters to constitute treachery—and if you've convinced enough of the other ruling households that that is the case—only one question remains. What are you going to do about it?"

The Knylenn Elder spoke, its voice a grating rasp from the amplified speaker mounted at the front of the cylinder housing the ancient flesh. "The bloodline of Kuat . . . must pay the price . . . for its crimes . . ."

" 'Crimes'?" The Elder's words seemed to enrage Kodir of Kuhlvult. She stepped forward from where she had been standing next to Kuat. "The crime is yours!" An accusing finger darted out, pointing directly at Khoss of Knylenn above her. "Your greed and ambition have led you to spy on and invent slanders against a fellow kinsman." Kodir lowered her hand, letting the same gesture sweep across the ranks of the other Knylenns and their affiliates. "And all of you share the guilt for letting these suspicions poison your minds. The galaxy is at war, the Empire against the Rebels, and like it or not, we find ourselves on the battlefield. Now is not the time to conspire against the only one who has a chance of leading us to safety."

"Lead us to ruin, more likely." Khoss of Knylenn tempered the severity of his voice, the better to draw back into line any of his followers who might have had second thoughts. "Kuat of Kuat hides from us that which we most need to know—and that which would absolve him of suspicion, if his actions are indeed blameless. There are things we need to know, which he managed to keep secret. All he needs to do is dispel the darkness that he himself has created, and then our objections to the way he administers Kuat Drive Yards will melt away like dew upon the forest's leaves." The last bit of poetry was accompanied by an unpleasant smile. "What say you, Kuat of Kuat? You may have your secrets—but not without suspicions. Or accusations."

The temptation was great to divulge exactly those things that Khoss and the other Knylenns demanded to know. *Tell them,* thought Kuat grimly, *and let there be an end to it all.* Upon the heads of the Knylenns and their affiliates, the blame would be as heavy as it was upon his own. Why should he be the only one to be crushed beneath this burden when all shared the benefits of his constant, unsleeping labors? He could feel the words splitting open his heart and rising to his tongue, the intricate details of his schemes forcing their way to the light . . .

Tell them the truth, thought Kuat. *And give up any hope of success. Any chance of survival, of saving Kuat Drive Yards from its enemies.*

That was the problem, the trap in which he was caught. Information flowed both ways; if the Knylenns were already in contact with spies and other shady intelligence sources, then anything revealed here would quickly find its way to those who would be even more interested in discovering the details of

Kuat of Kuat's schemes. Someone such as Prince Xizor would not have been grateful upon finding out that he had been the target for the net that Kuat had woven in hopes of trapping him within. And Xizor would have had ways of expressing his displeasure; ways that would have been personally unpleasant, then fatal for the schemes' instigator. It was the price that came with playing games with such high stakes. What burned inside Kuat was the awareness that the cost of his failure would also be paid by Kuat Drive Yards. The corporation would cease to exist; even its name would be wiped from memory, as it was absorbed into the fabric of the Empire. Xizor's intentions toward Kuat Drive Yards had been made plain long ago; all that he had lacked had been the pretext upon which he could convince Emperor Palpatine to seize the corporation's valuable assets and make them his own. The discovery of schemes such as those launched by Kuat of Kuat would have more than sufficed for that purpose.

A choice such as that which Kuat faced was no choice at all. Kuat knew that to use the truth to defend himself against an enemy such as Khoss of Knylenn would only deliver him, and Kuat Drive Yards, into the hands of an even more implacable enemy. *Better to maintain silence,* he decided, *and take whatever accusations they want to throw at me.*

"I keep my own counsel," Kuat answered aloud. "As do you yourself. You and your fellow conspirators did not seek the benefit of my advice before you saw fit to spy upon me. So be it. If all your prying cannot unveil what you seek to know, and if you cannot buy it with all the credits that my labors have put in your coffers, then you can hardly expect me to give you that information for free."

Khoss of Knylenn smiled as he nodded. "That is exactly the answer I expected from you. That all of us, who have chafed under your unbridled power, thought we would hear from you. It comes as no surprise that you will not—or cannot—defend yourself."

"He needs no defense," said Kodir angrily, "from baseless accusations."

The sneer returned to Khoss's face. "It's clear you've made your choice as to where you stand. If treachery can buy your loyalty, you'd better be satisfied with the price you got for it." As though dismissing her from his consciousness, he turned his gaze back toward Kuat. "You see the numbers arrayed against you." With both hands outspread, Khoss gestured toward his followers. "Rather an obvious majority, isn't it? And they've appointed me to speak for them—they have sworn oaths of liege fealty to the Knylenn bloodline. Those oaths are binding and irrevocable. It is on that basis that I thus make the wishes of the ruling households known to you, Kuat of Kuat."

"Ah! Is that so?" Kuat stroked his chin as he looked round at the wall of faces, then back up at Khoss. "That seems a great deal of power to be invested in one who is not, in fact, the head of the bloodline that he purports to represent."

Khoss's sneer changed to a dark scowl. "What do you mean by that?"

"It's very simple. And it is just as I say. You are not the head of the Knylenn bloodline; you are still but an heirling of that one from whom you will someday inherit the title. Those oaths from the other ruling households are not sworn to you, but to the person of another." Kuat gestured toward the ancient, withered visage of the Knylenn Elder. "Should he not be the one to state the charges against me, and the one to pronounce whatever retribution this world's heirs demand?"

A moment passed before Khoss replied. "Just so," he said, his expression even more murderous than before. On the raised platform atop the portable life-support system, he took a step backward, still letting his hands rest upon the shoulders of the metal-encased Elder. "If it is your wish to hear him speak, then that is something easily granted."

The Knylenn Elder's yellowed eyes balefully glowered at Kuat. "I am old . . ." His voice was heavy with weariness and loathing. "And have not the strength . . . that I once had." The sighing, gurgling noises of the life-support system formed a counterpoint to his words. "That is why . . . this younger one . . ." The Elder's head raised in a gesture indicating Khoss standing above. "He speaks the words . . . that I would speak. He speaks . . ." The last words seemed to be forced out of the Elder's mouth by sheer willpower. "With my authority. Doubt him not . . ."

"And is that your understanding as well?" Kuat looked across the faces of the Knylenns' affiliates, ranked on either side of the life-support system's machinery. "You listen to Khoss of Knylenn, because he speaks for the Elder of that household?"

He received a few nods from the affiliates. One of them, the Kadnessi Elder, spoke up. "Our loyalty is to the Knylenn Elder; he received our oaths long ago. But if he wishes his heir to speak for him, we have no objection to that." The Kadnessi Elder peered sharply at Kuat. "Do you?"

"Not at all," said Kuat. "Your oaths are sacred, and I respect them. But let us see if everyone honors them as I do." He strode across the small distance between himself and the portable life-support system, one hand reaching up toward the controls visible on its front panel.

"Stop him!" Atop the machinery, Khoss of Knylenn shouted, his gesture jabbing frantically down toward Kuat.

Before he could lay his hand upon the portable life-support system, another grabbed his shoulder and pulled him around. The former security head for Kuat Drive Yards gathered one side of Kuat's formal robes and pulled him close against himself.

"I know what you're trying to do—" The former security head's expression was set grim and tight as he reached with his other hand inside his jacket. "I didn't sell you out to these people just so I could watch you defeat them." A glistening vibroblade appeared in the former security head's fist. "You have to realize—I'm on their side now."

Kuat shoved the butt of his palm hard against the former security head's chin, pushing the other man's face to the side; with his forearm, he blocked the thrust of the vibroblade at his ribs. The former security head was younger and stronger than Kuat, too strong for him to break free of the other's bearlike hold across his shoulder and neck. The vibroblade slashed downward across the sleeve of Kuat's robe, parting the heavy fabric and slicing a millimeter-deep wound, precise as a surgical incision, along the back of Kuat's arm. Blood welled out and seeped across the chests of both men, pressed tight against each other.

The fist holding the blade slammed up into Kuat's solar plexus, knocking the breath from his lungs and forcing him a step backward. That gave the former security head enough space to draw his arm back and aim a slashing, fatal blow with the weapon, straight toward Kuat's throat.

The blow never reached its target.

Gasping in sudden shock and pain, the former security head dropped the vibroblade; clattering, the blade spun across the floor. The former security head's fingers clawed at Kodir of Kuhlvult's forearm, jammed hard against his windpipe. With the same move, Kodir had thrust the point of one knee against the former security head's spine; his shoulders arched backward in a tensed bow, his greater weight balanced against hers. Before he could act in any way other than pure, unthinking reflex, Kodir's free arm swung her fist into the man's temple, with enough force that the crack of bone was audible. The whites of his eyes rolled upward behind the trembling lids; when Kodir let go of him, he crashed unconscious to the gathering place's floor.

Under the luminous dome, the assembled crowd had been struck silent by the quick burst of violent action in front of them. Before any of them could move, Kuat of Kuat had already darted forward and snatched up the vibroblade that had fallen from the former security head's grasp. Blood trickled down his forearm and dripped from his elbow as he held the weapon up.

"I would advise everyone to continue standing very still." The rush of adrenaline in Kuat's veins had anesthetized him from the wound in his arm. The front of his formal robes, slashed open and spattered with red by the same blade that he now gripped, hung down toward the top of his boots. He kicked the scrap of heavy fabric aside as he stepped closer to the portable life-support system. "That goes for you as well," said Kuat; he held the vibroblade higher, its glistening point on a straight line toward the throat of Khoss of Knylenn. "Stay right there. That way you'll get a good view."

Khoss of Knylenn froze in place, as though hypnotized by the sight of the blade. Before him, the yellowed eyes of the Knylenn Elder watched from beneath
drooping lids, mouth slack and wet at its corners.

Kuat knew that he had only a few seconds before
the Knylenns managed to break free of the shock that
now held them. But that would be long enough.

He stepped close to the portable life-support system. The machinery shrieked, as though its metal and
silicon were capable of feeling pain, when the vibroblade sliced through the exposed cables and hoses.
The blood-cleansing apparatus sped up, then ground
to a halt as its workings ran dry; the recycled blood
and other floods spread in a glistening pool beneath
the machinery's tank treads.

Up above Kuat, the face of the Knylenn Elder
distorted in a frozen rictus, the cords beneath the
wrinkled flesh of his neck tightening and straining
against the confines of the cylinder's metal collar. A
red bubble formed and burst at the wet corner of his
mouth.

Another blow, this time with the point of the vibroblade, pried open the front panel of the portable
life-support system. Kuat forced it open wide enough
to get his fingers underneath the smooth edge of
metal. As he strained against it, he was joined by
Kodir of Kuhlvult at his side; the two of them managed to pull the front panel off the machinery and
drop it with an echoing clang onto the gathering
place's floor.

Kuat no longer needed the vibroblade. Now he
was able to reach into the workings of the life-support
system and disable it.

"Back off—"

Kodir's warning voice sounded from behind him.
Kuat glanced over his shoulder and saw that she had

scooped up the vibroblade. With her knees bent in a defensive crouch, Kodir used the weapon to keep the Knylenns and their affiliates at bay.

"Maybe you could hurry a little," said Kodir, glancing back at Kuat. "I'm not going to be able to hold them forever."

"This won't take long." A single motivator unit ran all the functions of the life-support system; Kuat grasped the top of the unit, gave it a turn to the right, and yanked it out of the center of the machinery's circuits.

An inhuman screech sounded from the amplified speaker mounted above. As if Kuat of Kuat had struck a blow at the heart of a living beast, the portable life-support system shuddered and sank lower upon its treads, nearly toppling Khoss of Knylenn from its upper platform. The grey, withered face of the Knylenn Elder showed no sign of animation as Kuat grasped the bottom edge of the cylinder and tugged it free. Like an ancient warrior's battle shield, it crashed on top of the other discarded sections of the machinery's exterior.

The vibroblade brandished by Kodir of Kuhlvult didn't cause the others in the gathering place to take a step backward, pushing themselves away from the hulk of unpowered devices in front of them. It was what they saw, revealed at the machinery's heart.

Inside the opened cylinder, the corpse of the Knylenn Elder hung suspended—not held upright by the tubes and wires of the life-support system's various components, but by a simple leather strap crossing the body's shrunken chest. The flesh dried upon the protruding bones was as cold and lifeless as the surrounding metal, as though the skeleton were merely some part of the machinery's framework. A last trace of the odor of decay had been released by the opening of the cylinder; a few of the Knylenns and their affiliates turned away in horrified disgust.

The Knylenn Elder had been dead for a long time; long before the portable life-support system had carried the disguised corpse into the gathering place. That much was obvious.

"Not a bad piece of work; very well designed." With an engineer's clinical admiration, Kuat pointed out the rest of the details. He pointed up at the wires and servo-linked pneumatic tubes running through the metal collar and into the base of the Elder's skull. "As you can see, there was no need to go to the expense of preserving all of the body in a lifelike state; only the head of the Elder was necessary to give the impression that he was still alive and functioning. A few simple, real-time animating devices, a synthesized voice, and a database of vocabulary and mannerisms, all under the control of the Level 1 droid intelligence that was supposedly monitoring the life-support system's components and the corresponding vital signs—basically, not an elaborate construct at all. But well done, nevertheless." Kuat looked up at the pallid face of Khoss. "Who did you hire to do the work for you? Must have been expensive." He slowly shook his head. "Offhand, I'd say it looks like a Phonane Mimesis Studios job—it's the kind of thing they specialize in. But it might also have been—"

"How did you know?" Khoss's hands were white-knuckled and trembling as they grasped what was left of the cylinder before him. His voice sounded more agonized than the fake Knylenn Elder's had been. "It was *perfect*. It's been over a year since the Elder died, and no one else has ever suspected . . ."

"They might have had their suspicions." Kuat cast an amused glance at the others in the gathering place. "Perhaps they just didn't want to say anything about it, since they had already decided to go along with your plans to wrest control of Kuat Drive Yards from me. And . . . I imagine you had a few accomplices." Kuat looked again at the person standing atop the dead machinery. "I remember the Knylenn Elder well; he was not a stupid individual. Whatever his own ambitions for the Knylenn household, I doubt if he could have been convinced to go along with this plan of yours."

"Is that how . . ."

"It was enough to arouse my own skepticism," replied Kuat. "But I needed proof—and that wasn't long in coming. It just shows that you're not cut out to be an engineer, Khoss; you rely too much on clever machines. Someone who works with and designs them always knows that the human element is inescapable. And decisive." He shook his head in mock ruefulness. "It's always the simple things that trip people up. You programmed the droid intelligence in that device of yours pretty well; it was doing a decent enough imitation of the Knylenn Elder. But it got the facts wrong. It would have been very difficult for the Elder to have sworn before our biological mothers that he would outlive me, since our mothers never met. Mine died in giving birth to me. I was raised in the household of Kuat by the father from whom I received my inheritance. So when your phony Knylenn Elder didn't catch me out in a simple falsehood—that's when I knew it wasn't really him."

One of the Kadnessi, the male who had spoken up before, looked puzzled. "I don't understand," he said. "Why would Khoss go to such elaborate lengths to make it appear that the Knylenn Elder was still alive? As soon as the word of the Elder's death would have gotten out, that would be when Khoss would have been acknowledged as the heir of the Knylenn household."

"That's not difficult to figure out." Kuat smiled. "It's not enough to inherit the title when the oaths of fealty from the other ruling households were given to the *person* of the previous Knylenn Elder. None of you has ever sworn an oath to Khoss of Knylenn." The notion brought a laugh from Kuat. "Why should you have? So for Khoss to proceed with his campaign to drive me out of the leadership of Kuat Drive Yards, he needed all the authority that went with the Knylenn Elder still being alive, without the inconvenience of the old man disagreeing with him about what should be done. The real question, of course, is . . ." Kuat's voice darkened with sly hints. "Just how convenient was the Elder's death? Perhaps our dear cousin Khoss might have . . . *helped* the process along. Just a little bit."

"That . . . that's a lie." Khoss of Knylenn's face had paled to a bloodless white. "If you're saying I killed him—that I had anything to do with his death—"

"A very serious charge," said the Kadnessi. He nodded solemnly, a gesture that was repeated by others in the crowd, including the Knylenns and their associates. "This will bear investigation. And if it should turn out to be true . . ."

"Then the murderer's own life is forfeited." Kodir of Kuhlvult spoke the words with evident satisfaction. "That is the law, as ancient as the ruling households themselves. It's a capital crime for a designated heir to take an Elder's life. And the punishment must be exacted, or the households would be awash in the blood of the victims."

Atop the disabled machinery, the ruined manifestation of his scheme, Khoss was reduced to sputtering incoherence. His fists clenched as his face distorted with the rage of the impotent and guilty.

Kuat knew what to expect; he saw Khoss's muscles tensing for one final act. It was no surprise to him when the defeated Knylenn heirling leaped from the machinery's elevated platform, his hands clawing for his enemy's throat.

This time, there was no need for assistance from Kodir. Kuat took care of the problem himself. The butt of one upraised hand caught Khoss at the edge of his jaw, snapping his head back; a blow from Kuat's other fist sent the Knylenn sprawling at the feet of his kinsmen. He didn't get up, though his chest could still be seen rising and falling, laboring for breath.

"Let me know," said Kuat coldly, "what you decide about him. It would probably be best, for Kuat Drive Yards' public relations if the execution were performed in as quiet a manner as possible. This kind of squabbling within the ranks is always seen as a weakness by outsiders." He turned and strode away, toward the gathering place's exit.

Fenald had just started to regain consciousness, and feebly raised a hand toward Kuat as he passed by him. Kodir planted the sole of her boot in the man's chest and knocked him back flat against the floor.

"I don't think the Kuat household is going to be needing your services anymore." Kodir smiled as she looked over at Kuat of Kuat. "I'd say the chances are good that there's going to be a new head of security at Kuat Drive Yards." She set her fists against her hips and regarded Kuat with her head tilted to one side. "And so . . . ?"

He looked back at her for only a second before making his decision. "All right," said Kuat of Kuat. He nodded toward the exit and the corridor leading to the docking area. "The ship's waiting."

14

On the flight back to the Kuat Drive Yards, business arrangements were finalized.

"This hasn't been done before," said Kuat of Kuat. The in-transit time wasn't long, so he had immediately gotten down to details. "At least, I'm not aware of a fellow member of one of the ruling households having served as the corporation's head of security. Certainly, with my immediate predecessors, there had always been someone hired from off-planet." He raised one eyebrow. "And after a considerable search and test of qualifications as well, I might add." His own words evoked a bitter laugh from Kuat. "Not that it did much good, it seems." The memory of Fenald's betrayal still burned deep within him.

Kodir of Kuhlvult leaned back in the passenger-area seat next to his. "You're wondering if I'm qualified for the job?" She smiled at him. "How much more proof do I need to give you?"

"None." Kuat shook his head. "You had enough moves back there at the ruling households' gathering place to indicate that you know how to act in an emergency. And . . . you hadn't gone along with the others and fallen for that scheme of Khoss's. Now, that either indicates a pretty sharp analytical mind—which is always a good thing for a security head to have—or perhaps . . ."

"Perhaps what?"

It was his turn to smile. "Perhaps a few inside sources? Khoss of Knylenn might not have kept everything as much of a secret as he would have liked—or as he thought he had. A little snooping around, a little following up of hints and leads—such as word of unusual deliveries to the Knylenn household, things like that—and a smart person might have known even before I did that the Knylenn Elder was dead."

"Oh, you're right about that." Kodir nodded slowly. "A smart person would have known about that. And . . ." She looked more than pleased with herself. "A smart person also knows how to keep her own secrets."

"Fair enough," said Kuat. "As long as it doesn't interfere with your duties. But there's more to determine than just your qualifications."

Kodir turned her gaze back from the small viewport beside her seat. "Such as?"

"I need to know exactly why you would *want* to be the security head for Kuat Drive Yards. My head of security."

She gave a shrug. "There's all sorts of answers I could give you. Maybe I should just say that wanting to be where the action is . . . that's sort of a Kuhlvult household trait. And right now, Kuat Drive Yards has a lot of action happening around it."

"If you just want action, go join the Rebel Alliance. Then you'll get all the action you could ever want."

"Saving our own skins is also something of a trait with Kuhlvults." Kodir shook her head. "I don't know if going up against the Empire is compatible with long-term survival."

"I don't know anymore if being on the Emperor's side is good for one's health." An old, familiar weight pressed again on Kuat of Kuat's shoulders. "I'm just trying to keep Kuat Drive Yards intact and independent, no matter who wins."

"That's one of the things I admire about you," said Kodir. "You demand loyalty from others, but you're not an idiot about giving it away."

For a moment, he wondered if she was being sarcastic. Then he had to admit the wisdom of what she had just said. "The loyalty that Emperor Palpatine extracts from his followers is not the loyalty of free creatures. It's no more than the fear shown by slaves."

"It would be worth your life," Kodir spoke quietly, "if I were to make your sentiments known to the Emperor."

"But you're not going to." All smiles had faded, from both his face and hers. "Which means either that you're not afraid of Palpatine, or you're loyal— enough—to me. Or . . ."

"There always seems to be another 'or.' "

"It's a complicated galaxy we live in," said Kuat. "Or you have your own reasons for being on my side. Things you want, that you would be more likely to achieve if I were to stay healthy and in charge of Kuat Drive Yards." He peered closer at Kodir. "So exactly what is it that you want?"

"Answers."

One word, flatly stated; Kuat nodded in appreciation. "Those can be hard to come by," he said. "Unlike questions, which are about as plentiful as hydrogen atoms in the universe."

Kodir gave a slight shrug. "Mine are pretty specific."

The personal transport would be at the Kuat Drive Yards docking area soon. And there were still a few things that Kuat wanted to settle with his new head of security before being surrounded by other creatures.

"Be careful," warned Kuat. "Sometimes questions are asked, and answers are given—but they're not the ones that you might want to hear."

No emotion showed on Kodir's face. "I'll take that risk."

"Then ask away."

She leaned closer to Kuat, as though the answers might be written at the dark centers of his eyes. A moment passed before she spoke. Then: "What happened to that girl?"

The question puzzled him. "I don't know what you're talking about."

Anger seeped into the flat tone of Kodir's voice. "Don't play around about this. We can have a business arrangement together, or we can be enemies. Your choice."

That flash of temper provoked his curiosity. *It's something important to her,* thought Kuat; he just didn't know what it was—yet.

"Tell me," said Kuat mildly, "just what girl you're referring to. And we can proceed from there."

"The dancing girl. At the palace of Jabba the Hutt."

It took Kuat a moment to recall what she was talking about. *The hologram,* he finally realized. From the hyperspace messenger unit that Khoss of Knylenn's spying had captured him watching. Back at the ruling households' gathering place, Kodir had watched that hologram-within-a-hologram replay of the past events at Jabba's palace. Watched, and had seen something in it that she considered important. But what?

"She must have died," said Kuat. "When Jabba

threw her to his pet rancor beast; that's what was in that pit with the retractable grid over it. And nobody survives coming into that close contact with a rancor."

"I'm not talking about that dancing girl." Kodir snapped out her words with impatience. "Who cares about some Twi'lek female? I mean, it's too bad, but that's not what's important. It's the other one, the other pretty one, that you could see there in the hologram of the palace—the one off to the side. That's the one I want to know about."

Kuat searched his memory, trying to dredge up the details that he had previously considered unimportant. His attention, when he had first watched the holographic replay that the hyperspace messenger unit had brought him, had been focused on the comings and goings of the bounty hunter Boba Fett in Jabba's palace. That had been the whole reason for the autonomic spy setup that had been smuggled in there; anything else that had been recorded was incidental to Kuat's original purposes.

"You're right," he said, nodding slowly. "I guess there was another dancing girl there." Kuat shrugged. "Jabba always kept a small troupe of them in the palace. Given the way he fed his pets, there was a pretty high turnover for them. It wasn't the kind of position that came with a high life expectancy attached."

"But that one lived." Kodir spoke with unexpected ferocity. "The other one, the one that Jabba didn't throw to the rancor."

"How do you know that?" He still didn't understand Kodir's interest in an anonymous dancing girl on some far-off world like Tatooine. "Something else might have happened to her before Jabba was killed. And even afterward . . . that's a pretty hostile environment for anybody to survive in."

"*I know she's alive.*" Kodir's words came through

her tightly clenched teeth. "I can feel it. Even this far away."

Puzzled, Kuat looked at the young woman sitting beside him. A few more pieces fell into place as he now managed to recall the face of the other pretty dancing girl in the hologram. The holographic recording had caught, for just a few seconds, the image of her watching the Twi'lek female fall into the rancor pit before Jabba's throne platform, and listening to the terrified screams that had preceded the unseen death in the darkness below.

Kuat saw now, as he gazed at Kodir of Kuhlvult, what he had missed before. But even this much of an answer only deepened the mystery.

"Yes," said Kodir softly. She had obviously discerned the realization in Kuat's eyes, his sudden awareness of the familial resemblance. "The girl, the other one there in Jabba's palace—she is of my blood, my family; the household of Kuhlvult. That's how I know she's still alive. She has to be . . ."

There was more, Kuat knew. Now he spoke softly, almost tenderly. "What is her name?"

Kodir squeezed her eyes shut as she answered. "Her name," she said, "her true name, is Kateel of Kuhlvult." The words came slowly, as though they had been lodged close to Kodir's heart. "But when she was but a child, and speaking as a child does, she couldn't pronounce such a name; she would just say *Neelah* instead." Kodir's voice had dwindled to a whisper. "And that is what we called her."

Kuat regarded the woman beside him with something close to pity. "And you think I can help you find her."

"Oh . . . you will." Kodir turned a fierce gaze toward him. "I don't have any doubt about that."

A glance out the viewport beside Kuat showed

that the Kuat Drive Yards docking area was already in sight. He turned back to Kodir. "My resources—and my time—are limited. I don't know how a child of one of Kuat's ruling households wound up in Jabba the Hutt's palace. And I have more pressing concerns than finding out the answer to that question."

"No, you don't." Kodir spoke with ominous certainty. "I assure you—there's nothing more important for you than this."

"You seem pretty confident about it."

Another nod from her. "I have reasons to be."

Kuat raised an eyebrow. "Such as?"

"Very simple," said Kodir, "and very compelling reasons. You've already spoken of your suspicions that I might have other sources of information—and good sources, too. The truth is that you're correct about that. It's how I knew that the Knylenn Elder was dead, even before you figured it out. I've spent a long time building up and working those information sources; some of them I inherited, as part of the Kuhlvult bloodline. And they're how I know things about you, Kuat of Kuat. Important things."

"Really." He gazed back at her coldly. "Go on."

"You've managed to keep it a secret from everyone else—including your former head of security. But I know at least some of what you've been up to. Khoss of Knylenn was right when he made his accusations that your schemes and plans had gotten you—and Kuat Drive Yards—into some pretty dangerous territory with the Empire and the Black Sun organization. But Khoss wasn't aware of what I've been able to find out about those schemes of yours." A trace of sympathy, and even of admiration, showed in Kodir's own gaze. "Khoss just wanted to use the little scraps of information that he had for his own ambitions, to take over control of Kuat Drive Yards. Even if he had been aware of what I know, he would still have tried to do that. But I know what you were trying to do with those schemes. They may have been dangerous, but you had no other options available to you. Not if you wanted to save Kuat Drive Yards."

Kuat leaned his head back against the padded seat. "So you do know."

"Enough," said Kodir. "Enough to see that it was an honorable thing you were attempting, Kuat of Kuat. For someone as close to the Empire as you are—close but not a part of it—it was possible to analyze the situation and deduce that the greatest immediate threat to the independence of Kuat Drive Yards was not Emperor Palpatine, but his underling Prince Xizor."

"Exactly so." Even the name of the Falleen nobleman set a hard stone of resentment in Kuat's gut. "Xizor coveted the power and the capabilities of Kuat Drive Yards; he wanted more than anything else to bring the corporation under his own dominion. And he saw the way to do that, through the suspicions of the Emperor. If Xizor had been able to supply evidence—either the truth or his own brand of lies—that the leadership of Kuat Drive Yards had been disloyal to the Empire, then Palpatine would have seized the corporation. There would have been Imperial battle cruisers, built in our own construction docks, encircling the planet of Kuat; we would have been taken over and crushed beneath the Empire's heel, as other worlds had been." On the arms of the seat, Kuat squeezed his hands into white-knuckled fists. "As *all* worlds will be, if Palpatine has his way."

"Careful." One corner of Kodir's mouth lifted in a smile. "Now you're beginning to sound like a member of the Rebel Alliance."

"If I thought they had a chance—any chance at all of succeeding—then I *would* join the Rebels. I would turn all the resources of Kuat Drive Yards over to the Alliance, whether the other ruling households agreed with me or not. But they don't have a chance." Kuat shook his head, more in sorrow than any other emotion. "The Rebels don't know what they're up against. They may be able to destroy a flawed construction such as the Death Star, but that is due more to the arrogance and the muddleheadedness of the Imperial Navy's admirals than to any real advantage that the Rebel Alliance might possess."

"I wonder about that. I've heard some things in the course of investigating and spying—things about some of the Rebel leaders." Kodir's voice went quiet and thoughtful. "On some worlds they speak of this Luke Skywalker as though he was the hero for whom they had been waiting since the overthrow of the old Republic."

"Sentient creatures can believe whatever they want—but too often they confuse their hopes and dreams with cold, hard reality." Kuat's expression had settled into a grim mask. "I don't have that luxury. As an engineer, I'm only concerned with what works."

"Too bad your scheme against Prince Xizor was a failure, then. Now you're left with the job of cleaning up the pieces that were left behind."

She had described the situation with admirable exactitude. "And you plan to help me with the cleanup, I take it."

"You got it," said Kodir. "Xizor wasn't the only one who could have profited from supplying damaging evidence. You did a nice job, from what I've been able to find out, putting together something that would have wound up involving Prince Xizor in some heavy difficulties. Synthesized Falleen pheromones tucked in with a sensory-enhanced video recording of an Imperial stormtrooper raid on a Tatooine moisture farm; a raid in which Luke Skywalker's only family, the aunt and uncle who had raised him from infancy, were gruesomely killed—a neat way of indicating, just subtly enough so it wouldn't seem like a plant, that Prince Xizor had somehow been involved in the raid. So there would have been a good chance that Skywalker would set out to settle the score with Xizor; he'd have been taking care of his personal accounts while he was also helping the Rebel Alliance by going after one of Emperor Palpatine's main henchmen." Kodir smiled in grim appreciation. "Only it was supposed to have been *you* who'd be the one who would really benefit from all that."

"That's right," said Kuat. "Me—and Kuat Drive Yards."

"Of course. Even if Skywalker didn't succeed in eliminating Prince Xizor, he'd have been more than enough distraction to have kept Xizor from advancing his own schemes against Kuat Drive Yards. At least, for a little while."

"Time can be a precious commodity." Kuat smoothed his hands out against the seat arms. "You buy as much of it as you can, whenever possible."

"Very wise, Kuat of Kuat. I'll try to remember that." The sympathetic look appeared again in Kodir's eyes. "It seems a shame, then, that all those clever plans didn't work out. And that you and Kuat Drive Yards would have been better off if they hadn't even been attempted."

"True. It shows that one cannot guard against every contingency. I had thought that Xizor was the one whose machinations I had most to fear. And then it turned out that Xizor had been his own worst enemy; his cleverness and ruthlessness only succeeded in getting himself killed. Too bad he couldn't have done that before I manufactured the false evidence against him."

With one hand, Kodir touched him lightly on the shoulder. "Now it's your life that's in danger, Kuat of Kuat; your life and everything you value. Your cleverness is turned against you, like a dagger against your breast. If Emperor Palpatine were to come into possession of that manufactured evidence, he would know immediately that it was false; he already knows that the late Prince Xizor had nothing to do with that raid on the moisture farm on Tatooine. So he would hunt for whoever had falsified the evidence—and it would inevitably be traced back to you, Kuat." She slowly shook her head. "It's not likely that the Emperor would look with forgiveness upon those kinds of schemes taking place under his very nose. He will extract a high price from the perpetrator. And get two things thereby: vengeance . . . and Kuat Drive Yards for himself."

The latter was the only thing that mattered to Kuat; he cared nothing for his own life. *Machines break and rust,* he mused, *and beings die.* Only those greater entities that built machines and that beings served and died for had a chance of surviving in this universe. The thought that his own hands and mind would be the instruments that brought about the destruction of his beloved Kuat Drive Yards—that set a raging spirit loose inside him. Kuat of Kuat had already vowed that, one way or another, he would make sure that Emperor Palpatine never held this corporation in his foul clutches.

"You have a most excellent understanding of my situation," said Kuat aloud. "I congratulate you,

Kodir of Kuhlvult. Your information sources—and your clever brain—have served you well." Carefully, so that his movements would not be discerned, Kuat reached one hand down into a small storage pocket at the side of the personal transport's passenger seat. "You do indeed have much to bargain with, to insure my assistance in tracking down this sister of yours who has strayed so mysteriously from her home-world." The puzzle of how a daughter of one of the planet Kuat's ruling households could have wound up a dancing girl in Jabba the Hutt's palace was one that intrigued him. Kuat imagined he might look into it someday. But he had other business to take care of right now; his hand closed around a grip of cold metal. "But as you say, I need to eliminate any evidence that would damn me in the eyes of Emperor Palpatine; even evidence that I was responsible for creating." He pulled the blaster pistol from the seat's storage pocket, brought it up, and aimed it straight between the eyes of the female sitting next to him. "Consider yourself honored that you'll be the first evidence that I'll have taken care of. Really—you know too much for me to let you go on living."

She moved faster than Kuat could ever have expected. Faster, and smarter. Kodir didn't try to make a grab for the weapon, or duck out of the way of its lethal beam; caught in the confines of her passenger seat, she would have had no chance of accomplishing either before a laser bolt had scorched its path through her skull. Instead, she slammed the butt of one hand against the thin structural panel just ahead of the seats that divided the passenger area from the transport's cockpit. That motion was just enough to instinctively draw Kuat's sight for a microsecond, and away from her. Before he could snap his gaze back to

Kodir, her other hand had grabbed the front of the torn, bloodstained formal robes that he was still wearing. She didn't try to thrust him away or knock the blaster out of his hand; she pulled Kuat *toward* herself. The press of their bodies together forced his pinioned arm upward; the hand holding the blaster jerked toward the ceiling of the passenger area. He managed to get off one shot before her other forearm clubbed him across the neck and the side of his jaw. The blow was strong enough to lift him partway out of the seat; dazed, Kuat barely managed to keep himself from toppling into the passenger area's narrow aisle.

The personal transport's alarm sirens wailed as Kuat shook his eyesight back into focus. When his vision cleared, he saw Kodir holding the blaster pistol and a charred, ragged-edged hole drilled through the ceiling panel.

"What's going on?" The pilot's urgent voice came over the transport's internal communications system. "Technician, are you all right? Answer and confirm—"

"I'm fine," Kuat responded. He pulled himself back the rest of the way into his passenger seat and flopped down into its padding. "We just had a little accident. Nothing to worry about." The bolt from the blaster, though lethal, hadn't been powerful enough to pierce the transport's hull. With one hand, Kuat tentatively rubbed his bruised jaw. "Carry on."

"We're just approaching the docking area. We'll be down and secured in a minute." The pilot's voice clicked off.

From where she sat, Kodir didn't bother holding the blaster on Kuat. The weapon sat loosely in her palm as she regarded him.

"I think," said Kodir, "we understand each other better now."

"Yes . . ." Kuat slowly nodded. The whole side of his jaw ached. "We certainly do . . ."

The personal transport docked. Summoned by Kuat, a pair of administrators from the corporation's security division accompanied their new head of operations to her offices. Kodir's duties were to begin immediately.

Even before he had returned to his private quarters and was alone again, his thoughts had returned to the same track as before. In the diminished light of the stars beyond Kuat Drive Yards, Kuat of Kuat returned the heavy formal robes to their stand and thought of the bounty hunter Boba Fett.

The key, mused Kuat of Kuat. *He is still the key . . .*

To the present and the future—if there was going to be one—of Kuat Drive Yards. And to that past that now seemed more mysterious than it had before.

Kuat sat down in the chair by his lab bench. The felinx jumped into his lap, and he stroked its silken fur, his musings distant in both space and time.

In darkness, he thought about the bounty hunter and the past.

15

"So how do you think the job went?"

The Trandoshan bounty hunter Bossk stood at the rear of *Slave I*'s cockpit, watching its owner and pilot make adjustments to its course and waiting for an answer. The cockpit's space was so cramped that the upper curve of its bulkheads pressed against Bossk's scale-covered shoulders.

Boba Fett's visored gaze turned round from the ship's controls. "I see no need," he said evenly, "for any kind of postmortem analysis on this operation. And 'postmortem' is an inaccurate figure of speech. We got the hard merchandise we came for, and"—even hidden by the helmet of the Mandalorian battle armor, Fett's glance seemed to sharpen—"nobody died in the process."

That's a judgment call, thought Bossk grumpily. If neither he nor Boba Fett had been killed while capturing the renegade Imperial stormtrooper Trhin Voss'on't, they had come as close to it as possible without actually winding up as blank-eyed corpses on that crummy mining planet they had just left. After Voss'on't's unconscious body had been dumped in one of the hold-

ing cages aboard *Slave I*'s main cargo area, Bossk had
gone straight to the ship's medical supplies locker and
had started patching himself up. Right now, as he
stood there in the cockpit, his breath was a little short,
due to the transparent compression bandage he had
wrapped around his torso, immobilizing the ribs he
had cracked when he had fallen from the crust-piercer
machinery. That whole sudden eruption of chaos
from beneath the abandoned mining colony's dismal
watering hole was going down in Bossk's memory as
one of the least pleasant episodes in his bounty hunter
career.

While he had been tending to his wounds, Boba
Fett had ignored the visibly worse condition he himself had been in—the crust-piercer's immense mass
had, after all, landed directly on top of him—and had
readied *Slave I* for takeoff. Bossk had grudgingly admitted to himself that that had been the smart thing to
do; there had been no telling what other defensive
measures Voss'on't might have had wired into place,
any of which could already have been triggered by his
capture. Better to get the ship and its merchandise out
past the planet's orbit, just to be safe.

Once that had been taken care of, Boba Fett had
taken the time to sort himself out, replacing the torn
and broken pieces of his armor and operating gear
from the stock of spares he kept aboard *Slave I*. Even
his helmet—its dark visor had been cracked by the
weight of the crust-piercer, but Fett had restored the
optical component, along with the side-mounted comm
antenna that had been broken off in the struggle. As
Bossk looked at him, the other bounty hunter appeared
just as experience-scarred as before, with the colors of
the ancient Mandalorian warriors scraped and faded
on the dented metal of the helmet—but he didn't look
any *worse* than before.

Bossk wished he could say the same for himself. As far as he was concerned, the only creatures aboard *Slave I* in worse shape were the battered ex-stormtrooper in the holding cage below, and the dead bounty hunter Zuckuss stretched out in one of the ship's storage lockers. Even if it had been necessary, the unemotional manner in which Boba Fett had put Zuckuss permanently out of the way still struck Bossk as cold. *Though that's what you get,* he supposed, *when you hook up with someone like Fett.* It was a lesson he had already taken to heart.

"So that's it?" Bossk watched as Boba Fett turned back toward the cockpit controls. "Nothing else?"

"There's no more to be discussed." Boba Fett's shoulders lifted in a slight shrug. "All that's left is payday." He leaned forward, the forefinger of one gloved hand punching some new numbers into the navicomputer. "If it's important to you, then you could say our partnership—our *temporary* partnership—has been a success."

"I'm glad you think so." Bossk drew something from his belt and set its point, with a sharp metallic click, against the back of Boba Fett's helmet. "Because I'm ending that partnership right now."

Boba Fett turned his head and found himself gazing into the muzzle of Bossk's blaster pistol. The thought of whatever surprised expression might be on his face, behind the helmet's visor, amused Bossk.

"What's this supposed to mean?" Fett's voice betrayed no sign of emotion.

"I'd give you three guesses, if I thought you needed them." Bossk kept the weapon aimed straight into the top-center of the helmet's visor. "But you don't. You might have been fool enough to trust me and take me on as a partner, but I'm sure you can figure out what's happening now." One side of Bossk's muzzle curled into a snarling smile. "As I said, this partnership's *over*." He stepped back into the doorway of the cockpit and gestured with the blaster pistol. "Stand up."

"Very well." Boba Fett swiveled the pilot's chair around. "But as an ex-partner, let me give you a bit of advice. This is not a good idea."

"Shut up. Turn around and face the viewport." Bossk had kept a careful eye on the other bounty hunter as he had stood up. "Don't try anything. This blaster's got a hair trigger—and so do I." With his free hand, he reached out and grabbed the various larger weapons from where they were slung at Boba Fett's back. He tossed them into the far corner of the cockpit, safely out of reach. Bracing the muzzle of the blaster between the other's shoulder blades, Bossk snapped the control lines for Fett's wrist- and forearm-mounted weapons. All the time he had been aboard *Slave I*, he had been carefully observing Fett for indications of any hidden gadgets. Now, as he stepped back again from him, Bossk was sure that he was completely disarmed. "All right," said Bossk. He drew back into the space outside the cockpit's hatchway, still aiming the blaster at Boba Fett. "Time to head below."

Fett was halfway down the ladder's metal treads when he stopped and looked up at Bossk holding the blaster on him. "Of course you realize," said Boba Fett mildly, "that you're taking some pretty big chances here. This is my ship; it's as much a part of me as any of those weapons you just took from me. Do you really think that I don't have other means of defense close at hand?"

"Not now, you don't." Crouching at the side of the ladder portal, Bossk reached with his free hand into one of his belt pouches. He brought out a fistful of miniaturized power sources, trigger mechanisms, and sensor relays. They glittered brightly and ominously in his grasp. "I've kept myself busy while I've been here on *Slave I*. I've had a good look around, and I came prepared to make a few little changes of my own. Let me tell ya, pal—you don't have any tricks left up your sleeve." Bossk motioned with the barrel of the blaster. "Keep going."

When Boba Fett reached the bottom of the ladder and stepped away from it, Bossk didn't bother climbing down after him. He jumped, landing bent-kneed and immediately snapping the blaster's aim at the center of Fett's visored helmet. "You see?" He straightened up, smiling. "You're not the only person capable of a few surprises."

"Apparently not." Boba Fett folded his arms across his chest. "I congratulate you. You must have been planning this for some time."

"You got that right. I was planning it even before I came and had my little talk with you, when you agreed to go in with me on this job." Bossk pointed with a thumb-claw toward the ex-stormtrooper Voss'on't, still lying unconscious on the floor of the holding cage behind Fett. "As nice as getting half the bounty for this particular piece of merchandise might've been, there won't be anything nicer than getting *all* the credits."

"Which is what you wanted from the beginning." Boba Fett slowly shook his head. "Not much of a partnership."

"Yeah, right." Bossk sneered at him. "It's breaking my heart just to think of betraying your trust and all. But you want to know a couple of things? One, I don't give a womp-rat's hindquarters what you think about it. And two—turnabout's fair play. You trusted me as your partner, the same way the old Bounty Hunters Guild trusted you when you came around and applied for membership. When all along you were planning on sinking a vibroblade in our collective back."

"Who told you that?"

"Nobody had to tell me, Fett; I could figure it out on my own." Bossk tightened his grip on the blaster pistol. "All I needed was some confirmation of my suspicions. And I got that through some contacts inside Black Sun. To make a few credits, they were happy to give me some interesting tidbits about what their boss Prince Xizor was hoping to do to the Guild."

Boba Fett's helmet turned to one side, as if the eyes behind the dark visor were peering harder at Bossk. "What's Xizor got to do with all this?"

"Don't play dumb with me, Fett. I don't have time for it." Bossk raised the blaster, bringing it level with the other bounty hunter's helmet. "And as a matter of fact—neither do you. You don't have any time left at all."

"What are you planning on doing?"

"The same thing I've wanted to do for a long time. Since the day we first crossed paths, I knew that this moment would come, Fett. And that one of us would be alive afterward, and one of us wouldn't. Guess which one *you* get to be."

Boba Fett radiated the same eerie calm as before. "That's a great deal of talk for someone intent on murder."

"I didn't," said Bossk, "want to miss my chance to say exactly what I thought of you. But you're right. So I've just run out of words. And now the fun starts." Bossk kept the blaster aimed at the other bounty hunter, and used his free hand to gesture toward the cargo area's exterior airlock. "I don't want to hear any more words from you, either. So you're going out where things don't make any sound. We're surrounded by vacuum now, Fett. Take a deep breath, because it'll be your last." Bossk's fang-lined smile grew wider. "I'm going to enjoy turning this ship around to take a look at what's left of you, after your blood's boiled away and your body's exploded from depressurization. I've heard that the process takes just long enough for you to feel it; maybe a second or two. I bet they won't go by fast, either." This time, he motioned with the weapon. "Get moving. You know the way out."

"Your thoroughness is commendable." Boba Fett took a step toward the hatchway. "I've been cornered inside my own ship before—some of the hard merchandise I've carried has been very resourceful—but I've never had *Slave I*'s internal defense systems disabled before. That's a new one." He stopped and brought his visored helmet's level gaze straight toward Bossk. "It's just a shame that you didn't think of everything."

"Yeah? Like what?"

"All it takes is to overlook one small detail." Boba Fett reached up and tapped the side of his helmet. "You left my comm system functioning."

Careful, Bossk warned himself. *The scum's playing mind games with you.* "Big deal," he said aloud. "Who're you going to call for help? We're alone here, and there's no other ship in this sector of the galaxy. Believe me—I checked that out as well." He pointed over his shoulder with a thumb-claw. "And a knocked-out stormtrooper locked in a cage isn't going to come to your rescue anytime soon. So go on. Have enough guts to get into the airlock on your own power. You don't have any other option."

Boba Fett made no reply. Bossk thought he heard

a muffled whisper, as though Fett had spoken into the comm mike concealed inside his helmet. A few seconds passed, then Bossk knew for sure that he had heard something. One of the storage lockers behind him had opened, its metal door unsealing and lifting upward.

"Nice try." Bossk didn't bother to turn around and look. "If you think a simpleminded trick like that is going to get me to take my eyes and this blaster off you, then I'm really disappointed. I expected better from you than just trying to divert my attention with a little comm-triggered noise."

"Okay. Is this better?"

He was surprised to hear another voice speaking, and from right behind himself. Bossk was even more surprised when he felt the unmistakable cold pressure of a blaster pistol's muzzle placed against the back of his head.

That was when Bossk recognized the other voice. "Zuckuss!"

The blaster muzzle didn't move from the base of his skull. "That's right," said Zuckuss, still behind him. "Now why don't you lower your weapon. I really don't like you pointing it at *my* partner."

"I'll take it." Boba Fett stepped forward and removed the blaster from Bossk's slackened grip. He gestured with it toward the holding cage. "Stand over there."

Bossk muttered a string of guttural Trandoshan curses as he backed toward the vertical durasteel bars. "Talk about dirty tricks—" His eyes narrowed into slits as he gazed at Zuckuss. "You weren't dead at all."

"I try to avoid it, when I can." The blaster in Zuckuss's hand was reflected in his large, insectlike eyes. "Though for one of my species, it's pretty easy to imitate." He pulled two miniature cylinders of compressed ammonia from the dangling tubes of his breathing apparatus. "When you come from a planet like Gand, where we've got both ammonia-breathers and oxygen-breathers, you have to be adaptable. In an oxygen-rich environment, I can shut down all respiration and external vital signs—usually just for a couple of minutes. But with a couple of these"—Zuckuss held up the air units—"I can go for days like that. It's actually kind of relaxing."

"And useful," said Boba Fett. "I've discovered that when dealing with Trandoshans, it's good to have *another* partner on hand."

"You slimy—" Words failed Bossk as his clawed hands squeezed into impotent fists. He didn't know which of the two figures in front of him he despised more. "How could you do this?" He snarled at Zuckuss. "We've worked together; we've been *real* partners—"

"Business is business." Zuckuss gave a slight shrug. "And Boba Fett here made me an offer I just couldn't refuse. We're talking forty percent of the bounty for the hard merchandise in the cage."

"*Forty!* I would've given you a straight half!"

"Yeah, but . . ." Zuckuss regretfully shook his head. "You're not exactly in a bargaining position right now."

Bossk fell silent, except for the grinding of his fangs and the pulse of blood hammering inside his head. The treachery of sentient creatures was infuriating.

"And you—" Bossk turned his red-tinged gaze toward Boba Fett. "This is what you were planning all along. Isn't it?"

"Just as you were making your own plans." Boba Fett tucked into his belt the blaster pistol he had taken from Bossk. He reached his empty hand over toward Zuckuss standing beside him. "Give me your blaster."

"Huh?" Zuckuss's large eyes goggled at him in puzzlement. "Why?"

"Just give it to me."

Zuckuss handed the weapon over.

"Thanks." Boba Fett did a quick check of the blaster's power cell, then raised and pointed it at Zuckuss. "Now stand over there with him."

"What—what're you doing—"

Boba Fett motioned with the blaster's barrel. "You can go over there with Bossk, or I can kill you right where you're standing. Your pick."

"I thought . . ." Zuckuss shook his head in dismay as he joined Bossk at the side of *Slave I*'s cargo area. "I thought we were *partners* . . ."

"You idiot." The disgust that rose inside Bossk was enough that he struck Zuckuss's head with the flat of his palm. "You don't *ever* hand over a weapon to somebody like that."

"How was I supposed to know?" Zuckuss rubbed the side of his head. "I trusted him . . ."

"That was your first mistake." Boba Fett kept both of them covered with the blaster pistol in his gloved hand. He turned his gaze toward Bossk. "Your mistake was in thinking that I would trust you. I could figure out from the beginning that you were planning on eliminating me as soon as we had the hard merchandise safely in our possession."

"All right." Bossk nodded as he spread his hands apart. "That's a fair assessment. You can't blame me for trying. And I did help you catch Voss'on't. So how about if we just forget this part of my plan, and we go ahead and turn him in to Kud'ar Mub'at and split the bounty fifty-fifty, just like we were originally going to do?"

"Hey!" Zuckuss's voice squeaked in protest. "What about me? What do I get?"

"Neither one of you is getting anything," said Boba Fett, "except a blaster bolt between the eyes. My patience is not unlimited."

"I think Zuckuss has got a point." Having a blaster pointed at him had sent Bossk's thoughts racing. "Fair's fair, after all." Bossk stepped behind Zuckuss and placed both his clawed hands on the smaller bounty hunter's shoulders. "After all, we weren't trying to do anything different from you. You know—just playing to win."

"You're right." The blaster didn't waver in Boba Fett's grip. "You played to win, and I played to win. The difference is . . . I won."

Bossk didn't say anything more. Instead, in one quick move, he lifted Zuckuss bodily from the floor of the cargo area and threw him at Boba Fett. Even before Zuckuss's flailing, panicked form struck Fett, Bossk was heading in a crouched-over sprint for the other side of the ship. A blaster bolt scorched past his shoulder as he dove for his one chance of escape.

He had spotted the auxiliary escape pod's rounded hatch when he had previously checked out *Slave I*'s fixtures. The escape pod must have been original equipment installed by the Kuat Drive Yards when the company had built the ship for Boba Fett— it was hard to believe that Boba Fett would have had much use for the device. Bossk wasn't even sure that the pod was in operational order; its external fascia seal had been unbolted and discarded, as though Boba Fett had already decided to strip out the pod and the connected launching mechanism. But it was still worth a try. Hot sparks lashed across his spine as another bolt hit the bulkhead above him; the escape pod's hatch popped open and he threw himself head-first into its dark, cramped space.

"You're not going anywhere, Bossk—"

From inside the emergency pod, Bossk peered around the edge of its open hatch. He saw Zuckuss lying flat on the cargo area's floor, covering his head with both forearms. The helmeted figure of Boba Fett stood over him, blaster aimed toward the pod.

"I've already signaled the cockpit and overridden that pod's launch sequence." The blaster in Fett's hand was level with the exact center of the pod's hatch. "That's a dead end for you. Literally."

"Maybe so—" Bossk called back out to Boba Fett. Drawing his head back, Bossk quickly searched through the pouches of his belt. He had no weapons, but there was something that could still be of use to him. He found the small object, one of the pieces of equipment that he had extracted from *Slave I*'s circuits when he had disabled Fett's onboard defense systems. When he pushed a button on top of the small cylinder, a row of tiny red lights began flashing down its side. Keeping his thumb on the button, he held it out so that Boba Fett would be able to see it through the open hatch. "Let's talk."

Outside the pod, in the center of the ship's cargo area, Zuckuss raised his head. "Bossk—" He had spotted the device as well. "What're you doing? You'll get us all killed!"

"That's the idea," said Bossk grimly. "I'm not going unless I can take everybody else with me." He held the flashing cylinder a little higher. "Fett—you know what this is, don't you? You should; it was part of your equipment here."

"Miniature thermal detonator," replied Boba Fett. "It's no big deal; I've seen creatures try to cut a deal for themselves using full-sized ones. When they're that small, they're only useful for jettisoning sections of a ship's fuselage that might have gotten damaged in an exchange of laser-cannon fire; that's the only reason there were any aboard *Slave I*." Fett shook his head. "You can blow yourself up with that thing, but it's not powerful enough to take out this entire ship."

"It doesn't have to." Bossk stayed prudently back from the edge of the escape pod's open hatch. "All it has to do is blow out a big enough gap in the side of the hull, and you're going to have a hard time making it back to Kud'ar Mub'at's web without laying over for some lengthy repairs. And you and I both know that the word has already gotten out about our having captured Trhin Voss'on't. Do you really want to be sitting out in the middle of empty space in a crippled ship, while every bounty hunter in the galaxy heads this way to try and lift that valuable piece of hard merchandise off you?"

Boba Fett was silent for a few seconds, then he gave a single nod. "All right," he said. "I'll make a deal with you. I'll activate the pod's launch sequence, and you can go. But when we cross paths again—then you'd better be ready."

"Don't worry. I will be."

"Engage the safety on the detonator and toss it out here."

"You gotta be kidding." Bossk barked out a short laugh. "I'll deactivate this thing when I'm safely on my way. And not a second earlier than that."

"As you wish." Boba Fett reached down with his free hand and grabbed Zuckuss under the arm. "Come on—you're going traveling, too."

"What—what're you—" Zuckuss sputtered in

confusion as Boba Fett dragged him toward the emergency escape pod. "But—but you *owe* me . . ."

"And I'm paying off the debt." Holding the blaster by the side of his helmet, Boba Fett kicked Zuckuss inside the pod with a single boot thrust. "I'm letting you live."

The pod's interior was barely big enough for both bounty hunters; Bossk's spine was crammed back against its curved wall, with one of Zuckuss's arms thrust across his face. He shoved Zuckuss aside as the hatch began to seal shut. He had one last glimpse of Boba Fett's cold, visored gaze—then he threw the detonator outside just as the hatch clicked shut.

Launch had already commenced, as though the pod were an archaic metal bullet being fired from some primitive tribe's gunpowder musket. The violent shock wave of the detonator's explosion, back aboard *Slave I*, tumbled Bossk and Zuckuss inside the pod as it shot away from the ship.

"What did you do that for?" The pod's velocity had taken it past the concussive effects of the explosion. Bleeding from a scrape on his brow, Zuckuss hunched himself over to one side of the cramped space. "If that thing had gone off a half second sooner, we wouldn't have gotten away!"

"We wouldn't have gotten away, either, if Boba Fett had been able to turn his ship around and blow us to bits with one of his laser cannons." Bossk leaned forward, wrapping his heavily muscled arms around his knees. "I wanted to make sure that he was good and distracted, until we were safely out of firing range."

"Oh. Good thinking." Zuckuss shifted about, trying to make room for himself inside the escape pod. "For a change," he said disgustedly, "I think I'm

going to scout around for a more dependable partner." His large insectoid eyes looked up, as though
seeking some indication of the pod's flight through the
vacuum of space. "Where do you think this thing is
going to wind up?"

"Who knows?" Choice of destination, Bossk was
well aware, was not a feature of such devices; they
were programmed to seek out and head for the nearest
habitable planet. "We'll find out when we get there."

The only thing he did know—a perfect certainty in
the brooding silence that filled his heart and every other
space inside him—was that one way or another, sooner
or later, he would find his way back to Boba Fett.

And then, vowed Bossk, *that scum is going to
pay . . ."*

Big time.

The damage wasn't extensive, and was easily contained. There had been a momentary drop in atmospheric pressure aboard *Slave I* as air had rushed out
from the hole created by Bossk's parting gesture with
the miniature thermal detonator. But the ship's own
homeostatic defense systems had been activated by
their sensors registering the explosion; the hull's structure and surface area near the escape pod's launch bay
had sealed themselves off like a rapidly mending
wound in a living creature's soft tissue.

Even before the ship's internal pressure had been
stabilized, Boba Fett had also been at work, minimiz-
ing the explosion's effects. The helmet of his Mandalorian battle armor contained its own emergency air
supply—only a few minutes worth, but enough for
him to have reached another onboard source if necessary. He had been more concerned with the welfare of
the hard merchandise inside the cargo area's holding

cage; the ex-stormtrooper Trhin Voss'on't was only valuable if he stayed alive. Fett had grabbed an oxygen canister from one of the storage lockers, then reached into the cage and fastened its tethered mask over Voss'on't's gasping face. Voss'on't's eyelids had fluttered for a moment, as though the anoxic shock had been enough to rouse him into consciousness; a quick blow to the side of his head had put him safely under again.

Taking care of the merchandise had prevented Boba Fett from retaliating at the departed Bossk. By the time the damage to *Slave I* had been contained and all systems stabilized, Boba Fett had gone up to the ship's cockpit and had found no trace of the escape pod on any of the scanners. *Just as well,* thought Fett. Mere vengeance was rarely a priority with him, and certainly not worth any time pursuing now. If he ran across Bossk again, he could take care of the Trandoshan at that time.

Right now, though, he had business to wrap up. The sooner he had dropped off the hard merchandise he was carrying, and collected the bounty for it, the more at ease he would feel. Bossk had been right about one thing: the longer he stayed out here, the more attention he would attract from other bounty hunters. He could undoubtedly fight them all off, but why go to the effort if it wasn't necessary? Leaning over the cockpit's controls, reading out the damage-assessment gauges, Boba Fett started figuring out what kind of navigable condition *Slave I* was in.

Less than a Standard Time Part later, he had his answer. *It'll make the trip,* Boba Fett decided, *but it'll be in bad shape when it gets there.* He had returned to the cockpit after a thorough check of the damaged hull sections, scoping them with a structural diagnostics kit from the cargo area. The ship's main computer had crunched the numbers he had factored in, and the results were not good. *Slave I* was in no imminent danger of disintegration, and could even travel for an indeterminate distance—as long as he kept it at sublight speeds. But the explosion had severely weakened the ship's tight-angle thruster ports and maneuvering capabilities; the stresses of a jump into hyperspace would rip some of the control surfaces completely loose from the hull. *Slave I* could make it to Kud'ar Mub'at's web, but the ship would be a limping cripple when it arrived.

He had no choice. Staying here in this sector, while making repairs, would make him a sitting target for everyone with an eye out for the hard merchandise he was carrying. The safety that would come with unloading his precious living cargo lay at the other side of the galaxy.

Safety . . . and an extremely large pile of credits.

No choice at all.

Carefully and precisely, he started punching the coordinates into the navicomputer, getting ready for the jump into hyperspace.

"The away scout just reported, sir." With a slight bow of the head, the Black Sun comm specialist reported the information. "His message states that Boba Fett's ship has left the sector in which it was last seen."

"Very well." Prince Xizor turned away from the main viewport of his quarters aboard the *Virago*. At the moment, nothing but stars and emptiness showed beyond. "Alert all personnel. It shouldn't be long before he arrives here."

"As you direct, sir."

"Be sure everyone understands." Xizor's gaze stayed for a moment on the underling before he resumed his contemplation of the galaxy's bright pieces. "We must be ready to welcome him. In the manner"—Xizor smiled to himself—"that he deserves . . ."

The comm specialist gave a quick nod of acknowledgment, then hurried away.

Prince Xizor folded his arms across his chest, letting his eyelids draw half-shut with the pleasure of his meditations.

A quick death, he thought, *but a sure one.* What could be more appropriate than that, for one such as Boba Fett?

16

NOW

"Did you find out everything?" Boba Fett glanced over his shoulder at the female standing in the cockpit's hatchway. "Everything you wanted to know?"

Neelah shook her head. "I decided to give Dengar a break," she said. "We left it right at a good part." She smiled maliciously. "You were about to get killed."

"Which time?"

"Does it matter?" The look on Neelah's face was almost one of admiration. "Telling your history seems to be a long process."

"I've been around a bit." There was little present need for him to mind the *Hound's Tooth*'s controls. The ship's course had already been set. "If other creatures think that's so remarkable, it's not my fault. I'm just going about my business."

"Murderous business, from the sound of it."

Fett shrugged. "It's a living."

"For you."

"That's all that matters."

Neelah gave him a disgusted look. "I'm beginning

to wonder if hanging out with you is such a good idea."

"It all depends," said Fett calmly. "You might be safer with me than anywhere else right now."

"What do you mean?"

"There's a lot going on in this galaxy." Boba Fett pointed toward the viewport. "I've been going through the data traffic from the major comm bands. There's a major confrontation shaping up between the Empire and the Rebel Alliance, somewhere near Endor. There's a lot of Imperial resources going into that sector. From the sound of it, could be something big. And decisive."

"So?" Neelah didn't seem impressed. "What's that got to do with us? The way I heard it from Dengar just now, you've always managed to survive no matter who was in charge."

"That's possible," said Boba Fett, "when there's more than one power dominating the galaxy. Much can be accomplished right under the nose of even a despot such as Emperor Palpatine when his attention is focused on enemies strong enough to challenge him. The Rebel Alliance has given him a great deal of trouble so far—but the Rebels' luck may be finally running out. Palpatine has had enough chances to figure out their weaknesses, and now he means to crush them once and for all."

"And you think that's what will happen?"

"I wouldn't bet against it." Boba Fett swiveled the pilot's chair back toward the cockpit controls. "And it will be a lot colder, harder, *and* more murderous galaxy when it happens. Whatever you might think about me, I am at least an independent operator. Profit is all that motivates me. With Emperor Palpatine, it's something different."

He glanced over his shoulder and saw Neelah slowly nod, deep in her own thoughts. Fett knew she was assessing her own chances in a galaxy such as he had just described. She wasn't enough of a fool to think very much of them. But he also knew that that wasn't going to stop her.

Just as it wasn't going to stop him.

Without looking around, Boba Fett knew that he was alone once more. Neelah had returned to the ship's cargo area. He leaned back in the pilot's chair, hands laid flat on its arms. Soon enough, the *Hound* would arrive at its destination. In the meantime, there was just waiting and readiness; that was all. That, and the certainty of death—his own or another creature's.

As there had been before, when his own ship *Slave I* had brought him to the trap where he had been meant to die.

Behind the visor of his helmet, he closed his eyes, letting himself fall into the truer darkness of his past.

How many times, wondered Boba Fett, could he die—and yet not die? Someday it would all be over for him . . .

But not yet, he whispered to himself. *Not yet.*

About the Author

K. W. JETER is one of the most respected sf writers working today. His first novel, *Dr. Adder*, was described by Philip K. Dick as "a stunning novel . . . it destroys once and for all your conception of the limitations of science fiction." *The Edge of Human* resolves many discrepancies between the movie *Blade Runner* and the novel upon which it was based, Dick's *Do Androids Dream of Electric Sheep?* Jeter's other books have been described as having a "brain-burning intensity" *(The Village Voice)*, as being "hard-edged and believable" *(Locus)* and "a joy from first word to last" *(San Francisco Chronicle)*. He is the author of over twenty novels, including *Farewell Horizontal* and *Wolf Flow*. His latest novel, *Noir,* is available from Bantam Spectra.